Nobody Tells Lia Anything

Carol Maloney Scott

Nobody Tells Lia Anything

Copyright 2019 © Carol Maloney Scott

This is a work of fiction. Names, characters, places, and incidents are products of the author's imagination or used fictitiously and are not to be construed as real. Any resemblance to actual events, locales, organizations, or persons, living or dead, is entirely coincidental.

All rights reserved. This book or any portion thereof may not be reproduced or used in any manner whatsoever without the express written permission of the publisher except for the use of brief quotations in a book review. For permission requests, please contact the publisher.

Formatting by Wild Seas Formatting (http://www.WildSeasFormatting.com)

http://carolmaloneyscott.com

For Benny
The sweet little dog I never thought I'd have

CHAPTER ONE

"It may be crass to speak of the...deceased...this way, but I swear, your mother was a fruit loop."

Mom cringes at her own words and jangles her many silver bracelets, while my father smiles, and nervously glances around the office of Edward Franklin, Esquire, located in the quiet, bucolic mountain town of Applebarrow, Virginia.

Only Paul DeLuca, Professor of Experimental Philosophy, would be okay with his wife making snarky comments at such a serious time. But after all, he is known to his students and colleagues at Langworth College as the 'Happiness Teacher.'

No one really knows what 'Experimental Philosophy' is. I triple majored in foreign languages, and even my degree is more marketable.

I don't like to think of my father as a 'Cult Leader' (my late maternal Grandpa's words), but I think 'Guru' sums it up.

I bite my lower lip as Mr. Franklin clears his throat. Clearly this appointment with the middle-aged hippies from Vermont (and their daughter), is cutting into his Saturday fishing.

The whole office is decorated in lures, reels, and plaques with sayings about fishing. There is even a cute embroidered pillow urging us to 'get out and reel 'em in.'

They were probably gifts from local clients. Sensible people who don't argue quite as much at Will readings.

Although, only my mother argues, since any negativity makes my father's 'chi' go out of alignment.

You would think being married to a noted authority on happiness would improve my mother's mood, but the giddier Dad gets, the more she looks like she wants to knock him in...

"Mrs. DeLuca, I understand that—"

"Ed, it's Mrs. Edelman-DeLuca, but since that's a mouthful, I wish you'd call me Sarah."

She smiles at us and continues, earning an encouraging nod from Dad, since she seems to have employed one of his ten 'Happiness Tenets' to take her tension down a peg or two.

"It's not that I don't think my mother-in-law has...had...the right to leave her estate to anyone she wanted, and Paul and I are perfectly happy with our share of the settlement."

Dad chimes in with the expected, "Perfectly happy!"

Mom's smile is now drooping under the strain of remaining in a Zen state, and I know she wants to yell curse words in Yiddish. That was the first foreign language I picked up as a child. Not Yiddish. *Curse words* in Yiddish.

Mr. Franklin stares longingly at his fishing rods and tackle box, with a stolen glance at the beautiful day outside his stuffy, conflict-ridden office.

If only Granana could have left a simpler Will, but the same brain that concocted this bizarre scheme was the same one that produced my father. She was an odd bird, as I once heard Grandma Edelman call her.

Whatever. At least Granana didn't keep plastic

on her couches, so your legs got stuck when you visited on summer vacation.

Before our weary attorney can open his mouth, Mom says, "I'm just worried about Lia. She's a young woman with her own life in Richmond. She has a job and an apartment and a boyfriend. She's supposed to uproot herself, and give all that up, to do what again?"

Since my paternal grandmother, Allegra DeLuca, passed away a week ago of natural causes, my parents have been a little weird. Weirder than *usual*. They aren't into small town Virginia, Catholicism, or leaving Vermont.

And they are dealing with all three this week.

Of course, Dad is beaming like the Dalai Lama no matter what, but I have a sneaking suspicion my 'holistic medicine' mother is itching for a prescription of her mother's 'nerve pills'.

Granana was ninety years old, and I'm guessing she would have lived even longer if she had eaten better and exercised, but her mind was sharp. We spent most of our visits speaking Italian, doing mind teasing puzzles, and baking.

Her husband, Grandpa Joseph, died three years ago, and I'd like to think they are reunited now (even though he was kind of a grump), however I don't like to presume such things.

We held the funeral last Thursday, the day before St. Patrick's Day. I didn't want to go out with my boyfriend and our friends, but my parents insisted that Granana would want me to enjoy myself. 'She lived a good, long life, and it was her time...blah, blah, blah...'

So, I went. I hate to be alone when I'm feeling sad. Or mad. Or even happy.

Okay, I really don't like being alone.

Jason (my boyfriend) attended the wake and funeral with me, and he provided so much comfort. This is the first real loss of my life, and when I told him Granana had passed away, he left work and rushed home to be with me.

And Jason is quite the workaholic.

However, on St. Patrick's Day, while sipping a green beer, he whispered in my ear, "So, the Will reading is tomorrow, huh?"

Suddenly I was worried that he now saw me as the heiress to the DeLuca Delicious Delights fortune.

When I didn't respond right away, he backpedaled and said, "I mean, I'm *sorry* she's gone, but don't you wonder what's going to happen to all that money? Your dad doesn't seem to be interested."

Jason isn't an insensitive prick (really, he's not). He's practical, not sentimental.

Therefore my mother loves him, and my father thinks 'that boy needs to slow down'.

Mom is a reluctant hippy at best, and she appreciates a go-getter, while Dad is smelling the roses.

Literally. He grows roses.

When Jason brought up the Will, I laughed at the thought of my father inheriting millions of dollars. He would probably start a Happiness Foundation. I hoped that my grandmother left him the money, and that he wouldn't be too stubborn to accept it. People like my dad can do a lot of good with the proper resources.

And I can't say that I didn't want *anything*. Who would say that? Well, other than people like my dad.

I never had an awareness of the wealth growing up. I knew my grandparents made a lot of money from the business (DeLuca's Delicious Delights was a household name), but I never saw much evidence of the money in their lifestyle.

My grandparents *did* have a big house in Applebarrow, but no servants. They had nice cars, but nothing extravagant. They vacationed in Italy, and a few other places in Europe, but they weren't jet setters.

I guessed that their minimalist lifestyle led Jason to assume that I was an heiress of a large untouched fortune, and that if he stuck with me, he'd be an heir.

But I still wasn't too upset with him. He loves me, and I know he hasn't spent the past five years with me so he could get his hands on the DeLuca fortune. And unlike my father, most people are quite happy to come into unexpected money. It's human nature.

And who knew where it would end up at that point? She could have left it all to a charity. The Church, maybe? And Jason had never mentioned it once before last week.

My grandparents started the giant snack cake company many years before, when they were first married, and moved to rural Virginia. Already in their thirties when they married, they had both done some traveling, and when they were looking for a place to settle, Grandpa Joseph remembered a trip to the Virginia mountains from his youth, and how 'those poor bastards didn't have a decent bakery.'

What started out as an adventure with two 'fish out of water' Italian New Yorkers moving to the small southern town and opening a bakery, ended up growing into a huge company with factory operations in Applebarrow, creating jobs and growth for the region.

My father was born in the early days of their marriage, and as he grew, he showed no interest in the family business, much to my grandfather's distress.

Only in very late life did he finally accept his son's choice to pursue a career in academia, a world that was completely foreign to his working-class Italian immigrant sensibilities.

Paul DeLuca met Sarah Edelman at college in New York, and my dad convinced my mom to give up nursing to become a massage therapist.

My Jewish, New Yorker maternal grandparents thought Paul DeLuca was a fruit loop.

Grandpa DeLuca closed the business right before he died because due to the 'health nut bullshit', the demand for unhealthy snack cakes was diminishing, along with Grandpa's health. No one in the family wanted to take over the business.

I was a senior in college and obviously was in no position to step in and run a factory, and my dad...well, I've already explained that problem.

Therefore, when it came time to read the Will, I honestly wondered how much money was left for any of us to inherit.

At the funeral, I heard talk of the factory building still sitting empty in Applebarrow, and speculations of my grandmother's net worth (such appropriate funeral conversation!), but as for Granana's actual finances, the only one who really knew was Edward Franklin, attorney, fisherman, and confidante of my grandparents for many years, taking over after his father and uncle retired from the law practice.

I fidget in my seat, and cross and uncross my legs, uncomfortable in the skirt I've chosen for this somber occasion.

My usually hippy-attired parents have been dressing up for all the funeral activities, and today is no exception. My father probably can't wait to get back to Vermont and break out his ancient jeans and sandals.

I'm putting on pajamas as soon as I get home. I'm even wearing lip gloss and mascara today, and my eyelashes keep sticking together. How does anyone wear this crap every day?

Mr. Franklin clears his throat and reopens the huge tome that contains my grandmother's final wishes. I don't think any of us have ever given any thought to this moment—it seemed like Granana would live forever.

By the way, I know 'Granana' looks like a careless typo, but it's not. I called her by that rather unusual name because when I was born my mother's mother boldly claimed the name 'Grandma' for herself, and my parents wanted Dad's mother to have a different name, so I wouldn't get confused.

Granana did not want to be called 'Nana' (something about her evil mother-in-law), so they compromised and made up their own name.

I often think my parents must have taken one look at me as a baby and decided I wasn't the brightest bulb, since they thought I couldn't keep two 'Grandmas' straight.

I turned out to be an honors student who has never gotten less than an A in any class.

However, I don't like to brag, especially in front of Jason. It's a good thing his profession relies more on the ability to schmooze than academic achievement.

Mr. Franklin interrupts my day dreaming. "So as I was saying, Mrs. DeLuca left the previously discussed sum of money to her son and daughter-in-law."

Fortunately, after much eye rolling and sighing on my mother's part, Dad agreed to accept the money and 'put it to good use.'

Money for money's sake is foreign to him, but my mother often points out that she would be happier with a bigger house.

I'm glad I don't live in Vermont, so I won't be a witness to the discussions about the distribution of this newfound wealth.

Mr. Franklin appears relieved that he can move on without any further complaints or questions. "The Catholic Church Mrs. DeLuca attended will receive a smaller sum, and then the remaining assets go to Lia, along with a substantial cash inheritance, based on the guidelines and requirements Mrs. DeLuca has detailed. I've given you all a copy, and Ms. DeLuca, you have until Monday to let me know if you will accept your grandmother's terms."

He takes off his reading glasses and polishes them. I notice this is a nervous tic of his because he's done it numerous times, and it's not like he's reading Wills in a sandstorm. How dirty are his glasses?

Everyone looks at me and I finally get a chance to speak. Normally I am the most talkative one in a room, but I've been rattled by the loss of my grandmother, and her odd request of me.

And my parents aren't helping. Well, mostly my mother.

"Well, I certainly appreciate that Granana thought so highly of me that she would leave me so much money, the factory, and the apartment complex. But Mr. Franklin, I don't know how to run an apartment complex. And it's only ten units? Can't we just hire someone? It would be giving a local person a job, and isn't the economy struggling in Applebarrow since the snack cakes plant closed down?"

My mother can't resist chiming in. "Yes, it is! And I think it's quite possible that the locals blame the DeLuca family for that. I hardly think anyone is going to roll out the red carpet for the snack cakes heiress. And she has *plans, dreams*...I don't understand how my mother-in-law could have spent so much time with Lia and leave her with such a mess."

Dad squeezes Mom's knee and says, "Ed, forgive Sarah. She's protective of Lia, as am I. All we want is for her to be happy, but I also value my mother's dying wishes. So, let me make sure I understand. Lia has to move to Applebarrow to run social events for the residents of the apartment complex, and then she'll receive her full inheritance in one year?"

"Yes, that's correct. Mrs. DeLuca specifically stated that she was saddened by the lack of friendship at Pentagon Place, the ten-unit apartment complex she owned with her late husband, and she felt that her granddaughter is the one to make a difference."

I squirm in my seat and curse the invention of panty hose. It would not have killed Mr. Franklin to see my bare legs—it's already warm here in March, but my mother insisted on professional dress.

"It's nice that Granana thought I would be up to this challenge, but I don't know if being a Resident Assistant in my college dorm is the same thing as planning social activities for a bunch of strangers from different age groups and demographics. What could all of them possibly be interested in? How can I motivate them to want to get to know each other if they haven't already done it on their own?"

Before anyone responds, the biggest question on my mind is blurted out by my mother.

"Ed, why the hell did Allegra *care* if her residents got along? It's not a commune, it's an apartment complex. If the people pay their rent and aren't assaulting each other, who cares? It's not even like she lived there. Her house is a good few blocks away from the apartments. I don't get it."

My father leans forward with his Buddha-like expression and says, "I think it's a lovely idea."

Mom and I both glance at him in surprise (hers is more of a glare), but I can't help but think of my sweet grandmother, wanting to bring harmony to the world—or at least her little corner of it.

I sit up straighter and ask, "Mr. Franklin, you knew my grandmother, didn't you?"

"Oh yes, very well. Lovely woman."

"So why do you think she wants me to do this?" I thumb through the pages of directions from the Will. "Monthly social meetings. Regular resident events. How will we measure the success of any of this? And am I really cut out of the Will if I don't do this?"

Mr. Franklin clears his throat again and says, "I'm not entirely sure. After all, Mrs. DeLuca had a sincere wish for people to be happy. Obviously, she taught your father those principals, based on his career choice."

My father smiles broadly and looks up to the heavens, while my mother rolls her eyes in the same direction and says, "I guess I should be grateful she didn't ask you to do this, Paul. Or I'd be packing my bags to move to this shi...little town and hosting hay rides and pot luck square dances."

Mr. Franklin ignores my mother's thinly veiled disdain for his town and says, "And while she did state clear requirements in the Will, it is my personal opinion that your grandmother will not cut you out entirely if you don't complete this mission."

My mother rubs her temples and says, "Well, don't you *know*? She's not here to tell us, and you're her lawyer. Isn't this a Will reading? I feel like I'm in a game of Clue, and maybe it was the butler in the parlor with the candlestick."

Mr. Franklin stands up and starts pacing. He's either getting ready to bolt out the door with his tackle box, or he's preparing to convince the jury (Mom) that I need to sign on the dotted line so he can...well...run out of here with his tackle box.

"Mrs. DeLuca grew up in an Italian neighborhood in New York City, as you all know. She had a large family and enjoyed the close-knit community. When Mr. DeLuca, may he rest in peace, brought her to Virginia, she deeply felt the loss of that community. As she became elderly, she started to notice the comings and goings at Pentagon Place, and she was saddened by the loneliness she perceived in the residents."

He stops and pauses a moment, holding on to the back of his chair. "Now, I ask you, is that so crazy? I don't know. I'm a lawyer, not a psychiatrist. But it was clear that Mrs. DeLuca felt she was too old to affect any change with the residents, but since it was important to her, she hoped that her bright, caring granddaughter would take the job."

"Did she say that about me?"

"Yes, she did. And I'm sure her motivations are more clearly expressed in the letter."

"What letter?"

For once, Dad, Mom, and I all speak in unison. This is getting awfully dramatic for a Will reading, but I guess Granana had a lot of time on her hands to plot and plan. She most certainly was not crazy.

"Mrs. DeLuca left a letter for Lia with specific instructions about her assignment."

"Well, let's see it then!" Mom's hands are flying so fast now she's about to go airborne off the tweed couch.

Mr. Franklin winces, but ignores my mother's shouting and sits back down. "Lia, you will get your letter once you make a decision about how you'd like to proceed. Again, please read the information I've provided, and understand that this is a one-year commitment. Once you've made your decision, I can read *my* secret letter, which will tell me what happens if you refuse the terms."

Now my mother is questioning how I'm supposed to decide without the letter. Why does the letter come after the decision? And the lawyer has a secret letter?

I must admit that it's confusing and cryptic, but she's freaking out and it's not helping.

"Ed, what is this, a game show? Lia must decide if she wants what's behind door number one or two, sight unseen? Can't we have Allegra declared insane by someone who *is* qualified?"

My father tries to calm Mom down, and I marvel at how he completely ignores her comments about his mother.

"And how will Lia earn money while she waits for her big payout, if she chooses door number one?" Mom's eyes are bulging.

Mr. Franklin explains that I will be paid a salary to act as the apartment manager, and it's more than I am making now, and I'll have free rent.

Not that I pay an equal share of the bills now, living with Jason, but he makes way more money than I do and insists on contributing more.

How will he react to this? He was thrilled when we moved in together, and it hasn't even been a year.

Will he view this as a step backward in our relationship? He does tend to think more like my mother, who is still hammering away at poor Mr. Franklin.

Now my parents have moved on to debating the fate of the snack cake business assets. I can't even begin to get my head around that right now. Or probably ever.

Those buildings are worth a lot of money, but only if someone wants to start a business and restore them to their former manufacturing glory.

None of us know a thing about running a factory—that hasn't changed—and my mother is not shy about pointing it out—again.

"Lia, are you listening? I know it's a lot to take in. I don't think we should even think about the business until you decide about what you want to do. What do you think, Honey? Do you want to talk it over with Jason before you give Mr. Franklin a decision?"

Before I can answer, Mom says, "Yes, why don't you go back to the hotel and call Jason? He's got a good business sense. Maybe he'll have some ideas. And you really want his buy-in—this will be a huge adjustment for your relationship. But who knows where the money will go if you don't accept this ridiculous deal? Paul, how are you not upset about this?"

My father pats my mother's hand while she breathes heavily. Mr. Franklin is looking around the room, either for a paper bag for my mother to breathe into, or that elusive escape route.

I find it hard to believe Granana would issue me an ultimatum, and possibly disinherit me.

I bet the secret letter will tell Mr. Franklin to give me the money no matter what I decide.

Mom stands up and offers Mr. Franklin her hand. He sighs as if he is thrilled that one of us has decided to end the marathon Will reading. I bet billionaires and rock stars can get their crap sorted out faster than my weird little family.

My parents and our attorney exchange goodbyes and other pleasantries, while I continue to hold Granana's proposal in my hands. I am dying for my letter, so I can better understand what's behind my grandmother's odd request.

Even though Jason and I aren't married, we've been together for five years, and we have plans. But I still think he'll want me to take advantage of any deal that could help us achieve our goals even sooner, and he'll respect my desire to honor my grandmother's final wishes, especially when he finds out that to refuse her is a huge gamble with an enormous fortune.

And it's only a two-hour drive from Richmond to Applebarrow. We were further apart my last two years of college, after he graduated.

Mom purses her lips and says, "Lia, are you okay? I know this was a lot to take in. Maybe I'm overreacting, and this isn't such a big deal. You could just do ice cream socials or something. And Jason can come visit on the weekends. Maybe you don't even have to *live* here?"

Mom looks hopefully between me and Mr. Franklin, and I say, "Yes I do. Read the proposal. I must become a resident of Pentagon Place, apartment number One."

I close the booklet and rise from my seat, feeling a little light-headed. I don't know if it's hunger, or I am feeling my life as I know it draining away.

All I know is, I need to get my hands on that letter. Granana will do a much better job of explaining herself than Mr. Franklin, and she didn't tell him everything. That's why she personally wrote to me.

Plus, I can't think with my parents...oh, there goes my phone now. I thought I silenced it.

It's a text from Jason.

"Hey, how'd the Will reading go? And how are you holding up with the 'rents? JK—love Paul and Sarah. Can't wait to see you—dinner tomorrow?"

I am not going to respond right away. There is plenty of time once I get back to the hotel to pack. I don't even know what to say right now, but I know this new commitment will involve much more than ice cream socials.

If I know my deep-thinking grandmother, this is a carefully orchestrated plot. My parents don't realize that Allegra DeLuca wasn't just a sweet old lady who sat home and made lasagna, while Grandpa built his snack cake empire.

No, she was smart. Shrewd even. I always wished both my grandparents and my parents had been younger when they had children, so that Granana would be alive well into my adult life. I valued her opinions about career, money, men…

I can't wait to read her wise words, and I trust that she had good reasons for making me jump through hoops to become a wealthy heiress.

Now, to get home and convince Jason that this detour from our plans is a great opportunity.

He likes money, but Jason isn't much for detours.

CHAPTER TWO

"**O**nce you get settled, I promise I'll visit most weekends."

Jason shifts his weight on the barstool and picks at the moist wrapper on his craft beer. "You'll see—the year will fly by, and then we'll be off on our next adventure."

I hold in my sigh and smile instead. I should be glad he's being supportive, but I'm a little uneasy about his dollar signs for eyeballs, ever since I told him that I stand to inherit a lot of money and assets, if I move to Applebarrow and complete Granana's mission.

I did come clean and tell him there's a possibility that I could decline the request, and still receive my inheritance, but that is not a chance he thinks I should take.

I keep reminding myself that most normal people like money. I can't expect him to pretend it doesn't matter, and it's not like he wished my grandmother's death so he could get his hands on her cash.

However, I also know that it won't be easy for him to get away every weekend, no matter what his intentions. He works so hard. I don't see much of him now, and we live in the same apartment.

But Applebarrow isn't that far, and I can probably even come to Richmond during the week...surprise him occasionally. Although, he's always working.

"We'll make it work—maybe I can visit you, too."

I play with the straw in my Fuzzy Navel, as Jason leans in for another kiss. As he moves on to rubbing my leg, his friends and co-workers return from a 'friendly' game of darts at the back of the bar.

From the looks on their faces, I would say that Amy has just crushed the guys, and Zach and Richard are not too happy about losing.

Not that I care about darts, or who is good at darts. Just an observation. I don't even like darts.

Jason holds his beer close to his chest, like a baby. I'm not even sure he likes beer as much as drinking it fits his 'young professional happy hour' image. He usually nurses one all night, but I'm glad he doesn't over-indulge. A drunk boyfriend is not fun.

I shouldn't be so hard on him, but ever since he graduated from college, he's changed. My mother reminds me that it's called growing up.

"Of course, we'll make it work. But I do work late most nights, and we don't know what your schedule will be at your new 'job'."

Unfortunately, he did the air quotes. This is something he would have made fun of in college, but now does all the time.

At least Jason's oldest friend from college, Zach, is here. He's an engineer and the friendliest of the bunch.

If only my own friends were still around. Jason's crew is okay, but since I graduated it's been hard for me to find my own tribe.

I watch Jason banter with his pals, and I smile when I think of all he does for me. Maybe I'm trying to pick a fight because I'm worried about leaving, and if I focus on his bad qualities, I'll be able to go to Applebarrow, and not miss him so terribly.

He may be turning into a bit of a pompous ass, but he brings home my favorite ice cream, and buys tickets to see bands I like. He even leaves me little love notes on his pillow when he leaves for work before I'm awake, which is pretty much every day with my retail schedule.

As I ponder the state of my relationship, Amy slithers, I mean *walks*, up to the bar and says, "Yes, Jason *will* be working late if he wants his weekends free. He's not going to convince Greta to open an overseas office in a year by working nine-to-five."

She tosses her blond mane and wipes her brow, as she orders a beer. She's making a huge show of how exhausting it was to defeat two somewhat drunk office workers at darts. It's not like she just won a cage fighting match. If I tried harder, I could probably...

No, never mind. If I threw a pointy object in public, I might poke someone's eye out. And yes, it's coincidental that I'm having this fantasy while staring into Amy's round baby blues. I am merely admiring her expert shadow application—she's a pro at the smoky eye. Her eyes don't stick together when she blinks.

Amy and Jason are both account executives at an up and coming marketing firm called Elevation. They have some advertising slogan about elevating your bottom line.

They wanted to use the U2 song, "Elevation", but they didn't want to pay for the rights. So, my friend Taylor wrote a snappy jingle for them.

She majored in Music Composition and lives in London now, working as a songwriter. If I told you who she's written songs for, you would die. Well, not *die,* but you would be quite impressed.

Our third college apartment-mate and best friend, Gabby, is in Costa Rica saving sea turtles.

While they are off on those adventures, I help upper middle-class women pick out their clothes at a department store while waiting for MY career to start. Yep, I spend my days suggesting a cold shoulder top for an edgier look, or a cardigan for chilly nights.

I am not interested in including Amy in a discussion of our plans, and she turns away from me when she sees I am not going to engage her on Jason's schedule.

Richard, the other, slightly older, account executive, is calling Amy a ball buster and complaining about these ambitious young kids who upset the status quo.

"She throws darts like she sells, though. You kids make me look bad."

Richard offers cheers to Amy and Jason, who is peeking at me out of the corner of his eye.

He knows his work talk bores me, but since my own friends are all over the world, and I'm stuck here, I make the most of the socialization available to me.

The women at the department store are nice enough, but they are either older ladies getting out of the house, or young girls working a part time job for extra money. There aren't too many college-educated, ambitious young women explaining that the bralette is a fashion statement, and it's okay if your underwear shows a little in 2017.

And now I'm off to Applebarrow to help a bunch of strangers join in friendship and harmony. Sometimes I feel like I left my social skills back at the University of Delaware.

Zach screws up his face at the conversation unfolding about Greta's micro-management, and plops down on the barstool next to me.

"How do you stand this bunch?" he says, while glancing at Jason, who is holding out his pinky finger while drinking his beer. That's new...and weird.

I laugh and say, "I don't know, they're okay. Just trying to make a buck, right? We can't all be scientists like you."

"I'm not a scientist, I'm an engineer. Remember? I build 'widgets'."

I almost spit my drink as he does the air quotes and imitates Amy, who earlier in the night made it sound like Zach was Bob the Builder.

"I'm glad I can make you laugh. You seem tense. Worried about the big move?"

"Yes. No. I don't know. It's not that big of a move, really. My job is a joke here. And Jason is so busy that he won't even notice I'm gone."

Zach leans forward and says, "Hey, none of that talk. That guy is crazy about you. In his own douchebag way, he thinks he's doing all of this for you. He knows how much you want to move to Europe and do...whatever it is you want to do."

He has always teased me for majoring in foreign languages. *'Lia, you know about Google Translate, right?'*

"Very funny. I'm not exactly sure what I want to do. I just know I want to be immersed in a foreign culture. And you're right—I do appreciate it that Jason shares my dream and wants to help build Elevation internationally. It's a perfect opportunity for both of us."

Zach rubs his belly and signals to the bartender for a menu. "I don't know about you, but I'm starving. Nachos? Cheesy fries?"

I nod and feel my stomach rumbling as well. We were supposed to meet for dinner, but then Jason had to work late, and I hadn't bothered to grab something on my own before meeting the gang here.

The Elevation employees (including Jason) are a bit image conscious, and they don't like to eat unhealthy bar food, but I'm not complaining. I don't want to hitch my wagon to a slob.

Not that Zach is a slob, but he isn't exactly concerned with his image with his scruffy red goatee and his untucked flannel shirt.

As I'm judging him, I look down at my own outfit and admonish myself. Most of the time I am wearing what amounts to street-appropriate pajamas, especially when I'm not working at the store.

Zach finishes placing our order and says, "I was thinking—moving to Applebarrow is almost like moving to a foreign country. Except I don't know if you speak the language of the locals there." He laughs again. "I'm only joking. I've done some riding out there and always meet nice people."

Jason appears suddenly and says, "You sure did, Buddy. Looks like you could use a little time on the trails again." Jason eyes Zach's middle and laughs. "I keep saying the trails out there are stellar and we need to start biking again. Hey, now that Lia's going to be living in Applebottom, maybe we could all visit. Your grandmother's house is huge. Right, Honey?"

Jason puts his arm around me as I imagine Amy in spandex, sleeping in Granana's house. Hopefully, Greta will keep them busy enough to avoid that fun weekend outing.

"It's Apple*barrow*." I can't resist correcting him. I suddenly feel protective of my new town.

"What did I say?" He laughs at his own dumb joke and adds, "But we do have to make sure that's not against the inheritance rules. Maybe the family manor is off limits. Once Lia reads the letter, she'll have a better idea."

All eyes turn to me and I reply, "Yeah, once Mr. Franklin gives me the letter, I'll be sure to let you know what we can and can't do."

I look up at the heavens and ask my grandmother to forgive me for lying. I do have the letter, and I'll read it when I'm ready. It's private—between my grandmother and me.

Later, back at home, Jason is snoring lightly. I don't tell him it bothers me anymore because he says it's impossible for a man of his age and fitness level to snore.

Since I prefer harmony, I usually put in earplugs, instead of recording him to prove him wrong.

I am more restless than usual. On the way home we got into a bit of an argument over the whole biking weekend idea. I haven't even moved yet, and he's already asking me to plan activities for him and his friends.

I don't think Jason understands that this is a

serious undertaking I am about to embark on, and that if it meant something to Granana, it means something to me.

He said he was sorry before bedtime, and that he's just anxious about the changes, too, and he's trying to think of ways to make it better, and wouldn't it be fun for *our* friends to visit so I don't get lonely...

I didn't say that they are not *our* friends, but his. And I don't know why everyone is so worried about me being lonely. I can enjoy my own company. If I must. I just *prefer* people around. I'm an extrovert.

It's normal.

The problem is that I haven't met many people I want to be extroverted with in a long time. Secretly, I am hoping that Applebarrow will be one of those welcoming small towns, like in the movies. If I don't romanticize a little, I'll chicken out.

Speaking of chickens, at least my grandparents didn't own a farm!

As my insomnia gets worse, and my thoughts crazier, I get up and move to the living room sofa. With Jason asleep in the middle of the night, it's just me and the raindrops on the windowsill of Jason's high-rise city apartment. I mean—*our* apartment.

I would never say this to Jason, but maybe this will be good for me. My life in Richmond has stalled and I'm stuck in a rut.

I've already agreed to Granana's terms and Mr. Franklin gave me the letter. It's a done deal.

It's times like these I wish I could talk to my grandmother, but ironically, she has presented me with a path, without even knowing I needed one.

Or did she know?

***

"She's his work wife."

Sassy Beauchamp tosses six dresses at me, as I stand outside the fitting room at the Richmond-based Pierce & Ludlow Department Store, where I work as a personal stylist to the (sort of) wealthy clientele who can't afford Neiman Marcus, but still want to feel pampered and stylish.

They will hire anyone to do this job, as *I* am not the least bit 'stylish'.

I buckle under the weight of satin, lace and organza. Sassy is searching for a dress for her husband's fall harvest party and is looking at prom dresses instead of evening wear more suited to her age.

Luckily for Pierce & Ludlow, Beau Beauchamp's company has a party for every occasion. Sassy's Groundhog Day outfit was stunning last year.

Okay, I'm kidding, but Sassy and Beau are really the names they call themselves. I think that's his real name (not sure what his parents were thinking there), but Sassy is a nickname. She is...well...quite sassy, so it makes sense.

"Sassy, come on. Jason is not cheating with Amy."

I put my hands on my hips after hefting the load of party dresses onto a chair in the mirrored waiting area. These seats are usually adorned with bored husbands and boyfriends in the evening, but they are free on a weekday morning.

Frankly, I wouldn't mind curling up in this nest

of dresses and not think about Jason, Applebarrow, Amy, or Granana's scheme.

"No Sweetie, his 'work wife'. You've never heard that term? Here—let me look it up on Wikipedia."

She fishes her pearl adorned reading glasses out of her purse and starts tapping on her iPhone. Her perfect blond bob sways as she shakes her head.

It's hard to tell if Sassy is in her thirties or pushing fifty, and since she has no children, there isn't even that age clue.

"Here we go. And I quote, 'A work wife referring to a co-worker, usually of the opposite sex, with whom one shares a special relationship, having bonds similar to those of a marriage.' See what I mean? It's not sexual. Beau has had tons of them."

I slump down in the chair and get poked in the eye by a stiff lace hem. As I smack down the pile of fabric, I sigh and say, "Well, that still doesn't sound good. I don't want him having a close bond with another woman."

I should ask my mother what she thinks, but I don't want her to think there's trouble with Jason.

Because there is no trouble with Jason. I am clearly overreacting. Sassy and Beau have been married a long time, and surely if having a 'work wife' was a problem…

"Oh, it's fine. You worry too much. Now, occasionally you can get one who oversteps her bounds and you must do some correcting, but I've only had to do that a couple of times. I would keep an eye on this Amy, but what could she possibly have that you don't have?" She blinks and continues. "Now, be a dear and get me these dresses in one size larger. But if you tell anyone I've gained weight, you will suffer the same fate as Beau's last poorly behaved work wife."

She starts cackling, and I join in with a nervous giggle. As I scurry off to fetch her frocks in a size that I know will still be too small (we usually start about three sizes too small—a little game Sassy likes to play called 'what, I had a big lunch'), I wonder what she did to keep her husband's work wives in check.

If Amy sinks her hooks into Jason, I may have to employ some techniques from a pro. Sassy is a bit of a kook, but she's still married, so she has *something* that keeps him interested.

But that's just it. What if I don't have more than Amy where Jason is concerned? I'm not successful, I don't understand his business, and my idea of cycling is going for ice cream on a bike with a basket and a bell.

However, to be fair to Jason, he doesn't seem fazed by her, nor does he look at her as if he's attracted to her. Maybe I'm making something out of nothing.

I should probably worry less about what Jason will be doing while I'm gone, and more about what *I'll* be doing when I'm in Applebarrow.

Sassy also assured me that she'll visit because she can't possibly dress herself without my input, and apparently Applebarrow has lots of cute boutiques that she wants to hit.

Plus, I think she wants to check up on me. And she's a little lonely.

I heave the next bunch of dresses over the fitting room door and go back to biting my cuticles and worrying.

What am I getting myself into? What kind of

people live in Granana's apartments? They might be nasty and belligerent, and I'll have given up life as I know it in Richmond for no good reason, other than possibly money.

And fulfilling my dear grandmother's dying wish.

No pressure there.

However, my life in Richmond is not all fairies and unicorns, that's for sure.

Granana's letter is currently in the zippered compartment of my purse. Once I'm done with Sassy for the morning (who am I kidding?—she's already planning on where she's taking me to lunch), I'm going to read it.

The suspense is killing me, and before I embark on this journey, I need to better understand the mission.

And why Granana thought I was the one for the job.

CHAPTER THREE

"Thanks so much, Dawson. You can put those over there by the bookcase."

I point to the corner of my new living room, and my helpful tenant places several heavy boxes down at once.

When we were packing the car in Richmond, Jason said his back hurt, and he couldn't even move one box by himself. Thank goodness he has friends, or I wouldn't have made it out of the city with my belongings.

"No problem, Miss DeLuca. Happy to help. My lazy brother has joined us out at the truck now."

Dawson tips his hat, which proudly displays his company's logo, Swanson Brothers Auto Repair. He and his brother, Tucker, own the business and are residents of apartment number Five, which is on the opposite side of the courtyard from my new dwelling.

As I remind Dawson to call me Lia (he's only a few years older than me, for God's sake), I survey my new place, which is decorated in mid-century modern furniture with sleek minimalist lines.

It's just my style, but the funny thing is—I didn't decorate or buy a single thing for this apartment. It was set up for me, which only makes my curiosity over Granana's letter burn brighter. After this move is complete, I am finally going to sit down and read it. I've put it off long enough.

Tucker Swanson is the older brother, and has the darker, brooding role down pat. Dawson must be the customer-facing partner in that business.

I smile at the elder Swanson, as he carries in more of my possessions. He gives me an odd look, and Dawson is right behind him with an equally puzzled expression on his open, almost childlike face.

"Miss…I mean Lia, are you okay?" Dawson stammers.

I scrunch up my face in confusion and reply, "Yes, I'm fine. Why do you ask?"

He shifts the weight of the boxes he's carrying to point out the writing on the side. "You just have an awful lot of boxes labeled 'pajamas'. You don't have one of those sleepy sicknesses, like narcolippy or monolukyosis?"

I suppress a giggle at his mispronunciations and feel my face flush. "Oh no, I'm fine. I just have a thing for pajamas."

Tucker walks by with raised eyebrows, and Dawson punches him in the arm. Maybe they think pajamas is a code word for sexy lingerie.

"Of course. Who doesn't like a nice soft pair of flannel…anyway, that's the last of it, Miss. Lia, I mean. We hope you'll be happy here, and may I say again it's a right shame about your Nan. She was a fine woman."

"Thank you, Dawson. And thanks to both of you for your help."

Dawson reiterates his earlier offer to help at any time, and Tucker tips his hat and ambles across the courtyard to their apartment. As I open the door, I can hear deafeningly loud rock music, and I strain to figure out where it's coming from.

Dawson sees my reaction, and says, "Oh, that's just the young couple over there across from our place. They're head bangers. We don't mind too much, but Molly and her girls are the ones who share a wall with them, so she blasts country music to drown them out. Sometimes we do it, too, and they get it from both sides."

I make a mental note to investigate the potential for disharmony there. Loud music is one of the main sources of conflict in multi-family dwellings. I read about it in the apartment manager's handbook I bought.

Plus, when I was an RA, it was a big point of contention among the students when someone was blasting music when others were trying to study.

I call out to Dawson as he makes his way home, "Don't worry, I'll look into it."

"I ain't worried. We just make a rock n' roll sandwich with two pieces of country white. Get it?"

He laughs at his clever joke, and I can't help but smile. So far, I'm not seeing any miserable people here, but it's early. And Tucker isn't all that friendly, but with a brother like Dawson, he probably doesn't get to talk much.

I go back inside, and I'm startled by my adjoining neighbor, Stan Featherstone.

Pentagon Place consists of ten two-story apartments, in pairs of two attached units, arranged in the shape of a pentagon. The five buildings face an inner courtyard, with green space and a large clubhouse.

Stan's apartment is attached to mine. According to the community records, he's forty-five and works as a court bailiff.

"Well hello, you must be the famous granddaughter. I'm Stan Featherstone. I see the wonder twins helped you move in?"

Stan shields his face from the sun, and gestures across the courtyard. He almost looks like he's saluting, resembling a military man with his cropped hair and excellent posture.

I look up at him (literally—he's tall) and say, "Hi Stan, nice to meet you. Yes, they were very helpful."

"Yeah, I bet. If you have a boyfriend, you better let them know right away. I wouldn't be surprised if they were fighting over you right now."

He smiles, and I realize he may be right. Dawson was especially attentive and concerned about my sleepwear.

"I do have a boyfriend, and he'll be visiting often. I'm not worried—they seem sweet and harmless. So, how long have you lived here?"

"About ten years."

His expression softens and I know what's coming. I'll have to get accustomed to this as I meet each neighbor.

"I'm sorry about Mrs. De Luca. She was a great woman, and one hell of a cook! I'm sure you miss her very much."

I nod and thank him, but I didn't realize any of the residents even knew Granana, but maybe it's just the polite thing to say. But how would he know she was a good cook?

"She spoke highly of you, and I'm sure you'll do a terrific job here. Let me know if you need anything, Neighbor."

I absentmindedly murmur thanks, as I now feel the need to read the letter even more urgently. Mr.

Franklin made it sound like Pentagon Place was inhabited by a group of unhappy people and Granana was unable to reach them, but so far that doesn't seem to be the case.

Mr. Franklin is a lawyer, though, so who knows what speech he was asked to recite for the occasion. Granana has some explaining to do in her letter.

Or maybe the residents are afraid that the big city heiress will raise their rent, and they want to get on my good side from the start.

I push those cynical thoughts aside as I close the door to my new apartment. It's a nice duplex with an upstairs—bigger than the place I share, or should I say *shared*...with Jason.

However, it's just more space to feel alone. I hate to be a downer, but this is an abrupt life change and I'm still not sure why I'm doing this, other than it was obviously important to Granana. And there's a lot of money at stake.

At least the neighbors seem nicer than I was expecting, but I don't know if I'll have anything in common with anyone here.

I started to read the tenant files, and in addition to the Swanson brothers and Stan, I am living among a waitress with two daughters, a young couple who apparently plays loud rock music, a craft shop owner, a librarian, a retired county government worker, a middle-aged empty nester couple who work at the post office and the hospital, and a bartender.

Maybe the librarian or craft shop owner are nice. They're women and close to my age. Maybe we could become great friends and do girls nights out.

I sigh and sink down on the sleek gray sectional, holding Granana's letter in my hand with the reverence it deserves.

I know everyone in my life is dying to know what it says, especially my mother and Jason. Dad is too peaceful to be anxious about it, but I'm sure he'll want to know what his mother had to say to his only child. He didn't complain that he didn't get a letter, but he may feel slighted.

I finger the gold envelope and smile. Granana was a lover of the sparkly and outlandish. We'd joke that she wasn't rich enough to have a gold toilet, but she was thinking about it.

I run my fingers over the perfect script—what a lost art form in our generation. If I have children, they may not even teach them how to write at all. They'll just give them little tablets in kindergarten and start with typing class.

I may be young but spending a lot of time with my grandmother helped me to appreciate the past, and the way things were done long before I was born. Granana said I was an old soul.

I cross my legs and sit up straighter, and suddenly realize that opening this with my fingers is going to ruin the envelope, and I want to preserve this treasured heirloom. I don't know if I have a nail file. I don't do much with my nails.

I glance at the desk in the corner of the living room, which I didn't look at carefully when I plopped my laptop and other electronics over there this morning.

I know Granana had a letter opener, but I'm sure her personal items are back at the house—everything here seems to be new.

I also don't understand when she set this up,

and how Mr. Franklin claims he doesn't know. I could ask one of the residents, but I don't want to appear weird to them—like my family is full of mystery and intrigue.

Except, it seems that we are.

Underneath the mail I tossed next to my computer, I see it. I would know that handle anywhere. It's worn but beautiful. It's mother of pearl and inlaid with colorful butterflies. I pull it out and see there's a small note attached.

"Use this to open the letter, Sweetie. That stationary is expensive."

I drop the letter opener and note like they're on fire, and my heart is pounding. If seeing my grandmother's handwriting on such a practical, simple note has me freaking out, how I am going to feel when I read the *letter*?

Well, it's time to find out. Being a baby isn't going to get me the answers I need.

I grab the letter opener and slip the note off, tucking it into a corner on the desk. It's another thing to save, and it's funny. I can hear her talking about the expensive paper. She would save wrapping paper at Christmas, even though she was a millionaire.

Slowly I walk back to the couch, resume my comfortable position, and slice open the gold foil paper.

My hands are shaking as I pull the letter out, and I almost wish I had paid more attention when my father tried to teach me how to meditate. My breathing could use some calming right now.

Wait...today is April 1st. April Fool's Day. Could this be a trick?

I shake my head and feel a stab of guilt. Obviously no one, especially my deceased grandmother, would plan an April Fool's hoax of this proportion.

I blame Jason for making me watch too many scary movies. I especially don't like the ones about ghosts. I remind myself that ghosts aren't real, and that this is just a letter written by someone I love, *before* she died. There is nothing creepy about that.

Here goes.

Dearest Lia,

Did you find the letter opener? I hope so because this paper is expensive, and you'll probably want to keep this artifact to hand down to my descendants. Hahahahahaha...

Anyway, hello Sweetie. I hope you're okay because if you're reading this, I have kicked the bucket. I know you're probably sad, but I have faith that I am in a better place now. I checked it out ahead of time and it seems legit. I know you're confused, but it will all make sense—I promise!

I know you're wondering why I asked you to move to Applebarrow as a condition of the Will, and I hope you don't think I would have cut you out if you had decided not to do it. Mr. Franklin has a different letter for that scenario, but it's sooo boring.

The other letter says the same things I'm writing here, but without the juicy parts. I hope now that you've made the move that you'll stay and make me proud (yes, I am guilting you a little, even from the grave). Hahaha...I crack myself up.

So, just do what Mr. Franklin asked you to do in the agreement—shine your sunny self all over Pentagon Place and help those people have some fun. I know you can do it!

I must stop writing now because my arthritis is

acting up, and this letter is too private to ask anyone to help me write it. I usually ask that nice young man to help me, but I don't want him to know what I'm plotting.

Please don't cry and try your best to keep an open mind. Oh, and tell your father and mother that I miss them and love them very much. But you're the one I hope to see soon.

All my love,
G

P.S. If those bitches from my church stop by don't believe a word they say, and keep a close eye on them, and whatever you do don't let them in my house! A couple of them look like they might have sticky fingers, if you know what I mean (wink, wink).

P.S. #2 Also if you meet someone nice, give him a chance. I know you love Jason, but you're a young girl, and sometimes he's a bit of a cretino.

Okay, that's all my words of wisdom for now.
What the freaking hell?????

I sink back into the couch and rub my temples. I know my grandmother was not senile, but what the hell is she talking about? I'm more confused than ever.

She checked out the afterlife ahead of time? That doesn't sound very Catholic. And what nice boy helps her? And she hopes to see me soon? Before my parents??

She couldn't possibly hope that I DIE before them.

And she called Jason a 'jerk' in Italian? I thought she liked Jason.

And the weirdest thing—that's all for NOW. Are there more letters, or does she have more to tell me when she sees me? Soon. And what parts are juicy?

I place the letter calmly on the coffee table and take a deep cleansing breath. Okay, this makes no sense at all. I should call Mr. Franklin and ask him if he's sure this letter came from Granana, but it does look like her handwriting.

I thought the letter was going to tell me why she wants me to help the residents, and why she asked me to come here, but instead I get warnings about church bitches? And criticism of Jason.

And if this is her *only* letter, how will I know what to do now?

Wait a second...I grab the letter and find the part that is most worrisome—what the hell could she be plotting? Plotting is an active term. Dead people can't plot, unless...

"Ding dong..."

I jump as the doorbell rings. I wring my shaking hands, after carefully placing the letter back in its expensive envelope.

I glance around the room, but I don't see anything unusual. What do I think I'm going to see?

I begin chanting 'there is no such thing as...' when the doorbell rings again. My heart is beating like I'm running from a bear, but I manage to get up and answer the door. After all, only living people ring doorbells.

I continue to breathe like I'm in labor, and sigh deeply when I see an ordinary looking man smiling and extending his beefy hand. The stocky, jovial guy looks to be in his late thirties.

"Good morning, you must be Miss Lia DeLuca. Your grandmother spoke so highly of you. We're so pleased that you're here."

I shake his hand and say, "Thank you. And you

are?"

He laughs and slaps his denim clad thigh. "Sorry, I'm Pete. I forget that everyone doesn't know me, I've been here so long. I'm the maintenance man here at Pentagon Place."

Mr. Franklin did tell me there was a part-time handyman. I think he's only part-time because he has another job, and there *are* only ten apartments. How many appliances can break at once?

As if reading my mind, Pete launches into a speech about how he has another job and that he would love to do this full time, but it doesn't pay enough. He has four kids, and his wife's business isn't steady. The worst part is that he lost his full-time job, along with so many others in Applebarrow, when the snack cakes plant closed.

Pete is not shy when it comes to sharing, and I ask him to come in because it feels rude talking to him at my open door.

I don't have a problem with him not being available all the time, although maybe that *is* a problem. If a resident has an overflowing toilet, I don't want them to be kept waiting. Or call me.

Although I guess I could just call a plumber. Or maybe I could raise Pete's salary and find more projects for him to do.

Once I talk to Mr. Franklin again, I'll hopefully have a better idea of my budget here. Granana only addressed the great beyond, my boyfriend's shortcomings, and suspicious church ladies.

Pete declines my invitation to come in, but asks me what I'm doing for Easter, which is in a couple of weeks.

"Oh, I'm not sure. My boyfriend might come from Richmond. We haven't talked about it yet."

I loved Easter with Granana. My mother is Jewish, and my father only believes in happiness, but apparently that didn't extend to coloring Easter Eggs, a fake bunny who brings you treats, and wearing a fun hat to church. They had no problem letting me visit Granana and indulge in all the traditional activities.

Pete stuffs his hands in his pockets and says, "Well, if you're in town please come to our house. Donna and I would love to have you, and I'm sure she'd enjoy reminiscing with you about your grandmother. It will be a shame to have a holiday meal without Allegra's Italian cooking."

I ignore the fact that Pete pronounces Italian, 'Eyetalian', and wrinkle my brow.

"You had holidays with my grandmother?"

"Not the actual days, obviously. She spent those with her family...and friends. But Mrs. D put out quite a spread for her holiday parties at the clubhouse."

While Pete salivates over the memories of lasagna and chicken parm, I glance around for a hidden camera. *Was* my grandmother's plotting a big joke? It IS April Fool's Day but unless we are on a reality TV show I don't know about, none of this makes any sense.

"So, you're saying my grandmother hosted parties for the residents?"

"Oh yes, they were great fun."

I open my mouth to question Pete further, but I realize it's fruitless. He probably doesn't realize that her parties were unsuccessful, and while people may have liked the food, the neighbors still didn't get along or have any fun together.

"Well, thanks for stopping by, Pete. I'll let you

know about Easter."

"Sure thing and bring your fella if he's in town. Donna loves to work with new people, and she'll be able to tell you if you're getting a ring soon."

Pete laughs as he waves goodbye and heads back to his truck.

What the hell is Donna? A detective?

I'm a little leery about bringing Jason to meet people here, especially if I haven't been to their homes first. He has become a bit of an urban snob. Plus, who knows if he's going to make it out here at all. Easter isn't something he's interested in, either.

Regardless, I am not eager to have some woman I don't know questioning my boyfriend about his intentions. I can't believe how old-fashioned people are here.

I look around my new apartment at the boxes that need to be unpacked, and dive in. I need something to do to channel this nervous energy.

I start opening boxes of pajamas and lounge wear, since that comprises most of my wardrobe. When I was an RA, I spent a lot of time in the dorms, and even for classes, I got away with clothes that were very pajama-like. Victoria's Secret makes some stylish ones that are comfy and fine to wear in public.

Jason was always excited when he saw VS bags in my room and would then be so disappointed when there was nothing sexy in them. He has tried once or twice to get me into some frilly, itchy thing, but I resist. I bet Amy wears lingerie like that.

Why I am thinking of Amy? She poses no threat, and Jason is handling this move so well. I'm just jittery because of Granana's cryptic letter.

I am a bit peeved that she seems to want me to doubt Jason. This is starting to look like a plot to get me to rethink our relationship, but did she think I wouldn't see that? Of course! That's the plot. She's trying to get me to question our relationship by making me move to Applebarrow.

But why?

I could be mad, but I forgive her. It's not like she can do anything to meddle any...

Now my phone is ringing, and it startles me. Why am I so jumpy? It's probably stress and lack of sleep. Next thing I'll be seeing things and hearing scary noises when I'm alone at night.

I see that it's Jason calling and feel a pang of sadness. To appear cheerful and not so needy, I answer the phone brightly.

"Hello, Honey. How are you?"

"Hey, little sweetie. How's my country girl?"

Granana is wrong. Was wrong. Jason is a good boyfriend. No man is perfect. And she's one to talk—she didn't get along with Grandpa so well.

I update Jason on my move-in, and the people I've met so far, and he says, "Ha, should I be jealous of the redneck guys? Just kidding. I'm glad you've met people there to help you. I was worried they'd be total assholes based on your grandmother's assessment."

I wish he wouldn't call the residents 'rednecks' because that's not nice or fair, but this world reminds him of his country upbringing. I rarely brought him here when I visited Granana, and therefore she didn't know him very well.

We laugh about how little he has to worry about, and I ask him what he thinks about me planning my first event as a potluck at the clubhouse.

"It sounds like that's what your grandmother did, and maybe that's all you'll need to do. I wouldn't bend over backwards for these people. Just feed them your grandmother's food and they'll be happy."

"I can't cook like Granana!"

"Lee, just get some cheap jar sauce from the grocery store, or better yet get some pizza place to cater it. They won't know the difference, believe me. My mother thinks Chef Boyardee is Italian cuisine. Don't get stressed out—it's not your job. Just get it over with so you can get the money...and come back home to me."

His tone is playful, but something about it doesn't sit well with me. I know part of my hesitancy comes from my idealist, hippy father and his distrust of wealth and anyone who seems to like it. Jason just wants us to have a good life and move forward with our plans. I should be happy he misses me and can't wait for me to come home.

We end the call with Jason telling me that he probably won't be able to make it for Easter, but he will definitely come when I have my first meeting. "I'd like to meet these people—my curiosity is piqued, that's for sure."

After we hang up, I get a sick feeling. Jason said it's not my job, but isn't it? I quit my job in Richmond to come here and do the job that Granana asked me to do. And if I don't put some effort into this endeavor, why am I here? And what am I supposed to do with all my time?

I know I should tell him that I'll receive my inheritance whether or not I fulfill Granana's wishes, but I don't like his flippant attitude about my role here. And he didn't even ask about the letter. Every time I talk to him, he seems so preoccupied.

Right before I return to unpacking, I have a quick thought and text Jason. Even though I'm annoyed with his comments, I still need his support.

"What if I throw a party and nobody comes? They don't know me."

The reality of how hard this is going to be has set in now. This isn't a college dorm. I have no idea what these people are interested in (except dueling musical tastes), and I suddenly feel shy, and even more alone. I wish Granana could continue to help me, but I must accept that I'm on my own.

I feel silly and almost embarrassed for texting Jason. I don't like him to see how insecure I can be at times. Amy would never do that.

And no, I am not worried about Amy. She is just a woman I see often, so it's natural that I would compare myself to her. My social circle is smaller now and...

Ah, another text. I need to silence my devices until I'm not feeling so jumpy. Just that little buzzing sound gave me goosebumps.

"Do a free rent raffle. They're only eligible if they show up. That'll get them—people are greedy. Aren't you glad you're in love with a marketing man?"

Not a bad idea.

But if people are greedy, isn't Jason one of them?

CHAPTER FOUR

I stare at my phone and consider calling someone. But who?

I've already talked to Jason this morning and told him that his idea worked. I have one-hundred-percent YES RSVPs for the potluck dinner/residents meeting at the clubhouse, scheduled for this Thursday night.

I thought a weeknight was a good idea, so I don't monopolize people's weekends.

He also asked me about the letter (FINALLY), and I told him the truth. He was supportive and said that it's not like we can move to Europe tomorrow anyway, so it isn't hurting our relationship.

I was wrong. I thought he would insist I come home. I can't help but wonder why he's okay with it, but I'm just being paranoid. It's not like he wanted me to leave Richmond.

Ugh...Granana's letter has planted a seed of doubt about Jason that should not be there.

I'm still lonely, so I could call my mother, but she's not going to appreciate my Easter stories from an afternoon spent at Pete and Donna's house. My mother was a good mom, but she's not super maternal. Pete and Donna's kids are so cute, and there are so many. Well, there's only four, but for an only child it felt like ten. And they move so fast—like a swarm of bees.

I would love to talk to someone about some of the odd things I discovered while there, but when it comes to Granana's memory and what I'm learning about this neighborhood and its residents, I am a bit confused and I want to hold some of this new intel close, until I can make some sense of it.

I just wish my grandmother had some close friends that I know well, like a nice next-door neighbor.

Even the church bitches might be able to shed some light...never mind. I can't tell them that Donna and my grandmother read tarot cards together. They might want to do a posthumous exorcism on her house, and lift some valuables while the priest is driving away the evil spirits?

Now I'm sitting in my car, in the parking lot of a local bar, alone and super awkward.

I'm just going to hold my new information about Granana close for now, and go into this bar and order a drink, like a normal adult.

Once you're out of school you can't spend your whole life with a mob of people. It's important to learn how to be alone. And it's less lonely in public than at home in my empty apartment.

I sigh and open the car door, staring at the sign for Tonic. When I asked Siri to help me find a place, it looked like the least rough bar in the area. It looks like a place that a lot of tourists would frequent in this artsy, mountain town.

I'm learning that Applebarrow has a split identity crisis. There are the locals—people like the Swanson brothers, Pete, Donna, and some of the other residents of my new apartment complex who grew up in this area.

Then there are the theater people associated

with the Shakespeare productions in town, and the local artisans and craftspeople, like Emma, one of our residents who owns a shop called The Crafty Owl.

Then there are the hikers and bikers who descend upon the town in good weather to take advantage of the beautiful mountains and cycling trails.

It creates a bit of disparity, and I'm interested to see if an intolerance for diversity could be part of the reason why Granana felt there was friction at Pentagon Place. I haven't met everyone yet, so it's hard to say.

Just a few more days and I'll be leading our first meeting, and serving pasta with jar sauce, and chicken parm and garlic bread from the local pizzeria.

I picked one way on the other side of town, closer to the Shakespearean theater, hoping the residents don't travel that far for their Italian fare.

According to Jason, they order Domino's or open a can. I thought he was being a little jerky (not a cretino, though!), but I have seen the cheap cardboard pizza delivery guy in our neighborhood several times.

I don't normally go to bars, unless it's with Jason and his crew for happy hour. I hope I don't feel out of place, and the only people in here on Easter evening are hard core drinkers with nowhere to go.

Maybe there'll be a female bartender and we can exchange...what? Recipes? Fashion tips? Ugh...

The dimly lit space is surprisingly packed for a holiday, but the dark wood floors, twinkly lights, and long, polished bar are modern and inviting.

I glance down at my outfit and it seems okay for this crowd. I changed into black leggings and a purple, long tunic top for my visit to the Bennetts' house today. Donna was wearing a flowing multi-colored, peasant dress and a flower in her hair.

The whole gang was eager to adorn me as well. The little girls put flowers in my hair, and I had to wear bunny ears and a tail all day. It was fun, though. We colored Easter eggs, but they didn't mention anything about church, but who knows if they went before I arrived.

I still can't believe my devout Catholic grandmother played around with tarot cards, runes and crystals.

I tried to divert my attention back to the kids because while I liked Donna, I felt like she was capable of turning me into a newt. Or at least conjuring up some spirits. She kept talking about Granana as if she is still with us. It's a nice thought in some ways, but also a super creepy one.

Since I must sleep alone tonight—again—I think a drink...or maybe even two...are in order.

Donna did tell me that Jason will eventually propose, but is that fortune telling? We've been together for five years—why wouldn't we get married some day?

I walk up to the bar and locate a seat that isn't too close to the large crowds, but not so far away that I look like the weird, lonely girl.

The bartender comes over and takes my order, but not until I ask her a few questions about the drink menu.

After a few minutes, I see she's getting antsy and blurts out, "Honey, pick something while we're all still young!"

She's just like one of those funny, sassy ladies that worked at our favorite college bar in Delaware. You would think my friends and I would have preferred cute guys, but some of the women were hilarious and great to talk to, especially if you were having guy troubles.

I glance at her nametag and notice that she's taking deep cleansing breaths, although I don't know if she would call them that. I better order something before I lose my chance to grab a friendly ear. I'm thinking that talking to a stranger tonight would be a better idea than calling anyone I know. I need impartial feedback.

"Okay, I'm sorry Janet, is it? I'll have a Long Island Iced Tea."

She wrinkles her brow and says, "You sure about that?"

"Yes, I remember one of the girls in my residence hall drank them all the time. She said they taste just like iced tea." I lean forward and decide to build a little secret rapport with my new friend, Janet. "You see, I don't like the taste of alcohol that much, so I would rather drink something that disguises the flavor."

Now Janet is smirking. She probably thinks people who don't like alcohol are odd, but she's about my mom's age and it may be a little endearing to her. It's possible that I remind her of her own daughter.

"Okay, I'll whip one up for you, but let me ask you something. The friend from college?"

"Yes?"

"Was she stumbling around drunk off her face a lot?"

"Now that you mention it, she was, but so were

a lot of the girls. But I'm only going to have one, maybe two tops. I'll be fine. Really."

"Alright then. They are a bit on the strong side."

Just as Janet looked like she was going to share more drinking advice, a loud male voice yelled her name, presumably from a back room.

"I'm gettin' this nice young lady her drink. I'll be back in a minute." She shakes her head as she begins making my drink and says, "You know, he's lucky he's somethin' to look at, although at my age what's the difference, right?"

I laugh along with Janet, and then get distracted by my phone. It's just a text from Jason telling me that he's too tired to talk tonight and he'll call me tomorrow. I write back with smiley faces, but I don't tell him I'm at a bar alone. He might worry.

Oh, how sweet. He wrote back and wished me luck with the event prep and reminded me that he'll be here Thursday night for our first resident meeting and Italian potluck.

I'm a little worried about my menu. It might need an addition. I should ask Janet.

I jump a little as she bangs the glass down on the bar in front of me. I don't think she's mad or anything, she's just a purposeful woman who gets things done. My father always says that Granana was that way when she was younger.

"Thank you, Janet."

I hand her my credit card and let her start a tab. I feel so adult doing that on my own. In college it was always Jason who took care of paying. Even now, he does it all. I offer to contribute, but he always declines. But I'm sure now that I'm an heiress, he'll let me help more.

Janet hands me my card and heads to the back room, where she is being summoned again. The boss sounds a little demanding, but what do I know about running a bar? Or an apartment complex? Or a factory? Or anything? I sigh and slump in my seat a little as I take the first taste of my drink.

Wow, that's delicious! It tastes just like iced tea. I can barely even taste the alcohol. There must be so little in it. And I'm pretty thirsty, so it's nice to drink alcohol that's refreshing.

I shouldn't have been so responsible with my RA duties in college and let loose with the girls a little more. Truth be told, I was a little bit of a nerd. But so were my closest friends. That's why they're so successful.

Crap, why I am so unsuccessful?

I stare around the room and now I realize that someone from the apartment complex might see me here drowning my sorrows, but I don't recognize anyone. And anyway, I'm an adult and I can take myself out for a solo drink. There's nothing wrong with that.

I should perk up. Everything is fine. So what if my grandmother had a side to her that we don't know about, and she left me a confusing note? Who knows, maybe it will make sense in time.

As I look back at my drink, I see that I've hit the bottom. Shoot, I wanted to order a snack. I had a nice Easter dinner with the Bennetts', but the ham, potatoes, yams, assorted vegetables and six dinner rolls are wearing off now. There was good pie, too.

Now my stomach is rumbling. I grab a menu and signal to the young male bartender—I guess Janet must still be in the back talking to the boss...oh no, there she is at the other end of the bar. I hope she's not ignoring me—I thought we could bond.

"Hey, can I order another drink from you? Janet was helping me."

The cute blond guy (what? I can look) smiles and grabs my glass. "Sure, whatcha' drinkin'?"

I ask for another Long Island Iced Tea and an order of the loaded nachos. It will be a ridiculous amount of food that I won't be able to finish, but who cares.

He nods and walks away to give my food order to the kitchen. At the end of the bar I see him talking to Janet, and they both look at me. I catch their eyes and smile and wave.

Oh that's sweet, Janet waved back. Maybe when it's less busy I'll ask her if she knew my Granana. I doubt she frequented local bars, but my grandparents were prominent people in this little town.

After a few minutes, the bartender—his name is Tim, I think...or Tom, brings me my order, and suddenly I'm so tired. My eyes are getting a little blurry. My contact lenses always get a bit dry late in the day, and I did do those crafts with the kids. I was going cross-eyed with the detail, but they were so cute. The youngest one, Cassidy, insisted upon putting purple glitter on my bunny tail because I was wearing a purple top. So cute...

Wow, these nachos are salty, but so tasty. Good thing I ordered another drink to wash them down. I can't believe how much this tastes like iced tea.

I polish off my snack and realize how hungry I was. I left a little on the plate but now I feel a bit sick, like a little kid who eats too much cake at the birthday party.

I was that little kid because my parents wouldn't allow any food with refined sugar into our house.

As I climb off the stool, I notice there aren't many people left in the bar, but it's a Sunday night after a holiday weekend, so of course people have to go home to sleep so they can go to their jobs.

My only job is to prepare for this stupid...I mean fun party. I wonder if I should make lasagna. But that would be so much work and I'd probably screw it up. My pants feel so tight now—I can't believe I ate all that food.

The hallway to the bathroom is dimly lit and I stumble a little, but I'm fine. I only had two drinks. I'm not that much of a lightweight.

In the ladies' room I almost run into a woman who just finished drying her hands.

"Oh excuse me, I didn't hear you come in. Hey, are you okay?"

I don't know why she's asking me that. I'm a little sleepy, but I'm fine. Oh, what's that wall doing there?

"Yes, I'm fine." Wow, my voice sounds weird in my ears. This bar has odd acoustics. I hope they don't have bands play here.

"How much did you have to drink, Sweetie?"

The nice lady looks so worried, but I don't know why. I look...oh holy hell. I catch a glimpse of myself in the mirror and I see what she means. I don't look good, but I *have* been under a lot of stress. I'm not going to try to explain it to her because if I don't get in the stall soon, I am going to pee in my pants.

"I only had two Long Island Iced Teas."

I walk into the door of the stall before I can open

it. It opens such a weird way, I can barely figure it out.

I still see the woman's feet under the stall, and I wonder if she's waiting for me. Maybe if I stay in here awhile, she'll go away.

"Um, just so you know, the bar actually won't serve anyone more than two of those drinks. They're strong. There are like five different types of alcohol in them."

Oh my God, she has no idea what she's talking about. It tastes almost like an iced tea in the bottle from a convenience store. Honestly, people can be so nosy and silly.

I yell out, "I'm fine." Or at least I think I am. This toilet paper is so hard to get off the roll. This bar kind of sucks. It looked nice when I first came in, but everything is a little off now.

The woman finally leaves, and I step out to wash my hands. I do look a little fuzzy in the mirror and my eyes are red, but once I get home and take my contacts out, I'll be fine.

I go back to the bar and look for Janet or Tim. Tom? Someone to settle my tab. "Hey, is anyone out here?" While I wait, I'll just rest my head on the bar.

Now I hear voices and it doesn't feel like I'm on the bar. It's too soft. So cozy.

"...well, I need to get home. Harold has a fit when I close every night. Just call her an Uber and she'll be fine."

"Seriously? She still has to walk into her house."

It sounds like Janet, and maybe the boss guy who was yelling. I wonder who they're talking about.

I roll over in my bed and realize that if I were in bed, I wouldn't be overhearing a conversation between people who work at the bar. I slowly open my eyes and am immediately blinded by insanely bright light.

"Oh good, she's awake. I'm out of here. Call the Uber. If you're really that concerned you can ride with her."

I see Janet leave the unfamiliar room and realize I must be in the back of the bar. With a strange man. Crap. I just have to hope that Janet wouldn't leave me alone with a bad man.

The hopefully good man walks over to me and slowly sits down on a stool next to the couch I'm lying on. "Hey there. You're Lia, right? Janet took your credit card and then called me when you fell off the barstool. Tim got to you before you hit the floor. Are you hurt?"

What is he talking about? I feel fine. I'm just tired.

I open my mouth to speak and it feels dry and sticky. I turn and see that my caretaker is laughing.

"What is so funny? Haven't you ever been really tired?"

"Yes, I have been...tired...just like you. Those are some pretty strong drinks. I told Janet she needs to make sure people understand what's in them..."

He rattles off a list of different types of alcohol, and as I sit up, I realize what he's laughing at. "I'm still wearing a purple glitter bunny tail. Aren't I?"

"Yes, you are." His eyes are sparkly for this hour, but he's probably used to working long nights running a bar. I'm so embarrassed now.

Thank goodness I didn't see anyone who lives at Pentagon Place. Or at least I don't think I did.

I explain how I was playing with the kids today doing Easter crafts, and he says he totally understands, and it looks like my car has arrived.

Before I can say anything else in my defense, he's in the car beside me and he's talking to the driver like he knows him. It makes sense—it's a small town and he runs a bar. I'm sure I'm not the first person to screw up and get drunk when they weren't planning on it.

Yes, I am admitting to being drunk now, but no one needs to know that. I just won't go back to that bar or take an Uber in this town again.

Problem solved.

"Hey, I do have one question." My voice sounds squeaky and gritty at the same time. "If you guys were going to an Italian party, would you expect lasagna? My Granana made an amazing lasagna, and I think everyone will expect it. Also, she died."

Now suddenly, my face feels wet. I'm crying.

This is why I didn't drink in college. How could an RA behave like this and ever command respect? And what if I had been wasted when Chelsea and Abby set off the fire alarm once a week, burning popcorn at three in the morning?

Now the bar guy and the driver are exchanging worried looks. I know men hate it when women cry. Jason claims it's emotional blackmail.

This bar guy is kind of cute—Janet was right. He looks nothing like Jason. Much taller and more muscular. Also, Jason has a bigger head. And darker eyes. Ha-ha...if Jason heard me say he has a big head, he would be sooo mad.

Before anyone can figure out how to console

me, I'm laughing.

Bar guy huffs a sigh of relief and says, "Yeah, I would think everyone would expect lasagna. I knew an old Italian lady once who made a great one. Everyone loved it. Right, John?"

John nods and agrees enthusiastically as he pulls into Pentagon Place. I don't remember telling them where I lived. The bar guy must have looked at my license. Wait...my license doesn't have this address on it. I just moved here.

Either way, I'm home. My new bed is screaming my name. Granana made sure to get me the finest linens. Seriously, when did she do all of this? Did she know for sure she was going to die soon?

I turn to ask the bar guy if he knows anything, and then I realize he doesn't know anything about my grandmother. He's also not in the car. Where did he go? His lasagna idea was good, though. He has a weird accent—I can't place it, but it's northern so he probably knows lasagna.

In the couple of seconds it takes for me to look around in confusion, the passenger door beside me opens and I see a hand reaching out. Oh, there he is.

"Thanks. I'm so tired."

I grab his hand, and he rests his other hand on the small of my back as he guides me to the front door. He's asking me if I have my keys, and I root around in my purse and drop a Chapstick, which rolls behind the bushes. He retrieves it before I even get a chance to say, 'Hey, there goes my Chapstick.'

He's so fast and I liked holding his hand but that's because I miss stupid Jason. Well, it's not his fault. It's my fault for coming here, but what else could I do? Granana needs me.

"Here you go—I'm sure your grandmother does need you. Now in you go."

How did he know I was thinking about Granana? I must be talking out loud. Hopefully he didn't hear the part about holding his hand. How embarrassing!

He opens the door for me and hands me my key. I stumble in and offer a smile and wave before I sit down on the ground and notice that the car is gone.

How is he going to get home now? I can't believe John didn't wait for him. Maybe he had another drunk person to go pick up, or the bar guy likes walking. He does look fit. But where did he go?

I can't believe I didn't get his name—I think John said it. Something with an N? A G? An A? Maybe an L?

At this rate I'll recite the whole alphabet before I remember. Good thing I don't drink and drive.

Can you imagine if I had to recite the alphabet backwards? Or forwards or sideways? Wait, that last one isn't a thing. So sleepy...

CHAPTER FIVE

"**M**om, it's not that funny."

I finally called my mother to tell her about the letter and update her on my adjustment to life at Pentagon Place. I don't have a lot of time, though, so I left some parts out.

Like the fact that I am apparently the only person who doesn't know that Long Island Iced Teas are lethal, tricky bastards. She doesn't need to know about that.

"It's sooo funny! I can picture you sneaking around the supermarket, loading your cart with frozen lasagna." She snort laughs and I can picture her wiping her eyes and jangling her bracelets. "Wait, did you wear a disguise?"

"No, Mom, I went to the grocery store on the other side of town." This town isn't very big—eventually I'm going to run out of hiding spots to conduct my business. I don't know why living here is turning me into a sneaky...

"Oh Lia, your grandmother would die if she...oh, poor choice of words. Sorry, Honey. Allegra would be *distressed* if she knew you were serving frozen lasagna to your guests and passing it off as hers. If that trick works, these people are clueless."

"Well, I don't know how to make it, and I don't want to. Plus, I don't know how to make the gravy, either."

Another loud snort laugh from my mother. "This is too much." She sighs and composes herself. "But seriously they probably won't know the difference, and it's not like she's going to know. If she's in a better place, she's not worried about earthly concerns like Italian cooking."

We both pause because if there was any earthly concern she would care about, it would be that.

"So, what do you think about the letter? You didn't say anything."

I took a picture of the letter and texted it to my parents. I expected the same type of shock and confusion I was experiencing.

"Well, your father thinks she may have been getting a little senile, but of course he was super positive about the letter. He doesn't think you should put much stock in her words. Old ladies have a lot of opinions, and she was voicing hers, one last time."

"Okay, obviously Dad is going to go all 'happy' with his reaction, but what did you think?"

No matter how much my cynical New York mother embraces her Vermont New Age girl, she has a strong opinion on everything.

"I thought it was a nice letter, and your father might be right about Allegra's mental state."

"Mom, she said she would see me soon! Doesn't that creep you out a little?"

"Maybe it was the way she ends letters. I don't know, Honey. Don't read so much into it. And it doesn't matter if you don't know more about her reasons for asking you to move to Applebarrow. Ed Franklin knows how much you're supposed to inherit and when."

"So, you think it's a matter of me going through the motions to honor her wishes?"

"Yes, I really do. You're going to drive yourself crazy with this, and your future is not in Applebarrow. And speaking of your future, I didn't know she disliked Jason but again—who cares? I hate to say it, but she didn't have such a great marriage."

I sigh and silently forgive my mother. It's too soon for me to hear my grandmother criticized, but I know that my well-being is my mother's number one priority.

And she's right.

"You're right. I don't remember Granana and Grandpa spending much time together, and if she really wanted to make an impact on my dating life, she should have brought it up while she was alive."

"Exactly. Now go have your Italian potluck meeting and do whatever you need to in order to fulfill your promise to Allegra. And then get the hell out of there."

"I will. And Mom?"

"Yes?"

"You don't think Granana would haunt me if she knew I was serving inferior Italian food?"

My mother laughs again and says, "Oh no, she definitely would. Let me know how it goes. Bye for now!"

I begin loading the catering cart (there was one in the clubhouse) with food and start wheeling it over to set up.

I feel a little guilty joking about haunting when Granana is only gone a short time, but she would want us to laugh and enjoy ourselves. She raised the 'Happiness Guru' and she has asked me to bring joy to others as her final dying wish. I can't do that if I'm always sad and taking everything too seriously.

Hmm...the cart is a little wobbly on the grass...oh there's a paved path to the door. I can't believe I didn't see that. My grandparents thought of everything when they built this complex.

The clubhouse is a large building for a ten-unit neighborhood. I guess they did want to create a community. My eyes are tearing up a bit as I approach the front door. Don't worry, Granana. I'll make you proud.

"I'll help you with that, Miss Lia. Why didn't you tell me you needed help? You can knock on our door any time."

Dawson is charming, but I think Stan is right—good thing Jason is coming today. That way he'll see I have a boyfriend and he won't continue to hover quite as much.

"Thank you, Dawson, and please call me Lia. No need for formalities."

He keeps on smiling and it's infectious. I still don't understand how Mr. Franklin painted a picture of a bunch of miserable people.

However, there are several residents I haven't yet met, so perhaps they are less friendly than the Swansons and Stan.

The clubhouse has a full kitchen that is much bigger than the space in our (Jason's) Richmond apartment—not that Jason and I ever cook much. My new, temporary apartment has a decent kitchen, but I should use this kitchen to prepare for parties from now on.

Who I am kidding? I'm not cooking for any more parties. I am counting on this meeting to be a brainstorming session where the residents come up with their own ideas for monthly community events.

I figure if I give one person the task of creating and planning an event each month, it will get everyone involved and contribute to diversity, just like in the dorm when I was an RA.

As I start unloading the cart, I can see that Dawson knows his way around the kitchen. "Dawson, did you do this for my grandmother, by any chance? Help with parties?"

He's already pre-heated the oven, and he knows where everything needs to go. Unless he has restaurant experience, he's helped host parties here a time or two.

"Yes, Ma'am, I mean Lia. I like to be helpful. But Mrs. D didn't do too much cooking in recent years. She was a pretty old lady...God rest her soul."

He looks up to the heavens and takes off his Swanson Brothers Auto Repair hat. "While we're alone, Lia, I was wondering if you would let me take you out to dinner. Preferably at The Stone's Throw in town?"

Stan was right.

"Oh Dawson, I'm sorry but I have a boyfriend, and he's actually coming here today for our meeting. But I'm flattered."

"I know you have a boyfriend. I'm sorry, I should have been clearer. I want a certain ex-girlfriend waitress at that establishment to see me with a beautiful girl like you."

I smile and say, "I see. You want to make someone jealous. That's not nice."

I playfully scold him, but I'm wondering if this waitress person deserves it. I can't imagine anyone breaking up with Dawson, although he is a bit of a puppy dog, and that can become tiresome. Jason may be a little over the top at times, but he's an assertive man.

"Well, it's not just to make *her* jealous. All the jealous skanks in this town would be green with envy if they saw me with a classy woman like you. It would raise my value."

"Why would you want to date jealous skanks?"

"Only the good ones, obviously."

I wrinkle my forehead and think about how to respond to that, when I'm saved by a "yoo hoo" at the clubhouse door.

"Dawson Swanson, are you flirting with this woman? She's our boss—"

"I'm not your boss. I'm just the—"

"And she's an heiress. And she has a boyfriend. What's wrong with you? And I told you that Pam isn't goin' out with you. She has a thing for the fry cook." The pretty, spikey-haired blond looks at me and continues, "I swear. These men, right? I'm Molly. I live next to those young people who play the loud rock music."

She extends her hand, and I remember that's she's in her mid-thirties and has two young daughters. I am assuming she's divorced. She works at a bar or restaurant, but I don't remember which one.

"I'm sorry about the noise—have you ever asked them to keep it down? I can have a talk with them." As an RA I am experienced in noise control.

Molly laughs. "Oh no, Sugar. I don't even notice half the time. It's a running joke we have about the rock n' roll sandwich on—"

"Country white. Yes, Dawson told me that joke. Cute. Anyway, as long as you're okay."

"I have two young teens, so I have my hands

full with a ruckus in my own house. Magnolia and Zinnia are supposed to show their faces here later, that is...the tops of their heads...always bent over those damn phones. Anyhow, let's get this food going. It all looks delicious."

I accept Molly's help, and she explains that she previously worked at Tonic, but now she works at The Stone's Throw, with Dawson's crush.

"I was just there the other night. At Tonic, I mean."

Why did I blurt that out? I don't want the residents to think I hang out at bars by myself. On Easter Sunday, no less.

But it doesn't matter because no one saw my behavior that night, and if I stay away from Tonic, my secret is safe.

Molly heaves the rest of the soft drinks onto the counter. "I'm glad to see you didn't buy any alcohol. Did Logan tell you he was bringing some from the bar?"

"No, who's Logan? Does he work at your bar?"

"No Honey, The Stone's Throw is a diner. I was sick of serving drunks."

Maybe the guy who brought me home is Logan. Sure, that makes sense. He's Molly's former boss, and she probably asked him to bring some alcohol over because he gets it cheaper. That's nice of him, but now he's going to see me, and may say something in front of Molly and Dawson. They don't seem judgmental at all, but it's still embarrassing.

"Logan is my old boss and he...oh, here he is. Logan, come meet Lia, Mrs. DeLuca's granddaughter."

Logan can barely see around the cart of booze he's bringing in for a residents' meeting with like fifteen adults. It's a freaking Thursday night! How much do these people drink? I guess my behavior isn't as scandalous as I thought with this crowd.

Logan stops the cart and says, "It's a pleasure...to meet you." He smirks and offers his hand.

I know my face is red, and it looks like I'm shy about meeting a good-looking man, when I'm worried about the man outing me for getting blasted on two drinks. Or he might protect my honor. It could go either way.

Molly says, "Lia said she was in Tonic the other night—what day was that? Lia?"

Logan looks between us and says, "You don't say? Well, I mostly work in the back and I'm very busy. Sorry I missed you."

So, this is how he's going to play it. Okay, he can enjoy teasing me. He'll get this cart unloaded and go back to his bar before the meeting starts, and anyone else arrives. I do appreciate him pretending he doesn't know me.

"Oh damn, I forgot the bottle openers and the wine opener. I'll go back to my apartment and get mine. I'll be back in a minute."

"Okay, thank you, but I'm sure someone who lives here has—"

"I do live here. In the apartment next to yours. Not the one that's attached to you—I'm in the unit beside you, attached to Fred's place."

Dawson chimes in, "Now, that old man is a hoot. Am I right?"

They start discussing Fred, the funny, old retired guy, and my stomach sinks. Logan lives right next to me. That's why the car was gone the other night. John, the Uber driver was dropping us both off in the same place. I should have finished reading the resident bios.

But how the hell did Logan know where I lived? Or who I am? Is this town that small that everyone knows the DeLuca's granddaughter has moved in to claim her fortune?

I can't keep thinking about Logan and my humiliation because the residents are pouring in now, and I must check on the food, although Molly and Dawson are doing a fine job of handling the kitchen.

Hmm...they might make a cute couple, but she seems a bit older than him, and they've obviously known each other for a long time so if sparks were going to fly, they would have already.

Ken and Beth Washington come over and introduce themselves. They are a middle-aged African American couple, and I notice they are the only black residents. I wonder if they like living here, but from talking to them for a few minutes it's hard to imagine they are uncomfortable in any way, which makes me feel better.

Why do I keep looking for problems?

I know. Maybe because I was told that everyone is miserable.

"...and Lia, I have saved so much money living here. Buying a house is a fool's game. I don't cut the grass or replace any roofs or anything. All my money is in the bank."

Beth Washington laughs at her husband's speech and says, "He thinks that's where it is," and they both crack up like long-term married couples do when they're teasing each other.

Beth is a nurse at the local hospital, and Ken is the Postmaster at the Applebarrow branch. They have a son who is away at college.

"Oh, so that's where your money is going." My out-of-state tuition wasn't cheap.

"No Ma'am, our Ken, Jr. has a full scholarship."

Ken beams with pride, and we chat a few more seconds about their son's achievements and then I move on to the next group of residents.

Olivia Daniels lives in the apartment attached to the Washingtons, across the courtyard, and she's a librarian. Late twenties, single. I try not to assume she has cats because that's such a dumb old-fashioned stereotype, but she looks like she has cats.

She's standing with Emma Barton, whose apartment is attached to the Swanson brothers, on the other side of the noisy young people (who don't seem to be here). Emma owns The Crafty Owl, and she's also in her late twenties. A little heavy with a pretty face, she looks shy as I approach, whereas Olivia looks bored.

"I run the Applebarrow Central Library," she tells me, "and I have three cats. Pepper, Princess, and Poppy. Please don't feed them if you see them out. They are fat enough already."

I hate when stereotypes are correct. She even looks like a librarian, with her shirt buttoned up to her neck and her hair up in a bun.

Her fat remark seems to have made Emma uncomfortable, and she looks away as I engage her in the conversation. Olivia shouldn't make those comments—she looks like she could gain a few.

"Hi, you must be Emma. I can't wait to see your shop."

Emma brightens at the mention of her business. "Do you like crafts?"

I try to remember a craft that I could pretend to like, but I am saved by Fred, the funny old guy that Molly and Dawson were talking about.

He's a recently retired widower and worked in the county clerk's office. He has that twinkle in his eye and seems to be okay after losing his wife. I don't know how long ago she died, and I am not going to ask. I'm sure one of the more gossipy residents will tell me.

I've almost met everyone now, I think. Stan comes in while I'm talking to Fred, smacks him on the back and they shake hands.

The local government seems to employ a lot of people here—I am wondering why there are no former DeLuca's Delights employees living here. I guess that's a dumb question—who would want to get paid by their employer and turn around and pay rent *to* their employer?

Plus, a lot of those people may still be unemployed or have been forced out of the area. Getting a viable business up and running in the old plant seems far more urgent than making sure these people like each other, especially when it seems like they already do, at least as well as any group of residents.

So, the young Santos couple is missing. Molly just told me in the kitchen that they married against her parents' wishes. Apparently, they didn't like their daughter dating a Mexican, and then Arielle rebelled and married Marcos. They're only nineteen and twenty-one! Wow, when Jason and I were that age...

Oh, a text from Jason.

"Hey, running a little late but I'll be there. Don't worry about saving food for me. Amy and I grabbed

a salad over work before I hit the road. See you soon—I'll save you from those boring country folk."

I try not to become too annoyed over him being late. After all, he's very busy and he's driving two hours to see me on a weeknight. And I know he's anxious to be alone with me.

I am oddly protective of the residents now, and I wish he wouldn't call them 'country folk'. It's so condescending. I know he's probably kidding, and he feels like he can say it because of his own origins.

In addition to the Santos', I notice the other brooding Swanson brother is missing.

Oh no, there he is. Tucker is drinking a beer with Logan. He must have found his personal stash of bottle and wine openers.

They are talking low and laughing. Logan better not be telling Tucker about bringing me home the other night. Especially not with Jason on his way. I don't want him to think I'm having a problem adjusting to being on my own, so I'm resorting to drinking alone in bars.

I'm not having a problem. I just moved here, and I'll have lots of friends soon.

Well maybe not LOTS, but I could have something in common with some of the younger women here. We could form a little circle, like in the dorm.

Olivia probably loosens up, and I love to read. And Emma owns her own business and probably has a lot of interesting things to talk about. She's a little shy, but I am so good at helping shy people out of their shells.

And Molly is a mom, so we don't have much in common, but she's friendly. Maybe she can be like a big sister. And maybe Arielle could be like a little sister and I could help her...

"Lia, the food is going to get cold, Honey. Did you want to start talking before we eat?" Molly leans closer and says, "The natives are getting restless. You know, they're dying to know who's going to win the free rent."

She pulls me back to reality with the reminder that I have brought them here with a bribe.

So much for the start of beautiful, genuine friendships.

I survey the chaos in the room and decide that I should make a few remarks and then let people eat and mingle. They seem to know each other well, which again seems contrary to what Mr. Franklin told me.

"Okay, everyone, can we please take a seat? I'd like to introduce myself and chat a little before we move on to dinner."

I smile more confidently than I feel. I'm comfortable with public speaking, but I've done it more often in a foreign language or to a group of peers at college. This is quite an eclectic and restless group of hungry apartment dwellers.

Make it quick, Lia.

I wait until the last person shuffles himself over to a chair, and I smile at Fred, so he doesn't think I'm one of those young people who rushes the old guy.

I stand in front of the room and regard everyone sitting at the folding tables, and Molly winks at me. I guess that's my cue to dive in.

"Hello everyone. Thanks so much for coming—"

"Well dear, you are offering a free rent raffle. Are we doing that before or after the food?"

Now Fred is annoying me a bit, but this isn't school, and I don't want to be too authoritative. I want these people to like me.

I open my mouth to say we're going to do it at the end—that was another one of Jason's marketing tips. If I wait to the end they'll stick around and be forced to interact.

I don't get the first syllable out before Ken Washington says, "I'm hungry! We're gonna need to eat first!"

His wife, Beth taps his arm and says, "You hush up, Ken. It's not anyone's fault you need to eat every two hours like a newborn baby. This girl is trying to talk to us."

I send her silent thanks, but Fred looks worried about the gambling portion of the evening, and Ken is turning as red as a black man can over his wife's public scolding.

"I have a fast metabolism!" Ken sucks in his stomach as he says this.

I interrupt the domestic spat and say, "I promise I'm not going to talk long, and then we can eat and draw the raffle at the same time. No worries."

Now they're all having separate discussions, and I'm losing control of the group.

I don't know what Ken just said to his wife, but now she's yelling, "Kenneth Washington, you know I am menopausal! Don't you dare...I am a delicate little flower!"

Oh wow, she might be...what's that poisonous flower? Oleander, foxglove, wolf's bane?

What? I read a lot. I've never poisoned anyone.

I search the room for anyone who looks like they might be both friendly and strong enough to gain control of the crowd, when I hear a shrill whistle.

All eyes are on Logan. "What is wrong with you people? No one ever behaved like this when Mrs. DeLuca came to talk to us. Now don't you think she would like us to afford her granddaughter the same respect?"

"That right there is a wise statement. You know, sometimes the dead can come back—"

Molly puts her hand over Dawson's mouth, and then wipes it on her pants in instant regret. Dawson holds up his hands in apology, and now everyone is staring at me.

"Thank you, Logan. And…Dawson for that reminder…about my Granana—"

Marcos and Ariel Santos have joined us during the fray, and Marcos interjects, "Is that like a banana flavored granola bar?"

He laughs and now his wife (I use the term loosely because they both look like bored teenagers), tosses her long red hair and says, "Babe, stop it. The lady is trying to talk. This is why my parents don't like you. You're such a wise ass."

I think I'm beginning to see what Granana meant, although until I started talking there didn't appear to be any dissent or marital discord.

Maybe it's because they don't like new people. Change can be hard.

I know—I'll recommend we read *Who Moved My Cheese*!

Never mind, these people aren't going to appreciate the business classics.

I take the brief moment of silence (Logan shot a warning look at Marcos) and continue. "I know everyone is looking forward to eating and the raffle, as

I said, but I wanted to introduce myself. I'm Lia DeLuca, and my Gran...mother asked me to manage this apartment complex as part of her last Will and dying wishes. I hope I can do a great job for all of you. I feel like it's a sign from my grandmother that's brought us together. I'm not sure what it means..." I sigh and say, "Yes, Dawson?"

He's raised his hand. Now they're acting like they're in school, which I suppose is preferable to a jail or the insane asylum.

Dawson puts his hand down and says, "By a sign do you mean like when you see Jesus in your toast?"

My eyebrows instantly wrinkle as Molly waves her hands around, "No, it's more like when you see Jesus in your Walmart receipt, like that one couple. Remember?"

Stan is holding his head in his hands and Tucker is smirking.

Apparently, I am not aware of the Jesus sightings in this part of the country. I'll Google 'seeing Jesus' later so I'm in the loop.

Tucker stifles a laugh that explodes when he adds, "I reckon you may also see The Lord in your bathroom mold. So, you better clean..." He's laughing too much to finish his thought.

I have no idea if they are making all of this up or not.

Finally, Olivia, the librarian, stands up and fingers the pearl buttons on her white collared shirt. "That is enough. Silence!"

Wow, she's good at that.

She purses her lips and stares around the room. "Miss DeLuca has the floor. The sooner you knock off this childish behavior..."

She shakes her whole body like a wet dog and says, "Now let our new apartment manager finish and then we will eat and do the raffle." She peers at me and adds, "And I'm sure the food will be delicious, and the raffle will be very fair."

Hmm, she's helping me out but there seems to be veiled mistrust in that statement. I will make a note to invite Olivia over to watch a movie or something. Maybe do a girls' night in.

I clear my throat. "Thank you, Olivia. Yes, I've prepared a handout that explains how we're going to run our monthly meetings. I think you'll see that it's going to be a lot of fun."

Logan takes the papers from me as I spot Jason by the door. I wonder how long he's been standing there.

Judging by the smirk on his face, long enough.

CHAPTER SIX

"**N**o, thank you. I don't watch silly movies. I read *books*." Olivia flips her head back, as if her hair is down in a cascading auburn sheath, instead of tied up in a bun that is clearly squeezing the nice part of her brain.

"Okay, well I read books, too. I just thought—"

Olivia silences me with her icy stare and says in a low whisper, "You know, I saw you at the grocery store buying frozen lasagna. I wonder what your dear *Granana* would think if she saw that."

Yeah, it's a good thing she doesn't know. But seriously, why does Olivia care? All I saw her eat tonight was salad.

She stands up taller and declares, "And I know why you chose Logan to win the free rent raffle. We're not all blind, you know. Also, some of us have insomnia."

As she glides out of the clubhouse, she casts a pointed glance at Jason and Logan, who are chatting at the buffet table.

Jason came in early enough to hear some of the mayhem, and I was a bit embarrassed at my lack of control.

He smiled and whispered, "I see Jesus in your ear." It made me laugh out loud, but then I felt bad.

My bigger problem is now Olivia. I asked her if she wanted to come over and watch a chick flick, after thanking her for supporting me with crowd control, and she turned psycho on me.

She must have seen me with Logan coming home from the bar on Easter evening, based on her 'insomnia' reference. She obviously thinks I'm playing favorites because there is something between us, and that's bad.

What I don't understand is why she has it in for me, unless she has a thing for him. I wouldn't blame her. He's tall and dark and...whatever.

She saw me choose the name randomly from the bowl! They put their names in the bowl, so unless everyone changed their name to Logan, or they all have secret fantasies about him...I mean, *I* don't have any but if I did...anyway, I didn't do anything wrong. And so what if I can't cook like an old Italian grandma?

Logan and Jason barely noticed her as she marched out the door of the clubhouse. I know Jason wouldn't give her a second look in her librarian uniform (not like the sexy librarian Halloween costumes), and Logan doesn't seem interested in her. I saw her trying to talk to him earlier and he excused himself to get another beer.

Not that I'm watching him, but I am a little concerned that he's going to mention my drunken behavior. I'd like to be respected by the residents.

Plus, I have a long-distance boyfriend, and I don't want to be perceived as a cheater. If I don't drink anymore, I'll be fine. Easy peasy.

Jason is talking loudly and gesturing with his hands, and Logan is searching the room looking like he needs the bathroom.

I know Jason can be overwhelming, but he's making my new neighbor look like he has to poop.

Not good. I hope he isn't bragging. He gets so excited about whatever he's involved in. He's passionate, but sometimes it comes across as braggy to others who aren't as accomplished.

As I make my way over to the guys, I am stopped by a few residents thanking me for the meeting. Stan says he can't wait to float his ideas to me for the May meeting.

He won the lottery to be the next organizer. I'm glad someone who appears to be emotionally stable won, because I am not looking forward to the obnoxious (almost) teenagers, or the bickering middle-agers doing the planning. I can only imagine what activity a 'delicate menopausal flower' will suggest.

"Hey, guys." I lean into Jason and link my arm through his.

Logan notices and I detect the slightest hint of a grimace. I'm not doing it to *prove* anything. Just showing my boyfriend, who I barely see, mild affection. Everyone is so touchy around here.

Maybe that's what Granana was getting at—she wasn't great with words, as evidenced by her letter. I still can't stop thinking about her saying she'll see me soon. I wonder if *she* can see *me*. She didn't say *I* would see *her*, right?

Logan interrupts the awkward silence as Jason gazes at me like he wants to devour me. I guess this is a sickening sight for others, but we've been apart for quite a while, and at least Logan isn't one of those jerks who yells out, 'get a room'.

"Jason was just telling me about your plans to move to Europe? When this nonsensical crap is over?"

I wince but hold onto Jason tighter. I have a

feeling those were Jason's exact words.

Jason takes this opportunity to kiss my neck and add, "Yes, I can't wait to whisk her away on our adventure."

Seriously, he's kissing my neck? He might as well pee on me.

And as if on cue, Dawson yells out, "Hey you two, get a room."

Why is everyone so predictable?

I slowly disengage from Jason and pretend I want another cannoli (these are TERRIBLE by the way—I bought them from a local 'bakery'—my grandmother would die again if she tasted these) and say, "Yes, we've talked about moving to Europe, if Jason's company opens a foreign office."

"Oh, they'll do it. That's why I'm working around the clock." He turns to me and says, "I'll be in your apartment. Can I have the key?" I hand it to him as he shakes Logan's hand. "It was a pleasure, Landon. We'll have to check out that bar of yours on one of my visits."

Hmm...that was an abrupt end to the conversation. Logan didn't bother correcting him.

I am taking that as my cue to leave as well, but I see Molly and Emma cleaning up, with Dawson at their heels, and I should help them, if I am ever going to get out of here and join Jason.

Logan says, "Hey, you can go. I'll help them close up. It's like the work I do at the bar. Us 'service industry' folks are good at that sort of thing."

He does the air quotes around 'service industry'.

"I'm sorry if Jason was a little bit of a—"

"Dick?" He laughs and says, "Too much?" He pauses and looks into my eyes, "Hey, I get it. Long-distance relationship, gorgeous girlfriend. He's bound to be a little territorial. He's clearly insecure, but I don't know him. Maybe he has a reason."

Before I can formulate Jason's defense, Logan continues. "And don't worry. I'm not going to say anything about the other night. Now, go ahead and ditch the Applebottom Hillbilles and join your man. He's waiting."

Logan winks, but I detect enough sarcasm to choke an elephant.

"He said that, didn't he? I'm so sorry."

"Stop, I'm teasing you. As you get to know me, and most of these people, you'll find that we don't care what people like Jason think. And I'm sure he's a good guy at heart. He won your heart, right?" He grabs the tray of crappy cannolis and adds, "And anyway, I'm from Chicago. Everything isn't always as it seems. Good night, Lia."

My face is burning. I'm not sure if I'm just mad at Jason, or embarrassed by his behavior? My own behavior? Annoyed with Logan for being so self-righteous?

Damn those Long Island Iced Teas.

One thing I know—my face is also flushed from excitement. Jason may *be* a bit of a dick, but I've missed...well, you know what I mean.

***

"BZZZZZZZ"

Uh oh. A buzzing noise.

I sit on the couch reading a book—well I'm sort of reading it. Truthfully, I'm bored. Reading Madame Bovary in the original French isn't as engaging in an empty apartment in the middle of nowhere, as it was when I took Nineteenth-Century French

Literature in college.

Maybe Jason is right. I'm not going to make friends here or fit in, and I should focus on getting out as soon as possible. After all, in no time I could be headed to an exciting life in Paris, Lisbon, or Frankfurt.

I'm not quite sure what I'm going to actually DO in those places, other than fluently speak their languages, but still—I will be *living* in Europe. With Jason.

"BZZZZZZ"

I drop Madame Bovary and the corner gets soaked in salsa. Crap...that's why my father always warned me not to eat snacks while reading first edition foreign classics.

I know, my family is weird.

I wipe off the edge of the book and set it on the coffee table, along with my bowl of salsa, next to the chips and Coke. If Granana could see me I'd get such a lecture about my eating habits. I sigh and sink back into my seat. I miss her, and I wish she could be here, even to chastise me.

"BZZZZZZ"

I jump and my heart pounds. Okay, calm down. It's probably a bee. It's not a sign that Granana knows I'm eating junk and feeling sorry for myself, alone on a Friday night.

"And anyway, cut me some slack, Granana. I just moved here, and Jason had to go back to Richmond. I have no friends!"

Now I'm bonkers—talking to a bee that I haven't even seen yet as if it were my... "AAAAHHHH!!!!"

The bee picks my moment of mental collapse to dive down right in front of my face. What the hell? Is it sniffing me? It's not a dog. Holy hell, I must get it out of here. I don't kill bugs. Especially if they might be my gran...AAAHHHH!!!"

Now the bee is heading back into the kitchen. That makes sense. I probably left something sweet out. Don't bees like sweets? I'm a linguist, not a biologist.

I look in the coat closet for a fly swatter, but if there is one it's probably in the kitchen and I'm not going in there unarmed. Crap, here it comes again.

I grab a magazine off the end table—where did a Cosmo come from? I don't read that nonsense... "AAAHHHHH!!!!!"

The bee is back in the living room, buzzing itself silly. I run to the front door, open it, and then jump back inside to shoo the bee out the door. Of course, I am not thinking that any number of its friends could be coming in while the freaking door is wide open.

Maybe if I stop screaming...

"Come on, little bee. I know you're not my grandmother, but I'm still not going to kill you."

"Who are you talking to?"

Standing in my doorway is Logan. I should have known some chivalrous man would come running when I screamed. It is the south, after all. Even if Logan is from Chicago.

"I'm talking to the bee." I point into the apartment as I join him on the front stoop, just now noticing that I'm wearing my Peter Rabbit bunny pajamas in honor of Easter month.

"Oh, the BEE! Of course. The bee that isn't your grandmother. Makes sense." He smirks and I'm not sure if it's because of my fervent conversation with an insect, or my festive, super cute sleepwear.

"Well, can you help me get it out of my apartment?"

"Are you allergic to bee stings?"

"I don't know."

"You've never been stung by a bee? Do you go outside?"

I push the magazine into his hand, and now I see that he thinks I've been reading about 101 Hot Sex Moves and how Ariana Grande doesn't need a man. Well, whoopy for her! I can't afford to hire someone to kill my bugs. At least not yet.

Logan takes the magazine and looks like he's going to make a snarky comment, but heads back into the living room to get rid of the bee.

"Don't kill it!"

"I know, on the off chance it could be your grandmother."

Even though he thinks he's being sly, he manages to get the bee out. For some reason (probably the fact that Logan isn't wearing a shirt—wow, he did run over thinking I was getting murdered—how sweet), I am frozen to the stoop. He grabs my hand, pulls me outside, and slams the door.

"Why did you do that? Ohhhh, so the bee doesn't get back inside. Right?"

He laughs and says, "Look at you, figuring things out in your time of distress. Is everything good now? Any other issues that might cause screaming? Other than your reading material?"

"I don't even...that's not...I don't read...damn it." Now I'm moving into the 'looks cute when mad' phase of my frustration response.

You would think I'd have learned to control this with the hippy happiness parents who raised me.

"It's okay, Lia. I'm teasing you. So, I take it Jason went back to Richmond?"

I sigh and say, "Yeah, he has to work hard so we can go to Paris or—"

"I know, Lisbon or Frankfurt. He told me, remember?"

"I'm sorry again. He can be a little overbearing when he talks about work, and I think he's a little worried about me being here on my own. And since you're such a...you know..."

"Such a...?"

"Well, you're such a handsome guy, he might have been a little jealous. I know that's ridiculous, but—"

"No, I get it. I am pretty handsome." He laughs and his eyes shine. They freaking *shine*. I wish I had a shirt to give him to put on. Well, not really.

"And Lia, don't worry. I know I tease you, but I will not say anything about your night at the bar, as long as you don't make a habit of it." He gives me the finger shake warning used by moms everywhere. "I may not always be around to rescue you."

"Thanks. I appreciate it. And Jason will be back in May for the next resident meeting, so you'll see him then. I'll talk to him about his attitude, but I think he'll be less of a jerk as time goes on."

I'm sure once everyone gets to know Jason, they will like him better, but I sound like an idiot with my lame defense. I can hear Logan thinking, 'Wow, he'll be *less* of a jerk—how awesome.'

Logan doesn't respond right away, and now it's becoming increasingly difficult not to stare at his bare chest, especially because I'm a lot shorter than him...and I am a bit flushed now, but it's only from chasing after the bee. I need more exercise.

"Well, thanks for coming to my rescue *tonight*." Now I giggle like a little girl.

Jason has nothing to worry about even if I was into Logan. My 4.0 average and excellent organizational skills are not showing themselves when he's around. All he's seeing is that I can't handle alcohol, I'm afraid of bees, I'm afraid my grandmother has come back as a bee, and I wear bunny pajamas.

Oh, and to add to the image, I read Cosmo for sex tips and defend my boyfriend's disrespectful behavior. What a catch I am!

"Hey, it's no problem. I'm surprised the rest of the men in our complex weren't lined up to help you. Especially Dawson. I'd say he has a crush on you."

I'm sure the other men are out on a Friday night. Even old Fred probably calls the numbers at bingo, or drinks beer at the American Legion Hall.

Hmm, I wonder why Logan is home.

"Um, I was wondering. Now that you're here and all. Would you like to stay and watch a movie? I was about to make popcorn."

I feel my cheeks burn as soon as the words are out of my mouth.

Boy, do I dislike being alone.

Why would Logan want to watch a movie with me? We've set our boundaries regarding my boyfriend, and it's only seven o'clock. He was probably getting dressed for a date, or to go to work at his bar, when he heard my blood curdling, overly dramatic screaming.

That's why he's not wearing a shirt.

He doesn't answer right away so I add, "Well, you could go home and get a shirt first because that would be...you know...better...for you I mean. But if you're busy..."

God, I wish the bee would come back and bring his friends, to divert attention from the stupid coming out of my face.

"You talk a lot, you know that?"

His eyes are so damn sparkly.

"Yeah, I know. My mother said when I was a little girl, I followed her around saying, "Mommy, I have sooo much to tell you."

"I'm sure you were very cute. As much as I'd like to watch *Peter Rabbit* with you, or maybe *Bambi*? *Who Framed Roger Rabbit*?" He presses his lips together to stifle his laughter, because I clearly don't appear amused.

"I'm sorry, but your face is...you're so easy to tease. Seriously, I have to go to work. So, I'll see you...around."

Now he's the awkward one, as he points his finger at me like a gun and heads back down the walkway to his apartment. Luckily, it's only about twenty steps from where we're standing.

"Okay, good night." I give him a little half wave and wonder how this exchange got so weird, so fast.

And who may have been watching the whole thing.

"He turns around and says, "Hey, you know there's a big screen in the clubhouse. We could do a movie night for the next meeting."

"That's a good idea, but Stan chose a book club meeting. He's supposed to tell me the book tomorrow."

"Oh, I can't wait. It will probably be some unsolved murder thing. And listen Lia, for what it's worth, I've never seen any woman rock bunny pjs like you."

He smiles and opens his door slowly, disappearing with his smirk...and that chest.

I let myself back in my apartment, quickly so as not to attract any more reasons to require rescuing.

Hopefully Jason will be back *before* the May event, but even if he isn't, he said he was going to read the book, come and participate, and stay for a few days.

He also wants to check out the old snack cakes plant. I'm avoiding these practicalities, but Jason will force me to face them, and that's one of the reasons I love him.

However, he also said he will be surprised if our new friends can read.

I won't be sharing that observation with Logan, or any other residents of Pentagon Place.

***

"I think this will be a good pick. It's a Bizarro novel, not horror."

Stan fidgets on my couch as he shares with me the details of some disturbing looking novel on his Kindle. It sure looks bizarre. Maybe letting the residents choose their own monthly meeting events was a bad idea.

It's Monday evening, and Stan called yesterday to ask if he could come over to discuss the novel for the book club meeting, so we could decide in time for everyone to acquire and read the book.

I put on actual pants for this discussion. I was not interested in any of my 'pajama' choices being mocked, even though they are perfectly appropriate to wear in front of others.

"Okay, it looks...interesting. Can you tell me what Bizarro is again?"

"Sure, it combines absurdism, satire and the grotesque. It's meant to show pop culture in a weird and subversive way."

I nod, as if that answer helps me. I am afraid to even read the description. I don't want to insult Stan, but I don't know if anyone else is going to like this. But perhaps I've been reading foreign literature for so long that I'm not up on modern contemporary genres.

I've always been a little out of the loop with pop culture. First by circumstances, growing up with odd parents in rural Vermont, and then by choice—once I deemed myself an intellectual.

Chick flicks don't count because...well...because other women like them, and I was trying to fit in. And I don't have a stick up my butt, like some people (Olivia).

I sigh and remind myself that I don't want to be perceived as a snob, or someone who is rigid. Who knows? Maybe sick and subversive books are super popular in Applebarrow.

Somehow, I can't see our head librarian getting behind this trend, but since she and I did not hit it off, I don't think I'll run this by her.

The other possibility is that no one will read it, and we'll have an alternate activity. I could have a movie ready to show in case it all falls apart, but then I'll be sad for Stan. He's so excited.

"What do you think? Pretty cool, right? And the book is only ninety-nine cents to download, so everyone will buy it."

"It sounds fine, Stan. Thanks for your enthusiasm and getting on this right away."

"Oh, I love a good book club meeting. Also, I was thinking for snacks we could do some with scary themes. Like Halloweeenish? I know it's May. But some things are scary any time."

"Yes, they surely are."

I am beginning to think Jason has a point. What am I *doing* here? I feel like I'm losing control of the mission before I get started.

The doorbell rings, just as Stan was most likely getting ready to show me his Pinterest board with Halloween ghoul and goblin treats.

Great, now what will we do when it actually *is* Halloween?

The fact that it's five months away, and I will still be here to deal with it, is a depressing thought. Maybe by then the residents will grow tired of this whole monthly meeting thing, and Mr. Franklin will let me off the hook, because I tried my best. That's all I can do.

"Stan, can we save that theme for Halloween? How about Mexican? People like that."

The doorbell rings again.

"I need to get that. Why don't you send me the links to some ideas for snacks, and I'll see if any of the other residents want to help with the food. And I'll send out the book link with the invite."

Stan stands and gathers his belongings. "Thanks, Lia. This is going to be so much fun. You'll see."

I open the front door to let Stan out, and Mr. Franklin extends his hand.

"Stanley, nice to see you. Keeping busy helping Miss DeLuca with her meeting planning?"

"Yes, he's going to lead a book club discussion."

"Wonderful. I do like a good mystery myself. Maybe I'll join you. Unless you're reading something romantic."

The men laugh while I try to conjure up any way there could be romance in the Bizarro book. I'm hoping there isn't, because grotesque romance is where I draw the line.

Stan says his goodbyes and I invite Mr. Franklin in. I have no idea what he wants.

"I'm sure you're wondering why I stopped by. Hope it isn't too late, but I saw your light on. Is everything going well here?"

It's only seven-thirty.

"Oh, it's fine. And yes, everything is going pretty well. I think everyone enjoyed the first event and seem eager to come to the next one. It's odd. My Granana made it sound like they hated each other or didn't interact, but it's not true."

"Hmmm...I suppose that was her perception. Or perhaps that was the hook to get you here and she has a different plan for you. I always found Mrs. DeLuca to be a bit mysterious."

He's either a great actor or Granana has him fooled, too.

"Granana? Mysterious? I'm sorry but I don't see that. She attended church at the same time every week, she ate the same foods, and we did the same activities when I visited. She wasn't the 'shake it up' type."

"Lia, don't you think it's possible, or even probable that there is a lot about your grandmother's life that you don't know? She was ninety years old. She lived a long life before you were even born."

I sink into my cozy armchair. "Yeah, that's true.

Maybe I didn't really know her. There was something in her letter that was disturbing."

"What was that?"

I motion for him to take a seat and he does, with a worried expression on his kind face.

"She said she would see me soon. It scared me because I don't want to die soon, obviously, and I don't see any other way she would *see* me. Unless she believed that she would be able to look down upon me from heaven?"

"Yes, I'm sure that was part of her belief system. She was a very spiritual woman."

"Thank you. That's comforting. It's hard to talk to my parents about this situation. My mother wants me to move on with my life with Jason, and my dad is too positive to critically analyze anything."

"I understand, but your parents surely mean well. Any time you'd like to talk about Allegra, just let me know. Oh, and Lia—the free rent thing. I understand why you did it but one of the residents came to me with a complaint about it. She said she felt there was favoritism."

"How could I show favoritism for someone I just met?"

I am hoping Olivia did not tell Mr. Franklin some embellished tale about my late-night drunken exploits with the hot bartender.

"I don't think it was because of you. Mrs. DeLuca had her favorites. You couldn't know that, not unless Allegra told you. I would be careful and try not to bribe them. The money truly will be yours to spend as you wish, but it would be nice if they come around on their own. Don't you think?"

I agree with him and ask him if he wants to stay

for tea. I know better than to suggest a movie. No one seems to be interested in that, plus he's our lawyer and old enough to be my father.

But I still get bored.

He refuses my offer, which is good because I remember that I am not my grandmother and do not keep tea in the house. He leaves with the promise to stop by the May event and see how things are going.

I can't believe that nice man is a con artist hired by Granana to help her meddle in my life from beyond the grave.

Right before he leaves, he says, "Lia, you're doing a splendid job. Don't overthink. I know your grandmother is proud, and I do think she's watching over you."

He looks up and following his gaze all I see is the top branches of the trees next to the building, and the gutters that look like they could use a good cleaning. Note to self to ask Pete to get on that.

Instead of letting on that his comments are freaking me out, I say thank you and close the door, with promises to end all resident bribery.

I lean against the door and listen. I don't feel anyone watching me.

In a way, it's oddly comforting that people can look down upon their loved ones, but I don't know if I believe it.

I'm also so incredibly isolated that my mind could easily start playing tricks on me. I don't see how I'm going to be able to read that Bizarro novel. My own life is bizarre enough lately.

And did I mention boring?

I hate to say that I'm bored because there is so

much entertainment in this world. I'm healthy, intelligent. I have a car and money.

But I am sitting alone in this apartment, thinking about whether my late grandmother is watching me, and not working hard enough to make friends.

Tonight, I am going to get a good night's sleep, and then tomorrow I am going into town and introducing myself to some of the merchants.

And I'll stop into Emma's store. She's likely to be more outgoing in her element. I feel like the rest of the residents intimidate her, and she's not able to make herself heard.

At the very least I can buy some hook rug and sock puppet kits to keep me occupied.

I *could* invite one of *my* friends to come for a visit, but everyone lives far away and is busy.

No, I can do this. I am tired of people saying that I'm not independent and I can't function without a huge mob of friends. That was college Lia. I can adjust to adult life.

I'm going to heat up some of that frozen lasagna and get to bed. Hopefully it won't give me bad dreams, but I am starving, and I won't be able to sleep on an empty stomach.

That's another solo issue I have—I don't like to eat alone so I often skip meals and then I'm starving right before bed.

That goes on my list of things to work on. With all this self-improvement I am going to be so ready to make Europe my bitch.

As I preheat the oven and pop in a reasonable sized portion of lasagna, I think of Olivia.

I hate it when people don't like me, and there's no good reason. She *must* have a thing for Logan, and she thinks I'm interested in him. That's the only sensible explanation. But Mr. Franklin insinuated that Logan was *Granana's* favorite, and that's ridiculous. I guess she could have loved him like a grandson, but she surely wasn't interested in Logan as a partner. That's sickening.

I shake my head and huff. Why am I thinking such things? I haven't even touched the Bizarro book yet and my own imagination is getting creepy. Too much idle time is bad. Maybe there are some foreign language meetups here that I could join? Or I could do some volunteer work. As much as I love this apartment, I'm going stir crazy already.

I can't help but smile as I sink my fork into the processed pasta, sauce, meat and cheese. Granana truly would have a freak out if she saw this. She did try to teach me how to cook, but I wasn't ever paying attention. I enjoyed speaking Italian with her and learning about our family heritage.

With a full stomach, I retire to my cozy master suite with the fluffy, soft bedding and hope to get some rest. Tomorrow is another day to reset my buttons and work on making my life better here. I'm sure Jason is fine and keeping up with his commitments. I can't fall apart just because I'm on my own.

After dozing off for what my phone tells me was a few hours, I hear a noise coming from downstairs.

I know I locked the door, so even though my heart is pounding there is no need to be so afraid of a little noise. Maybe I have mice. That's plausible.

And no one would break into our apartments. It's a small community where the units are close together and facing each other. It would be hard, and everyone would hear my screams.

I am almost certain each of the residents of Pentagon Place owns at least one gun, too.

Somehow the pep talk is not soothing my nerves because I still hear the noise. It sounds like it's coming from the kitchen.

It's probably a mouse. Or a bunch of mice. They travel in packs.

I won't be able to sleep if I don't check it out. If it's mice, I'll just call an exterminator. It's not like they're going to murder me.

I don't want to kill them, though. Maybe I won't tell anyone, and I'll order some of those humane traps, like my dad does in Vermont. Then I can drive them further into the country and set them free.

As I contemplate my fun road trip with rodents, I scan the bedroom for anything that could be used as a weapon, in case the noise is coming from a larger creature.

I think there's a fireplace poker downstairs. I could run and grab it, and then head into the kitchen.

I tip-toe down the stairs and realize I forgot my glasses. I wear contacts and I can't see a damn thing now.

I squint as hard as my eye sockets can tolerate, and locate the fireplace, gently pulling the poker out of its stand. It's a pretty lethal blade, but hopefully I am not going to have to poke anyone.

Now that I'm sneaking around in the dark, I'm thinking that staying upstairs and calling 911 would have made more sense. But then if it *is* mice, I will look like an idiot—'Officer, please arrest Mickey!'

I sneak into the kitchen and hear rattling in the pantry. Crap, that could be a whole family of mice. They may have run in during that stupid bee incident. I blame Logan for distracting me.

Not that he was distracting me with his looks or presence or anything. Just by him standing there teasing me when I only needed a bug eliminated.

I decide to go for it. If I ever want to get back to bed, I need to... "AAAHHHHH!!!!!!!!!"

I open the pantry door and there is a person in there! Well, I think it's a person. I don't want to beat her—it looks like a her. She looks old and she's touching things on the shelf. Is there an old folks' home for sleepwalking kleptomaniacs near here? Seniors with drug habits? Although if she's going to sell my cans of soup and...oh my God...

The woman turns around and I draw my weapon up higher, and she looks weird. Like a dream. This *is* a dream. Everyone says not to eat a heavy meal before bedtime. That's good common sense.

The figure is definitely female, and she's kind of fuzzy. I'm totally dreaming. I look at my weapon and realize it's an umbrella.

See, I'm dreaming. It's not just because I can't see shit without my glasses in the dark.

When this person turns around, I'll be sure of it, and then I'll probably wake up for real, get out of bed and slap some cold water...

She faces me, and with a menacing tone and a furrowed brow, says, "Jar sauce? And what's this I hear about frozen lasagna?"

I see the jar of Prego in her hand as I hit the floor.

CHAPTER SEVEN

"Lia? Sweetie? Please wake up. Oh, my goodness, if only I could touch you. Shoot, how I am going to get this thing on...?"

I open one eye and peek at a lady trying to put the kitchen light on but looking at it and jumping up and down, while I lay sprawled out on the floor. I would help her, but who the hell is she? And why do I keep waking up from a dream IN a dream?

"AAAHHHHHH!!!!"

Now she's right in my face. Her voice sounds so familiar.

"Granana????"

"Well it's about time. I see the problem. You jumped out of bed without your glasses on. I told you to get that Lasik surgery. I hope you'll do that now with the money...what's wrong, Dear? Oh, that's right. Silly me. I'm dead and that's weird for you. I'm used to it by now."

I jump up and run upstairs to get my glasses, hoping this thing that looks like my grandmother doesn't morph into a dragon while I'm up there. Ow, my back hurts. Did I really faint? Or is this still part of the dream? Can your back hurt in a dream?

Screw the glasses. I'm going back to bed.

That's it. If I go back to bed, then I won't have to deal with the lady in the kitchen.

I will never eat lasagna late at night again.

I climb back into bed and turn off the light, shutting my eyes tightly. I wish I could call Jason to talk me off this ledge, but one of the perks of a long-distance relationship is NOT middle-of-the-night calls from your girlfriend, telling you that she saw her dead grandmother in her pantry.

I start deep meditation breathing, and my heart rate is slowing down. I think everything is okay now and I should…

"Well now, I can't I turn this light switch on, either. I was able to touch the food, son of a gun. I guess I should have paid better attention in Haunting class, but the teacher is so boring—a real stiff. Hahahaha. How the hell am I supposed to be seen if I can't turn on a damn light?"

If I keep my eyes closed, it will go away.

"AAAAHHHHH!!!!!"

"Sweetie, I would hand you your glasses, but I can't seem to pick things up."

The Granana-looking thing is in my face again. I jump up, grab my glasses and turn on the bedside lamp in one motion.

Holy crap.

"There we are! Do you see me now? They told me I would appear a little fuzzy at first, but over time I'd get the hang of appearing more clearly. How do you like my outfit? Sweetie, close your mouth—you'll catch flies."

Closing and opening my eyes isn't helping to erase this image. Nor is smacking my head with the palm of my hand.

"You can't be real!"

"Oh, I am Lia. Well, not *real*. Not like you're real. But I'm here. I told you I would see you again soon. I guess I should have explained that better, but I didn't want to scare you."

"Oh no, God forbid you should *scare* me!" Is she for real? I mean, is she a ghost? A real *ghost*?

"How have you been holding up? I see you faked my Italian cooking. If you're going to serve the cuisine of our mother country, you have to do it right."

"I'm...sorry..."

I'm apologizing to a ghost. Is jar sauce and frozen lasagna powerful enough to summon the dead?

"Well, I don't want to keep you up all night. We all need our beauty sleep. Well, not me because I'm dead. Hahahaha...do you like my new look, by the way? Fashion in heaven is so freeing!"

She's wearing a tutu, a tiara, and her hair is pink. Is there any wonder I still think this is a dream?

"It's very...pretty. Wait, I had a Halloween costume like that—"

"—when you were three. Yes, my dear Lia. I'll be back again to see you. I was interested in checking out your pantry because I was suspicious about the food served at that party—"

"You saw the party?" What else can she see? This is too much.

"Yes, Honey. I can see the things I need to see. But nothing too private, especially if a certain young man comes around. I'm your grandmother after all, not some creepo."

She winks and the thought of her showing herself to Jason makes me cringe.

"So, yes, I wanted to check out the food and make sure you've been eating, and I planned on showing myself tomorrow in broad daylight so we could have a catch up. But this is more fun."

Oh, it's a laugh riot.

I don't know what to say to an old lady apparition who is wearing a grown-up version of my preschool ballerina outfit, and she's supposed to be DEAD!

"I know this is a big shock. I promise it will make more sense soon. Now try to work with Stan on the scary book party. He's a good guy...I know the Bizarro interest feels a little serial killer-ish...like he's one of those quiet ones the neighbors talk about on the news..."

I hadn't though that, but yay for new bad thoughts.

"...but it's actually an interesting genre. He lent me a few to read before the end, but my eyes were failing. I can see 20/20 now! No glasses!"

She does look different. Also, she's dead so...that's different.

"I'll probably pop in before the party. I'm not the strongest spirit yet. Apparently, it takes time, but I think I'll get an A on my first haunting...I mean visit. The word 'haunting' has a bad rap. See you soon, Love. And throw out that horrid lasagna!"

And just like that, I'm alone.

Maybe someone slipped something in my drink. Stan was here. Maybe Stan *is* a serial killer.

No, everyone seems to like him. But like Granana said, don't they always say you have to watch the quiet ones?

Except Stan is not quiet. I heard him talking to Fred about his digestive problems, and I know *way* more than I need to about what happens when he eats spicy food.

And she was so convincing. I think it is *sort of* possible that I just saw my grandmother.

And if so, then why didn't I ask her the vital questions, like why did she ask me to come to Applebarrow? And lie about the way the residents get along? And ask Mr. Franklin to do a one-man show at the Will reading?

And most importantly, how in the hell are GHOSTS real?

***

I need to remember not to call Sassy for advice.

"Maybe I should get a dog?" I reasonably suggest.

Sassy launches into one of her rants. "Lia, the last thing you need is a dog. They are dirty and loud and way too much trouble. It's bad enough you have a man to deal with. And why hasn't Jason been visiting you? Honestly, if I were you, I would take my perfect ass and puckered pout to the nearest watering hole and mingle."

My friend surely lives up to her name. And the last time I visited a 'watering hole' I was over-watered, and I wilted.

And why is Sassy recommending infidelity as a solution to boredom?

"I'm a little lonely, and you're right—I can't rely on Jason for everything. But I'm not going to cheat on him because he's busy. And he *has* visited. He was here just last week. It isn't his fault I moved away."

I get goosebumps when I think of who to blame for this situation.

"No, it's not his fault, and I'm only suggesting that you meet some new people. I know what we'll do. I'll come for a visit. When are you having your May event with the residents? I could come and show you how it's done. Mingling, that is. Don't ask me to cook or fold a napkin or put out a chair. What do you think?"

"That could be fun. I'll send you the info."

I can barely think about the next event, as I am still recovering from the last one. Let's just say between Stan's book, Jason's presence, and anticipating the return of a ghost—I am not sure I can do this for a full year.

"Ooh, how about a game night? Can we play the one where you put the word on your head? Or the dirty one? I love that one. I need a dress for an upcoming formal at the club anyway, and I can't dress myself. Those dummies at Pierce & Ludlow assigned me this drippy old lady as my stylist. I *could* go to New York, but why make a trip to the Big Apple when I can visit my favorite personal shopper in the Little Apple? Get it? Appleba—"

"Yes, Sassy, I get it. I'm not sure if the stores here will have anything you're looking for, but it would be great to have a visitor."

I would especially enjoy a visitor who is *alive*. As much as I miss and love my grandmother, I have been on pins and needles since I saw her in my apartment in April, and she still hasn't reappeared for our 'chat'.

As time goes by, I am more convinced it was a dream. I *did* wake up in my bed in the morning.

I am also a bit worried about Sassy at Pentagon Place. Jason is already doing a good job of alienating the neighbors. Wait until they meet the Belle of Richmond's Debutante Ball. I wish my more normal friends would visit.

Not that Jason isn't normal. He's just not a *friend*...you know what I mean!

I end the call with Sassy, and she promises to arrive with bells on (knowing her they will actually be ringing) and I am once again alone in my silent apartment.

I put on some Depeche Mode, my favorite eighties band, and try to summon up motivation to do something productive.

Jason hates Depeche Mode. He refers to them as 'that band with the singer with the creepy voice.' 'They're like a Halloween band,' he says.

Wow, I'm complaining about Jason a lot lately, but I know it's partly boredom and isolation.

I tried to engage Emma in friendship, but that was challenging.

I visited her shop and showed interest in her crafts, complemented her store, and praised her for being so independent and entrepreneurial.

I even bought a hook rug kit, which I have no intentions of actually doing, but I thought it was a supportive gesture.

Things were okay until I suggested we go to lunch. She started acting weird, as if I recommended that we go smoke crack in the park or run topless down main street.

I could see if I had suggested a drink and she was a recovering alcoholic, or someone who just doesn't drink for personal reasons. But everyone eats, so lunch seemed like a perfectly normal thing to do at LUNCHTIME.

Emma left The Crafty Owl in the capable hands of her elderly employee, Clara, and we walked two doors down to The Stone's Throw Diner, which is where Molly works, in addition to Dawson's crush, the jealous skank.

It's a cozy place and the food is great. Well, at

least *I* thought it was great. I brought Jason here the day after the book club meeting. He had stayed on through the weekend (which was blissful in more ways than one), but he was disappointed that we didn't get to tour the factory. The realtor wasn't available, so we postponed that adventure for a future visit.

I thought taking him to a nice local restaurant would be good. As much as I enjoyed our time in the apartment, I don't get out much, so I was prompting him to help me explore the town. There's a great local theater as well, but they are between shows at the moment. They do mostly Shakespeare, but I already know what Jason will say about that.

So, thinking that Emma seemed like an intelligent young woman who might enjoy Shakespeare (because who am I going to bring? Sassy?), I tried to tell her about it at lunch. At first, I thought she was also not a live theater fan, but no matter what we talked about she seemed uncomfortable.

"Emma, are you okay? I said. "You have barely touched your food."

I, on the other hand, inhaled my open-faced roast beef sandwich with mashed potatoes. I have a secret weakness for bland comfort food.

I was hoping this wasn't one of times Granana was watching me, if she is at all. Ever.

Emma shifted her weight and played with her food. I know some women don't like to eat a lot on dates, but unless I have given her the wrong impression, I'm not looking to be her new girlfriend.

"I don't like eating in front of people." She sat back and gazed mournfully at her plate full of barbecue, slaw and potato wedges.

"Oh, okay. Well, it's just me and who am I to judge?" I point to my empty plate, which is so clean they'll have to do a double take before washing it or putting it in the clean stack.

"I was teased a lot for my weight. In school especially...and some men have said things. Anyway, I get self-conscious. But I'll take this to go and eat all of it at home."

I know that for her health Emma *should* lose weight but being afraid to eat *anything* in front of other people is not emotionally healthy.

But instead of a diet lecture, I decided to order a big slice of peach cobbler and distract her through her meal with stories from my days as a resident assistant, hoping she'd become engrossed in my tales and start eating.

Girls...and boys can be cruel, and Emma's self-esteem needed a boost, just like my friend Gabby's. She struggled in college and it's taken her years to adopt a healthier lifestyle, so I told Emma her story.

She seemed to be interested, and asked questions about how she lost the weight. The distraction worked, and she ate about half of her meal and left the rest.

Wasted food isn't the best thing, but it was a start towards portion control, and she seemed to brighten at my suggestion of taking a little walk before she returned to the shop.

After lunch I felt a lot better about my attempt to make a friend in Emma, but we don't have much in common. The next night she invited me to her apartment, but she wanted me to bring my hook rug, and she was working on knitting.

And Sassy thinks *I'm* living an isolated life for a young woman.

There's nothing wrong with crafts, but it's not my thing. And Maybe Emma doesn't even need help. Everyone isn't like me.

One thing is for sure, we need a positive June event. May's book club was...um...memorable. I'm so glad Sassy couldn't make it. I hate to think what she would have said to Stan.

The book was INSANE! I tried to read it, and it was all over the place. Apparently, I don't get this genre because it has a 4.5-star average online, and like a squagillion reviews.

The main plotline is about clowns who turn into werewolves (as if each of those characters aren't bad enough on their own), and then they also drink scotch on the rocks and review movies, after killing people.

What the hell? It's like sarcastic and ironic, and there is political commentary thrown in, and disdain for organized religion. And then the clowns/werewolves are ripping people's arms off in the streets.

I was questioning Stan's sanity, and also my own, for allowing him to pick this book.

And for being here at all. In Applebarrow. In my life as I know it.

It was a bit much that a stupid, nonsensical book would be the catalyst for such existential thinking, but my grandmother may be a ghost, so...things are a little off right now.

While everyone was 'discussing the book'—Molly stared at the ceiling during Stan's speech on the symbolism of clowns in modern culture, and Olivia declared that we are going to hell for reading such 'mind-numbing evil'—Jason kept nudging me to get my attention.

I accepted that this was a train wreck of a meeting, but as its leader I felt obligated to at least pay attention and run interference.

The Swanson brothers almost started punching each other, arguing over who is tougher—a werewolf or their Uncle Bob. Judging from their hotheaded behavior, my money is on Uncle Bob.

I tried to silence Jason but he wasn't having it, so while Ken Washington was laughing and telling Stan that he might be the 'most twisted motherfucker in the civil service', and he doesn't even know anyone as messed up as him at the post office, I finally leaned towards Jason and in my most annoyed stage whisper, said "*What?*"

He leaned over and spoke quietly, hardly moving his lips. "This is fine and all, but when can we get back to your place?"

I almost blushed a little as I realized he was wanting to get some action before he had to return to Richmond, and I was all for that, even though I am a responsible property manager and social leader.

Just when I was about to whisper some suggestions for what we could do, he said, "I want to talk to you about when we can tour the plant. I have some good ideas, and maybe even an offer."

As soon as he said that something fell in the clubhouse kitchen, and my heart started pounding.

Did Granana hear that? I wish I could ask her what she wants me to do with the plant? It's so out of my element, but I'm not even ready to deal with it yet. I don't know why Jason is in such a hurry.

Jason was still talking with his mouth almost

entirely closed when I noticed Molly had taken control of the meeting.

"Okay, y'all, this meeting was a bit of a dud, but Stan tried with his little creepy book. Bless his heart."

Suddenly everyone started whispering about how it was true, and some of them wouldn't know of any better books, except Olivia, who said she isn't coming to any more meetings if they have anything to do with butchering the sanctity of literature.

I had already decided that I was choosing Molly to host next month's meeting, and I don't care if anyone accuses me of favoritism. I need some stability and level-headed ideas, and pulling a name out of the hat limits my odds of accomplishing that goal.

Hopefully Molly isn't going to suggest a turkey shoot or a drinking game. I need to get to know my residents better. Maybe I'll ask her if she wants to hang out so I can get some answers about what's going on here. And make sure the next meeting is a success.

A visit from Granana would help the most with my questions, but she may not appear to me again, especially if she doesn't like how I am running things. Old Italian ladies can be known to give people the 'evil eye'.

At least that's what my mother says.

Plus, she's not real. If I keep saying that enough, maybe it will be true.

The meeting was breaking up, and everyone suddenly seemed to be getting along. It's like these people love to hate each other, and then they're friends again.

I have so many questions, and I keep getting more confused. I was in no mood for Jason to pressure me about the plant.

He stood up and moved very close to me, invading my personal space. I normally wouldn't mind that, as our spaces are frequently intertwined, but at this moment I needed a break and he kept pushing.

"I will make it a point to come back to tour the plant. It's important for our future to get this figured out. Do you want to stay here with these yahoos longer than you have to?"

"Hey, so sorry to interrupt but I need to get back home. There's a dispute about crayons and my wife needs to leave for work." Pete stammered a bit and I felt bad that he seemed intimidated by Jason. To Pete, he must look like an important guy with his expensive clothes and city attitude. I don't know why Jason can't be nicer. He's usually not like this.

I jumped right in and said, "That's okay Pete. What can we do for you?"

"He looked down for a moment and said, "I just want to say how happy everyone is that you're here, Lia. You're doing a great job. Well, that's it. Oh, and the Mexican buffet was a nice treat. I was enjoying the tacos too much to notice what was happening with the weird book."

He laughed and I thanked him. He shook Jason's hand, and before Jason could say something snarky, Dawson walked over. He was quiet during the meeting, except for the argument with his older brother over werewolves.

"Hey there, Jason. Nice to see you here at the meeting. Hey, can you settle a bet for me?"

He leaned in closer and I saw Jason wince, as if Dawson smelled like motor oil instead of Irish Spring soap. I need to talk to Jason about his snobbish behavior. He comes from more meager beginnings than anyone here, I'd bet.

Jason sighed and said, "Sure, what's up?"

"Is it true your last name is Woodcock? Because if it is, you're one unlucky son of a bitch." Dawson laughed and punched Jason's arm playfully.

Unfortunately, Jason's last name really is Woodcock. If I were him, I would have changed it to my mother's maiden name, but he has some misplaced loyalty to his father. And he can't stand his mother.

It's so misplaced that they don't know where his father is currently physically located.

Jason gritted his teeth slightly and Dawson said, "I'm just playin' man. It's a cool name, especially if it refers to somethin' that can make your woman happy, am I right? Sorry, Miss Lia, but that's a *hard* comparison to resist."

I was willing Dawson to stop with my mind, but I don't think our minds work on the same frequency, because he continued as if this was a joke everyone was enjoying.

Poor Jason. He told me that when he was really little (before the more vulgar reference was understood), the kids all called him Woodchuck.

No one said a word, so Dawson continued. "Hey, my middle name is Shirley."

Jason screwed up his face and said, "Shirley? That's the middle name your parents gave you?"

"Yep. It was my Grandma's name and after I was born, Mama couldn't have no more babies, so yep. Tucker's middle name is Dex. I sure got screwed. So you see, I get it, Buddy. But of course, no woman has to take my *middle* name when we get married." His eyes widened as he pointed at me, and again I hoped he would shut up before he went there, but no.

"Lia, are you going to be Mrs. Woodcock someday?"

Before either of us could reply to that question, which was awkward on SO many levels, Logan appeared and said, "We're low on beer, and everyone is hitting it hard after the book discussion, and now Fred is saying it would be fun to dress as clowns and review movies."

Dawson cracked up, I laughed nervously, and Jason made another face like something smells. Where was his sense of humor?

Logan slapped Dawson on the back and said, "Can you give me a hand bringing in the extra beer from my truck?"

Dawson happily agreed, and Logan winked at me on the way out the door. Thank God someone has some sense. I made a mental note to ask Logan to plan a meeting soon, too. He and Molly might be the only ones with real social skills.

Logan obviously saw that Jason and I were trying to have a private conversation, and Dawson was oblivious.

Jason pulled me into a hug and whispered in my ear, "Seriously, we need to get you out of here. These people are nuts."

I pushed back gently against his chest and said, "I know, but they *are* nice people. And I promised my Granana."

"No, you actually didn't. You promised a lawyer

and your parents. Lia, this can't be what she wanted for you. I blame Ed Franklin for not contacting your father when she put together such a ridiculous Will."

I wanted to protest, but how could I tell him that I *may* have talked to Granana, and she *might* come back, and *maybe* then I will get my questions answered?

"Jason, I'm not ready to talk about this yet. Please give me more time to honor my grandmother's memory. That's all I ask."

Out of the corner of my eye, I noticed the guys were back with more beer, and Dawson was already raising one up in offer towards Jason.

Instead of accepting the gesture and engaging in more lively banter about his last name, Jason decided to bow out of our fun night and go home to Richmond, instead of using his namesake body part back at my apartment.

Crap, am I starting to think like a Swanson brother?

Jason sighed and hugged me again. "Okay, Honey. I don't understand, but if it's important to you, we'll wait. Right now, I have to go back to Richmond. I just remembered Amy and I have an early meeting with a client. I didn't think this meeting would last so long." He kissed me again and said, "I need to stay sharp so we can put our big life plans into action soon. Right?"

I managed a smile and Jason kissed me softly. I wasn't sure if he remembered the early meeting as an escape, or if he was telling the truth.

Either way, I was going to be alone again, and I wasn't looking forward to it.

As Jason made his hasty departure, I wandered

over to the remains of the Mexican buffet and smiled at the thought of what Granana would say about this menu.

"At least she couldn't accuse you of bastardizing her sacred food."

I was startled when Logan interrupted my thoughts as if he could read them. "Yeah, I'm not sure what she would say. I thought everyone would like something different. I guess my bad attempt to imitate her cooking was pretty obvious, huh?"

Logan cracked the top off a hard cider and handed it to me.

"How did you know I don't like beer?" I asked.

"Lucky guess. Also, you haven't been drinking any tonight. And I don't think most people had a clue about the Italian food, but Allegra sure would have."

"You're right." We clinked bottles and I wasn't sure if it was creepy or sweet that he was observing my behavior that closely.

"Hey, sorry that knucklehead Dawson was taunting your man like a kid on a playground. I don't know what happened to those Swanson brothers. I think they were both dropped on their heads."

We laughed as we watched them get into an arm-wrestling competition, which drew many spectators, and was better received than the book club meeting.

I returned my attention to Logan, who was casually leaning against the wall with his legs crossed in a relaxed pose that Jason would never strike.

Suddenly I had all the time in the world to chat. Logan and I didn't have early meetings, and there's nothing wrong with getting to know one of the less nutty neighbors a little better.

I'm sure Jason doesn't run from Amy when their business is concluded, and I needed a friendly ear.

CHAPTER EIGHT

It's Saturday night and I'm getting ready to go over to Molly's to discuss the June meeting, and have what she is calling a 'pajama party' with her and her girls.

Little does she know how much I love a pajama party from my college days, but since Logan made fun of my bunny pjs, and I guess it's technically 'inappropriate' to wear sleepwear out of the house, I am going with leggings and a big pink tunic shirt. Very close to pajamas, and I'm only wearing a sports bra. My girls can cope with less support for one evening in the company of other females.

As I gather my purse, making sure I have my phone for Jason's nightly good night call, I think about my conversation with Logan the other night.

I can't blame the hard cider, because unlike my drinking behavior on my first night in Applebarrow, I barely had a sip before I was sharing Jason's personal secrets.

In my defense, is it reasonable to hide your whole family from the world, and pretend to be someone you're not?

I never questioned Jason's refusal to publicly acknowledge his humble roots. I felt sorry for him because he was teased for being poor and having no father, and for having a last name that is a bully's dream.

But for some reason, watching him in Applebarrow has made me view him in a different light. I feel compelled to defend him, even though at the same time even I am offended by some of his behavior.

Therefore, in a moment of weakness and frustration, I told Logan how Jason grew up in Glossop, VA, which is only about twenty miles east of Applebarrow, and it's not a pretty town.

You can guess that by the name. It's like a hybrid of glop and slop, with some sauce thrown in. It reminds me of some kind of sludge that would get tossed into a chemical waste bin.

It's a linguist's nightmare.

True to the tone of its name, it's dotted with unkempt trailer parks, unemployed citizens, and seedy bars.

It was a rough upbringing, and while I think his mother did her best, (Pearly Woodcock's husband walked out on her and her boys), her salary as a clerk at the local laundromat didn't do much to support a decent lifestyle.

Jason's father, Ned, was a cheater, liar, gambler and all-around jerk. But like so many young boys who yearn for a father's love and acceptance, Jason idolized him and was disgusted by his mother and younger brother, Austin. He vowed to get out of Glossop and make a better life for himself.

Logan kept staring alternately between my eyes and my mouth while I was telling this story, which was causing me to feel warm in all the wrong (right?) places.

Damn Jason for leaving when I could have been back at my apartment with him, cooling my warm places.

If I didn't know better, I would think Jason was withholding his physical attention to punish me for being here. I also worry about whether his needs are being met at morning meetings with Amy. But that's another concern entirely. Back to *my* treachery.

Logan said, "Wow, that explains a lot. So, his mother and brother still live out there in the same trailer park?"

"Yes, and he hardly ever sees them. I've only met them twice and it didn't go well. He won't acknowledge them on social media, and when asked about his family, he changes the subject."

"Well at least he made good on his promise to himself. That's a big deal. He should be proud of that."

"Yeah, I wish he was a little more genuine and accepting, but I guess coming here has hit a nerve for him, and he's afraid of going backwards. Not that Applebarrow is anything like Glossop, but I think in his mind it is."

Eventually I remembered that Logan's good listening skills were due to bartending, and not a therapist's license, and I changed the subject before I got myself into more trouble.

I asked Logan not to share my revelations, and I do trust him. I don't want Jason to get even more annoyed with the situation if he finds out I shared his closely guarded secrets, but I felt that the need to explain Jason's behavior, at least in some small way, trumped the promise to keep quiet about his past.

I'm sure Amy thinks he attended private school and was a frat boy in college.

Jason is planning on spending the whole upcoming Memorial Day weekend here. He said he may need to bring his laptop and get on a couple of calls, but we should have lots of time to ourselves for hiking, biking (his favorite, but I'll do it), romantic dinners (not sure where yet) and some quality time in my apartment. I'm sure the residents have their own plans, and no one is looking to me to arrange their holiday weekend.

Hopefully Granana won't decide to appear and give Jason heart failure, but if she was a ghost, why wouldn't she have come back by now?

Unless she's enjoying her reunion with her husband, but based on their earthly relationship, I strongly doubt it.

No, I'm making it all up in my head. It's the shock of Granana's death, the Will reading, this big move, and now tension with Jason.

I was feeling upset with him after the meeting, but when I returned home, I saw that he had left me a sweet and sexy note on my pillow. It made me soften towards him. It doesn't take much.

I must remember that his life has been upended, too. He had a live-in girlfriend and plans for the future, and now he has to live alone and drive back and forth to the country and wait almost a year to get me back in his life full-time.

His interest in the money is a bit concerning (I think about the big lottery winners who lose their minds and all the money), but given his background, this is huge opportunity to have a life he never dreamed of, and he's worked so hard for us.

I think I will call Mr. Franklin on Monday and see if we can tour the plant when Jason is here. It doesn't do anyone any good to have it sitting there collecting dust. Jason is probably also thinking of what a boost it would be to the economy of the area to get it up and running again with a new product line.

Enough thinking. I toss my purse in my big tote bag and I'm off to Molly's. I wonder if her daughters are home. They didn't come to the book club meeting because Molly said she didn't want their brains warped before they hit their full womanhood.

I can see her point.

Magnolia and Zinnia are fourteen and twelve, and I am not sure what happened with their father. I'm assuming Molly is divorced, but who knows for sure.

I do hope the girls are home because I am great with teenage girls, unless they see me as old like their mom, even though I'm only a couple of years out of college.

Molly's unit is only two doors from mine in the next building to the left, when I walk out my front door. I hear a bit of noise as I lock my door, and almost run into Stan on the walkway, as he jostles a whole bunch of snack foods in his arms.

"Hey, Lia. Could you close my door, please?"

"Sure, no problem." I fiddle with the lock on the inside of the door, since he didn't give me the key, when he interrupts.

"Oh, don't bother locking it. I'm only going to the other side of the courtyard."

The Swansons' front door bursts open and Dawson yells out, "Hey, the Braves just scored, and Fred won the bet on this inning. Get over here with that grub, Man. I could destroy some Doritos right now. Oh, hey Lia. You're lookin' pretty."

I wave to Dawson and say thank you, while

Stan tells him he's coming and to keep his shirt on.

"What's going on over there? *Fred* is hanging out at the Swansons' apartment."

"Yeah, he hangs out with us sometimes. He's a good old guy. We can't leave him out."

"Oh, who else is there?"

"All the guys in the neighborhood. Marcos, Logan, Ken. Everybody."

Huh, that's strange. What an oddly matched group of ages and backgrounds.

This is driving me crazy. I must find out why Granana wanted me to think these people dislike each other.

I feel so useless with my stupid little meetings. Everyone probably thinks they're helping *me*, assuming I have no friends or real job, so my grandmother created a life for me.

"Well, I won't keep you. You're about to lose some pork rinds, if you're not careful."

I try to help Stan hold onto his bags of greasy salt, but he's doing okay, even though his arms and legs are in the oddest positions.

He laughs and says, "Yeah, have a good evening. Is Jason in town?"

"No, he's coming Memorial Day weekend. For the whole weekend."

I sound like a needy high school girl, and I turn away towards Molly's apartment. "I'm hanging out with Molly tonight. We're going to talk about the next community meeting."

Stan pulls a face and says, "Yeah, I'm sorry about the last one. I thought it was a cool book, but apparently this group isn't ready for the Bizarro genre."

"No worries, Stan. Enjoy your night with the

guys."

He says thanks and walks off, dropping bags no less than a dozen times. I could offer to help him get to the Swansons' door again, but I feel silly, like they might feel obligated to invite me in.

Plus, Logan is there, and I feel so exposed now that I told him about Jason's family.

I take a deep breath and ring Molly's bell. Her front door mat says, 'Sorry, the maid just quit.'

Cute. Her door knocker is decorated with a floral wreath with a bunny. I guess that's left over from Easter.

Bunnies. Ha! Thank God I didn't let *Stan* see me in my bunny pajamas. I can imagine the mockery that would ensue on baseball night at the Swansons'.

On second thought, men are interested in reporting when they've seen you in *less* clothes, not in flannel pjs.

"Come in, come in. Did you see my mat? The maid quit? Don't you love that? Zinnia's band was selling them for a fundraiser."

Molly pulls me inside, and tells me to put my bag wherever and come on in.

"I thought we'd start with a little cocktail and some appetizers."

"Wow, this looks amazing." Molly's spread would be the envy of the guys two doors down. Shrimp, quiches, homemade bread.

"Thanks. I love to cook. And then I thought we could talk about my idea for the meeting, but I also have a good idea for fun tonight."

I hope she isn't going to break out the Ouija board, especially since I have an actual ghost I may or may not be able to conjure.

"I can't wait to hear."

"Mom, is Lia here yet? Want us to bring the stuff down?"

I think that's the younger girl, Zinnia. Now I'm wondering if they are going to try to sell me their fundraiser wares.

Not that I don't like helping kids, but I don't want to go home with a giant tub of frozen cookie dough, scented candles, and a door mat with a snarky saying on it.

At least I know it's not a sex toys party with the kids here. Although, if Jason doesn't start coming to visit more often, I may need to find a store on the outskirts of town and invest in some solo merchandise.

I'll have to wear a disguise, though. Olivia was scandalized enough seeing me buy frozen lasagna.

The girls struggle down the stairs with more bags and packages than Stan, and it looks like cosmetics. Oh no, Molly must sell makeup on the side. I wear very little makeup.

"Hi, girls. What's all of this?" I figure the kids will give it to me straight.

"Hi, Lia. It's makeup." Magnolia gives me a look as if to say, 'what does it look like, bags of shit?'

But to be fair, some fourteen-year-olds' faces naturally look annoyed when anyone over the age of twenty-one speaks to them.

Zinnia jumps in and says, "It's Mom's makeup. And tonight, we're doing makeovers!"

The girls are both quite excited, but I'm having trouble working up the same level of enthusiasm. I thought we might play games or watch a chick flick, but everyone seems psyched for Molly's plan, so I'll have to play along.

I can always go home in the dark and wash my face before anyone else sees me, even if I look like a hooker working the corner by the liquor store on the seedy side of town, next to the sex toys shop.

"So, what do you think? I know you don't wear much makeup, but you're so pretty and you have amazing skin. Maybe your man might like it if we glammed you up a bit before his next visit."

Molly looks so genuinely pleased with herself I can't help but go along, even though Jason will not feel that way. The last time we visited his mother he was disgusted by her makeup, and said it looked like she applied it with a paint roller and removed it with a putty knife.

The girls lead me to a chair at a makeup vanity table in front of a huge mirror, which seems like an odd thing to keep in the living room.

I guess when there are no men in the house to complain, you can do what you want. I'm sure the Swansons' place is full of deer heads, beer steins, and model cars.

Zinnia drapes an apron over me, like they do at the salon, and Magnolia brings me a plate of assorted cheese, grapes and shrimp—along with a pink cocktail.

"Thank you, girls, but you don't have to wait on me."

Molly waves off my comment with her perfectly manicured purple talons and says, "Think nothing of it. They love this. We do Saturday night makeovers all the time, don't we girls? Now go put some music on and let's get to work on this beautiful canvas."

Zinnia runs off to obey her mother, and Magnolia starts sorting through the boxes of powders, potions, and brushes.

I don't even know what you do with half of that stuff. My mother and grandmothers wear/wore makeup, but minimalist. Black eyeliner, mascara, and red lips. That's the uniform. This is a rainbow of glitz and glamour.

"Do you sell makeup, Molly?"

"Oh no, Honey. I just love lookin' pretty and makin' others look their best. And not for men, mind you. I said that as a joke before. Isn't that right, girls? We don't get pretty for men, but for our own self-esteem."

The girls mumble 'yes, Mom' and Molly starts shaking her hips to the music Zinnia picked out. "Oh, this is my favorite song."

I listen closely to try to figure out what's playing, but I can tell by the twangy notes that it's country, and I have zero knowledge of that genre. Is he saying something about corn and whisky?

The girls are now singing into hairbrushes about how rain causes his woman to be frisky by making whisky. How silly!

But instead of jumping to judgment, I need to observe these cultural differences as interesting, like I was back in college and learning something new.

I might be able to jiggle around to this a bit, especially after a few more of these pink drinks. I've had a rough week, and I can indulge a bit.

I decide to go with the flow and give in to Molly's brushes and paints and enjoy the friendship. I've been so lonely.

***

Later, while admiring my new face in every mirrored surface I see, Molly has made coffee and the girls are up in their rooms, texting and watching You Tube videos about cats doing funny things.

I used to do that, and I found it mildly amusing tonight, but I could sense Molly wanted to talk about the meeting, and who knows what else, so I let them escape to their teenage activities.

"You have to try this blueberry crumb cake. I found the recipe on Pinterest. But it's one of the easy ones, not one that looks like a ballerina donkey and has a surprise baby inside."

Molly surely has a way with words.

"Sure, thanks." I'm going to have to stop eating like this. Maybe I can help Emma by asking her to be *my* weight loss buddy. When I was living with Jason, I did not eat like this.

Molly cuts a generous slice of cake for both of us and licks the extra crumbs off the knife. "I'll never be super skinny, but who cares." She smacks her own butt and plops down in the kitchen chair across from me.

"Now, my idea for the June event...a game night!"

"That sounds like fun! What game did you have in mind?" Wow, Sassy will be thrilled! I hope she chooses something clean. I don't want to appear to be a prude, but I know some of the residents will get upset, and with mixed ages and sexes...

I really want this one to go smoothly.

As if reading my mind, Molly says, "We have this game called Utter Nonsense. I play it with the girls and their friends."

Molly explains the premise of the game, which is to say nonsense statements in various accents.

It sounds silly, but also like it would be hilarious.

"And don't worry, we have the clean version. There's a hysterical adult version, but I know with some of these tight asses around here we can't have that much fun."

She smiles at me and then frowns. "Are you okay? Did I put too much makeup on you? You seem uncomfortable."

"No, I love my makeup. And I'm fine. Just having a bit of trouble adjusting to living alone, I guess."

"Yes, I'm sure you miss Jason. And it is odd that you came way out here to live. I mean, don't get me wrong, we love having you here, but we do wonder *why* you're here."

I explain the Will and the reasons Granana had as to why I'm needed here.

"And the most confusing part is that everyone gets along fine. No one seems miserable, and I ran into Stan on my way over here tonight, and the men in the neighborhood are at the Swanson brothers' apartment for baseball night. Do you have any idea what my grandmother was getting at with this plan?"

"Hmm, it's hard to say. I didn't know her that well. You should ask Logan. They were tight."

"Really? That's odd. I would think she would have been friendlier with the female residents."

"Well, I don't know the *whole* story, but they were as thick as thieves. I'm sure Logan would open up to a pretty girl like you."

"I don't know about that."

"Oh, I do. Don't you see the way he looks at you? Now he's a gentleman so he isn't going to infringe on another man's territory, so to speak, but

I can tell he likes you, Lia. So how are things with Jason?"

I sigh and reply, "It's complicated. Everything was okay in Richmond, but now with the distance and his schedule, it's hard. But he's working towards our future."

"Well that's nice and all, but I hope it's YOUR plans and not just HIS plans. My ex-husband had a plan too, and it involved sinking all of our money into a damn pyramid scheme and running away with the chick at the top of the pyramid."

My face must have fallen because Molly softens and says, "I'm not saying Jason would be that stupid or dishonest, but like I tell my girls, you have to go into relationships with men with your eyes, and *options*, wide open. Even when you're married, you can't rely on blind trust."

"Hmm...that's probably true. So, are you friendly with the other women in the community?"

I'm sick of talking about me.

"Not so much. Olivia is a bit stuck up, as if she thinks you need to have six degrees to read a book harder than *The Hungry Little Caterpillar*. Beth Washington is involved with the hospital and her church. Arielle is so young, and we don't have much in common. Now, Emma and I share our love of crafts and we have a great business relationship."

"Does Emma also work at the restaurant?"

"No, I sell my dolls in her shop. I'll show you them before you leave. It's more of a hobby, but I love making them, and the tourists seem to enjoy parting with their cash to bring them home, so it's a nice supplemental income."

We continue to talk about Molly's interests, and

I'm impressed. The residents are full of surprises.

Before I leave, she shows me her doll collection and they are stunning. Unique and not creepy at all (dolls can be a little Chucky-esque), with gorgeous costumes. I tell her I'll check them out in Emma's store. They would make thoughtful gifts.

At the door I stop, laden down with what feels like a few hundred makeup samples (Molly is a collector), and a tin foil package of blueberry crumb cake.

"Molly, I do still have one nagging question. Why do you think the residents haven't outwardly questioned what I'm doing here, and the meetings? I feel silly now, knowing that what I'm doing isn't even necessary."

She pats my shoulder and says, "Sugar, of course it's necessary. You're just trying to make people happy. It doesn't matter if they were happy to begin with, right? We could all use more happiness."

My father would love this woman.

"You're right. Thanks, Molly."

I open the front door and step out into the cool, crisp night air. May is a beautiful month in the Virginia mountains.

Molly leans against the doorjamb and says in a low voice, "Also, you have to remember that you're different from the rest of us. You speak, what six languages? And to some of us, you're an heiress from the city."

"Well, that's a bit of a stretch, and I only speak four languages fluently and—"

Molly shakes her head and interrupts. "You're different, Honey. Plain and simple. Some of us are impressed by you, like me. Some are intimidated, like Emma. Some are jealous, like Olivia. And some are infatuated, like Logan...and Dawson."

I sigh and take in what she's said as I hear more uproarious male cheering coming from the Swansons' place. They must be watching a second game by now. Even baseball games don't last four plus hours—usually. Maybe it's an extra innings nail biter.

They've got the front door wide open. I guess it's hot in there with all those sweaty male bodies.

I suddenly get a chill thinking about how my apartment contains exactly zero male bodies, sweaty or dry.

Molly puts her hand to her mouth and says, "Oh my gosh, I meant to tell you about the Memorial Day party. I didn't know if you would be interested, and the consensus was that you wouldn't be, and your man would want you to go to Richmond, but I said that we should ask you. I'll send you the details, since Jason is coming here that weekend. Now, it's late and you look like you're asleep on your feet." She moves to close the door and adds, "Oh, and I'll give you my friend Angie's number. You must go and get your nails done at her place. She's a star and such a hoot. You'll love her. She's a *Jersey Girl*."

I can't help but laugh at Molly's New Jersey accent impersonation with her underlying southern twang. Yes, the Utter Nonsense game will be hysterical with this group.

"Thanks, Molly. Say good night again to the girls for me."

"Will do, Sugar. Now hurry on home before I find you sleeping in the bushes on my early morning walk."

I wave and walk toward my place, but not before stealing a glance at the rowdy noise coming from the guys two doors down.

Crap, someone is leaving. I don't want to be caught gaping in that direction with my cake and bag of eyeshadow samples.

Logan spots me before I can make a run for it. If I bolt now, I'll look like an even bigger idiot.

However, it's not like he's a possible mugger, so I wave and walk to my place at a slow and perfectly normal pace.

"Hey Lia, is that you?"

I look over my shoulder to find him squinting, and then he does a double take. Do I look that bad? I know it's late, but...oh, I'm standing by the light from Stan's door and I remember my face.

I stop, as I see Logan intends to follow up his incredulous stare with a conversation.

"Wow it *is* you. That's a lot of makeup. Are you moonlighting somewhere? Wait, I know—you were auditioning with the circus?"

I purse my lips, and he snaps his fingers. "No, I got it. You just came from your dance recital."

He waits for my comeback and when none is forthcoming, he says, "What? Come on, that was funny. You look amazing. You never wear makeup, so I'm surprised. Where were you tonight? And hey, at least I didn't make any hooker references."

I raise my eyebrow, and he says, "Wow, I keep digging myself a bigger hole."

I laugh to put him out of his misery and say, "It's okay, I was at Molly's and she thought I'd like a makeover."

"Oh yeah, she's always trying to get someone over there for that. I told her I only wear eyeliner on stage."

"On stage?"

He shifts his feet and says a bit too quickly, "It's just an expression. Obviously, I'm not on stage. I work at a bar. Can I help you with any of that?"

He gestures to my packages and I wave him off. "No, I'm fine. You don't have to walk me to my door, but what a nice young man you are. Hahaha."

Why did I say something so stupid? It's like I'm channeling my grandmother.

Wait, is that a thing? Is she in my head now?

Logan smiles and looks up at the night sky. "That's funny. Your grandmother called me that. Anyway, your place is on the way to mine, and I was also on my way home. At least let me unlock your door."

My heart is pounding a little harder than it was when I left Molly's a few minutes ago, but it's silly. Granana didn't mean Logan when she was referencing 'the nice young man' visiting me.

She meant Jason. Well, maybe not if her letter is to be believed. I thought Granana loved Jason. He even brought her chocolates every time he visited.

"Earth to Lia. You must be tired. I hope you can stay awake long enough to wash that makeup off your face."

I regard his outstretched hand and realize he's waiting for my keys. I twist my body so he can grab them out of the hand that's holding onto the brick of blueberry cake. I could invite him in for some but...no, I would be unhappy if Jason invited a woman into our...his apartment. I can be naïve, even though I do trust Logan.

Maybe it's me I don't trust?

No, I'm tired and anxious to get inside and begin to scrape the five layers of product off my face.

As he works the lock, I impatiently move towards the door, expecting it to pop open. The key sticks in the lock, and I bump into Logan. It's awkward and clumsy, but also a bit forward. If anyone saw us, they would think I was pushing him into my apartment because I couldn't wait to rip his clothes off.

Maybe I do need to visit the shop on the bad side of town because my mind keeps going in one direction. I could wear this makeup or big sunglasses, and if Olivia sees me, *I* will see *her*, and that would be enough to shut her up.

Also, why do I have to hide what I'm doing from these people? I'm probably the only woman at Pentagon Place without a vibrator in her top drawer.

I sigh. Jason can't get here soon enough.

"Hey, somebody's in a rush to get inside." He winks at me and then laughs.

"I'm teasing you, Lia. My lock sticks, too. We should ask Pete to spray them with WD40. Or I may have some at the bar."

I sneak under his outstretched arm and say brightly, "Good idea! Yes, I'll call Pete right away. Well, not now because it's late and his kids are sleeping. And maybe he and his wife are busy. Sleeping probably. Okay, well I'm off to bed. Alone. Obviously."

If he would stop staring at me and smirking, I could end this cringeworthy exchange.

"Okay, good night, Lia."

Now he's talking to me in that 'don't upset the crazy person' voice.

"Hey Logan, wait. I'm sorry. I'm having a hard time…you know…adjusting, and some things are weird."

"Well that really clears things up."

It's not like I can tell him what's weird. Other than me—he knows that.

We both start laughing and now my multiple layers of mascara are about to 'racoon up' my eyes.

We stop laughing as abruptly as we started, and I will myself not to cry. I am not a big crier, but I'm tired and everything always seems worse at night.

I can tell by Logan's body language, that a potential hug is only a few feet away, but if I go there, I will melt into a puddle of goo, and who knows what else.

Logan moves closer to me and lightly touches me on the shoulder—right where Molly did several times earlier this evening.

Except when she did it, I didn't feel every nerve ending in my body screaming.

That's it—it's decided. I am staying in the house until Jason arrives next Sunday. I can do it. I'll order groceries or pay someone to shop for me.

"Lia, it's okay. We all have our crosses to bear. Your grandmother dying was enough of a loss, and now you're here and everything's changed. It's normal to be a little off."

I raise my eyebrows, and he says, "Okay, a lot off?"

His smile is so bright in the light of my front stoop. I never noticed the color of his eyes before. They're *so* blue. Dear knees, please hold me up.

Now I'm praying to my body parts. Terrific.

"I'm okay, but thanks." I take a step inside my

door and Logan closes it quietly behind me, but not before saying, "Hey, for what it's worth coming from me—your grandmother would be proud of you. Good night."

I drop the makeup bag and my purse on the floor and carry the cake like a prized possession to the coffee table before collapsing on my sofa.

That's one of my many questions—what *is* his view of my grandmother's opinion worth? What am I missing? Molly said they were thick as thieves.

"Granana, where are you? Oh my GOD!!"

A shrill beeping sound almost causes me to pee in my pants, and then I realize it's just my phone, and even if my grandmother is currently a ghost, she would just come out of the closet again. I doubt she still has her cell phone.

I grab it out of my purse, and even though I don't expect to see Granana's contact info, I breathe a deep sigh of relief that it's not her.

I don't need things to get any weirder.

"Hello. Why are you calling me so late?"

"Glad to see you're still up and not turning into one of those country bumpkins who needs to get to bed to rise with the farmers."

"Oh Sassy, I've missed you. What's up?"

I settle back into the couch and smile at her rooster reference and disparaging comments about my new home.

Hmm, why is it funny when she makes those remarks, and not when Jason does?

"Yes, I was just telling Beau—I must go see my favorite personal shopper. Hilda sucks. She keeps trying to get me to dress my age. Anyway, so big news. I'm definitely coming to the Little Apple!"

CHAPTER NINE

"**B**ruce is my God!"

Angie explains why her salon is covered in Bruce Springsteen photos and memorabilia. I'm hoping she isn't going to show me a pair of underwear that he signed in the eighties.

"Oh, I see. Hey, is the name of your shop a play on one of his songs?"

It seems vaguely familiar to me, and I can't think of any other reason someone would call her nail salon, Nails on the Edge of Town.

"Yes, silly. You need an education so you can also worship at the Church of Bruce. But you're probably one of those young people who listens to hip hop."

Angie is older than Molly—in her mid-forties. And every bit the Jersey Girl. Her black hair is huge.

"No, actually I don't, but the only old music I like is eighties New Wave."

"Oh yeah, with those funny British voices and the electronic sounds. New Wave always made me think of boating."

Angie cracks herself up but doesn't miss a beat on my nail design. I figured I'd go all out. I watch her draw flowers on my fingernails with the precision of a surgeon.

It's hard to believe this woman and Jason have

similar opinions of New Wave lead singers. I'm guessing that's where their tastes end (he's going to LOVE my fingernails—NOT!), but the irony is still not lost on me.

"What brought you to Applebarrow from New Jersey?"

"Have you been to New Jersey?" More cackling. "Seriously, I love my home state, but it's hard to live there—so cold and expensive."

"Yeah, I can relate. I grew up in Vermont with my parents. It's not that expensive, but the cold is unbearable at times."

Angie shivers and continues. "I know it! Also, my parents were sooo strict and Catholic. And every Sunday, thirty of my closest relatives came over for Sunday gravy and it was just too much."

I can't imagine that lifestyle, but it's how Granana described her youth, growing up in New York City. It was just me and my parents for Sunday dinner, and sometimes it was tofu.

"So why Applebarrow out of all the places in the south? How did you even know about it?"

"My family brought us down here to the mountains, every other summer. We couldn't afford to come *every* summer—probably because we were feeding half of the immigrant population from Sicily, but I was here every other year, from the time I was two."

"Let me guess. By year eighteen you refused to go back?"

"You're so smart! But I'm not surprised. Molly told me you speak like ten languages."

"Only four."

"You're precious! Only four, she says."

I look behind me to see if she's talking to a picture of Bruce. I'm pretty sure Bruce Springsteen is alive, so at least I know she isn't talking to a ghost. Speaking of ghosts...

"Angie, did you know my grandmother?"

"Of course! Everyone knew the DeLucas! We all got fat eating their cakes. Hahaha...that's a running joke in this town. Your grandma was awesome. Feisty, too. She came in to get her nails done every other week as long as I've had this shop."

"Are you serious?"

Granana's nails never looked like mine do right now. I almost need sunglasses to look at the bright yellow background, and the garden full of color on top.

"Serious as a heart attack." She puts her hand to her mouth and says, "Wait, she didn't die of a heart attack, did she?" Angie crosses herself and it reminds me so much of Granana.

"No, she didn't. It's okay. I was wondering why she never mentioned coming here?"

Or brought me here any of the countless times I came to visit? I am betting Angie has owned this shop for twenty years—almost all my life.

"I don't have any idea. She never wanted anything too fancy. Just basic pinks or reds, like they wore in the fifties. And the old guy she came in with all the time was hilarious!"

"What? My *grandfather* came to a nail salon?"

"Oh no, he was a grump. Sorry, Sweetie. Rest in peace, Mr. DeLuca." She blesses herself again. "No, it was another guy."

Now my brows are jumping up like my eyes are spring-loaded.

"I'm not saying your grandmother was...you

know...she would never do that. And obviously he must have been a *friend*, if she brought him out in public. He seemed artsy. I always thought he had something to do with the theater in town, but they never talked about it, and I don't like to be too nosy with clients."

She pauses a moment to examine her handiwork under a lighted mirror that looks like a microscope.

I wish she had been nosier with clients. I can't believe I know nothing about this. So much for my close relationship with Granana.

"He had a British accent. Skinny old guy. Wore a lot of black. Come to think of it, he reminded me of one of those British new wavers you were talking about."

This is too much to take in. Is this why Granana listened to Depeche Mode when I came over? I thought *I* influenced *her* taste in music, but was it the other way around? Back when I was a little girl and my memories are fuzzy?

"I shouldn't have said anything, and now you look worried. I swear it seemed perfectly innocent. My guess is that he was gay, and she liked hanging out with him. But if you really want to know, you should go see Donna?"

"Donna?"

"Yeah, she's married to Pete, the maintenance guy at your place."

This really is a small town.

"Oh, I've met Donna. They invited me to their house on Easter. What does she have to do with this?"

I did think it was odd that Donna and my grandmother spent time together. Granana was so piously Catholic, and Donna is so new age. Not that *I'm* shocked by that, having grown up in Vermont with my parents, but Granana? I don't see it.

"They were friends, but that's not why I'm sayin' you should see Donna. She's a medium."

I don't think she's talking about her dress size.

"Are you saying...?"

"She sees dead people. And talks to them. Now I'm not saying she can get you in touch with your Gran, for sure. Some people pass on and they're tired of this world. But it's worth a shot. You seem like you have a lot of unanswered questions."

I appreciate Angie's hand patting and sympathetic gaze, but she doesn't know the half of it. Every time I ask a question, it causes ten more to pop up. And Donna didn't mention this as one of her skills.

"I don't know if I'd be comfortable doing that, but I'll think about it."

I don't want to tell Angie that I've already seen Granana. Apparently seeing dead people is acceptable in this town, but maybe only if sanctioned by an expert.

Rogue sightings could peg me as a nutter. Or worse yet, they'll try to recruit me to talk to other people's deceased loved ones, and one ghost is more than I can handle.

Yes, Granana has been back to visit. I wish I could tell Angie about what happened the night I came home from Molly's, but it *may* have been another dream.

Now that I'm thinking more about it, it's ridiculous. I have never seen a single dead person prior to Granana. So why would I suddenly have this ability now?

No, I must have put that extra blanket on myself that night. I was cold, and so tired after talking to Logan outside. I just don't remember.

And I probably knocked the rosary beads off the dresser when I was getting ready for bed.

That's it.

I didn't wake up to find objects moved by a ghost, even if I did hear someone say something about the Mexican theme at the meeting.

And besides, according to my first Granana visit...I mean dream...she can't manipulate objects well.

It was my tired, restless brain playing tricks on me. I am not going to replay the events of that night anymore. I will simply forget them.

Easy peasy.

***

After insisting I stay to share a glass of wine with her ('it's almost five'), I pay Angie and stare at my nails on the way out of the shop. It's a little gaudy, but she is truly talented...owww!

I trip over my own feet and walk into...of course...Logan.

Why is he everywhere all the time? If I didn't see other people talking to him, I would think *he* was a ghost.

"Hey, steady there. Oh wow, I see you're mesmerized by your glow in the dark nails. I guess you just came from Angie's shop?"

We both turn to look at the glitzy storefront, and the proprietress is smiling and waving in the window.

Great, I love an audience for my stupid behavior. To make it worse, I give her a thumbs up, as if she's worried that I've sustained a bodily injury, and not that she's watching Logan massage the shoulder I smashed into his rock-hard body.

Now Logan places his hands on my arms, turning me to face the sunlight, and I squint.

"What are you doing?"

"You don't have anywhere near as much paint on your face as you did the other night. Is this the daytime look?"

"Yes...well...no...I need more lessons before I can recreate Molly's handiwork. I was playing around with some of the samples she gave me."

As if he's interested in discussing makeup techniques, and not teasing me again.

He finally releases his gentle grip and I still feel the warmth of his strong hands, as I look down at my own. "The nails are a little much, aren't they? I was so engrossed in our conversation, she could have tattooed me while I was in there and I wouldn't have noticed."

"Hmm...is Angie that interesting? I like her, but I always think of the movie, *My Cousin Vinny*, when I see her."

He scratches his chin and I'm struck by how sculpted his make-up free face looks in the sunlight. And then there's the stubble.

Jason shaves his face until it's as hairless as a newborn baby's. It does feel soft, but do I really want a soft man? I never gave it much thought before, but now all I can do is think, and about the wrong things.

"I'm sorry, what did you say?"

Ugh...I hate that I go into a trance when I talk to this man. I feel like Clark W. Griswold, in the *Christmas Vacation* scene where he's talking to the hot salesgirl at the lingerie counter.

Flustered, tongue-tied, and goofy.

"Angie? You, mean Marisa Tomei's character in *My Cousin Vinny*?"

He says, "It's hilarious. She just needs the gum and the black leather miniskirt."

I can't help but laugh at the comparison. And people act like *I'm* a city girl out of place in the country?

"She was telling me some unusual things about my grandmother." I glance at my wrist as if there's a watch there and ask, "Hey, do you have to be anywhere right away?"

He sticks his hands in his pockets and shakes his head. "Not really. I was going to grab a quick bite to eat before work. Would you like to join me?"

He's holding his arm out like he's going to escort me to a ball, and I feel like I asked him out on a date, which I, of course, did not.

He's acting like a friendly neighbor, so I should stop being stupid. I'm the one who becomes unglued when *I* see *him*, not the other way around.

"Sure, I'd love to. But hey, doesn't your bar serve food?"

"Oh, yes it does. Therefore, I prefer to eat elsewhere."

I've eaten at Tonic and they are known for great food, but I get it. If he tries to eat there, he probably gets bombarded with staff telling him they've run out of limes, or the beer truck is late, or the toilet is clogged.

We duck into a little café a few doors down from Angie's shop. It's early on a Tuesday, so it's just us and a guy with a laptop at one of the window tables.

The hostess seats us in a corner—I guess she

thinks this is a date, but I'm happy for the privacy since I am about to grill Logan about some private matters.

Angie and Molly may know gossip, but I have a sneaking suspicion that Logan knows some facts. I'm betting he wasn't Granana's favorite 'nice young man' for no reason.

I'm not the least bit hungry, but the French menu is familiar. I spent a summer in Paris in college.

I missed Jason so much that summer but come to think of it—he was fine with me being away then, too. He couldn't jump on a plane to visit me in Paris, but right now I'm only two hours away by car.

I *could* visit him in Richmond, but if all he's going to do is work, then I'll be even lonelier there. At least here I'm becoming part of a community again—like in college.

"I understand you speak fluent French. Care to help me with the menu?"

"Haha...since French speakers aren't common in Applebarrow, you'll notice the menu has easy-to-read English translations."

He pretends he didn't notice by holding up the menu to the outside light, like he did with my face on the sidewalk.

"Damn, I wanted to hear you speak French."

I'm not in the mood for joking, and my serious face wipes the smile off his. "Are you okay?"

"Yeah, but I have questions."

"Questions?"

The server comes over and interrupts. Her question is easy to answer. I order a salad and Logan orders a sandwich.

I am sticking with water. Alcohol is not my friend, and the last thing I need is to act any dumber than I feel.

I look out the window and see Olivia briskly walking past the restaurant window. She does a double take and I look down at my menu.

Why did she have to see us? Of all people? The *one* person in Applebarrow who seems to actively dislike me.

Hopefully I can keep her away from Jason this weekend. Not that I'm doing anything wrong, but I don't want to be forced to explain myself.

Jason doesn't seem to grasp my fascination with figuring out why I'm here, and what was going on with Granana. He wants me to forget about it and get the hell out. He doesn't understand family. It's not his fault, but it's also not my fault that he has chosen to disown his people.

"Lia?"

"Oh sorry. I suppose my questions are for my grandmother, but since I can't talk to her, they are for anyone who knew her...well."

That is technically true, because even though I've had two possible ghostly visits, I have no idea how to conjure additional time with Granana's spirit.

And if I know her, she won't appear for Donna if she can do it herself. And do I want people in this small town knowing that the heiress to the DeLuca fortune is communicating with the dead?

Jason would love it if I earned that reputation. He would tell me it was bad for his career, as if it were the nineteen-fifties, and he doesn't want to be embarrassed by my witchcraft when the boss comes over for dinner.

And since I'm not sure what I even believe, Donna could tell me anything and I won't know if it's true or not. Mediums don't bring the dead person into view, they talk to them. I think.

Really, they probably do nothing.

Logan looks out the window and then says, "Have you talked to your parents?"

"I guess they would be an obvious choice, but they didn't know her that well. I'm seeing now that I didn't, either."

"But weren't you pretty close? I mean, she asked you to come here in her Will, and take care of her...affairs. She wouldn't have done that if she didn't trust you. If she didn't have plans for you."

"That's it. What *are* her plans for me? It's so cryptic and mysterious. The residents of Pentagon Place clearly do not need me to do anything. We could have hired an apartment manager, and I could be in Richmond living my life."

"Is that what you want?"

I sigh and shake my head slowly. "If you'd asked me that even a few weeks ago, I would have said yes, but now I feel like there is more to all of this, and I need to get to the bottom of it. Plus, I do like it here. But please don't tell Jason that."

"Oh, I won't. I think he's already not my biggest fan."

The server comes over with our food in time for me to ignore that remark, and we exchange the normal dining pleasantries. I am not drinking much of my water because I don't want to be interrupted with a refill.

"Jason isn't happy that I'm here. I'm hoping he gets over it and...anyway, I didn't ask you here to talk about Jason. I know I've asked you this before, but how well did you know my grandmother?"

Once again, he squirms his way through this line of questioning and it makes no sense. It's not like he was having an affair with a ninety year old woman and he's hiding his shameful secret.

"So, you don't have any idea why she would have wanted me to live here?"

"People are complex, Lia."

"Really? I think people hide what they don't want others to know."

I immediately soften my tone. "I'm sorry. I have no right to pump you for information and insinuate that you know something. Angie told me about a man that used to accompany Granana to her shop. An old British guy. Do you know who that is?"

He leans back in his chair and rubs his face. "Lia, can't you let the past go? Old people have secrets, too. Things they want to keep private. And even if I knew, it wouldn't be right to spill them because Allegra isn't here anymore."

"You were on a first name basis."

"Yes, I'm an adult. And I grew up in Chicago, not the deep south. If you notice, I don't call you Miss Lia."

His playful tone will not distract me from my mission.

"Do you know an old British man?"

Now I sound like a secret agent. Maybe I should have had a drink. I am wound up tighter than Logan's lips.

I look at his lips and try to stay focused, but men shouldn't have lips that full and...oh my God, this is insane. It's like my sleuthing is at war with my sexual withdrawal symptoms.

"Yes, I do. His name is Axe. He lives in town. I

am guessing that's who your grandmother was with in Angie's shop. And that's all I'm saying."

"Was my grandmother having an affair?"

"I don't think so. An affair is a breaking of marriage vows, right?"

"Well, yes obviously."

"So, no. It wasn't an affair. Now, I really have to eat my sandwich and get to work. Why don't you tell me about the meeting Molly has planned? And are you and Jason coming to the big Memorial Day extravaganza? We put up a big blow-up pool and shoot off illegal fireworks. Oops, I hope the new property manager lets us do that."

I smile at his attempt to distract me with light banter, but my mind goes back to what he said about Granana.

What the hell does that mean—'a breaking of marriage vows?'

Were my grandparents not really married? That's impossible. I've seen their wedding pictures. They wore rings. Had the same last name. Surely my father would know if his parents were married.

As usual, my questions have created more questions, so I give in and discuss fire safety and party planning for the remainder of my meal with Logan.

It's all well and good that Granana wanted her secrets to die with her, but she pulled me into this web by demanding that I uproot my life and move to this bizarre little town.

Maybe I will go see Donna. My grandmother has some serious explaining to do.

CHAPTER TEN

"This is alpaca, isn't it?"

Sassy shoves a pair of socks in my face with llamas on them.

"I guess so. What does the label say?" I take them out of her hand and examine them. "Those are hiking socks. You don't hike."

"Well, that doesn't mean I don't like to keep my feet warm. And I could theoretically hike."

This mountain air is making Sassy weird. Well, weirder.

"I love these shops. I knew there would be interesting things to buy here. You should let me help you refresh your wardrobe."

"Ha, I thought *I* was the indispensable personal shopper."

"No, I just like you. You wear pajamas or garments that look like pajamas. I was so excited when Molly showed me the pictures she took of your makeover."

"So now you want to pick up where she left off?"

"Exactly. Now take these jeans and try them on."

"They have ruffles on the bottom and where's the zipper?"

"Lia, you are twenty-four, not ninety." She shoves a pile of trendy clothes at me and softens. "I'm sorry, I know your dear grandmother was ninety, but she wouldn't want you to dress like her."

The dressing room door closes in my face before I have a chance to tell Sassy that Granana would love to see me wear something other than leggings and sweatshirts.

I sigh and face the mirror, after laying the pile on the dressing room bench. Sassy couldn't wait to help me do my makeup this morning after she saw Molly's creation.

I did get her to go a little lighter on the color. I must ease into this new me. And I'm still not sure why I need a new me. I strongly doubt my grandmother wanted me to move to Applebarrow to up my fashion game.

Sassy is staying at Molly's place because she refuses to interfere with our privacy when Jason arrives. I have no idea where she's sleeping.

However, I do look good. It can't hurt to try to wear something a little more stylish. Growing up in Vermont didn't give me many fashion role models. And my mother still dresses like a New Yorker—mostly black.

An hour later and Sassy and I are on the sidewalk laden down with bags. I bought the cute ruffled bottom jeans with the high elastic waist and a top that clearly can't be worn with a bra.

Sassy insisted I wear the jeans and the top with the cutouts on the sides, and the purple lace bralette. I started to protest, but it doesn't matter. We're headed back to my place.

Sassy likes to take a nap in the afternoon, and I need to call my father back.

I decided that Logan is right. It's possible Dad knows a lot more about Granana's life than he's ever shared. After all, I'm still young. Maybe he thought it wasn't appropriate to tell me certain things, or he wanted to leave it to Granana to decide what to tell me.

Now that she's gone, I'm hoping he will be forthcoming with information. It's not like she can...well, she *could* pay him a visit, I guess.

I know he wants me to be happy, and as far as my parents know, things are going perfectly smoothly here. It's time to take on a family ally.

"Sassy, where are you going?"

She's sitting on a bench instead of walking to the car.

"Oh, I'm waiting for the delivery service to come and bring these bags back to the apartments."

"Applebarrow doesn't have services like that." As far as I know, Richmond doesn't either.

"Oh, that's where you're wrong. Money and charm make things appear."

"Sassy, what did you do?"

Just as she tries to look innocent, a truck with the Swanson Brothers logo on the side pulls up. And out jumps a teenaged boy I've never seen.

"You must be Travis."

"Yes, Ma'am."

Sassy has been in town for less than twenty-four hours, and she already has people working for her?

"Please take these bags to Ms. DeLuca's home. Wait, you don't have a key, and we don't want to give you the only one. Shoot. Mrs. Jenkins' home, then."

She gestures to me to relinquish my purchases to this eager young man. Am I supposed to tip him? He's like a mechanic-in-training/bellboy. Except without keys to the rooms.

"Yes, Ma'am." Travis loads the bags into the back seat of the truck and returns to his spot on the sidewalk like an eager puppy.

"Do you know which apartment Mrs. Jenkins lives in?"

"Yes, Ma'am."

If I didn't know better, I would think Travis was a country boy robot. So far there is no proof he knows any other words.

"Okay, and here you go." Sassy hands him some cash, and his excitement is evident.

"Thank you, Ma'am. I'll take care of this right away."

Okay, he's a real person.

As he drives away, Sassy says, "What? Last night I asked if anyone knew of an enterprising young man who would like to earn extra money performing some errands for me during my stay. And that delightful older daughter of Molly's, Petunia—"

"Magnolia."

"I knew it was a flower. Anyway, she told me that a cute boy works for the Swansons and I should ask him."

"So, you walked next door and banged on their door and asked the guys if you could use their employee to do your errands?"

"It was a Friday night. Obviously, they weren't in bed. They're virile young men."

Speaking of 'virile' men, I resist the urge to ask Sassy where Beau is this weekend, even though everyone is quick to give me grief for Jason's absence.

And I may get a little flustered when Logan is

around, but I don't go around calling men 'virile'.

If she starts some crazy cougar fling with a mechanic, I am calling Beau to come get her.

"So why couldn't we bring the bags home ourselves?"

"We are going to have a few drinks to celebrate. I saw the cutest bar on my way in last night and Molly says she worked there, and one of the residents at your complex owns it."

Logan *owns* Tonic? Why does Sassy already know things I don't? Nobody tells me anything. And I do nothing but ask questions.

"I normally don't drink in the afternoon, and I told my father I would call him back. Isn't it time for your afternoon beauty nap?"

"Nonsense, you can call him later. And this mountain air is so good for my skin. Doesn't it look younger and fresher?"

Again, she's been here since last night. We must have miracle air. Soon I'll look twelve again.

"Okay, one drink. And then I'm going home."

"Fine, I'll go drink beer with the Swanson brothers." She bursts into giggles at the sight of my shocked face, and she says, "Kidding! Well, not entirely but *you* must go somewhere and be seen in this outfit. You look amazing."

***

I didn't think Logan would be working. He seems to be at the bar more in the evenings, but of course with my luck he comes meandering out of the back room as soon as Sassy yells out, "My gorgeous young friend Lia and I will have blackberry mojitos."

The young bartender was explaining that they

can't make those because they don't have all the ingredients, when Logan appears and says, "I've got this, Mandy. It's okay."

Mandy scurries off in relief. I don't blame her. I wish I could escape.

"I'm Logan. You must be Lia's friend from Richmond."

He extends his hand and now Sassy says, "*You're Logan?* Well, now I can see what the fuss is about. Oww!"

I kick her under the bar stool and raise my eyebrows. The last thing I want is for Logan to think I've been telling Sassy about the hot bartender who lives in my apartment complex. He'll think I dressed like this to come here while Jason is away.

Sassy may be a good wing woman, but I don't want or need one.

"Everything okay under there?"

He smirks and pretends to peer over the bar to see what might have caused Sassy's yelp.

"Yes, I just banged my knee. So, your sweet bartender said we can't have my favorite drink. Can you help us?"

"I'm sure I can come up with something you'll love. You like berry flavor?"

He starts rooting around the bar and holds up a finger. "I'll be right back. I have a private stash in the back."

He leaves and Sassy watches his retreating butt.

I smack her arm, and she says, "You've become much more violent since you went country."

Through clenched teeth I say, "Can you please stop?"

"What am I doing?"

"You know damn well what you're—"

"Okay ladies. I do have what we need, so I'll whip up something delicious." Logan is back.

As he says the last word, his eyes rest on me. "Lia, you look beautiful."

Gone is the teasing and playfulness in his voice. He's looking at me like Jason did in the early days—when we were drinking cheap wine under the stars in a field, like in a cheesy country song.

"Thank you." I look down at my flowered fingernails and wonder when big mouth Sassy will jump in and help this awkward conversation along.

"Doesn't she, though?" Sassy looks back and forth between us and waits for someone to say something.

Logan's phone mercifully rings, and he excuses himself as he whips up our drinks.

Once again, I give Sassy the dirty eye, hoping she'll quickly finish this drink and get me out of here. I feel so self-conscious wearing a top that hugs every curve and shows a lot of skin and lacy bra.

I know it's the style, but I need a bit more support than this little number offers, and my cleavage looks more pronounced here than it did in the dressing room mirror.

"Everything okay?" Sassy says to Logan as he places cocktail napkins and purple drinks in fancy glasses before us.

"Yeah, that was my buddy, Jack. We were going to take our Jeeps four-wheeling in the woods today, but he was called into work."

"Oh, is he a bartender, too?"

"No, he's a surgeon."

"Oh, wow." Sassy looks surprised.

"Yeah, we need people to do all sorts of jobs here in the country." He winks at Sassy and I can see he isn't offended by her incredulous reaction. Hmm...but when Jason makes the same types of comments...

Logan points to the purple drinks. "How do you like my creation?"

I take a sip and Sassy says, "I have a great idea. Lia, why don't you go four-wheeling with Logan?"

I choke on my syrupy alcoholic concoction, and dab at my painted lips with a napkin. "Sassy, do you even know what that means?"

"Not exactly, but I have an idea. It sounds fun."

"I'm sure Logan would rather bring a friend."

"You're a friend. Right?"

She looks between us and we both nod and mumble our assent that yes, we are friends. I'm going to have one less friend after this because I am going to murder Sassy when we get home.

I wish Jason was here already, and we were back in my apartment. Alone.

Logan excuses himself to get his keys, after assuring me that it's okay if I don't want to go.

I think he's giving me the opportunity to bow out gracefully. Little does he know that he's leaving me alone to face Sassy's sales pitch without protection.

"Where are you going?" Sassy dangles my keys as she sees me get up to leave.

"Give me my keys!"

"I would, but I'm not going to. I am suddenly very sleepy, and I need to use your car to get back to Molly's."

I sigh and sit back down on the barstool. "Why are you doing this?"

"I am doing this because you're young and you deserve to have some fun. I know you are loyal to Jason, but this is perfectly harmless. And if you notice, Jason isn't here. And why is that? Really?"

"Sassy, you don't know him."

"You're right, but I've been through a lot of crap with men. Beau is my third husband. Wouldn't you like to make sure you get it right the first time? Logan seems nice and respectful, and I am not suggesting you have sex with him in the Jeep in the woods."

"Well, that's a relief."

"Not that it's not a nice thought. But please go and have a little fun. Jason will be here tomorrow, and he'll never know."

"That's dishonest."

"Do you actually believe that he doesn't do anything fun or social with other women? If that coworker of his, Amy the work wife, asked him to grab a drink after a late night at the office, do you really believe he would say no?"

I sigh and admit, "Probably not."

"So, there you go. Live your life. Have fun and don't do anything I wouldn't do."

Logan scares the shit out of me by sneaking up on us and says, "I'm guessing that gives you a wide berth."

I put my hand to my heart. "How much of that did you hear?"

"Enough. Listen, I don't know what her deal is, but you don't have to go. If I were Jason, I wouldn't want my girlfriend in the woods with another guy. I mean, even innocently. Not what she said. You know what I mean."

For once Logan is the one stammering, and now

I'm wondering if Molly is right. Maybe Logan is interested but too good to act on it. That would qualify him as a 'nice young man'.

I'm about to make my excuses, but then I think of Jason hanging out with Amy, and I know Sassy is right.

"You know what? I'd like to go if you want me to tag along. It will be an educational experience. The four-wheeling, I mean."

I clear my throat and silently curse Sassy for openly introducing the idea of me and Logan and...

"Okay, it's good with me. I just don't want to get punched at the party on Monday."

We both laugh. I do so nervously, hoping Jason doesn't find out and act like a bigger jackass than he has already.

However, I think Logan is laughing because he is about six inches taller and thirty pounds heavier than Jason, and he's not actually worried about bodily harm. Just a scene and problems for me.

I grab my purse and glance down again at my cleavage in this ridiculous little lace thing I'm wearing. To his credit, Logan has been looking me square in the eye the whole time.

"I have one request."

I can't even imagine what he's going to say— probably that I don't mention this to Jason, which is understandable.

"What's that?"

"No investigative reporting today. Let's stick to the fun and talk about movies and music."

"Fair enough. I'm disappointed though, because I was going to move onto a different line of questioning, like why you moved to Applebarrow and how long have you been bartending?"

"Sounds good. And I would like to know your bra size and when you lost your virginity."

"Okay, fine. We'll stick to the fun, but I don't see why you're so mysterious. You better not be a wanted man. I haven't been to the local post office yet."

"I think if my poster was there, Ken Washington would have turned me in by now, don't you think?"

"True. Okay, no questions. Just mud."

Those are words I never thought I'd speak.

As we walk out of the bar, there's a bottleneck of people coming in while we're trying to leave, and Logan rests his hand gently on the small of my back to guide me out the door. It's a small, innocent, gentlemanly gesture. He removes it almost as soon as he places it there.

So why do I feel his touch on the little spot of exposed bare skin long after he's removed it?

***

I truly had no idea what I was getting myself into.

I knew it would be muddy, but for some reason I assumed the mud would stay outside of the vehicle. I don't know why, because apparently the Jeep doesn't come with dirt protectors, like *windows and doors*. Logan's ride was missing those expected accessories.

At first, he moved slowly. With driving the Jeep, I mean! Nothing else happened at *any* speed.

Then I think he noticed that I was a little tense, so he sped up to gauge my reaction, like a little boy, and he took the game a bit too far.

And like the biggest cliché imaginable, we got stuck in the mud.

I mean, the vehicle *and* then our bodies.

Logan got out to push and had me step on the gas, which shot mud out of the tires. We had to leave the Jeep and walk back to town. Luckily it wasn't far. At one point he gave me a piggy back ride because my sandals were not handling the terrain very well.

So much for my fashion and beauty makeover.

I almost wished that we'd hit a spot of quicksand and it would swallow me up. At one point, I could taste mud in my mouth.

Since it was so hot, most of it dried by the time we got back to the main road and we could play a game of picking the mud off our skin and clothing in clumps as we walked.

If ever there was a less romantic outing, I can't think of one.

Not that I wanted romance, but this was a bit much.

I tried not to get too angry because Logan was very apologetic. And by the time we made it to the bar, I was so happy to be *anywhere* clean and dry, I practically wept with joy.

Unfortunately, I lost my cell phone in the mud, and Logan said that he doesn't bring his when he goes four-wheeling because he likes to 'unplug in nature'.

Next time I think he'll be sure to bring his phone in a plastic baggy and tie it around his neck with AAA already dialed, and the Uber app fully loaded.

Although I don't know how AAA, or an Uber driver, would make it to where we abandoned the Jeep.

Now I'm in the ladies' room trying to 'freshen

up' before Logan drives me home in his truck. He said he'll have to get his buddy with a monster truck to go out there and help him drag the Jeep out of the mud.

Personally, I would leave it there.

Now I'll have to borrow Sassy's cell phone to call my Dad back until I can get to the Verizon store and replace mine.

Hopefully Jason isn't trying to reach me. I'll have to call him, too, and tell him I dropped my phone in the toilet.

He'll believe that. At my college dorm, one of us did that almost daily.

And once I use Sassy's phone, I am going to run over it with my car. This is her fault. I'd like to see her picking mud out of her ears.

For the record, she's right. I never had any violent tendencies before moving to Applebarrow.

I take deep cleansing breaths, like my parents taught me, and try to clean up as best I can with water from the sink.

I hope the mud stains come out of my new clothes. What a stupid activity! Of course, if he wasn't showing off...

I toss a wad of mud-soaked paper towels in the trash, grab a fresh batch and try to wipe up some of the mud off the tile floor. Even though it's not my job or my fault, I still don't want the next woman who comes in here to deal with a huge mess or fall on her ass.

Unless it's Sassy.

Yes, I am not happy with Sassy right now, in case you weren't sure.

I take another deep cleansing breath and wipe under my eyes one last time. At least my face isn't that bad, even though I had to wash off my pretty makeup.

Back in the bar, Logan is wiping his face with a bar towel, even though it looks like he cleaned up in the men's room.

"Hey, how did you get so clean?"

"Oh, I have a bathroom in the back with a shower."

My mouth hangs open and he quickly adds, "I didn't think offering you a shower in my private bathroom would be practical, seeing as you don't have a change of clothes. Plus, it would be bad for the rumor mill. There isn't even a female employee on staff right now to supervise."

"I don't need a supervisor. I'm an..." What is that? Shit, now more mud dropped down my shirt. Where the hell did that come from? I look up from peering into my cleavage and Logan snaps his eyes back to my face. Ah ha!

"You were saying?" He folds his arms and concentrates on my eyes.

"I'm an adult and I can do what I want. Including shower, if I am dirty."

"Lia—"

"And furthermore, I don't care about gossip. And maybe Sassy is right. If Jason hadn't...what's wrong? Are you listening to me?"

Logan's head is snapping back and forth like the cat in the gif my friend Gabby calls 'nervous kitty'.

Oh no, I hope Granana hasn't decided to show herself...

Now Logan has his head in his hands, as I am suddenly spun around by a pair of strong hands. This is a disaster. I can't believe she would...wait, she's touch...

"Jason?"

"Glad to see you remember me." He steps back and looks me up and down. "I would ask what happened, but I ran into your friend Sassy while I was ringing your bell, and she told me you had gone on a little adventure today."

He's smiling, but in that way serial killers do in movies, right before someone loses a head.

"I'm sorry, but...wait, no I'm *not* sorry. Well I am sorry, as in I shouldn't have gone on an outing that shoots mud in your ears, but I'm not apologizing to you. I did nothing wrong."

"I'm not saying you did. Do you have a guilty conscience?"

Logan clears his throat and says, "Hey Jason...it's my fault. Normally this kind of thing doesn't get out of hand. I mean, the four-wheeling. You know, I normally don't get this dirty. As dirty as Lia is."

Jason glares at Logan, who backs away and says, "Okay, I have to get back to work."

"Thanks for the...ride." I wince at my choice of words and regard Jason with my hands on my hips.

He hates that.

Logan waves and disappears to the back room, presumably to give us privacy and to stay out of the path of flying glassware.

"Jason, I am not guilty of anything. And if you had come here today, like you originally said you would..."

"I'm here. I wanted to surprise you."

"Uh huh...why don't I believe that?"

I told everyone who asked (which was *everyone*)

that Jason wasn't coming until Sunday because of work. They must think he works at the White House or is a brain surgeon, given how often I use that excuse for his absence.

But this time it's a lie. We had an argument the other day because he wanted to tour the plant today, and I refused to call Mr. Franklin and ask him to work on a holiday weekend. If Jason can't make the time to come during the week to see the facilities, then I guess our future isn't that important.

Plus, he wants me to consider (accept) an offer we received from a subpar dog food company, and I am not prepared to do that.

I don't want to help someone make an inferior product, and I am not comfortable making a hasty decision. Whatever I decide to do with that plant will be my family's legacy.

I wish Jason wasn't so impatient and bossy. I may not have his business experience, but my GPA was a lot higher than his, and I have some common sense *and* a moral responsibility to the community.

Once I got off my soap box, as he put it (yes, I said *most* of that *to* him, not just in my head), he said he wasn't going to take time away from the office to come here on Saturday if I didn't want to make our plans a priority, blah, blah, blah...

We finally begrudgingly apologized to each other, after both of us stubbornly refused to give in. He said he isn't used to this side of me.

Well, that's because in Richmond I was wasting my time at a mind-numbing job with no responsibility and hanging out with his stupid friends (the guys are nice—I was just angry). Now I have people counting on me to make good decisions.

So now, after that big argument, he thinks that

surprising me is such a grand gesture that I should have been waiting for him at home, even though I wasn't expecting him until tomorrow.

Seriously? The nerve!

Instead of continuing the conversation in the middle of the bar, Jason takes my hand, grabs my purse (which is full of mud—yay!), and leads me to his car.

"I am not going to argue with you in public. Plus, we need to get you home and properly cleaned up. I guess I shouldn't be too mad, since you declined Logan's offer of a private shower."

Crap, I guess he was standing there awhile. I blame the mud in my cleavage. Logan would have spotted Jason sooner, if he hadn't followed my eyes down my shirt.

"He did not offer me anything. You misheard."

I stop in the parking lot, and now he looks worried that if he doesn't stop acting like a jerk, I am going to refuse to quietly get in the car.

"Okay Lia, I'm sorry. I overreacted in there. But look at you? You're not yourself since you got here. Where's my happy, carefree girl? And what the hell are you wearing?"

"She's still here, but she's a woman and she...why I am referring to myself as 'she'? *I* am a woman and I don't appreciate you talking to me like I'm a child."

"You're right." He pauses and lowers his head. "It's not an excuse, but I'm under so much stress and pressure at work. You have no idea. I guess I envy you this relaxed lifestyle, but I know you do have responsibilities, too. I'll try to be more patient. Okay?"

I lower my head to his chest, seeing as he has

closed the distance between us. "Okay. Take me home."

I want this argument to end so I bite my tongue. If he shared more about his work problems with me (instead of Amy), I would know about them. Sometimes he does treat me like a nineteen-fifties housewife.

Of course, my personal ambitions to date have not been impressive, and sometimes relationships suffer at times of great change.

Now I sound like my father—who I still need to call back, but my phone is in the mud.

Jason opens his car door and roots around for a towel from the backseat before I climb in.

Normally I would be opposed to sitting on a dirty gym towel, but most things are a lot cleaner than me right now.

I want to ask to use his phone, but maybe I'll wait until we get home. I don't feel like subjecting myself to a lecture about reckless behavior for losing mine. He apologized and I'd like to get home without another argument.

"I can't wait to get in the shower. Care to join me?"

Flirtatious talk is always a good way to divert Jason's attention.

He backs the car out of the parking lot and adjusts the air conditioning. "Wow, it's hot today. What did you say? Oh sure, but later. Right now, I want you to get ready to go out. With this heat, we'll both be sweaty again after the outing I have planned."

CHAPTER ELEVEN

"Lia, you have to talk to me."

I shoot daggers at Jason and say, "No, I don't."

With my arms folded across my chest, I know I'm acting like a child, but I don't care. All that's missing is my tongue sticking out.

He shuts off the car's motor, and now it seems my refusal to rehash the same argument over and over is preventing me from even leaving the former site of DeLuca's Delicious Delights.

Yes, that was the *fun* outing Jason had planned for us this afternoon.

I'd rather eat mud than hear his rationale for letting a company that practically poisons pets take ownership of my grandparents' business assets.

"Please be rational. This company has a lot of capital, and they'll bring jobs to the region. And you don't have a better idea or offer on the table, do you? And please don't tell me about Molly's dolls again."

I may have casually mentioned Molly's talents, and that if she had the right backers, she could expand her doll sales far beyond the reach of Emma's shop.

I was thinking American Girls, but for the adult collector. Her dolls are of all races and skin tones with authentic costumes. And not in a culturally offensive way. I could see these dolls selling in other countries, especially in Europe, where we are supposed to be *living* soon.

It's funny how Jason expects me to bow to his wishes with *my* business (yes, I have accepted that I almost own a business—yikes!), but I never get any solid updates on what's going on with his company and our plans, which depend on his success at Elevation. All he tells me is how 'stressed' he is.

"Jason, we do not have to make a decision about this right away. We don't *need* the money, and supposedly we're relocating with your company. I'll have a cash inheritance once the year is up, and we'll probably sell the house and I'll get some of that money."

"But the big money is in the plant site, Lia."

"Maybe I'd like to help out a single mother. You were raised by a single mother." I face him with a pointed look.

"Please, don't remind me. Comparing Molly to my mother is not the way to make me take this seriously."

I return my arms to their folded pose and say, "We need to go home. I have a headache and we've discussed this enough for one day."

I turn my head and look out the window, signaling the end of the conversation. I reach into my alternate purse (the muddy one is in the trash) to grab my phone out of habit, but of course it's not there.

I still haven't called my father. If my parents were the worrying kind, the police would be at my door by now. But knowing them, they're dancing around a bonfire, burning incense, and forgot all about it.

We drive home in silence, and Jason fiddles

with his phone to find some music to further annoy me with. All he listens to is Top 40 women singers who screech to show their range and do more dancing than singing.

It's bubble gum crap that sounds the same to me. He and Amy probably unwind to it after a long day doing—whatever the hell they do for fourteen hours a day at the office.

We arrive at the parking lot, and Jason barely puts the car in park before I bolt to my door. I don't want any public scenes at Pentagon Place, so I don't say a peep until we get inside.

I *am* angry, but I also don't want to ruin what little time we have together. Couples go through rough patches. We're not in college anymore, and this is our first big life change as adult partners.

I sit down and kick off my sandals. My muddy clothes are soaking in the laundry room, and the rest of my purchases are at Molly's with Sassy.

I'd like an excuse to get away from Jason for a few more minutes, but if I see Sassy and she asks me how my day went, I will flip out.

Also, *she* told Jason where to find me in the first place. Couldn't she have said I was *anywhere* else? Abducted by aliens would have been preferable.

Jason sits next to me on the couch and says, "I want what's best for us, but if you're not ready to make a decision yet, I understand. Maybe we can have Ed Franklin and the accountant review the paperwork and run some numbers. Plus, you could at least agree to *meet* with the dog food people. You're forming your judgment based on your father's opinion and no solid research."

I'm so tired of arguing, and my body is achy

from stress and being jostled around in the Jeep.
"Fine. We'll let the professionals advise us."
I know Mr. Franklin and Granana's accountant are not going to recommend we accept the first offer, and they have a big stake in what type of business relocates to this town.

"That's great, Sweetie. Thank you." He leans in to kiss me and I let him because anything other than yelling feels good right now, and it's been way too long...

He whispers in my ear, "Hey, want to go take that shower now. I, for one, feel gross and sticky after walking around that dirty, hot factory. Let's get wet."

When a man sticks his tongue in your ear and starts using the words 'dirty' and 'wet', it's hard to resist.

Logan may be hot, but Jason is cute and...why am I thinking of Logan?

I must ignore any thoughts of that man! Although, I would love to know if he was able to get his Jeep out of the mud. But I'll see him on Monday, and I'll find out then.

Sassy probably already knows the answer because she's back at Tonic, downing purple drinks and plotting more ways to interfere in my love life.

"Well, since you asked so nicely, I accept your offer."

I smile as he takes my hand. On the way to the stairs he says, "I'm so glad we figured that out. When your grandmother left us that property, I knew you wouldn't know what to do with it, and I was hoping you'd let me help."

Oh hell, no.

I stop at the bottom of the stairs and say, "Jason, my grandmother left that property to *me*. Not us. I know you know more about business, but I know more about my family."

I guess that killed the mood because his bedroom eyes darken and he says, "Oh, I get it. Everything was ours until you found out you were an heiress. It's funny, but I don't remember correcting you when you referred to MY apartment as OUR apartment. Your little job barely paid for some groceries and your pajama addiction."

"And *why* did I have such a shitty job, Jason?"

"Don't ask me. I guess because you majored in something useless and then did nothing with it."

I am sure steam is visibly coming out of my ears as I clench my fists by my side. "Are you kidding? I have lots of interests, but you promised me that in a short period of time we would be moving to Europe. Right? You acted like you were Prince Charming whisking me off into a bright tomorrow."

Jason grits his teeth and takes in a quick breath. "That's it! I have to get out of here. You are completely irrational and spoiled. While you're playing in the mud, doing makeovers, and planning parties—I am out busting my ass in the real world. And it's not easy!"

Jason bolts to the door and I yell out, "Where are you going?"

"I don't know, but please don't let me stop you from doing something *fun* this weekend. Maybe next you'd like to play in the sandbox. Knowing the maturity and intelligence of your new friends, they'll probably have one set up at the barbecue."

There is no smart retort for that statement because Molly told me that we are, in fact, going to have a big sandbox set up in the courtyard to simulate the beach, along with the previously mentioned blowup pool.

He's halfway to the parking area, and as much as I don't want to fight with Jason, I'm not seeing much chance for this weekend improving, and he has some nerve! I am *not* irrational or spoiled.

I could call him and try to reason with him, but I don't have a phone.

I hear a buzzing sound, and see that Jason left *his* phone on the coffee table. I am never one to snoop, but I would like to see who's calling. It could be the realtor from our plant visit today. Or the dog food people. Or work.

I take a casual glance, as if I saw it by accident.

'Amy cell.'

I am certainly not going to answer it. One, because I don't want to look like a jealous girlfriend. And two, because I want to talk to Amy as much as I want to lick a toilet seat.

But I could wait until the call goes to voice mail, and then use Jason's phone to call my father back. It's Jason's fault that this whole day was screwed up in the first place.

Well first Sassy's, then Jason's. And a little bit Logan, too.

Hmm…I'm blaming everyone but myself.

Hopefully Jason will cool off and realize that he needs to back off the factory plans.

I didn't *want* to throw it in his face that it's my inheritance, but we're not married, and he is getting way too bossy and territorial. He's never been that type of guy.

I'll use Jason's phone to call my dad. He'll be a calming influence.

I just hope he doesn't quiz me on his 'Happiness Tenets'. There are ten, and I can usually only recite about six or seven.

***

"What do I always tell you? You must breathe and put yourself in the other person's shoes. Arguments are never about what they seem to be, and it's just—"

"Negative energy, I know Dad. But when an overbearing person is breathing down your neck and trying to force you to bend to their will, it's not easy to stay positive. You wouldn't know what that's like. Oh wait, never mind."

"No, I've never dealt with that behavior."

We both laugh because my mother, and both of my grandparents, are/were argumentative and domineering. In a loving way, but still…

I don't know why I haven't reached out to my dad for advice since I moved here. I'm an adult, but I'm still fairly new to adulting and I need some wisdom.

Especially when my only local parental figure is Sassy.

"You know your mother and I both like Jason, but he's a college boyfriend, and sometimes things change. Or maybe it's only a bump in the road. Just remember the 'Happiness Tenets' and—"

"—you'll follow your bliss. I know, Dad. It's just…"

I wish I could confide in Dad and tell him what's really going on, but I don't want him to know there's another guy in the picture.

Not that there is. Well, I'm not sure *what's* going on.

Nothing. Definitely nothing. Logan is not the reason Jason and I are arguing—it's Jason's stubborn nature.

Also, I have a million questions about Granana. There's something weird going on here. I can't put my finger on it.

"What is it, Honey? You can tell me anything. Is it a woman's problem? Do you want me to get your mother?"

"Oh no. I mean, I would love to talk to Mom, but I don't have time, and it's not a woman's problem. I guess I'm having trouble coping with change. Are you and Mom coming to visit any time soon?"

What is that noise? I hear something outside. If Jason is back, I'd rather be off the phone, especially since it's his phone and I'd like to erase this call from the record, so he doesn't think I was snooping.

Things are bad when you don't want your boyfriend to know you were talking to your father.

Dad is talking and I'm only catching the tail end of it.

"—and I'm teaching a couple of summer courses to the advanced students, but we'll be free on the Fourth of July weekend. Why don't we come then? I'll ask Mr. Franklin if we can stay in Granana's house. Or would that be too weird?"

"Dad, we own the house."

"Well, not really. Legally, nothing has been inherited yet. Anyway, I'm sure he'll agree to us staying there."

"Of course. That will be fun. Dad, can you hold on for a second?"

I hear a voice at the door. It's probably Sassy.

I tiptoe to the door, and as I reach for the knob

my grandmother walks *through* me.

Talk about something you never thought you'd say.

"What are you doing? You scared me!"

I shake the strange feeling off. A *ghost* passed through my body—what the hell?

She's standing in the entryway dusting herself off, but there isn't a scratch on her.

"Lia, is everything okay? Is someone there?"

Dad is panicking because he thinks I may be in a dangerous situation. However, it's only a ghost pushing her way through my front door, while I'm on the phone with her son, and my boyfriend could come back any time.

Everything is super fine here!

"No, Dad. I mean yes—"

He obviously heard me talking so I must think of something to tell him.

Granana screws up her face and says, "Is that your father? Don't listen to him. Quick, we need to talk."

"It's the UPS guy, Dad."

"On a Saturday night? Honey, if you have company you don't have to make excuses on my account."

"They deliver on Saturdays, Dad. I promise." I glare at my spooky grandmother and mouth the silent words, "Can he hear *you*?"

"No, I don't think so. Only the person I've chosen to haunt can hear me. At least I think so. Give me the phone and we'll test it."

She reaches for the phone and her hand moves through it. Whew, at least she still can't manipulate objects very well. So, I guess I did put the blanket on myself the other night and knock over the rosary beads. Hmm...

Dad is babbling away as if I'm not talking to his dead mother. I suppose that's a good thing.

"Oh, I wouldn't know who delivers when. I don't buy things. Your mother buys things. All the things. I tried to make an earth-loving hippy out of the woman, but it's hard to get the New Yorker out of her."

"That's so true, Dad." I point to the couch for Granana to sit down before she causes any more trouble, but I'm guessing she'll melt through the furniture and end up underneath? Underground?

Granana gestures with her hands and moves her arms around to indicate that she can't attach herself to anything.

At least I think that's what she's doing. I'm a haunting novice.

"Fine, stay there and float."

Crap, I whispered that. And I've been told I am *not* good at whispering.

"What did you say, Lia? Something about a boat? This connection is horrible. I should go into town to use my cell phone. That's what we get for living in the middle of nowhere. So, a boat? Are you and Jason going out on the lake tomorrow? Oh, I forgot, he stormed off."

"Yep, that was the plan. I was just telling the UPS guy because he asked me if I had any big plans for the weekend."

"Okay, I hope Jason comes back. But remember, follow your bliss, Honey."

I'm finally able to get Dad off the phone, as I watch my grandmother float into the kitchen.

"Well, I guess you are real. Well, not *real*. You're dead, but here you are. I didn't dream you. I'm not going crazy. Yet. Granana, what are you doing in there?"

She's in my pantry again. With all the problems I have, she wants to maintain contact with me from the afterlife so she can spy on my cooking.

"Well, I'm glad to see you got rid of the jar sauce and the cheap cheese. I couldn't understand the tacos at the last meeting, but if you were going to bastardize an ethnic cuisine, I'm glad you moved away from my people."

"Gran, that's racist."

"How is that racist? I want the sanctity of homemade Italian cooking to be preserved by my only granddaughter."

"I guess you were at the meeting?"

"Yes, and I commend you for letting the residents participate in planning, but I hope you now see that's a bad idea. Some of these people are *folle*, if you know what I mean."

"Yes, I remember enough Italian. And yes, some of them are a bit crazy, but you told me to give Stan a chance with his book. And by the way, they get along *just fine*."

"Oh, do they?" Granana looks off into the distance, like a robot who went offline for a minute, but I'm not buying her act.

Changing the subject, she says, "Now Lia, I came here to talk to you about Jason."

She better tell me why she asked *me* to come here!

I sigh and hold off on further questioning until I hear what she has to say about my boyfriend now.

"You mean, my *nice young man*?"

"Um, well...yes. I suppose."

"Ha! I caught you. You were not referring to Jason in your letter. Granana, are you matchmaking from the grave?"

"No, I'm doing it right in your living room." She starts laughing and I want to tell her to be careful of her weak heart—but nope, that's not an issue any more.

"Lia, I can't help it if there are other nice young men who find you attractive in the world. I don't know why you would think I was matchmaking. I truly wanted you to help the tenants, but we don't have time to get into that right now."

I guess haunting has time limits, like Cinderella's coach and horses.

"Do you know where Jason is right now? Is that part of your powers?"

"I can see what I want to see, so yes I followed that little shit...sorry but I did not like his tone. I'm glad to see you stood up to him. Anyway, yes I know but I can't tell you."

"Why not? Is he having an affair with Amy?"

"I can't tell you that, either. It's a part of the *Code*."

I sigh and rapidly tap my foot. I'm already so tired of this game. You would think it would be joyful to see a loved one after death, but this isn't a heartwarming reunion with a sweet old lady.

"It's part of the *Haunting Code*. I'm in training. We can only haunt one person and I chose you. I can only tell you what you already know, *but* I can warn you about things *I* know."

"That's super helpful, and thanks so much for picking *me*."

"That's ungrateful, young lady. Aren't you glad you can see me?"

"Yes, Granana. I'm sorry. I'm sooo confused. Just tell me what you can. Please."

"Okay, he's hiding things. And I am hoping when he comes back, that he will tell you, although it's unlikely any man would make that confession. I'm hoping he'll start to tell you enough that you'll be able to piece it together. All I can do is serve as a guide and give you warnings, but you have to trust me."

"Okay, I'll try, but this is super weird."

"Don't I know it! I just walked through the damn door."

I glance at the door and shiver. That was one cold burst of energy flowing through me. "So, you can't manipulate objects?"

"We *can*, but I haven't gotten the hang of it yet, at least not consistently. I haven't attended school in years, and it's a steep learning curve. While other old spirits are off having fun, I'm working hard for you."

"The other night—I woke up with an extra blanket, and I knocked over the rosary beads. I wondered if that was you."

"Yes, I did those things." Now she's excited and talking with her wispy hands. "I had just come from class and I wanted to test my skills, but now I seem to have lost the knack again. I figured I'd do it while you were sleeping. When you're awake you ask so many questions and I need to be able to concentrate—"

"Well, wouldn't you have questions?"

"*Dolchezza*, please sit down. You are so fidgety."

I acquiesce and sit on my couch, staying far enough away from my ghostly visitor to avoid further contact.

I love Granana, but I like her better over there.

"That's better. Just because *I* can't bend my legs to the contours of a chair, it doesn't mean you should be uncomfortable." She purses her lips and says, "Oh, how I wish I could make you some cannolis."

Death has not changed her priorities.

"Granana, what did you want to tell me about Jason?"

"Oh, I wanted to say, he left his phone here. I heard him complaining about it, and I know you already know he left it because you were using it."

She points at the device as if it holds the secrets to life and the universe.

"What, now it's a magic phone?"

"Dear Lord, I'm not magic. I'm a *ghost.*"

Silly me! How could I not know the difference?

"Did you check the phone to see who's been calling him lately? Clearly you have suspicions. And in my experience, when a woman has suspicions, they are founded. You're a level-headed girl. Your father raised you well and—"

"You told me not to listen to him!"

"Yes, well he does talk nonsense, but he did a good job. Anyway, I'm assuming you didn't check the phone. You just used it to call your father because your phone is in the mud?"

"I thought you couldn't tell me things that you know?'

"Lia, you are an honors student." She sighs and looks up...not sure if that's a reaction left over from life, or if 'up' is really where she comes from.

"I can't tell you things *you don't know.* Try to follow. Obviously, you know your phone is in the mud. Please look at Jason's phone. And you need to get this Amy to come here."

"What are we going to do to her?" These rules are kind of stupid, but now I'm scared I will be punished by whoever made the rules. Crap.

Granana sighs and says, "Jesus, Mary and Joseph, I'm not an *assassin*. We aren't going to *do* anything to her. You are so naïve—I blame your father for raising you in Vermont."

"You just said he did a good job."

"He did, kind of. But he should have stayed in Brooklyn, where he was born."

"You moved him here!"

She shakes her head and says, "The point is that you need to open your eyes. Jason does have something to tell you and based on what I overheard tonight, I think he plans on spilling some of it. So, get him talking and give him a chance to grovel before you pound him. You'll get more information that way."

"I wish I knew what you're talking about."

"You will, I promise. Have faith. After all, you're talking to a dead lady and you're not *folle* in the *capo*."

Even when she taps her own head, her finger goes through her skull.

Great, a floating apparition, with no solid brain matter, is giving me advice about my love life. And telling me that I'm not crazy in the head.

Suddenly, loud knocking on the door causes me to jump. This is probably a living human, at least. Why aren't they ringing the bell, though?

"Okay, now there's the door." Granana gestures to her portal back to...who knows where.

"Is that Jason?" I look between the door and Granana.

"Do you know if it's Jason?" she replies.

"No, I can't see through doors!"

"Well, if you don't know then I can't tell you. Remember?"

"The *Code*. Yes, and now whoever it is can probably hear me talking to you. Super."

Hopefully it's just a neighbor reporting their overflowing toilet to the apartment manager.

The knocking is louder. "Lia! Are you home?"

It sounds like Logan, and somehow this feels like a matchmaking set up.

I can't believe my sweet, Catholic grandmother would encourage me to cheat on my boyfriend, just because we had a fight.

I wonder if she's been reunited with Grandpa, or if *she's* looking for a new man on the other side.

I stare at Granana and shoo her away. I can't open the door with her here.

"What? I'm not leaving yet." She looks as defiant as a floating being can appear.

I raise my eyebrows at her, and she slowly says, "No. One. Can. See. Me."

I sigh and raise my eyebrows higher. It's impossible to ignore her and talk to someone else, and maybe I'd like some privacy?

She points again, like the Ghost of Christmas Future (or the Grim Reaper), and says, "Lia, open the door before Logan's arm breaks off."

CHAPTER TWELVE

"Just get him to the couch, please. Is he okay?"

Logan half carries, half drags my inebriated boyfriend to the sofa, and he barely stirs when he's dropped onto the cushions.

I wince, but I guess Logan couldn't wait to deposit him somewhere.

"It depends on your definition of okay." Logan stretches his neck and shoulders. "Damn, I'm out of shape. I should be able to carry a little...anyway, he's just blasted."

"Jason never gets drunk. Was he drinking at Tonic?"

He explains how an infuriated Jason entered his bar, and while he was confident that he could take Jason in a fight, Logan was slightly concerned he could have a weapon, based on his swagger and menacing scowl.

"The last thing I need is to get into another fight, and in my own bar."

What has gotten into Jason? We just had an argument. Oh yeah, the four-wheeling incident isn't helping.

Wait? Logan gets into fights?

"Did he say anything to you?"

Granana says, "Oh, he said *plenty*. Make sure you ask him when he wakes up. Logan is too much of a gentleman to tell you."

I am assuming Logan doesn't hear her or see her floating around the living room in her long flowing gown. I guess she must be going through a princess phase in heaven.

Or wherever she resides when not making me crazy.

Logan sighs and nods towards one of my side chairs, and I motion for him to sit down.

Jason is moaning but he deserves his pain, and I intend to find out *how* much he deserves it.

Logan leans forward and steeples his fingers on his lap. "He did a lot of talking. He started out pretty combative, and said he only came back to Tonic because every other place in this town is a cesspool, and he was afraid of catching something."

"Yes, that's Jason's usual judgment of small-town bars. Okay, what else?"

"Look Lia, I do *not* want to get involved. I should never have taken you out in the Jeep today. That's on me. But you and Jason need to work this out without any interference from anyone else."

I was tempted to say something about Granana's interference, but then caught myself.

I guess I didn't correct myself immediately, because Logan asks, "Hey, what are you looking at? Are you crying?"

"No, I'm not crying. I'm frustrated."

I ball up my fists and then realize how ridiculously non-menacing I look.

Plus, I am totally crying, but blinking away the tears.

"I'm sorry, it was nice of you to bring him here. I'll talk to him when he wakes up. If he shared any secrets with you, he will probably confess, because he won't trust you to keep quiet."

"Yeah, that's if he remembers anything. I'm sorry he's so drunk. I think he was bullying a female server, and she was afraid to cut him off. I'll have a talk with her. We shouldn't continue to serve people who're this drunk, and she should have come to me to deal with him."

"I'm sorry, I know he can be an asshole at times."

Granana mutters, "That's for sure" at the same time Jason yells out, "Lia, baby I'm sorry!"

Logan jumps up and says, "Okay, that's my cue to get out of your hair. Make sure he drinks as much water as you can get in him, and if he's lucid enough to swallow a pill without choking, get a few aspirins in him, too. And good luck."

"Thanks, Logan. I owe you one."

"Nah, we're friends. Remember?"

He flashes a sweet smile and I close the door.

Did he look a tiny bit sad when he said that?

"I think he looked a tiny bit sad."

Oh my God, can she read my mind? Or are we both *really* in tune with Logan's emotions?

I shake my head and say, "You need to leave. Please."

She starts to protest, and Jason stirs. Crap.

"Baby, I can't leave. Don't have my car." He's speaking into the couch cushions and is whining like a baby.

"No, Jason I know you can't leave. I wasn't talking to you."

Hopefully he will think I was talking to Logan and not my dead grandmother, since his eyes are pressed into the couch and he won't know that Logan already left.

I point to the door, as if that's how she'll be

leaving (who knows?), and she glides over and says, "I'm going. I don't want to get in trouble with The Haunting Board, and if I stay a moment longer, I might say the wrong thing."

The Haunting Board? Another thing to add to my list of questions for the next visit.

"Just don't let him manipulate you. I can't tell you what you don't know, but I can come back and tell you if he hasn't spilled *all* the beans. And believe me, there are more beans in this situation than in that disgusting taco salad you served last week."

I wave at her and she drifts through the door in a huff.

I lay my forehead against the door and jump back as she sticks her head through again. I am going to have a stroke before this is over.

Will this ever be over? Too bad I can't ask The Haunting Board.

"And one more thing. Don't do that 'stand by your man' crap if he gives you a sob story. It's so Tammy Wynette."

And she's gone again. Who the hell is Tammy Wynette, and what did her man do?

I have no time to find out because Jason is looking green and moaning.

I hope Granana outfitted my new home with a bucket, or a large enough waste paper basket to...

"Leeeee!"

I give up on searching for a vomit receptacle, and sit on the carpet in front of Jason, ready to jump at the slightest gagging sound.

"Jason, do you think if I help you, you can make it upstairs? You need to drink water and take aspirin. You're going to be so sick tomorrow."

He slurs his speech, but at least his head is now facing me and not the cushion. "I'm so sorry about the fight. You're so good and I'm such a douche."

I'd love to pump him for information, but while he's in this state I can't trust anything he says.

I remember holding my roommate's hair back in college while she was getting sick, and she told me that she danced with a unicorn and made out with our math professor at a party.

I was there, and could attest to the absence of mythical creatures, and faculty members looking to get fired.

I regard his pathetic form and say, "It's okay, I'm not mad anymore. I'm going to the kitchen now to get you some water, and we're going to see if you can sit up to take some pills. Okay?"

He doesn't respond, but I go to the kitchen anyway. I hate taking care of drunk, sick people.

I should call Sassy and make her come over here and help me. This is all her fault.

Or at least some of it is.

Now where do I have aspirin? I rarely take medication, but I thought I saw...wait, what did he say?

I peek my head out of the pantry and say, "What did you say?"

He yells out, "I don't want to do it anymore. She's such a bitch!"

I feel colder than when Granana swept into the room, and that's really saying something.

"Jason, who are you talking about?" I rush back into the living room and yell, "Damn it!"

He fell off the couch and is snoring on the floor. At least I know he's not dead, but he's also not going to tell me anything now.

And it could mean nothing. Nonsense. Gibberish talk. He could be remembering something his mother made him do when he was a little boy, for all I know.

Well, he can suffer with a massive hangover tomorrow, and I'll go out alone, after I force him to tell me what the hell is going on.

I hope his head hurts tremendously while I grill him.

My own head is throbbing. I should resume my search for painkillers, but Jason's phone is vibrating on my coffee table again.

I don't know—maybe my grandmother is right.

Snooping *is* wrong in the general sense, but this suspicion I'm feeling isn't unwarranted. There are glaring red flags, so I think I'm entitled to look at his phone.

I've invested five years of my life in this man, and that's a large percentage of my twenty-four years. If he's a lying, cheating bastard, I need to know now.

I walk over to the buzzing contraption like it might bite me, now that my suspicions have deepened.

I take a deep breath and stare at the display. It's a text from Greta. Shit...it disappeared before I could read all of it, but it sounded like she was looking for him.

I wish I knew his passcode, but I have no clue. Wait, I know.

I pick up Jason's arm and drop it. If he doesn't respond to that, he's out cold.

Okay, if he wasn't *breathing*, I'd call 911, but he's snoring again. He's not waking up any time soon.

"Sorry, Jason, but you brought this on yourself."

I gently place his thumb on the screen to unlock the phone.

Now that I'm in, I go upstairs in case he wakes up. I don't want him to catch me in the act.

I sit back on the fluffy pillows in my cozy bed and do what I said I would never do.

Greta wrote:

"Jason, where are you, you naughty boy?"

I wince. That woman is a piece of work. What a way to address your employee. And on a Saturday night at eleven o'clock? Seriously? I start to scroll and see that it's his only text from her.

Hmm...she *is* old, so maybe she's only resorted to texting because he didn't answer her calls?

I move on to the Amy tab. Why not get right to the meat of it?

Amy wrote:

"Have you told her yet?"

"Jason, where are you?"

"What happened with the plant tour?"

"Now you're worrying me."

Ah ha! She's worried. She knows what he's doing. But the worst is—told *her* what? I have a feeling she's referring to me.

So obviously, the big thing he has to tell me involves Amy. Also, those are the *only* texts from Amy, and I know she texts him all the time.

Why would he erase the texts unless he was hiding something?

I guess I have my answer.

I drop the phone and sink deeper into my pillow mound, but then bolt upright.

Wait a second. Amy and Jason work closely together. Maybe she was talking about him telling *Greta* something—like about a client. And that's why Greta was hunting him down.

I bet he was avoiding both of them to focus on our time together.

And maybe Amy is just a nosy bitch and he casually mentioned the plant tour as a practical excuse to get out of working all weekend.

I am a little concerned about why he wouldn't save her texts, but maybe she annoys the hell out of him, and he doesn't want to keep them as a reminder of her nagging about work.

She's his work wife. Sassy was right.

Whew, I'm proud of myself for working that through in my head before starting another argument with wild accusations.

I'm not an idiot, and he could still be guilty of something, and according to Granana, he is. However, I am not sure of *her* motives. Although, Logan seemed to have something he was hiding about Jason, too.

Nobody tells me anything, but I don't want to jump to conclusions. That often happens in chick flicks. The woman confronts the man and then looks like a moron for being insecure and ruins her relationship in the process.

No, I am going to be level-headed and give Jason a chance to explain.

Even though I feel a bit better, I am not going to try to wake him now, nor am I going to sleep downstairs to watch him. He's an adult and if he wants to get blackout drunk because we had a fight, I'm not going to baby him. I'm not his mother.

Hmm...I wonder if there are any texts from his

mother. He rarely visits, but he does have contact. If there was anyone whose texts he would erase from his phone, it would be hers.

Okay, well there goes that theory. There is a text string going back to the dawn of time from his mother.

"*Do you still like spam? I'll make it when you come to visit.*"

"*How is that little girlfriend of yours? You should bring her here.*"

"*I won five-hundred dollars at bingo and your brother stole it.*"

"*The old guy across the street is watering his lawn with no pants on.*"

Only one text from his brother, Austin.

"*Hey J, do you have any money I can borrow? I wanna buy a boa constrictor.*"

Yeah, they aren't the brightest bulbs, but he saved *their* communications.

Ah, ha. Maybe it's just work texts he deletes on his personal….no never mind—there are a bunch from Richard, too.

I sigh and put the phone down. I'll sneak downstairs (probably not necessary with Sleeping Beauty's condition) and lay the phone back on the coffee table.

As usual, snooping only raises more questions.

What I'd like is to get Jason, Amy, Logan, and my grandmother in a room and hold them hostage until they tell me everything I want to know.

Great, now I'm plotting crimes against my loved ones.

And Amy.

Logan, too. He's not a loved one. I don't know why I thought that—I'm tired.

***

"Lia...wake up."

"I have ways of making you talk!" I yell in my dream, and smack Jason in the head. I wake myself up and say, "I'm so sorry."

He's holding his head and laying half on the bed, and half on the floor. "Jesus, I feel bad enough. But I guess I deserved that. And I *am* here to talk."

"I was dreaming. I don't talk like that in real life. What the hell would I do to make you talk? I'm not an FBI agent or a terrorist."

He crawls onto the bed and gingerly rests his head on the pillows. I scoot over to give him room.

He smells like a distillery and I can't imagine his breath, but if he's ready to talk, I'm not stopping him due to poor personal hygiene.

"So first, I guess Logan told you what happened?"

"He said you showed up at Tonic and drank too much. Oh, and that you told him a bunch of things he can't repeat."

"My God, he's like a fucking boy scout. Sorry, sorry. I'm jealous because I love you so much."

I dodge his embrace because...just no...I'm not getting sucked in that easily.

"You were saying?"

He looks up at the ceiling and I am tempted to turn on the light so I can see his facial expressions, but in his current condition I'm not going to be able to assess if he's lying. He can barely speak or move his head. And I can't imagine how bad his eyes must look.

He blows out a big breath and says, "You know how I was hoping that Greta would open an office in Europe, and we could move there?"

"Of course, it's all we've talked about since you took the job four years ago."

Obviously, this isn't a good start to this conversation.

"Well, it seems that Greta hasn't made the best business decisions and she's not going to be able to do that now. Basically, she tricked me."

I put my arm on his shoulder. "Oh Honey, I'm sorry. She's an awful woman."

Even though I'm not happy that he's been keeping this information from me, this is obviously devastating for him, and I'm sure he was dreading having to tell me.

"That she is. You don't know the half of it. I'm also not doing well there, either. Honestly Amy is the only reason I'm still employed. She covers my ass."

I wonder what else she does with his ass, but this wouldn't be a good time to go there.

"I don't understand. You majored in marketing. I thought it was your passion."

"I'm in over my head. You know I just got by in college, and some of that was because I had to work so much, but I'm not as smart as you…and Amy. She's carrying me right now and I feel like such a failure. And so trapped."

His choice of words is concerning. Is Amy helping him to improve the company and save her own job, too? Or for some other reason?

"How long have you known our plans weren't going to happen?"

"Since right around the time your grandmother died. So, you can see why I didn't say anything."

"Well, not really. If we're a team, we have to tell

each other everything, right?"

"Yes, you're right. I thought you'd be so disappointed in me, and I was hoping your inheritance could help us to salvage my screw-up. What kind of a loser does that make me?"

"You're not a loser, Jason." I prop up on one elbow and say, "We can come up with another plan. I was thinking. Maybe *we* could start a business here in Applebarrow? It doesn't have to be Molly's dolls. We could learn to run a manufacturing business if—"

"No way. If I can't handle creating marketing stories for clients' existing businesses, I can't learn manufacturing distribution, procurement, and all the financial stuff. That's a nightmare. Trust me."

I want to trust him, but the truth is...I'm not sure I do anymore.

"So, what did *you* have in mind?"

"I've given it a lot of thought, and I want to get out of the country. I mean, not like I'm running away from anything...just because I promised you and it's our dream."

"Uh huh." Why do I feel like Jason is running away from something? Or someone?

"Anyway, I was thinking that with your language and social planning skills, we could open a boutique hotel in Europe. And if it does well, we could expand and open them in your favorite countries."

"Isn't that the same thing as running the factory?"

"No, because we have the skills to handle this type of business, and we can hire a few people who are natives to help us run it. And I can do marketing for something like that—I'm not entirely useless."

"I never said you were—"

"So, what do you think? I could even do biking tours and you could offer language classes. I have so many good ideas and it would be such an adventure."

"It sounds interesting, but maybe we should try doing the bed and breakfast thing here first. In Applebarrow. Before making the bigger commitment. Don't you think Granana's house could be converted into a small inn?"

"Sure, probably. But don't you want to get out of this town?"

Hmm, I don't know. I would have said yes right after I arrived, but now...I feel like I'm forming a life here. Of my own.

"I guess I do, eventually. But I feel like I have unfinished business here. I want to honor my commitment to Granana. And won't it take a while to find a property in a foreign country? That sounds like a big undertaking."

"Sure, but we can move to the area and get an apartment before we start the business. If we get some revenue going here, we can afford to do that, and then soon you'll have your full inheritance."

He really wants to get out of town. If I didn't know better, I would think he killed Greta and buried her body in my backyard. However, unless Greta is an advanced ghost, she wouldn't be able to text him.

"I don't know. It seems hasty. I'd like to talk to a financial advisor and maybe get Mr. Franklin's opinion. And talk to my parents. It's a big step."

"I understand. It's just that soon I'll be unemployed, and I won't be able to afford my apartment."

I snuggle down next to him and whisper in his ear, "Then you can live here with me until we figure everything out properly. Now let's try to get some sleep so we can enjoy our day together tomorrow. Did you drink some water or find the aspirin?"

If he thinks I am running out of town to live in a foreign country with no plan, like a felon on the run, he's delusional.

And I am not satisfied with his reasoning. He may be having trouble at work, but I don't believe that's his only reason for wanting to accelerate this plan.

I need some face time with Amy. Granana is right. I can't stand by my man, like her friend Tammy did.

But I also don't want to throw away a good relationship out of fear, jealousy, or unfounded suspicions.

Hmm...I know who I could go see, but I can't believe I am going there.

Jason ignores my comment about living here and instead replies to my inquiry into his well-being. "No, I crawled up here to talk to you. Maybe you can get me some water? My mouth is like cotton and my head...Jesus. I'm sorry, Babe. You know I never get drunk."

"No, you don't."

Not unless this is another new development I'm unaware of.

"I'll go down. Why don't you try to get out of your clothes? You must be so uncomfortable."

"You might have to help me, but I'm not saying that in a suggestive way. I don't think I can pull my own pants off. Are you sure you want to do anything with a fuck-up like me?"

Am I?

"Yes, and you're not...that bad. Now try to stay awake until I get back upstairs."

As I walk into the hallway, he says, "Hey..."

I peek my head back in and he says quietly, "We'll get out of the country soon. You'll see. In the meantime, we won't fight anymore. We'll work together. Here in Apple Bottom Butter town."

I smile and shake my head at his further mocking of my grandparents' home.

He can say whatever he wants, but we're not fugitives from justice, and I am not going to be manipulated into leaving this town until I fulfill my promise to Granana and pump her for information about her motives and the secrets she's hiding.

It's a tall order, but I feel myself growing bigger in this little town.

I also intend to get to the bottom of Jason's bullshit, if there is any more beyond the obvious. I'm pretty sure this was the big secret both Logan and Granana were alluding to, and it's not that bad. But I just don't know for sure.

I was so caught up in Jason's stupid behavior, that I didn't even ask Granana the most burning questions—who's the British manicure partner? Is it Axe? How do I find him?

Once I get my phone back, I am going to set up an appointment to get some answers from a living person. Now that I know ghosts are real, why not mediums?

CHAPTER THIRTEEN

"**M**y head feels like little men are in there with hammers, trying to break out."

Jason says this as he practically leaps down the stairs, opens the blinds in the living room, and pours himself some orange juice—all in one motion.

I'm not sure how he's this perky with the head hammers. If it were me, I would be upstairs for the entire holiday weekend.

"I guess you're not letting a silly little massive hangover slow you down."

It's hard to stay mad at him when he's like this. This is a glimpse of the happy, energetic Jason I fell in love with.

"No, I am not." He grabs me tightly and starts dancing me around the kitchen. "We are going to have a good rest of the weekend. And I am going to the party tomorrow and I will be on my best behavior. For you. No matter what happens, I am going to suck it up and be a full participant in the redneck pool party."

I sigh and smile. I'd rather his enthusiasm not be tainted with continued judgment and insults, but he's a work in progress. I keep reminding myself that he comes from the country and has tried so hard to leave it behind.

"That sounds great. And what did you want to

do today? I have to replace my phone because of the...you know."

"Haha, the mud. I know. Logan told me how it flew out of the Jeep and he had to grab you to keep you from following it. Fun times."

I furrow my brow and purse my lips. Is he serious or mocking Logan? Me? It's hard to buy that he suddenly sees Logan as a fun scamp, and he's not the least bit mad or jealous.

"Really? So, now you think it was okay that I went four-wheeling with Logan?"

"Of course. I overreacted. We both have opposite sex friends and it's always been cool."

It has?

"We're young. People of our generation aren't like our parents. We're don't live by archaic rules." He kisses me again and sails back up the stairs. "We'll do whatever you want today. I know, let's go shopping for a new bathing suit for you for tomorrow. The skimpiest bikini we can find."

He leaves me alone in the kitchen to contemplate what the hell just happened. Some archaic rules are essential—like the no cheating one.

And he has always preferred that I dress conservatively, so why the sudden change?

I follow him upstairs to join him in the shower. Just for today, I am going to let it go.

He may have been reborn by whiskey, but it is still entirely possible that he's full of shit and telling me what he thinks I want to hear, so I forget what we argued about in the first place.

Therefore, I will call Donna later.

It can't hurt to rule out the more disturbing possible reasons for Jason's sudden attitude adjustment.

***

"I forgot how much I love cornhole!"

Jason runs across the field to give me a kiss and then heads back to join his team members.

Logan smirks and says, "Wow, somebody is feeling awfully good after cleaning me out of Jameson last night. What gives?"

"I don't know. Normally he would make fun of the amusements we've set up here today. Maybe he's feeling patriotic and it's put him in a good mood."

I glance over at the American flag waving at the clubhouse, and marvel at the irony of my statement. He wants to get as far away from the United States as he can, and as quickly as he can.

Logan says, "Hmm...interesting."

I look back and catch him looking at parts of me far below my eyes.

Gentleman, my ass. He's the same as every other guy, but I suppose that's not a bad thing. I *am* standing here in a ridiculously skimpy bikini. Thanks to Jason's personality shift.

"What's interesting? What I said...or something else?"

Great, now I'm flirting with Logan. Jason said he wasn't jealous, but that doesn't mean I shouldn't rein it in. Not that there's anything to rein in.

At least I was able to convince Jason that I should wear a coverup, but he picked out the flimsiest one they had, so basically, I'm half-naked behind a see-through shower curtain.

"Did you say something?" Logan grins and his face softens. He looks like he has something to say that should not be said.

I pretend to be exasperated and the moment is gone.

"Very funny. Seriously, I don't know what's up with Jason, but he did tell me what was going on at work, and I think he's trying to make it up to me."

"Wow, I'm glad he told you. Whiskey has been known to loosen tongues. I'm glad you're going to forgive him. It was a pretty crazy story, but—"

"There you are!" Sassy holds onto her straw hat as if it's windy, even though the air is perfectly still, and the sun is beating down on our little shindig.

"Yes, here I am." I have not forgotten that I am displeased with her.

"Oh, please, you're not still mad at me because I told Jason where you were?"

"I'm not?"

Logan backs up and says, "I'll let you ladies chat. That classy blow-up pool beckons."

"Don't be a stranger, Logan." Sassy turns back to me and continues. "He looks awfully nice in those shorts, and now he's going to take his shirt off, so don't say anything for a minute. I won't hear you." Her eyes follow Logan as he joins the others bobbing around in the water.

"Sassy! *Why* did you tell Jason I was with Logan? We have enough problems."

"Exactly, and you don't want problems in your relationship. What's that thing you kids say? I've got too many problems and one of them is a bitch? Something like that. You should be thanking me."

"You need to mind your own business. Where is your husband this weekend?"

"My point exactly."

"What are you talking about?"

"I don't even know where he is. And I want you to do better than me. Youthful relationships *can* blossom into lifelong love. Or they can crash and burn when you outgrow them. Why limit yourself?"

"Because I love him."

She grabs my arm. I thought she stepped in a hole with her impractical lawn footwear for a second, but now she throws her head back and I see she's laughing—the hysterical kind where you make no sound and then you suddenly honk...yep, there it is.

"Oh, you slay me." She wipes her eyes and it's a good thing Molly used waterproof mascara for Sassy's makeover. She might be mistaken for a football player.

"Lia, darling—love is the greatest deceiver there ever was. I'm not saying Jason is the devil—and he *is* awfully cute. But ask yourself—have you been deliriously happy with him? Even before you moved here? Because this is as good as it gets. You're young. No kids. You're not even married. Just think about it."

I sigh because even though she was laughing at me like a deranged hyena, she is making some sense.

And it's not like I've never been around other attractive guys before while Jason was away. We did the long-distance thing for two years after he graduated, and I was still at college.

This does feel different, but why do I feel conflicted now? Is it because we're adults and it's time to make major life decisions?

Or did Granana's death and the move to Applebarrow wake me up from some kind of fugue state?

But either way, Sassy is still an interfering pain in my butt sometimes.

"Okay, I want to be mad at you, but you do make some valid points. And Jason was acting like a total jerk yesterday. I guess it can't hurt for him to be a little jealous and worried about what I'm doing here."

"Exactly! You give him too much control. You don't have to sleep with Logan to get Jason's attention. Again, I'm not ruling it out entirely."

I give her a look, and she backs off.

"Kidding, I'm kidding. That will only make things worse. Just be careful. And I will say, it looks like Jason is behaving himself quite nicely today, so perhaps he had a little wake-up call and he'll be more appreciative from now on."

She looks me up and down as if she is seeing me for the first time today and says, "I love your new suit. It's about time you show off your assets." She leans in and whispers, "Mine would be on my lap in a top that flimsy."

And with that lovely visual, she's off to flirt with Stan at the buffet table. She'll tell him she loves his meat (he grilled it), or some other silly, flirtatious remark.

At least she picked one of the older men to chat up. I know age gap relationships are common, but I find them to be kind of gross, especially when an older person with more money or power goes for a much younger partner.

Plus, she's married! Although, it sounds like that isn't going so well.

But who am I to judge? I don't know what the hell I'm doing from one moment to the next.

I hear a bunch of cheering, and Jason and

Tucker are high fiving each other. Marcos and Dawson are apparently the losing team and they are dishing out the usual macho competitive nonsense.

Jason would call it, 'talking smack'.

I notice Logan isn't engaging in any of the sports activities today, including the rousing game of volleyball.

I'm not *opposed* to trying to hit a ball over a net, but in this outfit, I am sure to have a wardrobe malfunction.

Molly and the girls are playing volleyball, as are the Washingtons.

Emma is painting Arielle's face, and I make a mental note to spend some time with them today. I haven't given up hope on making friends here.

Not surprisingly, Olivia is giving me daggers while talking Logan's ear off in the pool.

Even the normally conservative librarian is wearing a bikini, but she gave me the evil eye when she saw her outfit was 'topped' in the sexy department, in more ways than one.

Let's say Logan has no problem looking *her* in the eye, and he appears quite bored.

Stan is manning the grill and laughing with Sassy, while Fred walks up to me and offers me a bottle of water.

"Hey there, little lady. Don't you look beautiful today."

He's being sweet and not creepy, and according to Molly, Fred is 'the salt of the earth'.

I don't know if he's had any dates since his wife passed away, but I would like to talk to him about it and see how he's doing. He seems fine, but it can't be easy living alone, with only a bunch of young people for occasional company.

"Hi, Fred. Thank you for the lovely compliment *and* the water. Are you having fun today?"

"Oh, of course. I love this community. We do so many enjoyable things."

There it is again. Why the hell am I here if everyone is so happy? The next time I see Granana I am going to pin her down.

Not physically because…you know…she'd melt through me and freeze me out again.

"Hey Fred, since you're a little older than the other residents…"

"Oh, I'm a *lot* older. I'm like the grandpa around here, but that's okay. They keep me young. What's on your mind, Love?"

"I was wondering how well you knew my grandmother? I mean, she was a lot older than *you*. Could have been your mother, probably. She was ninety, but I wonder how well you knew her…and my grandfather."

"They were good folks. I knew your grandmother a little better, but they had their ways, you know. Like everyone else. Very private people. People talk, but if you've heard anything, you should ignore it."

"Heard anything about what?"

"Oh nothing. I mean this can be a gossipy little town, and they were the richest residents. But they seemed happy and I'm not one to judge."

"Riiight. They did seem to have a bit of a tense marriage, though. Would you say that?"

"Like I said, I don't know about that. My marriage was blessed. God rest my Agnes' soul. Now listen, don't you worry about the past. Your Gran and Pop have gone to a better place. I look forward to reuniting with my love one day, but for now I'm going to hit that pool. It's a hot one!"

I smile at Fred and tell him that I'll join him in a little bit.

I'd like to ask Fred to elaborate on the gossip, but I have a feeling Donna will tell me what's going on.

Not only is she a self-proclaimed psychic and medium, but according to her and Pete, Granana spent a lot of time at their house.

If Donna told her bad things about Jason (through use of her gifts), that caused Granana to dislike him, then it makes sense that Granana would have shared her plans *for me* with Donna.

In short, I think they were conspiring.

And what the hell gossip would be circulating around my old grandparents? I doubt they were swingers or cult members.

It could be that Granana was having an affair with this British guy, although it's hard to swallow.

And then there's the mystery surrounding her relationship with Logan. What made him so special to her? And are any of these issues related?

I finish my water and toss the bottle in the recycle bin. Jason is coming towards me, enjoying a celebratory beer. Hmm...did the little men in his head quiet down?

"Hey, did you see my epic win?" Jason is sweaty but smiling. His headache must be gone or he's quite an actor.

He grabs me and pulls me in for a kiss. I break away and say, "Yes, I did. Congratulations. I didn't think you liked 'redneck games', like cornhole."

"They're fine as long as I'm not playing them with my idiot brother. He ends up throwing the bean bags in the woods and whining to our mother that he can't find them because of the pricker bushes."

I smile and remember how immature Austin can be. I've witnessed him stomping his foot and pouting, and I've only known him as an adult.

It would nice if Jason embraced the country enough to make amends with his family and his roots. He must have *some* fond memories.

"Okay, you're sweaty." I dodge more kisses, and he strips off his shirt, throwing it on the ground. "That's it, in the pool you go."

He picks me up caveman style, and I shriek in mock terror as he pretends to throw me in the pool, and at the last second, gently places me in the water.

Logan and Olivia move over to give us some room, and Fred smokes his cigar on the edge with his feet in the water.

"Wow, this is living!" Jason dunks his body under the shallow water, pops up, and shakes like a wet dog.

Logan raises his eyebrow and I shrug my shoulders. I agree, Jason is laying the change of attitude on a little thick. People are going to think he's on drugs or has a psychological disorder.

I'll have a talk with him tonight. I'm grateful for the improvements in his demeanor, but he needs to find a happy medium.

I also don't want everyone to think he's fake. That makes him a bigger douche than when he was being rude.

"Lia, get on my shoulders. Who wants to play chicken?"

I don't see where Jason is getting his strength

today. He's not a big guy and he often complains if he has to carry me, which of course rarely happens because I usually stay upright without any problem.

Olivia is climbing Logan like a spider monkey, so I guess we are going to try to push each other off the men's shoulders. How do I get myself roped into these shenanigans?

But since it's happening, that skinny bitch is going down. *'I read books, Lia.'* Who does she think she is? I graduated at the top of my class, and my arms are way stronger than her little spindles.

And based on the pained expression on Logan's face, I don't think Olivia is his 'chicken' partner of choice.

As Molly would say— 'Just sayin!'

***

"Hey, Logan were you a boy scout?"

I shoot Jason a warning look. He was doing so well.

"Jason, what are you talking about? He's making s'mores. That hardly makes him a boy scout."

"But he's a city guy. They don't make bonfires in Chicago, Lee." Jason points to Logan working multiple sticks in the firepit at the same time.

I don't know if it's the heat or the long day, but Logan's patience is running out. "Hey, Jason. Sometimes city people *leave* the city to do non-urban activities. And no, for the record, I was not a boy scout. I was the guy who made fun of boy scouts."

I find it hard to believe that Logan was a bully. He's probably giving it back to Jason because he's sick of his little comments.

At least they're not having a peeing contest. Or a 'whose dick is bigger competition'.

I am betting Logan would win the latter. I can't stop looking at his hands on the sticks. They're huge. His hands, not the sticks.

I look away and think of cooler thoughts. It was so hot today, but there is enough of a chill in the air to enjoy sitting around a fire.

Some people went home because they have work early tomorrow morning, like Ken and Beth.

Fred is snoring in a lounge chair. Someone will have to wake him, but I don't have the heart yet. He looks so comfortable.

Tucker is sitting beside him smoking a cigarette and zoning out by the fire.

Marcos and Arielle were making out and then disappeared. That would have been me and Jason a few years ago.

Molly is telling her girls they need to go home and get ready for school tomorrow and is receiving teen theatrics in response.

Sassy and Stan are looking *way* too cozy, but it's none of my business.

Emma is under a blanket, refusing Dawson's offer of s'mores, and Olivia keeps whining at Logan to make her another one.

"Logan, can you make me one more? I like mine hot and drippy."

I resist the urge to gag and can't help but make a disgusted face.

I was able to dunk her in the water about five times earlier, until she finally gave up and decided she was done with the game. She said she wanted to read her book.

Whatever. The real reason she threw in the proverbial towel is because on the fifth dunk she lost her top 'by accident', and none of the guys even noticed.

Except Dawson, who said, 'Oh come on, keep playin'. Lia might lose her top next. Hey Jason, how tight did you tie it?'

Jason high fived him, and it was in good fun. If I lost my top, Dawson would be the first one to bring me a towel. He's a sweet guy.

Around the bonfire, Jason leans over to me and says, "I wasn't being a dick, I was joking with Logan. I had a good time today. You're right. These people are great. I hadn't given them a chance."

He gives Dawson the thumbs up, and Dawson raises his beer. "My man, Jason!"

Dawson is drunk, and I notice he's gotten cozy with Emma. I'm not sure if there is anything romantic to that gesture, or he's making sure the shy girl doesn't feel left out of the fun.

Dawson would have made a great RA, if he had gone to college.

I look back at Jason...who is also drunk. Again.

After last night, I thought he'd be as sober as a Mormon today. Also, he has work in the morning, and it's after nine and he's still here.

He leans forward, almost slipping out of his chair, and says, "I am definitely taking you up on your offer to come for Fourth of July weekend with the gang for the bike ride. Just let me know if we can stay at your grandmother's house. If not, it's cool, but I don't know if everyone is going to wanna to spring for a hotel—since our jobs are going away soon. Well, except for Zach's, but he's an engineer, and who can do that much math? Am I right?"

Jason is drunk for sure.

I just wanted him to be polite and accepting, not regress to his teen years spent in the worst trailer park in the county.

I narrow my eyes and say, "So, you're not coming back to visit for six weeks?"

"No, I'll be here every weekend from now on. Fuck working all the time!"

He yells that out, and Molly shoos the girls towards their apartment and waves good night.

I'm sure that's nothing they don't regularly hear at school, but the drunken factor is an added bonus. Molly has been dealing with drunks for years at work, so I don't blame her for bailing.

I'm not looking forward to more of this behavior myself.

Does Jason now need to be drunk to enjoy himself? Or is he becoming one of those men who goes off the rails because his job is in jeopardy?

I have no role models for male insecurity. My father is the model of happiness, and my grandfather was a millionaire who never had a financial or professional setback in his life. Well, not until the end.

"You seem a little tired, Jason. Are you staying here tonight? I think that's probably best."

I hand him my keys, hoping he'll go to bed, and give me a little time to stare into the fire before joining him.

"Yeah, I think I'll turn in, but you stay here and enjoy the fire. I'm gonna leave early in the morning. Beat the traffic. Or maybe I'll go in late. Who fucking cares?"

He leans into me and kisses my cheek but mostly slobbers on my ear.

"Just wake me up when you come in. We can finish what we finished this morning...I mean start what we finished...again."

He makes himself laugh with his incomprehensible sex joke and walks off to my apartment. I hope I don't find him sleeping on my doorstep later.

I also hope that if Sassy went back to Stan's place that they're quiet with whatever they start *or* finish. We share a thin wall, and if I don't know something, I can't be asked about it.

Fred is still sleeping on the lounge chair. I rouse him and decide to help him to his apartment. Dawson joins me. Luckily Fred seems to be tired, and not drunk.

"Hey, after we deposit old Fred here, Emma and I will escort you home, Lia. We're going for a little walk."

Emma smiles and pulls her sweater tighter around her shoulders. Emma and Dawson make an unlikely couple, but I wouldn't be surprised if Dawson makes the quick trip from his place to hers tonight.

I say, "Thanks, guys. I'm going to stay a while and clean up, but I'm sure Olivia and Logan won't mind helping me."

Olivia is sulking in her chair because Logan has moved to the seat Jason vacated, waiting for me the whole time.

Hmm...

She jumps up and says crisply, "Well I'm off to bed, too. The library can't open itself."

Logan and I both quickly say good night and she lingers an extra moment, folding her chair. "I won't be asleep right away. I always read for a while. It helps me wind down. So, if anyone needs me, that's where I'll be."

Okay, weirdo. Who would need you? Can she be any more obvious?

Logan goes inside to get some water, after asking if we want any.

Great, here she comes.

"So, don't do anything I wouldn't do, Lia."

"I don't know what you're talking about, Olivia."

"Mock me all you want, but before you came to live here, Logan and I were forming a special connection. And now with you throwing yourself at him..."

"Ladies, is there a problem? I thought you were going to bed, Olivia?" Logan appears by my side and interrupts the tense, yet ridiculous conversation.

"I am. Don't forget, I'll be up a while." She walks off in a huff.

Why is there a mean girl in every group? I thought as an adult I wouldn't have to deal with this unpleasant social problem any longer.

I wish someone else was still awake, so there will be credible witnesses when Olivia tells Jason she saw something that didn't happen tonight. Does she think I don't hear her threats? If Logan won't visit her, then she's going to watch us. Got it.

"Why are you smiling?" Logan looks at me as if he wants to be let in on the joke, but I think he gets it. I'm sure he's been enduring Olivia's behavior for some time.

Changing the subject to something less intimate, now that we're alone, I say brightly, "So, do you want to help me clean up? Fun job, right?"

"It's not that bad. I've been tidying up along the

way. Kind of like at the bar, in anticipation of closing time. We can relax here and enjoy the fire for a few more minutes."

He settles back into his chair, but then glances towards my apartment. "Unless you need to get home. Jason *did* say you should wake him."

I feel my face growing hotter, and I'm grateful that I can blame it on the flames from the fire, and not the reference to my sex life.

"Oh, he's staring at the inside of his eyelids right now. Did you *see* him?"

"Yeah, he was a bit lit, but I'm sure he'll be fine to go to work in the morning."

I'm suddenly doubtful of that and hoping he doesn't blame me for being late. Then again, he seems to be embracing his inner rebel, now that he's shared his career troubles.

"I can't believe he was okay with you wearing that bikini today. I pegged him for the more jealous type, based on his previous behavior."

I changed into warmer clothes earlier, and I'm glad I'm not sitting here in that skimpy little thing.

"Jason picked it out and made me wear it."

"He MADE you wear it?"

"That was a poor choice of words. He doesn't control me. He wanted me to look...nice, I guess."

"Uh huh."

"What?"

"Oh, you looked beautiful. I'm wondering...but it's none of my business."

"Wondering about what?"

"You *looked* amazing, but you *seemed* a little uncomfortable."

"I don't usually dress like that in public. Was I acting weird?"

"No, I could tell he was kind of...I don't know...showing you off. If you were my girlfriend, I wouldn't do that if you were uncomfortable."

The longer I stay silent the more he seems to feel compelled to continue explaining himself. You would think he was a politician and not a bartender.

"It's okay to criticize Jason. He's not perfect. None of us are."

"Right, I'm not criticizing. Just observing. I guess I do that a lot. And hey, if you're both okay with it, it's not my business."

I stare at the fire for an awkward moment and say, "Do you know anything about Molly's doll making?"

I know the sudden change of subject is jarring, but I would like to move on to a safer topic.

Since Jason may be a bit more malleable to the idea of assisting Molly, now that he has admitted why he's so desperate to get out of town, I intend to use my newfound leverage to help her.

Logan does seem surprised by the odd turn of conversation and says, "Um...yeah. She's very talented. Why do you ask?"

I explain how she showed me her work, and that Jason and I (white lie) are interested in offering to help her with production, but I'm wondering about her current process.

"You'd have to ask her, but I'm pretty sure she buys the heads in bulk and then makes their costumes and hair. She has sketches for what she wants their faces to look like, but that would require manufacturing."

"Okay, I'll talk to her. I'm so excited."

"She's a great artist. She could have easily gotten into my...I mean, she would love to be able to make the dolls look more unique, especially ethnically."

Okay, he's observant of everyone. Not just me.

"I think we're in a position to help her. We'd have to hire someone and get investors. And I agree with Jason—I don't think the whole plant is needed, but maybe we could separate a portion of it."

"Maybe Jason would like to take this on as his project. Seeing as he's losing his job. Couldn't you two move into your grandmother's house?"

I don't want to tell Logan that Jason wants to get out of Virginia, and apparently the country, like he's being chased by a pack of wild boars.

I want to go to Europe, too but...

"We're floating around a bunch of options. But honestly, I think we'll be here for a while."

Logan smiles and his eyes take on a warm glow.

If I was warm before, now I am boiling in my University of Delaware sweatshirt. But if I take it off, I'll be sitting here in my miniscule bikini top. And that is not something I want Olivia to see out her window with binoculars, or a paparazzi, night photo camera lens.

Logan breaks our gaze and says, "I'm glad to hear you're not leaving right away. I spoke to a friend of mine who works in the school system and told her about you and your language skills."

"Wow, really? Why? I mean, that's kind of you, but I don't think I want to teach, and I'm not certified."

"No, I was thinking out of the box. Like maybe you could start an after-school tutoring program for languages. Maybe name it after your grandmother and do it as a charitable thing?"

My eyes start to water, and I quietly say, "That is such a nice idea. Granana would love... would have loved that."

I must be careful of speaking of Granana in the present tense, but I am touched by Logan's thoughtfulness.

"How did you know I'd be interested in something like that?"

"Come on, Lia. I know you're bored here. And a little lonely. I get it. And as far as I can see, you haven't gotten a chance to use your skills since you graduated. It sucks when you can't use your gifts. I know that."

I want to know what gifts he isn't using, but I recall the last time I tried to ask Logan personal questions, and it didn't go smoothly.

"I would be honored to help the school system. It could start small with me volunteering, and then I could recruit students from nearby colleges to do it as an internship."

"See, I knew if I gave you an idea, you'd run with it."

I am feeling too emotional to say much more. This is one of nicest things anyone has ever done for me, and I am struck by how unconcerned Jason has been as to the state of my career, or lack of one.

He's been saying all along that our goal to move out of the country with his job was because of me, but in the meantime, he thought it was fine for me to do nothing with my education and passions.

I even suggested teaching once, and he said it was a waste of time to put in the effort to get my license because we'd be off to Europe soon.

I thank Logan for his thoughtfulness, and as I stand up, I forget what it was he said a minute ago that I wanted to ask him about. Something about Molly being talented enough to go...somewhere?

Boy, this has been a long day, and even though I'm annoyed with Jason, I can't wait to get to bed and snuggle up to him. I know he cares—he's so Type A and focused on his plan. Our plan. It's hard when everything is in transition.

Applebarrow has upset his apple cart.

Crap, I must be exhausted if now I'm making bad puns about the name of this town.

No matter. I'll remember what I wanted to ask Logan. Probably in the wee hours of the morning, when Jason is up and cursing in the dark, getting ready for work with a gigantic hangover.

And it isn't like Logan is going anywhere.

That's the most comforting thought I can conjure up tonight.

I hope after we clean up and I head off to bed, that I don't 'conjure' up anything else.

Or *anyone* else.

At least not until after Jason goes home, and I see Donna.

She'll help me shed some light on my ghostly grandmother, and the residents of my temporary new hometown.

CHAPTER FOURTEEN

"Angie is so talented. I told you so."

Molly is inches from my fingernails, examining my game night manicure.

Angie went all out this time. We decided to go with a beach theme. My nails are pale aqua blue, and there is a nail on each hand with one of five designs—a lobster, a beach umbrella, a flip flop, a starfish, and a boat.

It's a bit much, and took forever, but it's fun and I had a chance to have a nice heart to heart with Angie.

Molly and I are prepping the clubhouse for the big game night. She brought the game we're playing, but I insisted she bring a couple of back-ups, in case things go sideways like they did with the book club.

The residents may get along well, but their tastes in entertainment vary widely.

Molly places a big pile of napkins on the counter and says, "Angie is a hoot. Did she tell you about her husband?"

"Yes, she did. She said when she left home to come down here, he came to visit her every weekend and tried to convince her to come home—until he gave up and decided to stay in Applebarrow."

"It's a such a sweet story and he's a great guy." She quickly adds, "Just like Jason. He's been here every weekend, right?"

"Yep. It's been wonderful."

Little does Molly know that he's about to be unemployed and is leveraging my resources to get out of the country as quickly as possible. That's his main interest in visiting Applebarrow.

I know he does want to be with me, but I can see he can't wait to leave this town. Unfortunately, the more he works on getting us out of here, the more I wish we could stay.

I connected with Logan's friend at the school, Maureen, and we're working on setting up an after-school foreign language program in Granana's honor.

I regularly spend time at Molly's house, and even Emma and I have gotten a little chummier. Dating Dawson has been amazing for her outlook on life. I guess it's true that a healthy relationship can improve your attitude.

I am ignoring the little voice inside my head that keeps saying, 'If that's true, then why am I stressed and jumpy?'

Luckily Granana did not visit the night after Logan and I had our awkward, but nice, bonfire chat.

And I am assuming Olivia was all talk because no pictures surfaced, and Jason didn't seem fazed when I told him that Logan and I had talked about Molly's dolls and my new language endeavor.

It's almost like he suddenly refuses to be jealous. If I didn't know better, I would think he read a self-help book or started therapy. Or consulted with a psychic. Someone to tell him he has nothing to worry about.

And he doesn't. Logan is a nice guy, but there are lots of quality men in the world, and you can't fall for every good-looking guy who shows you some attention and kindness.

If that were the way to go, my mother would be screwing around with Javier, her massage therapist partner, and Granana would have been sneaking around with the British guy.

I choose to ignore the fact that either, or both, of those possibilities could be true.

At any rate, I am going to see Donna next week, and hopefully she will help me with some answers that the others in my life refuse to provide.

I am staring into space, putting out the plastic cups, while Molly and her girls sashay around the room, greeting everyone and telling them how much fun they're going to have.

As always, Marcos and Arielle appear skeptical, especially Marcos.

They're closer to my age than anyone here, but they keep to themselves for the most part. I *could* get my hair cut at Arielle's salon. I would like to have more friends.

I feel ridiculous admitting that I'm lonely during the week when Jason isn't here, but I am.

I still haven't become fully accustomed to life after college. There I was surrounded by familiar faces, and as an RA, I was needed. I was the go-to girl, the shoulder to cry on, the mediator, the cruise director.

I sigh and catch Jason out of the corner of my eye. He's helping Logan carry in the beer. Now they're laughing and he's shaking his hand.

Granana and Sassy are wrong about Jason. He's under a lot of stress, and neither of them can understand. I don't think they ever worked at a real job a day in their lives.

Jason catches my eye and excuses himself.

"Hello, beautiful girl."

He kisses me and pulls me close. He has that freshly laundered scent, even this late in the day, and his face is still smooth.

And he's not even late. I asked him if he thought he could leave work early and he said...well, I won't repeat what he said. But it had a lot of words that would get censored on network television, while describing how much he feels like working a full day at Elevation.

Clearly things are falling apart fast at his company and he's eager to be here. There's nothing wrong with that.

I'm his partner, and I don't care what Granana says. I looked up that 'stand by your man' thing, and it's a song. While I'm not a country music fan, it's still a good life policy.

And after all, didn't Granana stand by her man? She never even dated after he died or showed the slightest interest in another man. Unless...no, if I can have a male friend so could Granana.

I extricate myself from Jason's bear hug and say, "How was your drive?"

He starts telling me about the idiots on Route 64, and Molly interrupts us to start game night.

The game is hilarious. We're playing in smaller groups so everyone can play at the same time, and we're switching tables after each round.

We decide to do it randomly, to break up couples and people who spend more time together, so they can connect. I am still mindful of my role here, and I want to add value wherever I can.

Now I'm at a table with Logan, Olivia and Fred. Fred is oblivious to any sexual or bitchy tension, so he isn't noticing that Olivia is looking at Logan likes she wants to eat him for dessert, and at me likes she wants to fork my eyeballs out.

It doesn't make it any better that Fred can barely see the cards and doesn't understand the game, and Olivia is so funny, but not in a good way. Her southern accent is cultured but prominent, and we laugh when she tries to imitate a rapper.

"Well, I'm sorry. I don't spend my time listening to that trash."

As if listening to it would improve her skill level. Rapping is impossible.

"Lighten up, Liv. We're supposed to laugh at ourselves and each other. That's the point of the game." Logan tries to make her feel better, which only causes her to scoot her chair closer to his.

I ignore them and continue to say my nonsense phrases in whatever accent I pick from the cards. I'm okay at 'mob boss', and terrible at 'valley girl', but before long I'm laughing so hard, my face hurts.

Logan is incredible at this game. Almost scary good. I have learned enough languages to change my voice, but I don't know where Logan gets his talent. He could be a voice-over actor, or on stage somewhere.

Fred cracks up at Logan's spot-on British accent. "Wow, that is amazing. You should audition for a play at the…oh, never mind. Time to switch tables."

We move on to our next groups, but now I'm dying to find out why Fred hesitated. Was Logan an actor? He's surely good-looking enough.

But if so, why hide that? It's not like a shameful secret.

Olivia is boring holes through me and is now seated at a table with Jason, Molly and Tucker. Olivia keeps laughing at everything Jason says.

He's not that funny, and I know she's doing it to make me jealous. I wish we could set her up with someone, but I only know the residents of Pentagon Place.

The only men not taken are Tucker, who isn't cultured enough for her, and Stan, who may or may not be fooling around with Sassy.

When she left after Memorial Day weekend I did not ask and she did not tell, but Stan was glowing. I swear he skipped to his car the next few mornings.

I look around the room, and the game is a rousing success. Everyone is laughing, even Marcos, who often has that brooding, 'everything is lame' look left over from his teen years.

After we're done playing, we share fried chicken and traditional southern comfort food.

I asked Logan to cater this event, and he was happy to do so. No one had to cook, and Granana can't visit me with any Italian food scolding.

That leaves her other forms of scolding, to include bashing my boyfriend and my lifestyle. She wasn't nearly this critical in life.

It's been said that old people drop their filters as they age. So, I guess once you're dead it's truly out the window, and you can say whatever you damn well please and then disappear.

Nice trick. And she's even taking classes to learn it. She's either super bored, or she thinks she has something to teach me.

Normally I would discount relationship advice given by a woman who is more than sixty years older than me. However, she's a freaking ghost. She can see me when I'm sleeping or awake, like Santa Claus, only she is REAL.

Therefore, I can't completely shake the nagging doubt that there's something to her warnings.

Jason is heading back to Richmond tonight. Even though he isn't too worried about being named employee of the month, he doesn't want to piss Greta off too much, and Amy counts on him to help her on their projects.

I'm beginning to think Amy is innocent and it was in my head. If they were having an affair, she would have told me by now, and Jason has been here every weekend and calls me every night.

"Bye, Sweetheart. I'll see you on the weekend."

Jason is all over me again with hugs and kisses, and on this visit, I am happy to note that he is sober.

I was a little worried his work problems were going to spiral him into bad habits, but he seems to have stabilized nicely. After Memorial Day weekend, he was fine.

Everyone drinks a little too much occasionally—look at what I did on my first night in Applebarrow!

I hold his hand and walk him out to his car. "So, you and the gang are coming Fourth of July weekend, right? We're going to open up the house."

"Excellent. We can't wait to hit the trails. And don't worry, we won't lose you. This is going to be a nice, casual bike ride."

As he gets in his car, I think of the last 'casual' bike ride I participated in with the gang.

I define 'casual' as riding eight miles per hour tops, on a bike with a bell and a basket, stopping to pick flowers or buy apples at a roadside stand. That was my childhood biking experience, and it never involved spandex, excessive panting, or scraping your arm along a narrow bridge that you swore you wouldn't be coordinated enough to navigate.

Olivia startles me as she suddenly appears beside me, watching Jason drive off and joining me in waving.

"Oh, hey Olivia. Did you have fun tonight?"

"I thought the game was utter nonsense." She laughs at her joke, since that is the actual name of the game.

"Yes, it was silly, but everyone seemed to enjoy it."

Her smile grows more forced and she says, "Jason is coming around. I'm so happy to see it."

I look beyond Olivia to see a crowd has formed at the clubhouse window. Do they know something I don't know? Unless she came out here with a weapon, there will be no girl fight to watch.

"What do mean—he's coming around?"

"Well, he seems happier. Lighter. Freer. Don't you see it? I'm so happy you two have your new plan worked out. Jason said you should be living in Europe before school starts in September. I bet Amsterdam is gorgeous in the fall."

I try to disguise my shock at multiple parts of that speech. Amsterdam? I don't speak Dutch. Why the hell would he pick a location without consulting me? And tell people about it before me?

And he knows I'm working on the after-school language program. Does he think I'm going to abandon that endeavor before it even gets off the ground?

And why the hell is he in such a rush?

One thing is for sure. Olivia is not going to know she's blindsided me.

"Yes, it's very exciting. Thank you. I need to help Molly clean up now. Have a great night!"

I begin walking back to the clubhouse and Olivia says, "You know, Lia, there's a lot you don't know about Logan."

I can't help sighing. This is getting old. "Okay. Why are you telling me this?"

"I've noticed you spend a lot of time together. I know you think I'm jealous, but there's a lot you don't know about Logan's past. He's been through a lot and I understand him."

"Good night, Olivia."

Now she's yelling and I'm sure the gawkers at the window can hear her. "I would hate to see you mess up your plans with Jason for a guy who can't commit."

I slam the door to the clubhouse, and everyone suddenly springs into action, as if they weren't spying a second ago.

All except Logan. He's washing dishes, and he's clearly been doing it for a while. He either didn't hear Olivia, or he's not interested in feeding the beast with attention.

I mutter under my breath, "Let it go, Lia."

"No, don't let it go!"

I jump and expect to see Molly or Emma, or one of the other women standing before me, but instead it's the biggest nosy snoop of them all—my dearly departed Granana.

I hiss at her. "Go to my apartment now."

Molly walks over to me as I'm talking to myself (Granana) in public again. She says, "Are you okay,

Honey? Can I get you anything? That Olivia can be such a bitch, between you and me and the fence post."

"Thanks. I'm okay. She has an issue with Logan and I'm staying out of it."

Molly agrees that's the smart course of action and resumes clean-up duty.

I can't worry about Logan, with all my Jason concerns wearing on my mind.

I may not be happy about Jason's timetable or lack of communication, but all couples have issues in times of trouble. Jason is about to be unemployed. This is when we need to roll up our sleeves and have some good honest communication.

I glance around and Granana seems to have listened to me and vacated the clubhouse.

Thank God! My nerves are shot from her sudden appearances.

One thing is for sure—I'm not going to Amsterdam in September, but maybe I can negotiate for Paris or Lisbon next spring. I'll make Jason understand my commitment to Granana, and if I must, I'll find more ways to slow things down and keep him occupied until I'm ready to leave.

He loves me and I know he'll ultimately do the right things. We just need to talk it out.

As I join Molly in putting the room back together, I realize the most obvious thing—Olivia could have made every bit of that story up to start trouble.

Since Granana has plenty of time and appeared uninvited, I walk over to Logan and say, "Do you need me to dry?"

***

"All I can say is thank the Lord for bitches with loose lips. And since I'm on the other side now, I can do that in person."

While I would love to explore the mysteries of the afterlife with Granana, she is focused on the here and now, and meddling in my life as much as possible.

Whoever we should thank, I will not thank them for enrolling her in Haunting School.

"Olivia is a bitch, but I don't see how her harassment is any kind of blessing...hey, you're actually sitting on the couch. Holy crap!"

"Yes, I've been working on it diligently, and practicing ever since you banished me from my own clubhouse and sent me here to wait for you."

She winks at me and adjusts her tiara. Yes, now she wears a tiara. I didn't know she had such a penchant for finery. Her ballgown barely fits on my mid-century sofa.

"Well, good for you. I guess. Anyway, I'm tired. I don't want to talk about Olivia's comments, unless you're going to fill me in on the truth."

I slump in the chair across from Granana and try to formulate a good way to ask her about the British guy.

Before I get up the nerve, she says, "Oh, you know speaking of bitches, have you heard from the church ladies? Never mind. I shouldn't call them that. It's not their fault they are the way they are. Olivia reminded me of them. She could be one of their granddaughters. Sticks up their butts, all of them."

"No, I have not heard from any of your church friends. They were at the funeral, but I did not speak to them other than to shake their hands in the receiving line. Now please get to the point of this visit. I'm exhausted, and my head is pounding."

"Okay, *Dolchezza*. I'm sorry. I forget you are bound by sleep and all that boloney."

"Also, I thought you were religious? Why are you against the women from your church?"

"It's quite complicated, I'm afraid. But unfortunately, I'm not able to share much on that topic. Rules, you know."

"Why am I not surprised? Sooo?"

"Oh yes, my reason for visiting today. I wanted to tell you that you must trust Logan and not Jason."

"Why can't I trust Jason now? He told me what's going on with him."

I want to ask her if Olivia was telling the truth, but I am getting sick of her saying she can't tell me what I don't know. This is such horseshit.

"Hmm, he did tell you *something* but no, you can't trust him."

"If you can't tell me why I can't trust my boyfriend, there is no point in these conversations, Granana. I love being able to see you, but this isn't good for me."

"Okay, what can I tell you that will make you see reason?"

"You can tell me why I'm here."

"Well, I know by now you know how that happened. Your parents loved each other very much and then they—"

"I don't mean how was I born! I mean why did you summon me here to Applebarrow in your Will? I know your stated reason is a bunch of crap."

She laughs. "I love your feisty spirit. That needs

to come out more when you're dealing with...people who don't have your best interests at heart. I can't tell you anything about other people that you don't already know, but yes, I can tell you why I wanted you to come here, since it's only between you and me."

Now I'm not sure if I want to know.

"I wanted to change your life. Shake things up."

"What was wrong with my life?"

"Lia, come on, Sweetie. A dead-end job with no opportunity in sight to use your gifts? A boyfriend convincing you to wait for him to produce this magical life in Europe, and not pursue a real life in Richmond? No friends other than his?"

"Well, when you put it like that, I did need to make some changes. But if you had just given me my inheritance, we could be in Europe now. Jason wouldn't be in a terrible situation at work and—"

"Don't you wonder why he's in a terrible situation at work?"

"He told me."

"Did he now? Since you're still on his side, I am guessing he did not tell you the real reason. Before I died, I obviously couldn't know everything about other people's lives. But with a combination of my old lady wisdom and Donna's psychic abilities, I was convinced he was up to no good. And now I know for sure."

"Why can you tell me Donna is psychic? Doesn't that fall under the category of something I don't know about other people?" I'm hoping she believes I don't know so I can catch her in breaking her own rule.

"You *do* know that. Angie told you. You can't put one over on me. Remember, like Santa Claus,

I am everywhere? Except of course in your bedroom when you have that man here."

Thank God for that. This is getting way too weird.

"Lia, the only way I could help you was to write my Will in such a way that you would be forced to look at your life from a different perspective and make some changes."

"Why didn't you say all of this when you were alive?"

"I didn't want to ruin our relationship, and I didn't know if I would ever see you again. Donna assured me that I'd be back, but I thought maybe she was nuts. Who knew? So, when I knew my earthly time was growing short, I put the plan in place."

"So that's it? You wanted to upset the status quo and make me reevaluate? Nothing else?"

"Well, I also wanted you to meet Logan. I figured if there was something there, it would happen naturally."

"Why do you like him so much?"

"That I can't share, other than that you can see what a wonderful person he is. I'm so excited about the language program at the school. Please make sure my name is on a plaque somewhere."

She rubs her hands together and I notice they look more solid. It's a bit unsettling. It's like she's becoming more alive the longer she's dead.

I don't want to talk about Logan anymore, especially because she's not going to tell me anything I don't know.

I would like to ask her more about her life, since she can tell me about that without breaking the rules, but I'm not sure how to ask my grandmother if she cheated on her husband.

And what does it matter? She's dead, and what terrible thing could there be to discover about Logan? Everyone loves him, so it's not like he could have killed anyone, and they don't let felons work in bars. At least I don't think so.

My focus needs to be Jason and our future. I'm worried about what else he might be hiding, but I still don't think it's an affair.

All this meddling is insane. Granana is bored, and maybe she's a bit jealous that her marriage wasn't good, or she's trying to protect me from making her mistakes. Either way, it's my life.

"I'll make sure you are properly honored, Granana. Don't worry. You and Grandpa. It was his money, too. Are you with him? Where you live now?"

"Yes, he's here. Having a ball. Now Lia, I have to go. But let me ask you this."

Papa is having a ball? I don't remember him even smiling often. Maybe they were secretly very much in love, and he was a private person who doesn't show public affection. He *was* old-fashioned.

I sigh and rub my temples. "What do you want to ask me?" I'll never get to bed unless I give her something.

"Would you honestly want to go back to your old life now?"

I feel those words in my heart, and my answer shocks me.

"No, I wouldn't."

She's up off the couch and back to floating. "Exactly. You know you're not disinherited if you leave right now, but you're still here."

"That's true. Granana, I know you love me and want me to be happy. But stop showing up when other people are around, please! I know my best life is not waiting for me in a mental hospital."

"Fair enough. I'll try to work on my impulse haunting. And don't worry about your grandfather and me. We are buried and in a better place. Focus on this place, right here. Your life. Make is sparkly, *Dolchezza.*"

And she's gone in a poof of...sparkles.

CHAPTER FIFTEEN

"I'm so glad you're here. Look at her aura, Pete."

Donna grasps my hands and her many bracelets jingle and jangle, like my Mom's.

I feel a jolt of energy, but I'm sure it's just my own excitement and not some special psychic juju.

"I see. It's very...pretty."

The happy couple explodes into a fit of knowing laughter. Pete can't read auras.

I smile and allow myself to be dragged into the living room.

"Where are the kids?" It's eerily quiet in a house that is normally bustling with electronics, yelling, and the movement of young bodies.

"Pete's mother takes them to church on Sundays. And then they go out for brunch."

Interesting. So I guess they did go to church on Easter morning. "Do you guys go to church?"

Pete grabs his car keys and says, "No. My mother likes the company and she makes it fun for them. We're trying to cover all the bases. We're not one-hundred-percent sure Donna's witchcraft is the way to go."

They both start laughing again, and I feel the awkwardness of someone who is not privy to the inside jokes. I guess all long-term couples have these special, shared stories to laugh at together.

I just can't think of mine and Jason's right now.

I'm nervous about being here. I rescheduled this appointment three times since the June residents' meeting a couple of weeks ago, and finally settled on sneaking out today, before Jason and his friends show up for the Fourth of July weekend.

They were originally supposed to come yesterday, but collectively decided they should attend Greta's company cookout at her house, before she goes on her Independence Day cruise. So, we're doing the bike ride tomorrow, and the picnic on Tuesday.

My first inclination was to think, 'must be nice to go on a cruise', but then I remembered that soon I'll have a lot more money than Greta.

Also, I'm surprised she's spending any money, if her business is about to go under. I'll have to ask Jason about that.

Pete excuses himself to run some errands and leaves us alone for our 'hocus pocus' session.

Donna is still laughing when she returns to the living room, after kissing her husband goodbye. "You do realize I'm not an actual witch, right? He loves to tease me. Not that there would be anything wrong with me being a witch..."

I sit up straighter in the cozy purple armchair I've occupied and say, "Oh, not at all. I mean, whatever you are is great. I mean, you're just you. Can you tell I'm nervous?"

Donna smiles and tells me to relax, and to think of this as a friendly conversation, except one that may or may not involve visits from dead people.

She didn't phrase it quite that way, but since she seems to have no idea I've already been visited,

I am questioning her skills. Maybe her communication only goes one way and we have to tap into it. Or something.

She leaves me alone with my insane inner ramblings to get us some tea. I don't even like tea, but since she might need the tea as part of her ritual, I'll go with the flow.

She returns and sits on the chair opposite mine, pours the tea and asks me why I'm here.

I tell her that I have more questions than answers—about my grandmother, Jason, where my life is headed.

I don't mention Logan because whatever he's hiding is irrelevant to my life.

Donna smiles and stares off into the distance. Finally, she says, "That's a lot to take in. Let's start with Jason, since we don't have to summon him."

She laughs again. Do all psychics find their gifts amusing? Or is she some kind of mystical comedian?

"I do sense that Jason isn't telling you the whole truth. I also feel a strong desire on your part to keep the relationship going until you find out something that causes it to end."

I put my tea cup back on the saucer and say, "I guess I am a loyal person, and we've invested five years in each other."

"That's a mere blip in your total life span, but I understand why you don't see it that way at your young age. I do think it's important to be loyal, but I see a temptation for you. One you are trying to resist?"

"Crap, I can't lie to you, can I?"

"You can, but what purpose would it serve?"

"Good point. Yes, there is a minor temptation.

Very minor. Teeny tiny."

I pinch my thumb and forefinger together, leaving the smallest space possible to indicate how incredibly small and insignificant this temptation is.

I don't think Donna's buying it.

I ramble on. "It's easy to find comfort and excitement with a new person when your relationship isn't working out, right?"

That didn't sound good.

"Yes, very true. Lia, you need to ask yourself, 'even if Jason was being completely honest and has no secrets to hide, do I have enough comfort and excitement with *him* to sustain the relationship long-term?' That's a very telling analysis."

"I'm not sure, but I'm not ready to give up. Is that bad?"

"There is no good or bad. Only what is. And in time it will become clear. In the meantime, keep your eyes and your ears wide open. I see a bumpy ride ahead of you before the smooth sailing."

I perk up at her last comment. "So, you do see smooth sailing ahead?"

"I do. So, I wouldn't worry. You have your grandmother's strength and resilience."

Whew, that's a relief. I'm sure whatever Jason is hiding is no big deal, and we'll work it out and be off to Europe soon.

Granana loves me, but she doesn't like Jason and she adores Logan, and who knows why? Can I trust the guidance of a ghost? She looks and talks like my grandmother, but is she the same woman I grew up with? I have no way of knowing. The advice of a living person is much more useful.

Even if I must learn Dutch, it won't take me long. It's not like I have to find a job right away.

We'll hire bilingual people to help us get our business off the ground.

I'll talk to Jason about it soon, if he doesn't tell me first. I don't want to confront him. He's almost certainly going to sit me down this weekend and go over his new plans, especially since he's told other people.

Although it was kind of odd that he chose to confide in Olivia. I don't know why he did that, but he was probably excited and wanted to tell somebody his good news. I'm sure he asked her not to say anything, and he has no idea she has fashioned herself into my nemesis.

Who else is he going to tell? Olivia is a disinterested party. It's like telling your bartender or hairdresser. I am making this way too complicated.

"Thank you, Donna. I feel like I am...um...channeling my Granana a bit lately."

I search Donna for traces of knowing, but she still seems focused on smiling and glowing in her chair, sipping her tea and dispensing wisdom.

"So, tell me about your grandmother."

"I was hoping you would tell me about her."

"Really? What do you want to know?"

It seems so gossipy and shallow to start questioning this woman about my grandmother's private life and possible affair.

Granana had a point. They're all buried and in a better place. Why do I care? It's not like I will judge her or love her less. And my commitment to her legacy and respect for her wishes won't waver.

I suddenly don't want to know anything (or at least I have decided I should drop it for now), yet I'm sitting here with someone who can supposedly facilitate communication with the deceased.

My curiosity is piqued. Can she really get Granana here, front and center in her new age decorated living room? Or will she claim to be talking to her, and I will see and hear nothing? And if she can summon her, it serves Granana right for all her meddling to be forced to appear. I'm beginning to think her 'haunting rules' are convenient excuses to disappear whenever she's asked a question she wants to avoid.

I quell my hesitation and reply, "I want to know if she's happy. If there is an afterlife and what she's doing in it. If she's been reunited with my grandfather. That sort of thing."

If Donna can conjure her, she will be quite annoyed with these questions. But in all fairness, I feel like I need to throw Donna a bone.

I also don't want her to think I'm so grief stricken or fearful that I can't face my grandmother's spirit. She'll never let me off the hook if she thinks she can help me, and I won't let her.

Donna beams her serene gaze upon me, and I know she's ready to roll with some spirit communing.

"Join hands with me, Lia. Let's focus on Allegra's loving spirit."

I take her hands and feel a chill. Is Granana here already, or does Donna just have cold hands?

What if she summons my grandmother and she's not the same spirit I've been seeing? How will I know who's the imposter ghost?

I can't believe the thoughts going through my head.

"Oh yes, I feel something. Do you feel it?"

Donna grasps my hands more tightly and now she's doing some weird humming thing. Her eyes are closed, but I'll be damned if I'm going to face whatever is coming without an immediate visual warning. I've seen my share of scary movies.

"Um, maybe...what should I be feeling?"

Suddenly, I see an outline of a figure before us, hovering over the coffee table. If Granana had fully mastered the touch thing by now, she'd be able to knock over our tea cups with her long, red velvet gown. She's also wearing long black gloves and pointy shoes. And a black hat.

Is she going for witch or vampire? And why is appearing to Donna a reason for a Halloween costume? Being a freaking ghost is enough of a spooky parlor trick.

Donna opens her eyes and based on her reaction, I'm worried she may have soiled herself.

I am now wondering how often Donna's 'gift' produces a spirit *sighting*, because she looks damn surprised. Maybe she normally only talks to them in her head.

I suppose spirits are only summoned when they want to be summoned—since now I know that they must enroll in Haunting School, and most souls would rather enjoy their perpetual rest instead of annoying their loved ones for all eternity.

Not that I'm bitter or anything.

"Allegra, is that you?" Donna's mouth is hanging open. I hope she has a healthy heart.

"Yes, it is I. Allegra DeLuca back from the dead."

Oh my God, what a nut she is. She's talking like she's the leading lady in a late night black and white horror flick.

"Wow, I guess I do have powers." Donna is whispering but smiles at me encouragingly. "Lia, are you okay?"

I ignore Donna and blurt out, "Granana, why are you dressed like that?"

Oops, that's not the most credible reaction upon seeing my dead grandmother for the first time. I need to feign shock, and cry or fall over. Something more dramatic.

I'm a terrible actress.

"I mean, it didn't look like you for a minute. You look so...beautiful...and spirit-like. I can't believe you're here."

Donna keeps smiling so my incoherent mumblings are being chalked up to shock and dismay, instead of annoyance at Granana's game playing.

I bet she'll get some laughs from her fellow ghosts at Haunting School when she tells this story.

Unless appearing to Donna is a violation of the rules. Who knows?

"Allegra, Lia wants to know that you are well and with her grandfather. Right?" She glances at me for agreement, so I nod.

I want to know if she was having an affair with a British dude, and why she liked Logan so much, and what Jason is up to.

I seriously doubt Donna has the power to draw any of that out of my stubborn grandmother.

"Yes, I am well, and so is my husband. My dear Lia, I am grateful you have heeded my wishes and moved to Applebarrow. It is all a part of a master plan."

"And what is that plan exactly?"

She floats around the room and says, "I'm afraid I can't share that. It would be a violation."

"Yeah I know, the Haunting Board will put you

in jail."

Oops...my bad. Again.

Donna looks at me quizzically. "Did you read that in a paranormal text, Lia? I know you probably studied a lot of interesting subjects in college, but I have never heard of a Haunting—"

Again, with the creepy voice, Granana says, "My granddaughter needs to stay here in Applebarrow. And Jason Woodcock is a fraud."

Donna says, "His last name is Woodcock? How unfortunate."

Some psychic she is!

I sigh heavily and say, "Donna, maybe you can ask my grandmother *why* Jason is a fraud."

Donna wrings her hands and says, "Oh my, okay. Well, *you* could ask her. She's right here."

I stare at Donna as if to say—that's your job, woman!

She clears her throat and says, "Allegra, what do you know about Jason? I do sense he is hiding something from Lia."

"Oh, he is, but I'll be damned if I am going to tell you. Lia is right. I will get in trouble if I share too much of the spirit world's knowledge with the living. I can't interfere in free will."

Well, that's a laugh. She fell out of her creepy, ghost character pretty damn fast.

I compose myself and continue to put Granana on the spot.

Hey, she showed up, and I think it's clear that Donna did not summon her, so I can hammer her all I want now.

"Granana, how am I supposed to do anything about this if you can't tell me the truth?"

"You have to trust, dear one."

This is such bullshit. I'm trying super hard not to roll my eyes and keep up *some* level of awestruck fear and wonder, but Granana is the most ridiculous caricature of a ghost.

And what the hell is the point of haunting me if all she's going to do is give me stupid cryptic warnings?

And why go to all this trouble? I guess she has time on her hands, and being dead must become boring, but she was never manipulative when she was alive.

"I have so many questions, Granana. For instance, why did you like Logan so much? Everyone says he was your favorite."

I shoot Donna a look to see if she knows anything from the regular town gossip mill—the information that requires no psychic powers.

She does look a little squirmy, but of course there's a dead lady dressed as a vampire/witch floating around her living room.

"Lia, you must be patient. You will learn all of this in time."

"But I want to know now." I am moving into the petulant little girl role, but Donna will buy that reaction—I'm a young woman pleading with my grandmother's ghost.

"Allegra, is there anything you can tell Lia about your life. Lia, you had some questions you said you were saving, right?"

When we talked on the phone, I told Donna that Granana's life was becoming more mysterious after her death, and I had questions.

I take the bait and say, "Yes, I want to know about Axe. Was he a special friend of yours? Where can I find him? You must be able to tell me about your past. That couldn't interfere with the free will of the living."

"Well, Axe *is* living, my dear, so therefore it is most surely a violation for me to tell you about him. I wish everyone in this town would keep their big mouths shut and focus on the present."

Donna appears jarred by Granana's further slip out of her gothic scary character, and back into the tough old lady she was in life.

"But Allegra, surely you can tell Lia who he was. Is. You don't have to tell her anything too private…or…*scandalous.*"

I am betting Donna doesn't know about Axe, or she wouldn't be so eager to coerce a dead lady into spilling the beans. She's not that bold.

Granana rustles her filmy ghost skirts and says, "If you two think I am going to risk going to jail, in a place where I am free to eat ice cream all day in a pool of chocolate with a cabana boy serving me, you are sadly mistaken. Now Lia…just keep your eyes open and don't make any rash decisions you can't change."

She waves her cape like a Dracula impersonator and slowly disappears while saying, "Just listen to your grandmother."

She's returned to the creepy voice at the end to make herself sound more mysterious and ethereal.

She's lost her mind. Well, technically her mind is dead, but I feel like she was way saner in life.

And who would have thought my elderly, church-going grandmother's idea of heaven is a cabana boy swimming in chocolate?

I shake off the possibilities of that horrific image and study Donna's face, which is as white as…I would say a ghost, but Granana does not appear any whiter than she did in life.

"Wow, that was amazing. I haven't conjured such a strong spirit in so many years. You and your grandmother have a strong bond. Perhaps you should heed her warning. I know it's frustrating, but we can't know everything about how things work on the other side."

I keep my eyeballs firmly in place (no eye rolling) and smile at the enthusiastic spirit summoner.

"Yes, you're right. I will respect Granana's advice, and maybe she'll appear to me again. If I come back here, of course. Thank you so much, Donna. What a gift you've given me."

"You're so welcome. But we shouldn't tell anyone about this. People act funny when you tell them you've seen dead people."

I stand up and feel a little wobbly, which is good as part of my act, but more a function of my wedge sandals and Donna's uneven wood floors.

I am exhausted and annoyed. I can't wait to get home and see if Granana shows up before Jason gets here, so I can yell at her for appearing to Donna like a total weirdo but saying nothing of use.

I suppose it's nice for Donna that Granana's appearance validated her skills.

However, between Granana's concern about preserving her fun times in the other world, and Donna's tight-lipped and/or clueless position in this world, I am out of luck on getting any new information.

I'm tired of asking questions of people who won't tell me anything. I'm going to live my best life and use my own wits to figure this out. I can sharpen my own detective instincts.

Of course, it's not easy when you learned your

crime-fighting skills watching the *Power Puff Girls* with your best friends, but those big-headed cartoon chicks had some formidable adversaries. But is Jason as bad as Mojo Jojo?

If he ever knew I was comparing him to an evil, cartoon monkey man...

One thing I know for sure—I miss the support of my best childhood friends.

It's time to bring Buttercup (Gabby) and Blossom (Taylor) in on this case. Bubbles (me) is out of ideas.

Yes, I wanted to be the cute one. Five-year-old Lia was smart, but too sweet to be the tough one or the leader. I can only lead if it involves planning parties, or refereeing roommate disagreements.

Shit, some things haven't changed, but I can count on Gabby and Taylor to hit me with some tough love, and hopefully a new perspective.

CHAPTER SIXTEEN

"**O**ooh, I remember Zach. He had that woodsy look to him. Like a lumberjack."

Taylor is pulling a face as Gabby reminisces about Jason's college friend, after I mentioned that he's one of the guests I'm expecting any minute.

Predictably, Jason texted to say they were running late when I was leaving Donna's, so I decided to Skype with my girls before the Richmond biking crew descends upon me.

Gabby says, "What? I can see you, Taylor and you *know* he was hot. You're used to those pasty Brits now. So, Lia, seriously how is he looking these days?"

I laugh and say, "He's still cute. I think you'd approve."

Gabby and Taylor were college friends, but we go way back to kindergarten in Vermont. Gabby's mom was a nurse at the local hospital, and Taylor's dad was a music teacher. They were both single and ended up getting married, so they are technically stepsisters now.

They continue to reminisce about the past, and they update me on their lives in London and Costa Rica. Such different and exciting worlds.

"So, Lee enough about us. What's going on with you? We've been dying to know!" Taylor corrals us back to the original purpose of this call, which was for me to share my mess with them and ask for their take on the current state of my life.

I'm closely watching the clock because I want to get it all out before Jason arrives, and I won't have a moment to myself for the rest of the weekend.

"Wow, I thought you were going to tell us about quirky southerners, and how the town has only one stoplight and you can't find good cannolis. What the hell? You think Jason might be cheating, your grandmother was living a secret life with some old British dude, and you think her Will was written to manipulate you from the grave?"

"That about sums it up."

Taylor clicks her tongue and says, "I don't know. It's hard to believe Jason is cheating but you never know. I would keep a close eye on this Amy chick this weekend. When I was working on their jingle, I felt like she was a bit bossy with Jason. But that doesn't mean she's sleeping with him."

Gabby chimes in, "She could be blackmailing him with their secret and forcing him to do her bidding."

Taylor shakes her head. "I don't know if it's quite that sinister, but Lee, I would pump Amy for info this weekend. Isn't there another guy coming, too?"

"Yes, Richard. He's an account executive at Elevation."

"I would try to get some dirt from him. Are there any hot women there who could pry it out of him?"

"Gabby, that is so devious. I can just ask him."

Gabby and Taylor begin to argue amongst themselves about what I should do, when Taylor says, "Hey, I just thought of something. I know an old guy named Axe. Did you say he was in the music business?"

"I didn't say that, but I suppose he could be. Although, I don't think Applebarrow is a popular hideout for famous music industry people."

"True, but I'll do some digging. Anyway, I think we're avoiding the bigger issue here. How do you feel about this big plan of Jason's for your future? You're set to inherit a lot of money, Lee, and it seems like he's poised to benefit from it with no strings attached."

"What do you mean by strings?"

Gabby pipes in with, "He hasn't put a ring on it, right?"

I wince at her old-fashioned gibberish. "Gabby, since when are you marriage minded?"

"*I'm* not, but you are. You wouldn't be with the same guy for five years if you weren't, and when we were little you were the one who wanted to play bride, while I was catching turtles in the pond and Taylor was banging on her keyboard like that character in the Charlie Brown cartoons."

Wow, they were even more career focused than I was at *that* age.

"Okay, you have a point, but we're still young. I'm sure he'll propose eventually."

"So, hint around about it, just to see his intentions. Apply a little subtle pressure. If he's cheating or embroiled in some messy shit, he will not want to hear about rings and seating charts, that's for sure."

We decide that it's not a bad idea. It *is* interesting that he hasn't mentioned marriage, now that we're moving forward with our life plan, AND he could benefit far more from my money as my husband. If anything, that makes him seem less guilty of...something. I think.

I'm still so confused.

However, I refuse to believe he's trying to benefit from Granana's death and dump me in another country, without the hassle of a divorce. No, that's not the man I love. There must be a better explanation.

"All I'm saying is if you do marry him, get a prenup." Gabby is shaking her finger at the screen and Taylor is nodding in agreement.

"There's one more thing I don't get, Lee." Taylor is twirling her long auburn hair and says, "Why don't you visit Jason? You're not in jail. What gives?"

Gabby hops in her seat and points at the screen again, "I know, I know! There's another guy, isn't there? There's always another guy. Is it Zach? Wait, he lives in Richmond so that makes no sense."

I sigh and say, "No, it's not Zach. And I could go to Richmond, yes. But...I don't know...I was sick of Richmond. My job sucked. Jason's friends suck, except for Zach, but he can't be my girlfriend. And Jason works *all the time*. I was curious about what it would be like here, and now I've made some friends and I have mysteries to uncover."

I surprise myself with my honesty. No wonder Jason is acting like I up and abandoned him.

I want to honor my Granana's request, but it's obvious now that it was her attempt to get me away from Jason and he must sense that's the case.

I'd be pretty pissed off if someone was trying to pull Jason away from me. Maybe this is more my fault than his.

"Have you made any hot friends, though?" Gabby isn't going to let this rest. She was always the over-sexed one anyway. I'm sure she'd be happy to give Zach a free vacation in Costa Rica.

I think of Logan, and if she saw him...well, let's just say she would forget Zach. And her name.

But I am not so easily swayed. I'm a loyal, committed woman. It's a bit unfair for me to be suspicious of Jason's behavior when my own isn't so squeaky clean. Well, at least my thoughts.

"There is a cute guy here, but...he's not for me. I think my Granana may have wanted to match us up, but that's not an issue now. I'm focused on Jason and what to do about the factory and the rest of this crap."

Taylor and Gabby get into it again, with Taylor trying to take control of the conversation and lead it back to the real issues at hand, while Gabby wants to know about the hot mystery guy.

I should ask if she has some time off and wants to come meet him. That way it would remove my temptation and get my ghostly visitor off my back.

However, there are plenty of women right here who would be happy to date Logan. I don't understand why I never see him with anyone. Hmm...

Taylor puts her hands up in the time out signal. "Listen, I think you should use the opportunity this weekend to dig deeper into what's going on and improve your communication with Jason. And I'll let you know what I find out about this Axe guy, but Lee...do you really want to know if your grandmother was messing around on your grandfather? She's gone and it's not like you can ask her about it."

If they only knew...and asking Granana anything has proven to be fruitless.

"You're right, but I can't help but feel like there's something going on here and I'm left out of the loop. It's hard to explain."

It's not easy to make my friends understand, since they don't know Granana is very much...not alive...but present, and if she wants to meddle in my love life, I can dig into hers.

And I can't help but suspect that Granana's secrets and Logan's are related.

Before the girls can offer any more thoughts, I say, "Jason and company will be here in a few minutes. He just texted and said they're getting off the exit right now. So, I have to go. Thanks for listening. It's hard to deal with all of this alone."

They both admonish me for not calling sooner, and they aren't that far away, and they would love to visit...blah, blah, blah...

I know they mean it but the sea turtles and hit records don't save and write themselves.

With Granana visiting at unexpected times (actually all visits are unexpected), it's not easy to entertain anyone. And if I can't control myself from speaking to a ghost in front of other people, I will be solving these mysteries from a padded cell.

I close my laptop after promises to update the girls on my situation, and then hear a noise out front.

I step carefully to the door as I don't want my grandmother sailing through my body again, and if it's her she better get going before my company shows up. It's difficult to ignore her when she's floating in my face, AND I have so much to say to her.

I slowly crack my door and don't see any dead people, just Fred, my older neighbor, outside Stan's door.

"Oh, hi Fred."

"Good afternoon, Lia! I was seeing if Stan was home. Wanted to grab a coffee or something."

I know Fred gets invited to the neighborhood guys' game watching nights, but I think Stan is the only one Fred talks to on a regular basis.

I have an idea to find some companionship for him.

"Oh, I think Stan went to Richmond for the weekend." Sassy seems to have stolen Stan away, and she has announced she's divorcing Beau. She promised they would be back here on Tuesday for the picnic, and we'd talk more about it.

Fred hangs his head and his sad smile kills me. I could invite him in, but I'm not exactly an ideal friend for Fred.

"Hey, Fred do you know any of the ladies my grandmother knew from church?"

He brightens slightly and says, "Oh yes. They came by a good bit to see Allegra, especially when she was sick. But that's all I know about your grandparents. Whatever they did was their business."

All I wanted to know is if he knows Granana's church friends? Why is he acting so funny?

And what were my grandparents doing that he most obviously DOES know?

"Were they younger than Granana? The ladies?" Even though that's not the question I want answered, I know better than to directly question anyone anymore. I've learned that it's futile in this community.

However, there is no sense in trying to set Fred up with women who are twenty-five years older than him, and matchmaking *was* the original purpose of this conversation.

"Oh yes, they were more my age. A fun group. Hey, I know. Should we invite them to the Fourth of July celebration?'

That's exactly what I was thinking, Fred.

He's ready, and I'm thrilled to help. Plus, meeting some gossipy old women who might have something interesting to share isn't a bad reward for my thoughtfulness.

***

"You always look so cute in your helmet."

Jason kisses me and playfully pulls on my low ponytail, sticking out of the bottom of my hot pink, expensive bike helmet.

I had a cheaper one, but it squeezed my brain, so I upgraded. It's bad enough how much my ass hurts from the seat, and this bike has the tiniest sliver of a butt cradle.

We are preparing for our 'casual' bike ride, and I am already annoyed. Plans have changed, and this is no longer the ride I agreed to, and I'm tense. And tired. Why do we have to start riding at seven in the morning?

As Jason, Amy, Zach and Rich fuss with their tire pressure and water bottles, I hop down from my bike and lean against the car, mentally reviewing the weekend thus far.

Yesterday, as I was talking to Fred about organizing his potential harem (hey, they're grown-ups!), Jason and his friends came bolting through my door. Amy had to pee, and Zach threw himself on my sofa, and Richard raided the refrigerator and couldn't understand why I don't stock beer.

Apparently, he hasn't seen Jason when he's had too much to drink.

Everyone was chatting about the drive, work, and the upcoming bike trip. I was thrilled (not thrilled at ALL) to find out they had decided to turn this into a road bike trip.

"I thought we were going to ride on the off-road trails?"

That's hard enough for me, but the hybrid bike has a more upright riding position, and it's less stressful than riding on the road with traffic.

Plus, if I get behind, I don't have to worry about getting lost. I can follow the marked trail.

Jason put his arm around me and said, "We changed our minds. Amy found a terrific country route that winds through fields, and there's a winery we can stop at and kick back for a few hours. It's gonna be great. I brought Amy's spare road bike for you."

Amy was smiling, but all I could think was I hoped Jason checked it to make sure she hadn't rigged it, so the wheels fall off mid-ride and I get thrown into oncoming traffic.

Granana and Donna are right. Something is off here, but I'm not sure what. My own intuition tells me Jason is acting weird, or I wouldn't be so suspicious.

I'm not convinced it's Amy. It's too obvious. She didn't seem the least bit interested in Jason, other than to give him grief about his driving and her need to get to Granana's house to take a nap before dinner.

Then I remembered that I had to take them

somewhere for dinner.

We debated that decision for a few minutes, and I tried my best to steer them away from Tonic. Jason and Logan are not a good combination for numerous reasons, and I'd like to have a peaceful weekend.

We settled on a fancy bistro in the touristy area and then headed over to Granana's house, where they would spend the night.

Hopefully, they would spend it alone and not with any visitors from beyond.

I suppose they did spend an uneventful night, because nothing odd was reported.

Jason came back to my place to stay with me, and we had an okay night. We didn't do a lot of talking, but we both needed to release some sexual tension, and I managed not to think about Amy while I was enjoying myself.

If he was having an affair, surely Jason wouldn't be so sex-starved. We barely made it home from dinner before he was taking my hand and leading me upstairs.

I'm sure our bedroom activities kept Granana away, which is fine. I still want to talk to her about her performance at Donna's, but that can wait.

My parents are also coming down this weekend, which is good *and* a bit problematic. It will be nice to see them, but I don't want my attention pulled away from keeping my eyes open and observing Jason's behavior.

However, I'm sure Jason will be monopolized by his friends, and a rousing game of cornhole.

My dad confirmed they will also be staying at Granana's house. It's plenty big enough, but I don't know if I want my parents and Jason's friends in such close proximity.

Although, my mother notices everything, and if anything suspicious occurs, she'll be the first to take note.

"Sweetie, are you ready?"

Jason interrupts my daydreaming, and Amy looks perturbed that I'm making her wait to get moving. She probably started her riding app, and I'm messing up her perfect record-breaking time.

I could have bowed out of this activity, but it doesn't help me in any way to shun Jason and his friends while they're here.

"Yep, I'm good. I'm following you? Is there a route I should put in my GPS or anything?"

Zach laughs and I screw up my face. "What? I can follow a GPS!"

He reminds me of the time in college when they all fell asleep and I ended up driving us to Virginia instead of Atlantic City because I drove in the wrong direction.

Amy smirks and I give Zach the evil eye. I wasn't used to driving on interstate highways. My town in Vermont had one road running through it that led us to anywhere we needed to go in the whole state.

And if I recall, that mishap was how we decided that Richmond was a cool place to settle after graduation.

So, it's my fault we met Amy.

"Hey, leave my woman alone. She can't help it if she's not a born navigator." Jason makes a mock pouty face. "We're teasing you. I'm sorry. Just follow me, and it'll be easier. We're gonna do a nice slow pace. Right, guys?"

As he turns to the others for agreement, they

are already halfway down the road and almost out of sight.

I don't want Jason to miss out on the fun of riding with people at his skill level. "It's okay, go ahead and catch up to them. You can always circle back around and ride with me."

He always employs that tactic on rides and claims he's fine with getting in some extra miles, and I insist I don't mind a little time riding alone. I don't, and it usually works out fine.

Except there was that one time I got lost, but he found me quickly.

Jason kisses me and thanks me for being 'the coolest girlfriend' and pedals off to catch up with his fellow speedy riders.

It's fine. He'll come back for me and it's a beautiful, sunny morning in one of the safest places. What could possibly go wrong?

As long as Granana doesn't start riding next to me on a ghost bike, everything will be fine.

CHAPTER SEVENTEEN

"Thanks a lot, assholes!"

I'm not exactly *hitchhiking*, as that would be a bad choice in 2017 in the middle of nowhere (or anywhere), but it would be nice if a car full of women could stop and see if the girl sitting on the side of the road, with torn cycling pants and no cell phone, was okay.

Bitches.

So, yes. I got lost. Jason has not come back for me and my phone is somewhere in a bramble of pokey wildlife and I saw a snake, or maybe a large lizard, while I was looking for it and decided I would take my chances with the sparse traffic as my rescue plan.

A girl who grew up in the country should be better at identifying and interacting with nature, but I stayed pretty much in town. I blame my Brooklyn-born mother.

I was doing okay on the ride, and I was enjoying it so much that I veered off at the fork in the road and pedaled off our planned route. I saw some damn wildflowers and was distracted!

Virginia also has this fantastic thing they do where roads have the same name but stop and pick up somewhere else entirely. One time I spent an hour thinking I was on Primrose Lane, and a local at the gas station told me I wanted the *other* Primrose Lane on the south side of town.

And this kind of thing blows Siri's mind, so there's no help there. Especially today with my phone lodged in the underbrush of the reptile nest.

RIP Siri.

So, thanks town zoning people! I need to ask Fred what gives with that. He was a county something or other.

I'm out of water and I haven't seen another car go by lately, so I stand up, wincing in pain at my scraped knee, and decide to hunt around for my phone.

In all fairness, this is my own fault. Jason can't circle back to meet up with me if I cycled miles in the wrong direction.

And if I wasn't looking at the bunny on the side of the road, my tire wouldn't have caught a broken bottle and spun out, flinging me into the woods.

It's hot as hell! So much for riding in the early part of the day to avoid the heat. I bet that nice wooded trail isn't baking, and I wouldn't have had any forks to choose from. I could be sinking my fork into a nice lunch somewhere.

I shake my head as I pull back the pokey bushes and pray the snake creatures are napping, or whatever they do in the sun. I can't remember if they like heat or they hide from it.

I am annoyed with Jason for dragging me out on this stupid ride, but I did agree to it. I'm sure I have a bunch of messages from him on my phone, and if I can retrieve it, he'll be out here with the nice cool car in a matter of minutes.

I could even be near the parked car now, not that I have the keys.

Everything looks the same on the outskirts of this town, and who knows if I rode in a circle. I am not walking anywhere to find out because I may pass out from dehydration and starvation. Amy's spare bike doesn't have a bag, so I let Jason carry my disgusting energy bar that tastes like soil.

Okay, I see my phone. Crap, it looks like the screen is cracked. I'm just about to reach for it, when I hear a male voice and a raccoon grabs my phone and runs off with it. What the...?

"Oh my God, I'm so glad you found me. A raccoon just stole my phone, and I'm filthy. I hope you're ready to go home and get in the shower."

I knew Jason would come for me, but as I push the prickers out of the way and emerge from my wildlife cocoon, it's not Jason.

"You don't have to keep getting this dirty. If you want to use the shower at the bar, you just have to ask nicely."

***

"It's not like we dress like Hooter's girls around here, not that there's anything wrong with that, of course. If you want to make tips...anyways Honey, you'll fill this little Tonic tank top out nicely, and I'll give you the pants because the shorts are a little cheeky, and more suitable for the late-night crowd. We're about the same size, I think."

Nicky, one of the bartenders at Tonic, is providing me with some clean clothes to change into after my shower. It's a bar uniform, but it's clean and perfectly serviceable to wear home. Although the cleavage spillage on this top is a little much.

Nicky reminds me of Molly. I wouldn't be surprised if they were friends. Everyone seems to know everyone, and everything, in this town. Except for me. Hmm...

"Thanks so much, Nicky. I feel so stupid for falling off my bike and getting lost."

"Oh, think nothing of it. I haven't been on a bike since I rode to the ice cream stand after school in seventh grade. Now come on and let me show you the back room, and get you cleaned up. There're fresh towels somewhere. I normally don't come back here and disturb the lord and master."

She says that with a smile, so I am assuming she's not insinuating that Logan is difficult to work for. Everyone at Tonic always seems happy, and I've never once seen him lose his temper with an employee, or even an irate or drunk patron. He even *brought Jason home*!

As she leads me into the room way at the back, I am speechless when she opens the door to a master bedroom suite. It's not like it's opulent—no gold or glitter, or mirrors on the ceiling, but it's an awfully nice space for the back room of a bar for emergency clean up and rest.

Nicky appears to read my mind and says, "Pretty snazzy, huh? I guess when you're the owner, you can do whatever you like."

She hands me some super soft grey towels and points to the bathroom, where I can already see a jacuzzi and a rainfall shower.

"It's a beautiful space. Does he stay here some of the time?"

"I don't think so, Sweetie. He's got one of those nice duplex apartments over in Pentagon Place in town, but there are lots of late nights in this business. Plus, a guy like Logan might like to have a private place to bring someone, if you know what I mean?"

No, I don't know what she means. He lives in his apartment alone. Why would he need a *more* private place to bring someone?

"Sure, Pentagon Place can be a gossipy neighborhood." I'm assuming that's what she means.

I explain who I am, and Nicky holds her hand up to her mouth. "Oh, then you know the whole story. You know Logan received this bar as a gift after all the...nastiness...that went down here a few years back?"

"Um, no I didn't actually. I just moved here and—"

"Nicky!!!!"

A shriek from the front of the bar reverberates off the walls, and she places her hands on her hips. "Dear sweet Jesus, that boy is going to be the death of me. He's only been here a week and he's dropped more expensive glassware than I can count."

She cups her hand around her mouth and screams, "Comin' Josh, don't cut yourself."

She says, "Now you take your time in there. I'll lock the door behind me, so you'll have your privacy. Logan would never barge in on you, but sometimes we have wandering drunks."

"Thank you."

"Anytime Sugar, and you know that Grandma of yours was a real peach. The old man, too. Hahaha..."

And she's gone. What the hell just happened?

I sit on the edge of the gorgeous bathtub and go over the disjointed and confusing information Nicky spouted.

It sounds like she's saying something bad happened to Logan and someone *gave* him the bar. But who? Why?

And Logan needs privacy to bring members of the opposite...or maybe *same* sex?

She couldn't mean that, but sometimes I'm naïve about these things. In college, there was a guy who I thought was hitting on me and he really just liked my shoes.

If Logan is gay that would be a good thing for me, and I certainly am not the least bit homophobic. I grew up with the most liberal parents imaginable. If I had been gay, they would have had a rainbow painted in my room.

It's hard to believe, though. The way he looks at me...but maybe I'm reading something into it through my own heteronormative lens. And for whatever reason, he doesn't want to come out to the neighbors.

Or I'm reading *way* too much into Nicky's comments. She might just be insinuating that he hooks up a lot after hours.

I put my towels on the bar next to the shower and turn the taps on full power. The rainfall blast is strong and steady, and I could stay in here until everything makes sense, which may be a long time.

***

"There she is, all fresh and clean. Did Nicky get you everything you needed? That outfit looks great on you. You sure you don't want a job?"

Logan is smiling and looking at me appreciatively.

Hmm...after what Nicky said, I don't know if his compliments are man to woman observations, or girlfriend to girlfriend remarks. Everything can be taken both ways.

It is true that in the almost three months I have known Logan, I have not seen him with a woman, and he's an attractive man, and an amazing person.

"Yeah, I think I have enough jobs for now. And yes, she was great."

We stare at each other awkwardly and start talking at the same time. I ask for a drink, and he asks if I want a ride home now.

"Oh, no I was thinking I'd like to hang out here awhile, if that's okay. My parents are coming soon but my apartment is kind of...lonely...and Jason is...has he called here, by any chance?"

I sit on a barstool and regret looking needy. Logan must be thinking Jason is such an uncaring asshole to lose me on the ride *and* not come looking for me. However, he may be out doing that right now, but I don't feel like making Logan drive me all over town looking for the lost bikers.

He pours me a glass of water from the tap and says, "Is this good?"

Since I'm not a big day drinker, I nod. It is five o'clock somewhere. Actually, right here. This day has flown by.

Where the hell is Jason? If he doesn't show up by the time my parents arrive, even my father might get mad.

Logan comes around the bar and walks me and my drink back to a table in the corner. Hopefully he's not going to tell me they found Jason's body, and I need to go to the coroner's office to identify it.

Before my grandmother became a ghost, I swear my mind never tended towards the macabre.

Once we're sitting, Logan says, "So, I was doing my errands this morning. I had to pay some bills in town and pick up some supplies for the bar in the next town over. And on one of the county roads, this red-headed guy on a bike flagged me down."

"Did you stop?"

"Yeah, I thought he was in trouble. His name was Zach, and he was looking for you. That alarmed me in all sorts of ways, since it implied you were missing *and* some big dude with a red goatee I've never seen before was looking for you."

Does Logan's nervous smile mean he thought Zach was cute, or that telling this story is going to be embarrassing for me?

I'm sure it's the latter. I must stop thinking such silly thoughts. Logan's not gay.

"He was alone?"

"Yeah, he told me you'd all gone on a bike ride and you had gotten lost. Then I remembered you had said Jason was coming and bringing friends from Richmond. So, I relaxed, and we chatted a bit to try to figure out where you might have gone wrong. We decided to split up, and he went one direction and I headed out in the other. Obviously, I could cover more ground in the truck, and there you were."

I lean back in my chair and wrinkle my brow. "So, you were looking for me? Where was Jason? And the others? Also looking?"

"Well, I probably shouldn't tell you this, Lia. I personally know what it's like to be the subject of gossip in this town, but—"

"Hey, guys! What's shakin? Why you sittin' over here? Uh oh, I'm interrupting something, ain't I?"

Dawson's timing is not very timely, and I want to ask him to leave, but he's so nice. I sigh and say, "We're just talking, Dawson. How are you? I got lost on my bike today and Logan rescued me."

Dawson pulls up a chair, as if Logan wasn't about to tell me some big truth about Jason, my life, and maybe even solve the mystery of his sexual orientation.

Dawson says, "Is that so? Are you okay?" He peers at me as if he's inspecting me for signs of injury.

Logan explains how he found me and how I am apparently not good at navigating in the country. Of course—let's all have a laugh at dopey little Lia. I could curse them in multiple languages if I wanted to!

I take deep breaths as I wait for them to end this conversation, and Dawson either gets the hint and excuses himself, or Logan asks him to give us some privacy.

I am assuming privacy would be best, since he brought me into the corner.

Dawson says, "That's hilarious girl, but I'm sorry you got hurt. Truly I am. I can't believe a country girl like you can't figure out how to get around in these parts." He stands up and laughs his goofy guffaw. "Well, I'll leave you two. Looks like somethin' serious was goin' on over here. Sorry for interrupting."

"Hey Dawson, I moved here from the city. You know that. Why do you think I'm a country girl?" I can't believe I am prolonging his presence, but I never told anyone I grew up in Vermont. I guess Granana must have told them.

Logan interjects and says, "It was in the bio."

Dawson is distracted by a group of rowdy women cackling on their way to the restroom and turns back to us and says, "Say what? You're *bi*?

We don't look down upon that here. Right, Logan? This is a very gay-friendly place."

He slaps Logan on the back and stands up straighter, as if attesting to his own heterosexuality, and walks off towards the bar with a wave.

"What did he mean by that? But just so you know, I am also gay-friendly. I mean, if someone told me they were gay I wouldn't be weird about it...not that it's true about *me*, obviously. But if it was true for someone else..."

I study Logan's face and he's looking even more nervous now.

I also make a mental note to explain to Dawson that I'm not into women.

"I don't think he knows what a bio is, plus he's a little deaf from working on engines all day." Logan runs his hands through his hair and says, "Look, Lia, I like to keep my life private, but if I'm not mistaken, I think you're assuming I'm gay, and that is the exact opposite of the truth, and what I want you to think."

I wave my hands around, the Italian and Jewish sides coming out of me when I get agitated, almost knocking over my water. "No, I mean...maybe...but it's none of my business, and I can see how in this town it might be easier...I don't know. I'm rambling. I will shut up now and let you talk." I sit on my hands but then lean forward to sip my straw because my mouth has gone dry.

"As I was saying before our friend interrupted us, *your* friend Zach told me that Jason and the others were at the winery. When I gave him a judgmental look, he quickly said that Jason wanted to stay in one place—in case you made it there, since you knew that was the destination."

"Uh, huh...." That son of a bitch. Sipping wine with Amy and that douchebag Richard while I'm sweating on the side of the road with snakes, pricker bushes, and phone stealing wildlife.

"Zach agreed with me that it sounded like bullshit, and that you deserved better. He said he's been friends with Jason for years and he's changed. He also said that Jason's phone was ringing off the hook and he said it was his boss, and they needed to have an emergency business meeting at the winery."

"You'd think they were all international billionaires or drug lords. It's ridiculous. It's always like this, and they were with Greta the other day at her house. Why is work so significant if the company is going out of business?"

Logan isn't going to have any answers. I'm talking out loud.

"I don't know, but I thought you should know the truth. Or at least what I know. You deserve better, Lia."

"Thanks. So, you're not gay?"

We laugh about that, but Logan says, "No, I am definitely not gay. I've been thinking about a girl I can't have a lot lately."

"Logan—"

"It's okay. I get it. I'm not going to try to break you and Jason up. That's why I didn't want to tell you anything bad about him. It makes it look like I'm trying to be the hero. I figure he'll crash and burn on his own, and if what your grandmother wanted is meant to be, it will happen."

The mention of my Granana chills me as it always does lately. Has she been visiting Logan, too?

"What do you mean?"

"Well, I shouldn't tell you this either, but I've had enough of the games. Allegra wanted to set me up with you when she was alive. She said you had a boyfriend she didn't care for, and that I should meet her beautiful, intelligent, sweet granddaughter and sparks would fly."

"Wow, that explains a lot." Granana is in sooo much trouble. If only I knew how to report her to the Haunting Board.

"Yes, so of course I told her she was being silly, and I would never break up an established relationship. Allegra was quite stubborn."

"That's for sure."

"I didn't give it much thought, and your grandmother was getting old and sick, and I felt I owed it to her to humor her a little bit."

Oh boy, he *owed* her. "Did she buy this bar for you?"

"No, your grandfather gave it to me."

"That makes no sense."

"I know, but they both loved me. They wanted to reward me. It's complicated."

"Reward you? I can see they were crazy about you, but why? Not that you're not a great guy, but what happened to make them so Team Logan?"

For the next hour, Logan explains his story and my mouth is hanging open by the end.

It seems Logan came to Applebarrow from Chicago five years ago to work at the theater. He was a set designer. He majored in Theater at a well-respected art school back home in the city, and wanted to do small theater, and was especially interested in Shakespeare.

The theater has apparently always been a bit out of place in this area. The touristy parts of town draw a different, and more liberal crowd, than the locals who've lived here all their lives.

Logan had a good friend, one of the actors who was brought here to play the lead in Macbeth. His name was Thomas.

Thomas was gay and had no intentions of hiding it, just because he was in a less than gay-friendly town.

One thing led to another and the harassment grew, and one night a few rough, intolerant assholes from the next town over cornered Thomas and beat him up badly.

Logan says, "They would have killed him, had I not stepped in. Unfortunately for me, one of those assholes tripped and hit his head on the sidewalk and ended up in a coma. His father was a judge."

"Yikes, what happened?"

"I went to jail."

My mouth is hanging open again (so attractive) and then he quickly adds, "Your grandparents bailed me out of jail, and hired the best lawyer they could find. All the charges were dropped, and the other guys were prosecuted and convicted."

"So why did Grandpa give you this bar? I don't see the connection."

"Your grandfather had bought it right around the time he closed the plant, just for fun. They said they were too old to run it, so they were giving me an early inheritance."

My eyes widen. "We're not related, are we?"

As I search my memory for possible long-lost cousins, Logan smiles and says, "No, we're not. How can I put this? They wanted me to stay in Applebarrow, and they were very grateful for what I'd done. It meant a lot to them."

So, was I related to Thomas? I still don't get it. I know my grandparents were good people, but this is over the top.

I have so many questions, so I continue with an easier one.

"Why didn't you return to the theater?"

"The production had ended and set designers don't make much money in small theater. I was all set to go back to Chicago and they offered me this opportunity. I had bartended in the past, and it seemed like an interesting adventure. I like it here, despite all that happened. Most of the people are great. And I knew I could sell it after they were gone, if I wanted out."

"But here you are."

"Here I am. What your grandparents did for me was unbelievable, Lia. I can never repay them."

"So, that's why you're so nice to me. I get it."

"No...that's not why. Maybe at first, but not now."

"They're both gone now."

I desperately wanted to know why he's still here, and at the same time wishing my asshole boyfriend would arrive and tell me he had been abducted by aliens at the winery.

I don't understand why my grandparents would do this for Logan. How did they even know him?

"Why were they so touched by what you did? I mean, it was an awesome thing to do, but it seems like they were personally involved. Did they have a gay friend? Or family member I don't know about?"

I'm really fishing here, but I'm wondering if it had anything to do with the mysterious Axe.

"They were supportive of the gay community, and they were patrons of the theater. Oh, look.

Here's your man now."

Jason is frantically searching the room. Logan sits back and folds his arms, as if he doesn't want Jason to think our conversation was intimate, but also challenging him not to worm his way out of an explanation for his very long absence.

"There you are! Thank God. I've been looking all over for you. I finally went back to your apartment and Dawson was outside and told me you were here."

To his credit, Jason is still in his biking clothes and at least has the decency to look sweaty and disheveled.

"Yeah, did he tell you how I got lost and fell off my bike? And broke and lost my phone?"

"Yeah, he was rambling on and on. That guy can talk. But I don't understand. Why are you here, dressed like you work here? Couldn't you get a ride home?" Now he's narrowing his gaze at Logan.

Here we go again.

"I'm sitting right here, man. You know perfectly well that I offered her a ride home. But it seems once she heard where you were, she decided she would rather clean up here and wait, instead of going home alone."

"I think she can speak for herself." Jason pulls himself up to his full height, but at five-foot-seven, it isn't much.

Logan rises and towers over him. "You're right. She can. I'm going back to work. We'll talk more tomorrow, Lia."

I grab Logan's wrist and say, "No, wait. Explain to him how Zach told you—"

"Lia, stop. I don't want to get involved any more than I already am." More gently he says, "I'm just glad you're okay."

He walks off and ignores Jason.

"I don't get it." Jason throws his hands up in the air. "I was trying to stay put so you would know where I was. I assumed that somehow you had lost your phone yet again, but I didn't think it had anything to do with *that* guy."

He points towards the bar in disgust.

"He rescued me and—"

"Oh, he *rescued* you! Come on, Lia. Can't you see what's happening here? You're pissed at me all the time, and *you're* the one who wanted to come to this town, knowing how much stress I'm under trying to make our dreams come true. And I'm *always* the bad guy. I can't help it if you took the wrong fucking fork in the road!"

"You were supposed to come back for me!"

People are staring now, but I don't care. It's about time...oh shit, I guess Dawson told my parents where I was as well.

"Lia, what's going on? Jason, why are you yelling at my daughter? And what happened to your hair?" Leave it to my mother to notice the appearance of the person cursing at her daughter.

"Ahhhh!!!" Jason lets out a cry of frustration, and now Logan looks like he's getting ready to act as bouncer, so we stop scaring his customers with our domestic dispute.

I'm guessing the local cops are not among his favorite people.

"This is terrible energy! I demand to know what's going on here." In an uncharacteristic burst of anger, my father steps between me and Jason.

"Hello, Paul. Sarah. I was just explaining to your daughter that I can't find her on a bike route if she goes the wrong way and loses her phone, then gets rescued by another man and comes back to his bar instead of her home, or the winery, where she knew I'd be. Also, she is freshly showered and wearing clothes that aren't her own. So yes, I am upset and have questions."

He folds his arms, after attempting to tame his hair.

My parents both stare at me and I look at my smug boyfriend. "You shouldn't have left me to ride alone in the first place."

Jason covers his face with his hands and grits his teeth. "You *told me* to leave you! I suggest you think about your passive-aggressive behavior. I am not the bad guy here. You haven't come to visit me in Richmond once. There are no bars on the windows in your apartment."

My father puts his hand on Jason's shoulder, which seems to instantly calm him. "Jason, what are trying to say?"

"Paul, I think you should have a talk with Lia about what's going on here. Also, before you blame me for everything, Sarah, as women often do, maybe you should talk to *that* guy."

He points at Logan, who is shaking his head and sighing behind the bar.

We watch Jason storm out of the bar yelling, "I'll be at your grandmother's house when you're ready to have an honest conversation."

I am speechless. Me, have an honest conversation? He's the one hiding something. Or maybe…shit…he had some points.

And why did Jason have to show up right when Logan was about to tell me why my grandparents were rainbow flag wavers?

I hate to say this, but I'm glad my mom is here. If anyone can help me figure out who's manipulating me, it's Sarah Edelman-DeLuca.

I hope we don't discover that I'm doing it to myself.

CHAPTER EIGHTEEN

"**I** don't want to go!"

My mother pulls off my covers and reveals my pajama-clad body curled in the fetal position. The way I feel, I may as well be sucking my thumb.

Jason returned to the house last night, and my parents stayed here with me until late evening. They said everyone was in bed when they arrived there, but I didn't ask them to check who was sleeping with who.

"You're going! You are the one who insisted on honoring Allegra's delusional request by coming to this town, and these people now count on you. And I didn't come all the way from Vermont to sit in this apartment or eat hot dogs with strangers. Now get up!"

I sit up in bed and slam my fist on the bed like a sullen teenager. "Fine, but I am not talking to any men, except Dad. And Fred."

Mom sits on the edge of the bed and pulls my long, sandy mane out of my face. "Oh Honey, you don't know what you're doing with men, do you? You were so shy in high school, and Jason was your first real boyfriend."

"So, lots of people stay with a first boyfriend. That's not the problem."

"Well, it's not helping. You know I like Jason, but I don't like the way he's affecting you lately.

You're not even old enough for a quarter life crisis until your next birthday."

She smiles but I'm not feeling like joining her. "Mom, I don't know what to do. Jason had some valid points, but I'm afraid he's trying to divert my attention away from his behavior."

"Uh, huh...that's possible, but I do think the guy behind the bar might have a part in this." She raises her eyebrows and I blush.

"I am not cheating on Jason. Or even thinking about it."

"Lia, I did not just fall off the turnip truck. That Logan is a hot tamale, and it seems like you've bonded with him since you've been here. And after everything you told us about him last night, it sounds like Allegra hoped you two would get together."

"But she's not here." I glance around after saying that, because you never know when she'll pop up.

"No, but you obviously respected and loved her very much. It's natural to be swayed by her, even now. I think you need to get out there in your hot bikini and enjoy the day. You don't have to make any decisions right away, and at least we can enjoy that fun inflatable pool together."

She takes my hand and I get out of bed, heading for the shower.

"Okay, Mom. I'm still not sure what to do about Jason, but I can't let my relationship fall apart every time I meet a good-looking man. Right?"

I keep saying this, but it seems that's what I'm doing.

Mom smiles, squeezes my hand and says, "That's right, Honey. If I did that, Dad and I would have been divorced years ago."

And off she goes to don her own bathing suit and huge sun hat. "Paul, let's grab some rays!"

I close the door behind her and anticipate Granana again. She must have heard me say something potentially positive about Jason out loud. She hates that.

I am *not* admitting how I feel about Logan out loud to anyone.

As far as I can tell, ghosts can't read minds.

***

"How do you like the theme, Lia?"

Arielle is proud of the work she and Marcos have put into the Fourth of July extravaganza. They went with a chili cookoff, but there are grills set up with hotdogs and hamburgers cooking as well, and tons of side dishes and desserts.

I feel a sudden gush of pride for the young couple, even though I'm barely older than them.

"Everything looks so great! I'm sorry I've been too busy lately to help."

Meaning, 'I'm sorry I've been preoccupied with a ghost, the mysterious past, an irate and possibly cheating boyfriend, and a growing heat I feel every time I look at a certain bartender'.

Just as I was about to find Jason to get this talk over with, Olivia accosts me and says, "Oh yes, they did a splendid job. I burned my mouth on that pot of flaming beans over there, and *what* is this music?"

I listen closely. Hmm...this is also a heavy metal picnic.

Hey, everyone gets a shot to do the events their way.

"Olivia, when it's your turn, you can play chamber music and hand out cucumber finger sandwiches."

I turn away from her icy stare.

"Hey guys, can you label the spicy chilis, and maybe switch up the music a little bit. Metallica is super cool, but some of this sounds like demons being tortured."

They both smile, and Arielle gives me the thumbs up, while her husband plays air guitar and bangs his head.

Kids…ha-ha…

Now where's Jason?

"Lia, there you are. Did you get my email about the organic dog food company I found for you?"

Sassy is wearing a quite 'sassy' looking bathing suit. I guess a new man warrants a sexier wardrobe.

"Why do I need a dog…ohhhh, you mean for the factory?"

"Yes, silly girl. I know you're embroiled in a sizzling love triangle, but you also have business to attend to."

Sizzling love triangle? Who has she been talking to?

"I hardly check email. You should have texted me."

"Oh, you kids. You're an important woman now. Be a grown up and check your inbox. We'll talk about it tomorrow when I'm back in Richmond. We need to set up a meeting. It's perfect—Jason will jump at it."

I wince at his name and continue to search the crowd for him.

"What are you looking for? Jason is playing his

new favorite game. That silly 'cornball.' Of course, my Stan looks sexy throwing that bean bag thing."

I'm beginning to feel like I am surrounded by 'cornballs.'

"Sassy, I need to talk to Jason. We had *another* argument."

I give her the rundown on recent events.

She says, "You do have yourself in a pickle. My advice—protect your assets. And I don't just mean the ones spilling out of that bikini top. You're a soon-to-be rich girl. And a bit of a naïve one. Use your noodle."

She taps my head and I watch her run over to the cornhole area and launch herself at Stan.

Jason looks over at me after she says something. I wave and he smiles broadly.

Yes, it's time for a talk. Then I am getting in that damn pool!

And yes, I wore the sexy bikini again. I always obey my mother.

***

Molly adjusts her bathing suit strap and leans back against the edge of the inflatable pool. Her spiky blond hair is perfect, despite the humidity. "Jason, that sounds amazing. Thank you so much, but I have so many questions."

Jason brings his beer bottle to his lips and says, "It's no problem, and it was all Lia's idea. Next weekend let's meet at your place to discuss a plan to move forward."

Cradled in front of Jason's body to keep most of me in the water, I close my eyes and soak up the sun, and the good vibes.

Once Sassy alerted Jason to my presence, he

came over and we both started apologizing at the same time. I told him the truth about why I wanted to come to Applebarrow, and why I've stayed.

He was shocked that I wasn't happy in Richmond and was remorseful about being so caught up in his own problems that he didn't notice mine.

"I was trying so hard to succeed for us. It was temporary, and when I let myself think about it, I always rationalized that you were fine with waiting for your life to begin. But I was kidding myself, and now I've blown it."

I told him it wasn't all his fault, and I let it happen. I promised to be more forthcoming about what I want in the future, like not being dropped on bike rides because I'm slow, and more time to get my affairs wrapped up in Applebarrow before we leave the country.

Then I mentioned my intention to begin visiting him in Richmond every other weekend.

"No, Babe, you don't need to do that. That place is a dead end for us. You're right. I should move here when I'm done at Elevation, and we'll make this work. I don't think it'll be long."

We kissed behind the clubhouse for quite a while, but regained control of ourselves in case my parents, children, or old people happened to see us.

Plus, I wanted to get to the party and enjoy the day, as my mother instructed.

As we walked around to the front of the clubhouse, I saw two people scurrying from opposite sides of the building.

Clearly, they had been spying.

Or maybe there were plausible reasons for

them both to be alone, within earshot of our conversation.

Amy was probably texting on her phone, or maybe she wanted a moment alone. I see nothing suspicious between her and Jason on this trip.

Logan could have been escaping the party, but maybe he wanted to make sure I was okay. He doesn't think too highly of Jason, and he did confess his feelings for me.

Well, he alluded to his feelings in a puzzling way.

There is way too much of that going around.

In the pool with the sun on my face, I decide to revel in this newfound peace with Jason. If people want to spy on us, it's because their own lives are lacking.

I'm happy that Jason is on board with helping Molly now. I told him that it was important to me to invest in Molly's doll business, and he's jumped right on it.

And better yet, Sassy told him about her lead on the organic dog food company, and he was punching numbers in his phone to get the meeting set up.

I am a tiny bit concerned about giving him so much control, since as my friends pointed out—I have a lot of money coming my way and Jason and I aren't married.

However, after our conversation I was sure he has every intention of moving in that direction.

I scoot out from under Jason and climb out of the pool, grabbing a beach towel off the stack Arielle has so thoughtfully provided.

Wrapping it around me to soak up some of the water, I wring out my hair and tell Jason, "I'm going inside for some water." I kiss his cheek and connect with the side of his mouth, as he turns his head.

Inside the clubhouse, Amy is on the phone. I hate to interrupt, but this isn't her private office and I'm parched.

"He's in the pool. Submerged in water. No, I am not telling him that." Amy spots me and says to the caller, "I have to go. We'll talk about this tomorrow."

"Hey, Lia." She slips the phone into the pocket of her sundress, and gestures to the food, "This is a great party. Thanks for having us."

"You're welcome." I grab a water out of the fridge. "Can I get you anything?"

"Oh no, thanks. Um...I was on the phone. As you heard. It was Greta. She's—"

"Looking for Jason?"

"Yes. She's relentless. I'm trying to run interference while we're here so Jason can enjoy his time with you. Sorry about yesterday, by the way. These roads *are* confusing. We should have looked out for you, though."

I take several big gulps of cold water and reply, "I don't understand why Greta is bothering any of you."

"Well, she's kind of a bitch. You must know that much."

"Sure, but if you're all about to lose your jobs anyway, shouldn't she be focused on what she's going to do next? I don't get trying so hard to save a sinking ship."

Amy blinks several times, and now I feel guilty for being so forceful.

"I'm sorry, Amy. That was insensitive. It just

seems odd that if the company is going out of business that she would—"

"Lia, do we have any limes in this joint? Oh sorry, Miss. I was looking for something for my woman to suck on."

We must look taken aback by Dawson's choice of words. "You know what I mean." He wags his finger. "Get your heads out of the gutter, ladies. It's just that Emma is on a diet. Not my doin'—I think she's a nice handful the way she is."

I open the fridge and hand him the bag of limes. "Here, take these."

I shouldn't be short with Dawson, but every time I'm dragging information out of someone, I get interrupted by someone else who is oblivious to my frustration.

"Thanks very much." Now he's looking at Amy and saying, "She's a beautiful girl, my Emma, but you know how it is when you like Twinkies too much. Those things should have a surgeon general's warning on them. I know more people who've Twinkied themselves to death than smoked—"

I swivel him towards the door. "Yes, you're helping Emma *so* much. Now Amy and I were having a chat, so bye-bye."

Dawson doesn't know what hit him and follows directions, smiling as I strong arm him out the door.

Amy clears her throat and says, "I better be getting back outside. Richard and Zach are probably arguing about something, and I'm the only one here to referee." She smiles weakly.

"Amy, is your company going out of business?"

"Is that what Jason told you?"

Crap, I hope I'm not telling her that she's losing

her job and she doesn't know.

I can't let my petty suspicions break Jason's trust in me. He asked me not to say anything to her, and here I am shining a lightbulb in her face the first chance I get.

"Well, he said things were...difficult. Anyway, yes let's get back to the party. I love your flips flops. Did you get them in Richmond?"

***

Fred and the church ladies seem to be going back to his place, and I refuse to read anything into that.

I briefly met the three women who were my Granana's friends. I will make it a point to connect with them personally, especially now that they've been invited back to their old pal's neck of the woods, as Gladys put it. Martha and Tammy are sisters who live together, and Gladys is their neighbor.

They seem like nice enough ladies, and I'm not sure why Granana was so adamant about keeping them away.

None of them mentioned the house or any of Granana's belongings. I'd like to reminisce with them and see if they have any idea why my grandparents were such strong supporters of the gay community.

Although, maybe that's a better question for Donna. I am learning more and more that my grandmother lived separate lives. This Granana is not the woman I knew in life.

For now, I say good night to the party-goers. A Tuesday holiday means back to work for everyone tomorrow.

I'm excited about continuing to work on the after-school program, and we've already decided that Dawson and Tucker will plan the next resident event for August.

I am hoping it isn't going to involve Nascar, or any other auto-related entertainment.

Jason comes up behind me and rests his head on my shoulder, while wrapping his arms around me.

"God, I wish I didn't have to go to work tomorrow."

He nuzzles my neck and I am thinking the same thing, but I don't want to be selfish.

"I know, but you should go back home to your place now, and not do that long drive in the morning. Friday will be here in a few days, and we'll have a nice reunion."

He spins me around, "That's what I love about you—always looking on the bright side. You understand that I need to keep up this work façade until we're let go formally, right? Greta is trying to squeeze out any revenue she can before we fold. If she can keep a few clients for herself, she may be able to give us severance. I'm just playing the game."

He kisses me and relief floods my core. This is the most harmonious we've been in weeks.

Logan's voice pulls me out of my bliss.

He's been making himself scarce all day. Olivia must be thrilled to see that he's stopped paying attention to me. Too bad he doesn't seem the least bit interested in her. He needs a sweeter woman, anyway.

"Hey, great party, Lia. Jason."

Jason shakes his hand and says, "I'm off. Have

a great week, Logan."

At least they're being cordial and pretending nothing ever happened, but there's no point in lamenting the state of their relationship. We won't be in Applebarrow long enough for it to matter, and it's not like Logan wants to be friends with the boyfriend of a woman he's inappropriately falling for.

Did he actually say that? Or am I reaching? No, I think he made it clear that he has feelings for me and it's best to keep these two men separate.

I would love to maintain our friendship while I'm here, but it's hard to be friends with someone when you want more.

And I'm talking about Logan. *I* don't want more. He does. Only *him*.

"I'll walk you to your car after you grab your bags." I release Jason's hand and he says goodbye to my parents.

Fortunately, they are fairly forgiving, and there is no fallout from the scene at Tonic.

I inhale deeply and smile at Logan. Sure, we can be friends. It's easy as...what did he just say?

"I'm sorry, what did you say you're doing?'

"I have a date. You know, when a man and a woman—"

"Yes, I think I know what a date is. I didn't think you were going to your apartment to eat dried fruit."

He looks at me quizzically and I say, "You know dates are like raisins? Anyway, bad pun. Is it anyone I know?"

"No, Lia. She isn't." He leans forward and says quietly, "If making up with Jason is what makes you happy, so be it. I wish you well."

"That doesn't sound sincere."

"It is. I loved your grandmother, and contrary to what you now seem to believe, I did not set out to fall for you. I was only looking out for you. But even out of respect for Allegra's memory, I am not getting my heart broken chasing someone who keeps getting lost."

My eyes feel wet and I reach up to touch a tear escaping onto my cheek. What the hell? I didn't even cry when Jason and I made up. Or fought.

He leans back in and says, "And I'm not referring to your poor sense of direction on a bike."

He walks away and I have nothing to say. What could I possibly say to that? He didn't set out to *fall for me*?

And why do I feel seething anger building when I think of him on a date?

I swipe at my eyes, which are luckily already squinty and sweat-covered from the sun and the water.

I don't think anyone saw that exchange. Most of the residents have headed home, or they're helping clean the clubhouse and put away the party paraphernalia.

My dad is helping dismantle the pool and that's a sight. He's not the handiest guy and Tucker is keeping a check on his patience, watching my dad smile through the annoying process.

Mom walks over to me and gives me a hug. "Now aren't you glad you got out of bed today?"

We laugh and I assure her that I enjoyed the day, which was her goal.

"Now if I can get your father back to the house so he stops impeding the cleanup process. Look at him. He's hopeless." We both watch my father and laugh.

"Come on Paul, or that old man will be complaining again about people coming in too late and disturbing his sleep."

Mom turns to me and says, "I swear, your grandmother's neighbor is a character. He must go to bed at eight o'clock. I don't know how long he's been here. Maybe he's on British time."

"British time?"

CHAPTER NINETEEN

I forgot what a slob Jason can be at times. His personal façade of perfection is a good cover for his messy nature at home. I was forever cleaning up after him. I'll have to talk to him about this before he moves into my new place.

I'm standing on the front porch of Granana's house, wrangling several bags of trash, which I have assured my father I can handle on my own.

I think my mother was eager to get me out of there, even though my clueless father was jabbering away about how happy everyone was at the party, and how fulfilled he felt helping with the cleanup.

As much as it grosses me out to think of it, I think his happiness is about to increase now that everyone has vacated Granana's house.

The soda cans and beer bottles jangle against my leg, while the lovely scent of jalapeno dip and cigarette ashes waft up through the top of the bags where I did a poor tying job, in an effort to get the hell out of there.

Yes, I am eager to ditch this trash into the cans on the side of the house, (and find out who was SMOKING in my grandparents' beautiful home), but I am way more anxious to see if I can run into the guy who is on 'British time'.

Luckily, the trash can storage area is on the

side next to his house, another stately Victorian manor.

My mother said his name was Max, while my father was sure it was something more unusual, like Jax.

I think we all know the truth. At least about his name. I am hoping to get the rest of the story out of my Granana's mystery neighbor.

Once I get to the bottom of this, I'll be able to fully focus on my present and future and let Granana's memory rest in peace.

And yes, I know I'm following her meddlesome ways, but she's the one who decided to plan her haunting of my life before she was even dead. And it will be nice to meet a friend of Granana's.

This mission is also a good diversion from imagining Logan on a date. However, I keep telling myself it's excellent news, despite the way it makes my stomach do unpleasant dances.

I take a deep breath, and walk down the porch steps, letting the bags bang against the railing. I wish I had on noisier shoes. It's rather late now, so I'm sure my target is in his sleeping cap and gown.

I don't know why I imagine old British guys dressed like Scrooge in *A Christmas Carol*.

I'm hoping that I'm right about his sexual identity, and he's more likely to be sleeping in silk pajamas and an eye mask.

It's obvious that I've lived a sheltered life. But in my defense, even though our Vermont town had a large homosexual population, I didn't attend any gay sleepovers.

Yes, I am convincing myself that Axe was Granana's cool gay friend, like on *Will & Grace*. Logan basically admitted it before Jason showed up.

Fortunately, the floodlight on the side of the house could light up a football field, and the trash cans are the old heavy metal variety that clank and clang when you barely touch them.

Here goes—sorry old guy, but I'm sure you're retired, and you can take a nap tomorrow.

I embark upon a clanging bang-fest with the trash cans to rival the street performances of the urban youth outside the Richmond Coliseum on concert nights. They do have way more rhythm, but I can ratchet up a solid racket.

It doesn't take more than a second for my mother to appear at the window in her paj...nope, nothing at all.

At least it's not my father, since the master suite has floor to ceiling windows.

I signal to her to go back to...yuck...you know...and she quickly darts away.

I turn around to see that it isn't me she was hiding from, but a grumpy old man with his head sticking out his upstairs window.

I'm glad to see my mother isn't so liberal that she wants to give Axe a peep show. But he's gay so...never mind.

"What is that infernal, bloody racket? Who are you, young lady? I told the grownups last night that you kids were making too much noise!"

"Oh, I'm so sorry, Sir. The lids on these trash cans are so heavy. It's so clumsy of me to make so much noise. I'm Lia DeLuca. Allegra's granddaughter. You met my parents last night."

"What? You're Allegra's granddaughter? And that was little Paul? I didn't put it together. The woman was so eager to get the man in the house, I didn't even hear what they said. And then there were all those other young people—very confusing. And loud."

He disappears back in the house. Is that all he has to say?

I continue to stare at the window when I hear a voice say, "Well, why are you just standing there gaping? Come to the porch."

Behind me is an old man in perfectly normal pajamas, smoking a cigarette, and fiddling with a device in his ear.

"I don't always wear these damn things because I find most of what people say is bloody rubbish anyway." He moves the burning cigarette to his left hand and offers me a firm, bony handshake.

"Well, I can't believe it. You look like her a little, in this light. Come on and tell me about yourself. I'm Axe, by the way. Like the chopping tool...and that ridiculous rubbish the teenage boys spray on themselves."

I follow him to his porch, after turning out the light on the side of Granana's house to give my parents some peace...and privacy.

I laugh at his joke and say, "Axe, I'm so happy to meet you. I understand you were a friend of my grandmother's? I don't understand why I've never heard of you until now. Did you come to the funeral?"

He flicks his ashes into the bushes, which is a fire hazard, but this man hardly looks like a guy who wants safety lectures from someone he views as a child.

His smoke blows into my face and I fight the urge to wave it away. I don't need to breathe. I can breathe later, once I have more information.

He waves the smoke away and tries to blow it

towards the house, despite the wind having other ideas. "I'm sorry. I'm guessing you don't like fags very much."

"Excuse me?" I blink hard. I'm not acting that uncomfortable, am I? "Oh, you mean the *cigarette*."

I read *Bridget Jones's Diary*, the classic British chick lit novel, at my mother's urging, and just now remembered their slang word for cigarette is 'fag'.

I could crawl under the porch and hide or tell him he needs to adjust his hearing aid, but he's laughing so hard he's started coughing.

Now I may have gone from insulting him to killing him. My mother knows CPR, but her mouth is preoccupied right now.

Why do I insist upon conjuring images that make my stomach sicker?

"Are you one of those silly Americans who thinks all British men of style are gay? Too hilarious, my dear."

He sits on his porch rocker with his legs crossed at the knee, grinning and displaying perfect teeth.

Is he not gay? Is he teasing me? All I know is that he was Granana's pal, and Logan's story must indicate that Axe was the reason for the DeLuca's love of the rainbow banner.

"I'm sorry, but here's why I was wondering—"

I am rudely interrupted by another voice—the one only I can hear.

Hopefully.

"NO, NO, NO! It's my job to meddle, not yours, young lady!"

Granana is decked out in a bikini. And no, being a ghost does not restore your body to its earlier glory. I might throw up off the porch rails and douse the burning embers from Axe's cigarette.

Also, I can't believe she picks NOW to show up.

"Don't you have a cabana boy to—"

Before I can figure out how to explain to Axe who I am talking to, I see that he's dropped his cigarette on the porch, and I stomp on it (how has this man not caught on fire?).

But he's not careless this time, he's in shock. "Allegra, is that you?" His eyes are as round as saucers and he's clutching his chest.

Shit, I haven't replaced my phone yet and his head is about to hit...

"Well, now you've done it! I hope you do go to ghost jail."

I'm yelling at no one as I see that Granana has instantly disappeared.

Supposedly, appearing to anyone but me is a huge no, no.

Now I'm positive that the old man spread out on the porch in his flannels, with his hairy legs sticking out and his glasses crushed, is none other than Granana's former lover.

She wouldn't risk Haunting Jail for any other reason.

Before pure panic sets in (I can't find his pulse but I'm not much of a nurse), I luckily (or unluckily) see my undressed parents in the window again.

I'm sure they have their phones handy. Let's hope there's a spare robe or two nearby.

***

"Dad, you guys can go now. You're not wearing any clothes."

My mother ties her bathrobe tighter, and since

it's a silky number, some body parts aren't adequately covered.

My father, on the other hand, seems to have brought his 'summer robe' (AKA way too short to wear in public or in front of your sickened daughter), and lacks control over its tying mechanism.

My parents have always been a little loose with their dress code, especially at home. It seems to be getting worse as they age.

Come to think of it, I don't think my mother was concerned about Axe seeing her in the window. I think Dad was calling her back...ugh...

I push them both towards the door and press their car keys into Dad's hands.

"Please go back to the house. The doctor said Axe is stable and I am not going to leave until he wakes up."

"Well, if you insist."

"Yes, I insist. You have a long drive tomorrow and you were...busy...when you were interrupted."

"Are you sure nothing happened to cause this? It's so odd that he would come down to talk to you after you woke him up. And have you ever taken out trash before? Paul, I told you we should have made her do more chores growing up."

As usual my father doesn't engage in petty arguing. He kisses the top of my mother's head and says, "It's all fine. We're going to leave for home now. We have a stop we'd like to hit on the way. Let us know how Mr. Axe is doing."

Mom sighs at her husband's never-ending optimism and says, "Well who knows, I think all of the houses are haunted anyway. Maybe he saw a ghost. Oh sorry, that was insensitive, with Allegra being...anyway, keep in touch."

I hug and kiss them both goodbye with promises to give them an update.

As they walk out the automatic hospital doors into the parking lot, they garner a few looks from incoming people, but I think the most baffling thing is where the hell are they stopping on the way to Vermont in nothing but their bathrobes?

I turn around and almost bump into Beth Washington. I'm relieved to see a friendly face. I had forgotten she was a nurse at this hospital.

"Slow down, Girlie. I just got here and saw you talking to your parents. Now who is this gentleman you brought in here? Oh, and also, in case you're wondering, there's a nudist colony about an hour outside of town. My bet is that's where your folks are headed. But try not to think about that. It's not good for your brain."

I allow her to lead me back to the waiting area, and I quickly explain the situation.

"Why are you so worried about what your grandmama was up to?" She puts her hand over mine and I squirm.

I know she has a point. I can't tell her that I learned meddling from the best, and she's still around stirring the pot.

"I don't know. I feel like there's something more to this whole thing, and I'd like to know her better. I miss her."

My acting is improving. I should ask Logan if he still has any connections with the theater in town. Shit, now I'm thinking about his date again. Is he home and all tucked in alone? Or did it turn into a late...no, no, no! Focus, Lia.

Beth mistakes my weary expression for grief.

"Of course, you miss her. But she was an old Italian lady, not a wild woman."

I smile and she gives me a hug. She's sweet, but she doesn't have all the facts.

Of course, neither do I.

"Now, since you're the only one here to visit that poor old guy, I am going to let you in to see him. It's after hours, but I can sneak you in. Those wenches working tonight wouldn't dare question me."

I make a mental note not to get on Beth's bad side.

She leads me down the corridor to Axe's room, informing me of his condition on the way.

"He didn't have a heart attack or a stroke or anything. He should stop smoking, but other than that he hit his head pretty good. He needs to wake up every hour, so you can wake him up in (she looks at his chart) thirty minutes. I'll tell the nurses I'm taking care of him, and you let me know when you leave."

I nod in agreement, and she slowly opens the door and whispers, "Also you are not a family member, so I told you nothing and was never here."

The door slams and I'm in the room by myself. Well, me and my new friend.

And he's awake.

"Lia, come here. I'm so grateful you were with me when I fell. I'm guessing you must have connections at the hospital, since it's after visiting hours."

"Um, yes I do. I can go if you want to rest." I point towards the door as Axe points towards the chair next to his bed.

I dutifully walk over and sit down, placing my purse on the antiseptic hospital linoleum.

Axe smiles at me and I vow to God, or Granana, or whoever can hear my thoughts that I am not going to cross examine this man in the hospital bed.

He has a possible concussion and he saw a ghost. I don't know if he remembers that or thought it was real, but either way I am keeping my big fat mouth shut and letting someone else talk for once.

And if one of those nurse wenches comes in here and interrupts any voluntary information Axe decides to spill, I will scream!

"You're a curious little bird with big questions. I can see that. And meeting you knocked me off kilter. If you can believe it, I thought I saw your grandmother. In the flesh. In a *bikini* no less."

"Wow, that's something. I guess that explains why you passed out. Do I look that much like her?"

I've seen photos of my grandmother, but few when she was my age. That would have been in the fifties.

"You do resemble her quite a bit. I think I know why you came to see me."

"I didn't. You just heard the trash cans and..."

He purses his thin lips and raises a surprisingly manicured white eyebrow. "Let's cut the crap, little bird. Somehow you heard about me and wanted to find out how I knew your grandmother, and if there is some sordid tale she took to the grave."

"Is that bad? I feel guilty for being so eager to know, when you say it that way."

"No, I think it's perfectly natural. You and Allegra were close. I told her for years, especially once you were grown, and after your grandfather died, that she should tell you the story herself. Before it was too late. But she was a bloody stubborn old bird."

I nod my head in agreement and tighten my lips shut.

"Lia, what I'm about to tell you isn't probably nearly as shocking as your mind is imagining, and it's technically not my story to tell. However, your grandfather is gone and so is Allegra. I truly believe that his desire to keep everything secret no longer matters to him. He's in a better place with his true love for all eternity."

"I always thought my grandparents weren't close. At least not romantically. And where do you fit in all of this?"

"Well you see, your grandfather's true love isn't your grandmother. He did love her, but not in the way that can sustain married life."

"So, Grandpa was the one who had an affair?"

"Yes...and no. I don't know why I'm talking to you like you're seven years old. Forgive me, I never had any children, and you're a grown woman."

"Sooo...I don't get it. Can you spell it—"

"Your *grandfather* was gay."

I can feel my face contort into a screwed-up...oh my God...*what* did he just say?

"What? I thought *you* were gay. Or you and my grandmother were having the affair. There is no way on earth my grandfather was gay."

"He was gay. I promise you. He was in love with Arthur Franklin."

"Was he related to Ed Franklin, the lawyer?"

"Arthur was his uncle. He and Ed's father ran the law firm together, until they passed it to Ed. I assure you, Arthur and Joseph were lovers for many years."

"Why didn't Granana leave him? Did she

know?"

"Oh, she knew after a while. Not long before I came to town. In the old days, the theater downtown wasn't a Shakespearean playhouse. They did musicals and booked live touring musical acts. I was in the music production business in London. I came here with an act I was working with and decided to stay awhile. I was quite nomadic in my younger years. I only bought that house after Joseph died three years ago."

"Right, I remember a family with kids lived there, and then I guess I never noticed that they moved. How old were you? You seem a lot younger than my grandparents."

"It was fifty years ago. I was only twenty-five. Your Granana was forty and Joseph was forty-five. He didn't want Allegra to divorce him. It was 1967 in a small southern town. He was afraid it would destroy his place in the community, and the booming business he worked so hard to create."

"So, what are you saying?"

"I'm saying in the plainest English that I was in a relationship with Allegra from that time until her death. I didn't want to settle down and have a family. It was perfect for both of us. She and Joseph decided to remain married and share their home, business, and family, and lead private, separate love lives."

"This is insane! Are you sure they didn't say you suffered brain damage tonight?"

"I assure you it's all true. We had wonderful times and I don't think any of us regretted it. I know it's hard for a young person like you to understand."

"But times *did* change. Wasn't there ever a time

that Grandpa could have...? I guess not. He was too old-fashioned and proud. They attended church every Sunday."

"Right. It's okay, though. Everyone was happy. I don't think Joseph will beat me up too badly if he finds out I told you. He's sipping cocktails, watching old musicals and flying around with Arthur on rainbows, I'm sure of it. And one day I'll join Allegra, but I'm not in a big rush, and I'm sure she's finding plenty to keep her occupied."

Yes, cabana boys and interfering in my life.

"You don't think you actually saw her on the porch, right?"

"Oh no, of course not. Between you and me, it could also have been something I smoked earlier." He laughs and reaches for my hand. "You do look like her. I would like us to become friends, Lia. If you'll have me. We *are* sort of related."

"Sure, I'd like that. You should rest now. When you get out of here, we'll talk more."

"Excellent plan. And Lia, don't be too hard on your grandparents, especially Joseph. You have to respect their decisions, as I'm sure they always respected yours."

I stifle a big laugh (my decisions are thwarted at every turn) and say, "It's a lot to take in, but I can't thank you enough for giving me the missing puzzle pieces."

"Yes, now Allegra, Joseph, and Arthur can rest in peace, and you can go back to your life, little bird."

Hear that, Granana? It's time to rest in peace.

I stand up but then sit back down. "I'm a little tired. If you don't mind, I'll rest here awhile as you go to sleep. I want to make sure you're okay before

I head out. And I'll tell Beth it's her turn to watch you when I go."

"Okay, if you'd like to stay a bit, I'd like the company. Just remember, your grandparents, me, Arthur—we were all only human. People are people."

He closes his eyes and I rub my hands over my greasy face to try to wake up. I wish I could take my makeup off...wait...what the...?

People are people? He's British. In the music business. Is he the one who played the New Wave music when I was a little girl?

No, he said he had never met me. But maybe Granana allowed it before she thought I would be old enough to remember.

And how did they hide all of this from my father?

Despite the crazy story I just heard, there is something even weirder happening. Or not happening.

The whole time Axe was telling his story, I was expecting Granana to appear. She was awfully concerned with stopping our earlier conversation.

Where are you, Granana? I hope she's not in big trouble for appearing to Axe.

I *do* want her to stop meddling, but I don't even want to think about what Haunting Jail looks like.

CHAPTER TWENTY

I wake up to a poke in my arm. "Ow!"
An annoyed Nurse Beth Washington greets my sleep-crusted eyeballs.
"It's a good thing I came in here before I was scheduled to leave, Sleeping Beauty. Some nurse you are. How many times did you wake the patient?"
I rub my eyes and smear what's left of my makeup. "I'm sorry. I fell asleep."
"No shit. Now get your pretty little ass out of here before anyone important sees you. Luckily Mr. Axton is still alive."
Mr. Axton. That makes sense.
I thank Beth and she gives me one more maternal hug, so I know she's all about tough love and she's not mad at me.
I stumble out into the light of day and shield my eyes from the blinding sun rays. In my car, I grab my sunglasses, which are scratched. And my windshield is filthy.
I need to work on my self-care.
As soon as I start the car, my favorite Depeche Mode song, "People are People", kicks on, and I am drawn back into Axe's story.
I wish Granana would show up, so I know she's all right. Unless she was waiting for me to leave so she can yell at Axe for spilling the story.

I would hope she loved him enough to let him live a little bit longer. She can always nag him for all eternity once he lives out the rest of his natural lifespan.

Also, didn't she realize that meddling in my life after her death would cause me to find out all her secrets?

I can't wait to get home, have a long shower, and sleep a little more.

Oh crap, what's that noise? And that smell? Son of a bitch!

My stupid car has decided to choke and die on a country road. I think it might be the same one where Rocky Raccoon ran off with my phone. They honestly all look the same. If I didn't have a GPS, I'd drive into a lake or off the side of a mountain in this part of the state.

I lay my head on the steering wheel. There is something more pressing I have to do than shower, sleep, or worry about Logan's date or Granana's double life. The guy at the Verizon store is going to love seeing me again.

If it's the same area I was stranded in last time, then a short walk through the woods leads to Tonic. And Logan.

Wait, bars aren't open this early in the morning. Is there a donut shop or a gas station on that street? Coffee shop?

I glance over at the thick woods, already heating up in the morning sun. There are spiders and ticks aplenty in there.

If I had listened to Jason and gotten a AAA membership, I could call a friendly tow truck guy for free. Oh wait, no I can't.

How did people live before cell phones?

I'm sure someone will come along, and it's not like it's unsafe to sit in the car, and I don't have any wounds like the last time I was stuck on the side of the road.

About twenty minutes later I am hit with the desperate need to pee, and two cars have whizzed by me. I thought country people were friendlier and more helpful.

Applebarrow is proving to be a contradiction to that stereotype.

I get out of the car and survey the woods again. I have only peed outdoors once, and it was in high school after attending one of my rare outdoor drinking parties.

I was sick for days from the booze, and I scratched my butt on a sharp rock when I lost my balance while crouching.

"Don't tell me you lost another cell phone?"

An all-too-familiar male voice startles me, and I think a wee bit of...well 'wee'... has escaped my body.

Great. Now Logan is here to see me looking like an extra from the Walking Dead, and I peed my pants.

"Oh my God, you scared me." I wobble on the way back to the road and almost twist my stupid ankle in these flip flops. They are an outdoor version of slippers.

"Sorry, I saw you standing there looking at the scene of the last...incident. Are you okay?"

"Yeah, my car died. Are you stalking me?" I mean this jokingly, but it comes out a little sharper than intended.

"Yeah, I'm up at the crack of dawn to stalk you.

If you must know, I am on my way home, and apparently you are too?"

"I was at the hospital. It's a long story. Can I use your phone?"

A few minutes later we are sitting in Logan's truck with the air conditioning running, waiting for Dawson. He said he'd come take a look at my car and get me a good deal on a tow if I needed one.

"I think you're the only person in this county who stops for women in distress."

"Hmm...could be. Good thing you have me. You're in distress a lot."

I tell him why I was at the hospital. Well, not the part about Granana almost killing her former lover.

He smiles and says, "So you met Axe, huh?"

Of course, Logan knows their whole history, which I disclose once he searches my face and says, "He told you, didn't he?"

I *knew* Logan was holding something back.

"I think I may be the only other person who knows. Other than Ed Franklin. But I didn't find out until after my incident with the law. Once your grandparents helped me, they brought me into their confidence."

"I still can't believe my grandfather was gay. I never would have guessed it in a million years. I would have pegged you as gay sooner."

Logan's eyes widen and I immediately add, "But I mean that in a good way. Meaning you are *so* not gay, but I would still think of you that way before my grandfather. He was quite manly."

"Okay, I'll take that as a compliment."

"I'm sorry I'm keeping you from getting *home*, you said?"

"It's okay. I don't work tonight. My assistant manager is on."

I look at my fingernails and then out the window. Don't do it, Lia. Mind your own business.

Logan says, "Hello...is there a reason you went mute?" He's staring at the back of my head. I can feel it.

"I was wondering if you were out all night? Or slept at the bar? After your date?"

Realization dawns on his face and he sighs. "I see. You're wondering if I spent a first date having a wild time in my secret sex lair."

"It's none of my business."

Why doesn't that stop me?

Just as Logan starts to speak, we are jolted out of our moment by a hard knock on the driver's side window.

Logan powers the window down and Dawson says, "Hey, kids. What's shakin'?"

We get out of the truck, and for once I'm grateful for the interruption. I should not question Logan about anything and be grateful that he's moving on. If he gets into a solid relationship, he'll forget about his silly crush on me, and maybe one day we can all double date.

Okay, that's a bit much, but it would be nice to kill some of the awkwardness.

We are both distracted by Dawson's non-stop yammering as he checks out my broken down, piece of junk car.

"So, me and Tuck decided on the August resident event. Are you ready?"

Oh boy, Nascar here we come!

"Sure. I can't wait to hear." I glance at Logan and he's trying not to smirk.

"At first we were set on the Monster Truck show. But then we said no, people will be whining. 'Oh, my ears hurt! I can't take these fumes!"

I nod my head. "Very true." Especially Olivia.

"So, we nixed that idea, and bought our own tickets, because we don't miss the Monster Truck show. Then we thought about a nice hike, because me and Emma have been hittin' the trails lately."

Logan laughs and says, "But then you figured the same whiners would say, 'Dawson, you bastard, my feet hurt, and bugs are attacking me.' Right?"

Dawson high fives Logan and says, "You bet, Buddy. So, then we got to thinkin' and decided on a road trip."

Oh, that could be bad.

"Flying Squirrels baseball in Richmond. A road trip to the big city. Nice, right?"

Logan agrees that it's a great idea, and I do too. Some people may not like it, but then they can stay home. Yes, I'm talking about you, Olivia! Nobody wants a library tour or an Elizabethan tea time.

"Now as for your vehicle here, it's toast. So, I'm gonna call my cousin, Zeke. He has a used car lot and—"

Logan interrupts. "Thanks, man, but I'm sure Lia would like to look at new cars."

Why do all men think you must buy a new car?

"No, that sounds fine. I don't need a fancy car, and when I get my full inheritance maybe I'll want a Lamborghini. So, I need something to hold me over until then."

They both laugh at the idea of me zipping around in a flashy sports car and Dawson calls Zeke.

"Okay, you're all set. Logan, can you drop her off there? It's only about a mile east of here. I gotta get back to the shop. My brother's gonna rip me a new one if I don't help him with this transmission job."

Logan looks at me tentatively and when I nod, he says, "Sure, I'll take her over there. Thanks for the help."

Dawson eyes my car and says, "You shouldn't leave anything of value in there, you know?"

"Oh, I'm not that worried. If I keep the doors closed, the raccoons can't get in."

"Well, my tow guy might not be able to fit you in for a while. He likes to have a long breakfast at the diner. Let's just grab your valuables."

Before I can stop him, he's ass up in the car, grabbing my scratched shitty sunglasses and a pile of old CDs.

"Here you go. You don't want to leave these in there. They might melt. Hey, who's Depechee Modee?"

His mispronunciation makes me laugh. "It's Depeche Mode. They were a popular eighties New Wave group."

Dawson's eyes light up with recognition. "New Wave? You mean like beach music? My mama dances to those tunes down at the shore every year at that festival they have down there. This is probably a little more modern, though."

He hands me my assorted possessions and salutes us as he gets back in his truck.

"Later guys. Zeke will take care of you. Tell him if he doesn't, I know where all the bodies are hidden."

Since he's laughing, I am going to assume

that's another one of Dawson's favorite sayings, and not an indication that the guy I'm about to buy a serviceable used car from is a murderer.

"Wow, he is clueless." I smile at Logan and he winces a little.

"Well, yes and no."

We walk back to his truck and I say, "I'm sure you know that New Wave isn't beach music."

Logan closes his door and clips his seatbelt in place. "Yes, I do. However, Dawson isn't an idiot."

"I didn't say he was an...okay, I guess I did. That wasn't nice."

"He has different knowledge. He didn't say you were an idiot for not knowing what was wrong with your car, right?"

He steers the truck down the road, and I get quiet, appropriately chastened. Someone is suddenly irritable.

I blurt out, "I think we're both grumpy from lack of sleep."

No matter how stupid I know it is, I can't help goading him into returning to our previous conversation about his activities last night.

"Lia, I slept just fine last night. And that's all I am saying on this topic. Okay?"

"Fine, drop me off at the car lot and I'll be out of your hair today."

"Um...no. I am not letting you pick a used car by yourself. I don't care how much Dawson threatens this Zeke guy—I am not interested in rescuing you from the side of the road anymore this summer."

I can't argue with that logic.

***

"I guess you must be looking forward to seeing Jason tonight."

I give Logan the side eye as we drive to Richmond for the Flying Squirrels minor league baseball game.

I was hoping Dawson and Tucker had chosen a weekend game, but they wanted to do a weekday event because they're having a sack race contest at the seventh inning stretch. The prize is free tickets to some country music festival.

It's almost worth going just to see the Swanson brothers falling out of pillowcases and pumping their fists if they win. Apparently, they've been 'practicing'.

"Yes, I am looking forward to it, as a matter of fact. But since he's come to Applebarrow every weekend since the Fourth of July, it's not like I haven't seen him."

Logan shifts in his seat and says, "Okay, I was making conversation. You don't have to get all defensive."

It's been this way ever since the Jeep buying incident, after Logan found me stranded on the side of the road with my deceased car.

Yes, I bought a Jeep. Jason still doesn't know.

That's how much he wants to drive around in his BMW. He's visited every weekend and still does not know that I have a new vehicle. I'm waiting for him to notice, but I'm in no hurry to hear a lecture about safety and rednecks, and him making the connection to my unfortunate off-road mud experience with Logan.

Fred leans forward and interjects, "Now kids, don't bicker. You'd think you two were an old married couple. I mean...well...you know what I mean.

I know that I sure wish Martha could come, but her sciatica is acting up, and she said she can't sit her ass on those hard seats for hours."

Fred smiles and looks dreamily out the window. I guess he's thinking about Martha's ass, which is fine. Good for him. I was so pleased that he *did* end up making a love connection from the informal dating game I helped him set up at the Fourth of July party.

Martha was the clear winner, and I haven't seen Fred smile this much since I met him.

Logan, on the other hand, goes back and forth from being super sweet and helpful, to being pissy and sarcastic. It's like he has his period *all the time.*

All of the Pentagon Place gang is on the way to the game—even those who have to work early tomorrow. They're all such good sports at every event.

I paid for the tickets with petty cash from the apartment fund. They're super cheap, and that's all it took to bribe the early risers into getting a little less sleep tonight.

I also think they expect free hotdogs, but that's easy, too.

Fred is the only one riding with us. The other cars filled up quickly and I think he wanted to save a space for Martha, in case her butt was back in working order in time to attend.

I increase my music's volume to signify the end of the conversation for now. Fred is lost in dreamland, and Logan is scowling and looking out the window.

I don't get it. I know he said he was developing feelings for me, but he barely knows me. And he's obviously been dating some mystery woman for weeks now. He's hardly ever home, and I've started to notice how frequently his parking space is empty early in the morning.

If he's moved on, he could be a little nicer.

The day of my car's death, Logan accompanied me to Zeke's car lot to help me pick out a new ride and provide a buffer against the possibility of me being cheated.

I took offense at first, but I had to admit Logan was right. I had been driving the first car I had ever owned for a long time. My dad bought it for me when I was sixteen.

I have never had much interest in cars and have never even accompanied Jason when he's bought a new one every two years.

Zeke was a good guy and I don't think he had any intentions of cheating me. He showed me a bunch of cars like the one I had owned—a black Nissan Sentra.

But then I saw it. A yellow Jeep. 2015. Barely driven. It looked so cheerful and sunny sitting there in a sea of black, grey and white.

Logan tried to steer me back to something more practical, but for some reason I was drawn to this rough riding, rugged vehicle. It screamed 'new life in the country', but it's not like I was planning on taking it in the woods and crawling around in the mud again.

Although if I'm being honest, that was kind of fun.

However, I did not want Logan to know I had any fond memories of our escapade and didn't want to encourage him by being the least bit flirtatious.

I am not one to self-sabotage. It's one of my father's 'Happiness Tenets'—be your own best friend.

Well, usually I'm that way. Or I used to be?

We took the Jeep for a test drive and I was hooked. I knew Jason would have something to say, but I didn't care, and assumed he wouldn't even notice. I was right.

He is incredibly preoccupied at the moment, but at least he's working hard on *our* stuff now, and not as much on his dying company's last projects.

He assured me that Elevation is going under, and that Amy doesn't know yet. I apologized for saying something to her and promised to let it go.

Really, what do I care if Amy is informed? She's never been all that friendly towards me, and I still think she has a thing for Jason, even though I am now sure of his loyalty.

Seriously, I am sure.

Mostly sure.

No, I'm sure.

So, I bought the Jeep and I cruised off into the sunset with my new, fun ride. By the time we finished the transaction (people don't move quickly in Applebarrow), it was well past lunch and moving into 'blue plate special' dinner time in these parts.

My stomach was rumbling, and Logan joked that he was going to chew off his own arm if he didn't eat soon. The candy bars from the dealership vending machines were expired, so we were desperate.

It seemed silly not to grab something to eat with Logan. We had spent the whole day together and it wasn't like it was a date, or anything even resembling a date.

I wanted to buy him a meal to thank him for helping me. I kept telling myself that it was perfectly fine, and Jason wouldn't be jealous.

Logan even has a new girlfriend, although that situation is still shrouded in mystery.

We ended up at the only quaint Italian restaurant in Applebarrow. We were the first ones seated for dinner, and on a week night it wasn't hopping. A lot of the restaurants do most of their business on the weekends when the tourists are here.

The locals are happy with frozen lasagna, as evidenced by the success of my trickery.

Thinking about that night made me think of Granana. I still hadn't heard from her and it was concerning. Even now on the way to the game, I have not heard one peep from her.

I'm scared that the price of gaining information from Axe has cost Granana her ability to visit me, and maybe even her heavenly freedom.

I can't share any of this with the occupants of the Jeep, so I go back to my memory of dinner with Logan.

It felt intimate. Close. Dark. Ugh.

He told me about his childhood. He was raised by a single mother, just like Jason. And instead of a brother who still lives at home and hasn't amounted to much, he has a sister in the same situation.

It's like the Mackintosh family is the city version of the Woodcocks.

I thought of how mean Jason is to his mother and brother, and how Logan apparently still loves his family. He said he frequently visits them in their rundown Chicago neighborhood.

It's hard to know what's true, and maybe Logan isn't the perfect son and brother he claims to be, and I shouldn't be comparing the two men's situations.

It's just that I've always been disappointed in Jason's treatment of his family, but I've made excuses for him because of them as well.

He blames them for any bad behavior he ever displays. 'Lia, it's the way I was raised. I didn't have a family like yours...' Blah, blah, blah.

But who am I to judge? I do have a stable family, and everyone is affected differently by their environment.

Jason loves me and he's committed to our future. We were strolling in downtown Applebarrow last weekend and he asked me to look in a jewelry shop window full of diamond engagement rings and tell him which ones I liked.

And he's been so wonderful about helping Molly. He's hired a consultant (with money from my estate, of course) to help get that business off the ground, and to meet with Sassy's organic dog food friend to get that endeavor in motion.

We also talked about what Olivia said about moving to Amsterdam, and it sounds awesome. Jason said he was sorry he hadn't told me first, but he was working on a deal to buy a property there and wasn't sure if it would work out.

As I suspected, he asked Olivia not to say anything because he wanted to surprise me, and she couldn't keep her big yap shut.

I can easily learn Dutch, and once I'm in Europe I can travel anywhere on the continent with ease.

Jason is right—I will embrace the money we have coming our way and enjoy our new life.

I can picture us biking in the cycling-friendly city and running a little hotel. I may even buy wooden clogs and run through the tulips to a windmill, and Instagram the moment.

And since I've been busy creating my after-school language program, I've gotten Jason in direct contact with Mr. Franklin, and he has my full authority to speak to him regarding my inheritance as it relates to our future business plans. Ed has the authority in the Will to release funds for the business assets right away. At least Granana didn't intend to hold the whole community hostage, waiting for me and Logan to fall in love.

I haven't approached Ed about what Axe told me, but it's on my to-do list. It's amazing how busy I am without a job.

While I'm daydreaming, I almost miss the exit.

"You almost missed the exit." Logan states the obvious and holds onto the passenger's door handle, as if my sharp turn was going to send him careening into my lap or out the window.

Hmm...no, those are both bad images.

I should have let Fred sit up front, but he insisted that Logan, with his long legs, should have the best seat.

We navigate to The Diamond and park in the sparsely populated lot. I see most of our friends are already here, stretching their legs and waiting for the rest of the residents.

I spot Jason talking to Dawson, and Amy is on her phone. I didn't know she was coming, but I did tell Jason I was getting extra tickets in case he wanted to bring a friend.

I wrongly assumed it would be Zach or Richard.

But no matter, I'm not worried about the blond. She's got her own problems, whether she knows about them or not, and there's no reason why I can't be pleasant, and show Jason that I'm not jealous. After all, I want the same from him with my friends.

As Jason spots us and starts to walk over, I see a flash of movement in my (supposedly) empty Jeep and a voice calling, "Don't you go in that stadium yet, young lady. I have exactly five minutes of parole to tell you what's going down."

Great, now she sounds like a ghostly gang member.

CHAPTER TWENTY-ONE

My nerves are shot.

It's Labor Day and I'm up early, watching the guys of Pentagon Place set up for yet another inflatable pool barbecue.

I thought it was a little overdone, but Emma insisted she wanted her event to be outside. She's doing a craft party/art show. There are some interactive stations set up, as well as merchandise from her store, and some of her own creations.

Molly has a table set up with her dolls, and we have invited more people from everyone's lives outside of the neighborhood. I don't see how the pool is going to hold up, but I'll let someone else worry about it.

Jason is sound asleep upstairs and I know he'll stay there awhile.

Granana hasn't been back since the night of the baseball game, which was a few weeks ago. She scared the crap out of me, and I had to pretend my phone was ringing in order to get in the Jeep and make believe I was on a call, so no one thought I was talking to myself again.

I am getting so much trickier since a ghost entered my life.

Fortunately, I had taken the time to get a new phone right after I bought my Jeep. Talking into my hairbrush wasn't going to fool anyone.

I told Logan and Fred to go without me and waved to Jason, pointing at my phone. He grimaced but then blew a kiss.

I got back in my Jeep and worked hard to talk into the phone and not look at my grandmother, who was dressed in a cheerleader's uniform, circa 1945.

"Isn't this a cute outfit for a prison uniform? And so fitting since you're going to a sporting event, but I can't stay."

I spoke into my phone with my eyes straight in front of me. Luckily the crowd had moved into the stadium, and I had my own ticket, so it's not like they needed to wait for me.

I'm sure everyone was hot and complaining that they needed a beer, a hotdog, etc.

Granana explained that she was in big trouble for appearing to Axe, but that her punishment was time away from the living world and her sentence is spent in a white void. She was also required to wear the uniform with a big red BG on the top, which stands for 'Bad Ghost'. She said it's boring in the void, but not painful.

Sometimes I think she's making all this up to mess with me, because I would have no idea if she was telling the truth or not.

She said she only had a few minutes and then she had to get back, but that soon she would have served her whole sentence and she'd be back on a regular basis to help me 'figure out this messy love triangle'.

I told her there was no love triangle, and that Jason and I were fine, and we had worked everything out. *And* Logan had found a girlfriend, so there was nothing more to that story.

She said I was delusional and that she would be back to help me.

As soon as I protested and started to question her about everything Axe had told me, she said, "That man has a big mouth! But I did dearly love him. In a way, I'm glad he told you, but we need to talk more when I get back. Just don't make any rash decisions until I can talk some sense into you. I was told by a fellow spirit that you were seen looking at engagement rings."

What the hell? How many spooks are watching me?

I didn't have time to ask, and I frankly didn't care at the time. I had found out everything I needed to know and solved all the mysteries. It doesn't matter what Granana adds. It's done.

As for Jason, I don't think Donna is perfect in her psychic skills, and Granana had another agenda entirely.

Jason *had* been hiding information from me about work, and his plans for our future, but I can forgive him for that.

I was no longer worried about Amy. It's possible she *was* an issue at one time, and she isn't anymore. I was thinking he shut her down and it was over before it began.

It's not like I'm telling Jason that Logan has (had) a crush on me, so if Amy was pursuing him, he wouldn't tell me, either. I was sure that I would know if he was cheating, and his odd behavior was easily explained by his work troubles.

Logan continues to be adversarial towards Jason, making snarky comments. He's also still quite bipolar in his dealings with me. Some days he's distant and weird, and other days he's sweet and kind.

Last week, Axe and I had a nice lunch at Tonic, and Logan came out and chatted with us. We laughed and they told me some stories about the days when my grandparents were alive.

Apparently Granana thought it was hysterical that Axe was nicknamed for the middle school boys' favorite personal care brand, even though he earned that moniker decades before kids were walking around wearing cheap pheromones to attract girls and repel insects.

It was fun to hear them reminisce about the theater, and I wished I had been included in this hidden part of their lives.

I still haven't talked to my parents about Axe's revelations, but they are here for the week, and I think it's time to let them know and hopefully introduce them to Axe as…who he really is.

It was a pleasant afternoon, but after Logan returned to work and left us alone, Axe started questioning me about my love life.

"I'm just an old man who lived his life in an unconventional way, but I'm not dead yet. If *I* felt the electricity between you and Logan, I know *you* feel it, too."

I said, "No, you're mistaken. We do get along, but I swear, it's not what you think."

He leaned forward and said, "His eyes don't leave you for one second. And you put a lot of effort into avoiding them."

I sighed and began to protest, and he said, "I will bet you a thousand dollars that if you glance over there, he's looking at you."

I shook my head and quickly turned around to prove him wrong, and my eyes locked with Logan's immediately.

Flustered, I made an excuse to leave Tonic as soon as I could, and I've tried to avoid Logan lately.

Just because we have an attraction doesn't mean we need to act on it. I promptly called Jason that night for a status update on our plans, and I'm going to talk to him again later today about the timeline for our move.

He's been handling the details, and I want to be out of the country by New Year's. Everyone here is doing great, except me and Logan, and we'll both be better off with an ocean, and thousands of miles, between us.

I'm hoping the Labor Day party will be uneventful, and I put on my more modest polka-dot, high-waisted bikini. No need to be flaunting my goods.

I'm glad there'll be a larger crowd today, and I'm hoping Logan invited some of *his* other friends to keep him occupied.

What I mean is that I hope he brought his new girlfriend so I can get a look at her. I can't help being curious.

I pull my sundress over my head and slip on my sparkly flip flops, the ones Sassy made me buy at a boutique in town to replace my boring black ones.

Jason is still out cold in bed, and that's fine with me. The party is right outside my door and he can easily join us when he's ready. He obviously needs his rest.

As I step outside, I see the party is already in full swing.

Several groups of people are looking at Emma's displays and Molly's dolls. Logan is explaining something to Molly's girls, and they're looking at him as if he invented art. I'm sure they have adolescent crushes on him.

I sigh at the irony of my own crush, but I am determined to fight it. Jason will be down soon, and he will be my focus.

I check the inside of the clubhouse and everything is beautifully laid out. The food is surprisingly healthy.

Dawson comes up behind me and says, "Hey, Lia. Emma wanted the food to be healthy, so we went with vegetables and fruits, and she's got us grillin' veggie and turkey burgers."

"Oh, that's nice, I guess. I'm sure some people are going to be missing the more traditional cookout food."

"We've got that covered. Come 'ere."

I follow him behind the clubhouse, and there's a secret grill and table with potato salad, cole slaw, pasta salad, and all the less healthy dishes most of our residents and friends would expect at their end of summer blowout.

"Stan and Ken are out here mannin' the grill, and Molly is keepin' the fixin's stocked, here on the table. She's also got some apple and pecan pies, and cookies for later."

I survey the setup and shield my eyes from the sun. Crap, I left my sunglasses in the apartment. "Hey guys, isn't Emma going to be upset when she discovers your covert operation?"

I'm surprised Dawson would risk being involved, since he seems so devoted to Emma and her fitness plan.

Dawson says, "Oh hell no, I don't know anything about this, and if anyone outs me, they're not gettin' any more work done at my shop. They'll have to go to the next town over and risk those nitwit Thompson brothers dropping gumdrops in their carburetors."

There's a story there, but with Dawson there always is, and I am more concerned about Emma's reaction when she sees people shoving ribs and slaw down their throats, while she's eating hummus and celery.

Ken laughs and says, "Listen, I will take the full heat. I am not eatin' any of that health crap when my wife makes the best biscuits in town."

It's a good thing his wife can use a defibrillator.

He holds up a fat cheeseburger and adds, "And not only that, Emma does not need to lose weight. A little meat on a woman is a good thing."

He elbows Dawson in the ribs, and he agrees but runs off to make sure Emma is still doing face painting.

I ask, "How does she not smell this? Jason will probably smell it in my apartment and wake up drooling."

Stan nods and says, "Well, I think those art supplies and face paints are pretty strong, and she's clear over on the other side of the yard. In fact, if you'd go and get on line for your face painting, we'll have enough time to finish this batch of chicken wings. Don't worry—we'll save you some."

I wrinkle my nose and say, "Fine, but first I'm going to find Sassy. You better hope *she* keeps your secret—that lady has loose lips."

Stan says, "Oh, I'm not worried about that. That woman is putty in my hands."

I'm a little tired of hearing the 'putty' activities through my walls every time Sassy visits.

When her divorce is final, I'm sure they'll get a

place in town, and then I am renting Stan's place to someone old and quiet.

However, by then I'll be gone, and *my* apartment will be available, too. That's one more thing on my list—find an apartment manager.

I spot Sassy in her big straw hat, talking to the church ladies about Molly's dolls.

"Oh, these are beautiful. My granddaughter would love these. Look at the one with the pretty African robe. Oh, and the little Dutch girl with the wooden shoes."

They pick up the dolls and show each other, as I hear Sassy quoting the prices, and that they should get their originals because soon they will be mass produced.

I know why Granana didn't want the church ladies near her house! She is still hiding Axe from them.

Sassy spots me and says, "Hey, here's a woman who's going to be a little Dutch girl soon. How is Jason's hotel idea coming along? You do know that prostitution and all sorts of debauchery are legal in Amsterdam, right?"

"Yes, Sassy. I don't think that's Jason's reason for wanting to move there."

"No, I'm sure not, but you're such an innocent little thing—I feel the need to warn you about such things. And, make sure you get that pre-nup."

"We aren't married or getting married."

"Oh, *please*. He's going to lock you in before he lets you get away with all that money."

"I'm not getting away, and Jason's not like that."

The sun is hurting my eyes and I glance over to my apartment door. I could text Jason and ask him to bring my sunglasses down.

"You say that now, but you want to cover all your bases. The lawyer will advise you of the same. Oh, and have you seen that lovely young woman painting over there?"

My eyes follow Sassy's head tilt, and I see a young African-American woman with gorgeous skin and her curly hair pulled back into a sloppy, yet perfectly executed ponytail. She's wearing a long white cotton dress, and it's hanging off one shoulder, revealing an intricate floral tattoo.

"Who is she here with?"

Before Sassy can answer, Logan comes up behind the pretty artist and rubs her exposed shoulder.

I quietly say, "So I guess that's his new woman."

"Yep, she's an actress at the theater in town. She's here playing Desdemona in *Othello*."

"I love *Othello*. We should go."

Sassy waves her hand and says, "Really? That's your only reason for wanting to go?"

"Yes, of course."

She doesn't look convinced. "Shakespeare is boring. Why don't you see if you can get Jason to go? Or better yet, *let it go*."

"What do you mean?"

"I think you know."

She strolls off, asking Molly if her girls happen to have the Twister game, and if she and Stan can borrow it.

It seems wrong to borrow a child's game for what I bet will be an X-rated Twister session.

I watch Logan with this woman, while Ken is sneaking Beth behind the clubhouse for their own version of naked Twister—a feast of ribs and biscuits.

Emma is painting faces and Dawson is sitting beside her, chatting with the guests and complementing her work.

Even Fred and Martha are looking cozy on the lounge chairs, sipping their Bloody Marys.

Suddenly I want Jason and I want him now. Plus, I need my sunglasses so if I wake him up, I'll have a good reason.

I could go over and interrupt the happy couple and introduce myself, but I'd rather wait until Logan isn't kissing her neck. Awkward!

I walk past the art booths, smiling at everyone but the new lovers, who don't notice me anyway.

I am off to see if my lazy boyfriend is awake. Plus, I think my sunglasses are in the bedroom.

I quietly open my front door. If I'm going to wake him, I'd rather do it gently.

I tiptoe up the stairs, not detecting any noise along the way. The muted din of the party is faint, but enough to wake someone who didn't overindulge on the margaritas last night.

Jason has been in a celebratory mood again. It was fun for a couple of weekends, and I'm happy that he's been visiting regularly and making lots of progress on our plans. If he works hard, he deserves a little fun time. Right?

I'm sure once we launch our new life together, he isn't going to be stumbling home drunk in Amsterdam, along the banks of the canal.

That reminds me, I need to buy the Rosetta Stone for Dutch, because Jason sure as hell isn't going to speak anything but English. *'Everyone speaks English, Lee'.*

No, they don't.

I admonish myself for negative thoughts about the man I intend to ravish and remember that I am practicing compassion for Jason's transitional place in life (as my parents would say).

He's definitely still in bed, and as I push open the mostly closed bedroom door, he drops his phone off the bed and immediately dives onto the floor to retrieve it.

"Hey."

That's my opening line. Not smooth, but when you've been with someone for five years, it's not necessary to be eloquent. Plus, he probably has a headache and isn't going to be interested in talking, which is fine by me.

I walk over to his side of the bed and sit down. I have to shimmy a bit because he's barely making room for me.

I don't want to kill the mood I'm trying to create with nagging, but we may need to have a talk about the drinking and late nights. He's lying there like an immobile slab, and that's not going to work at all.

I lean down to whisper in his ear. "I know you're not sleeping. I saw you throw your phone on the floor and hurl yourself off the bed." I nip at his ear teasingly, and he jumps up and knocks me on the floor.

"Jesus, Lia. You scared me."

Grateful that my Granana had plush carpet installed in the apartments, I pull myself to standing with my hands on my hips. "What? I know you weren't sleeping. What's the matter with you? Why are you so jumpy?"

Before he can answer, his phone starts bleeping in rapid succession, signifying text messages from someone who is quite insistent, and possibly irate.

We both glare at it and he silences the tone, getting up out of bed, phone in hand.

"Jason?"

"What? I have to go to the bathroom. And you know how you don't like an audience for that, so neither do I."

"You need your phone for that?" I purse my lips, both because he's behaving suspiciously, and the mood is killed, at least for now.

He runs his free hand through his messy bed hair and says, "Why are *you* in a mood? Shouldn't you be outside entertaining?"

He points beyond the bedroom window, and all I can hear is the happy sound of people having fun.

That sound hasn't found its way inside the confines of my apartment since I've moved here. Jason may be in crisis, but he doesn't have to be a total dick about it.

"I hate to be that girl, but who is texting you? Is it Amy?"

I regret the accusation as soon as it leaves my lips.

"You know, I am acquainted with people other than Amy. I never question who's calling you, or who you're spending time with, for that matter. Like Logan, for instance."

"Okay, never mind. This is an excuse to pick on the guy who has done nothing wrong."

"I bet if I look out the window right now, he's waiting for you like a sad puppy dog."

Jason stomps over to the window, cracks the

blinds and says, "Oh, I see the problem. Logan has himself a new friend. Nice, Lia. So, you're taking that out on me."

"What are you talking about? I came up here to spend some time with my boyfriend, who was once again too drunk last night to…well, you know."

I point at Jason's malfunctioning organ and he stomps into the bathroom, still holding his phone, and slams the door.

I am not chasing him. The image of him on the toilet is not appealing, and I'm sure he's already locked the door, like a big baby.

Things were going so well. How did we get back to this bullshit again?

I open my nightstand drawer and root around for my sunglasses, blowing on them and rubbing them on my dress, even though I should use the eyeglass cloth.

I count to ten and walk to the bathroom door, ready to say something to diffuse this tension, so at the very least he will come outside and pretend everything is fine for the sake of appearances.

Instead, I change my mind, and run down the stairs and back outside. I'll have more fun without him.

I head for the secret grill and ask Ken to cook me the most fattening thing he has on offer. He grins and starts slapping more meat on the grill. "That a girl!"

Then I walk back over to the art stations and ask Emma to draw a butterfly on my cheek. I describe the one on Granana's antique letter opener.

I suppose I'm also thinking about flying away from here and all the trouble I've had since I arrived.

But only after I eat my chicken wings.

Who am I kidding? I'm like a butterfly stuck to fly paper.

It's hard to keep still while Emma paints my face, and my eyes keep darting to my front door and over to the grill.

I can't retrieve my greasy, delicious meal until Emma and I part company. I don't want her to be disappointed that few residents are happy with hummus and carrots. I think Olivia is the only one who eats like a bird. Everyone else is sneaking real bird behind the clubhouse, slathered in sauce.

My eyes are also drawn to Logan and his new friend. I can't move my mouth too much to talk, since it will mess up my butterfly, so like a ventriloquist I say, "Hey, do you know anything about Logan's girlfriend? She looks nice."

Emma smiles and says, "Oh, Carla. Yes, I met her. She's sweet. And so beautiful. Isn't she?"

"Hmm..." I can get away with that non-response, since I want Emma's best work on my cheek.

"She's an actress in the theater. They're doing *Othello*. I'd go see her, but I find Shakespeare to be mind-numbing. I can't believe the amount of people that flock here to see it, but the tourists sure give me a lot of business, so go Bill! Right?"

That's the longest string of words I've ever heard Emma speak. She's so happy, and I am suddenly filled with remorse for my chicken order, when I should be supporting Emma's healthy metamorphosis in the solidarity of sisterhood, by eating gross raw vegetables.

She shows me a mirror and I thank her for the adorable, colorful creature she's painted on my face. "That is so cute. Thanks, Emma."

"My pleasure. And it's the symbol of growth and change, so it was a good pick for you."

I smile and let that comment slide. Knowing Emma, she only meant it in a positive way, and she has no idea what I'm facing in the 'growth and change' department.

Stan peeks his head from behind the clubhouse and performs hand signals that either mean my chicken is done, or it's safe to land the plane.

I'm glad to see Arielle behind me, lined up for some face art. While she and Emma begin discussing what image would look good on her face, and not clash with her gigantic chest/neck tattoo, I take the opportunity to sneak off to my secret banquet.

Of course, Jason picks now to emerge into the light, sunglasses on and phone nowhere in sight.

I would love to blow him off, but people are always watching. I don't know why, but I'm treated a bit like a local celebrity here. I do nothing to deserve it, but I guess being the newcomer and an heiress makes me interesting.

Plus, Jason's sparkling personality makes for some good gossip.

No matter how nice he is, or how much he participates in activities with these people, I feel like they are always waiting for us to roll around on the lawn, with him trying to restrain me from kicking him in the balls.

Or that's my repressed fantasy.

I think a good long talk with my mother is in order tonight, after Jason leaves for Richmond, and another super critical work week at his supposedly doomed company.

He walks over to me and puts out his hand. I take it because I can already feel the eyes upon us. He leads me to a couple of lounge chairs by the pool, away from most of the crowd, which is still merrily eating, drinking, and indulging in the arts.

"I'm sorry." He takes off his sunglasses so I can see his eyes. If I didn't know better, I would think he'd been crying. But tequila and tears can both produce red eyes.

"What's going on with you?" I'm not feeling eager to accept his apology until I get a bit more information.

For instance, is he sorry for being a jerk? Hungover? Late to the party? An enormous fucking liar?

He lowers his head and says, "It was my mother texting me."

"Is she okay?"

"Yeah, but you know how I hate it when she starts hammering me to come visit. She knows I'm out here every weekend."

"Oh, well we should go see her. I don't mind coming with you."

And now I'm being nice and supportive again, just like that. Did I overreact before? Or am I a sucker?

But if the texts were suspicious, wouldn't he have turned the sound off right away, before I sat down on the bed?

"I know you don't mind visiting my family, and you're so sweet to try with her. But I need...to get away. I'm hanging on by a thread, Lia—with work and struggling to get things tied up here, so we can move. But I know you're suffering for it, and I'm sorry."

He didn't mention the drinking, but I don't need to rub salt in his wounds. Eventually he will have to get a grip or seek help.

Life is full of problems, but if I say that then he'll remind me how MY life has always been easier than his, and I don't want to get into *another* argument.

He pulls me into a hug and says, "I need to go to Richmond tonight. Well soon, actually."

I pull back and say, "Why, Jason? I wish you would let me in on what's really going on."

"You know what's going on."

"Yes, your company is going out of business. So why is it—"

He leans back and sighs, "Lee, I don't want to burn bridges. Don't you get that? I am not going to abandon a sinking ship, just because my *girlfriend* is about to inherit a boatload of money."

He emphasizes the word 'girlfriend' as if he wants more from this relationship, and I'm the one who's stalling.

I'm not going to propose, so if he wants more, he needs to man up and get moving.

But this is hardly the time for a marriage conversation, and I don't want our semi-public makeup session to unravel into the lawn brawl I described earlier.

"Okay, Jason. You're right." I stand up and take a deep breath. "I know nothing about your business and I'm not being fair. Let's try to have some fun today."

I extend my hand and lead him to the contraband food area.

I do this as a goodwill gesture—Jason normally loves some ribs, but also there's a tiny part of me who hopes the smell of grease cooking will make his hungover stomach unhappy.

I accept his apology, but I'm still not thrilled with this pattern of jerky behavior.

I see my parents happily chatting with my new friends and remember that I have other things to talk about with my loved ones, other than Jason's work problems.

As I watch Jason rip off a big piece of barbecued chicken and lick his lips, it dawns on me.

There is one loved one with whom I have neglected to share my grandparents' secrets. It never even occurred to me, until now, to share the revelations about my family's past with the man I love.

That can't be good.

CHAPTER TWENTY-TWO

Sitting outside Ed Franklin's law office in my new yellow Jeep, I take a few minutes to review my messages.

Ed and I are meeting this morning because I have finally found the courage to approach this rather serious, middle-aged man about his gay uncle and my gay grandfather, and how in some bizarro world (not like Stan's book club genre) this makes us related.

I've been so preoccupied with my own problems, I've almost forgotten that Granana hasn't been able to visit.

That's an insane level of self-absorption when it slips your mind that the ghost who visits you has been AWOL.

Although since I know she's sitting in her blank white void with pom poms, I don't feel too sorry for her. She's not being harmed.

Just bored to death, and since she's already dead, she has time to kill. Maybe she'll contemplate her decision to scare the man she loved most in life half to death.

I could almost excuse her if I thought she was desperate for him to join her in eternity. As twisted as that is, it's still romantic.

But no—she was desperate to keep me from knowing the truth about her life. And Grandpa's.

If I hadn't found out, when Axe and Ed die, no one would know except Logan. And it's not like our paths are going to stay entwined for much longer. I never would have found out.

No, Granana can stew for a while, and I'm sure she'll be back. I doubt they give life sentences in Haunting Jail. In the case of the afterlife, I think that would be called HELL.

I glace around the parking lot and still don't see Ed's car, but I'm early. I was so anxious about this meeting that I couldn't sleep, and I woke up with the birds.

I even applied some makeup, including what Molly told me is a trendy nude lipstick color.

My lips feel weird, but I want to look like a grownup. Therefore, I tapped into the wardrobe Sassy forced me to begin acquiring, and I'm wearing red cotton skinny capris and a white V-neck sweater. I even ditched the flip flops for the wedges.

I don't know why talking about our gay relatives requires dressing up, but I suppose I want to be taken seriously.

I return to my messages and try to get through a string from Beth Washington that came over throughout the night.

I guess the night shift must have been slow. Either that or the other nurses are too scared to challenge her liberal cell phone usage on the job.

I am going with the latter.

Beth is eager to get the Halloween party planned, and she keeps sending me ideas she found on Pinterest. They all look cute, and if she needs any help with crafts, I'm sure Emma and Molly would love to help. I will remind her to ask others if they want to be involved, especially Olivia, who looks for things to bitch about like it's her job.

At the Labor Day party, everyone was so appreciative of Ken and Stan for hooking them up with traditional, unhealthy cookout fare, that several residents came up to me privately and recommended that Ken and Beth be selected to host the next event, which is the resident Halloween party.

We've quickly gotten away from our Thursday night monthly meetings and have moved into scheduling parties and events around holidays, but that feels more natural.

Besides, once I realized Granana's reason for bringing me here has nothing to do with the residents not getting along, it made sense to let them take the lead.

They don't need me at all.

Luckily Stan has already had his chance to plan, so he was not eligible to host Halloween.

I breathed a secret sigh of relief—after that book selection I would be scared to see what he would plan for the spookiest night of the year. We only have one medical professional in attendance at these events, and Beth can't resuscitate multiple people at once.

The Labor Day party ended with a bang. Literally.

The illegal fireworks were brought in and I turned a blind eye. I'm not an RA anymore. These are grown adults, and yes, this is technically my property, or at least my family's, but I didn't have the energy to argue with them after my argument with Jason, and his subsequent early departure.

If people wanted to risk blowing off their fingers, Beth said we needed ice and something to transport the severed digits until she can get them to the hospital. We prepped the triage area in the clubhouse and let them shoot themselves silly. If someone called the cops, I'd be in bed.

When Jason finally packed up and left, we had moved to a place of détente. I forgave him. Well, at least I went through the motions of absolution, even though I don't like the way he's been handling his stress level. I told him that being under stress is not an acceptable excuse to pick fights and brood.

I truly wanted to believe his story. I know his mother does push his buttons, and he's not in a good place right now. I must figure out how to suggest that he go to therapy.

However, after that conversation, I might need therapy.

So, I decided to go with trust and patience, yet again.

That is, until I made a phone call.

The next day I called Jason's mother to invite her and Austin to Thanksgiving dinner.

I already know we're going to host a huge meal at the clubhouse. All the residents and immediate family members, friends, or whoever they normally celebrate with are invited. I wanted to let everyone know we were doing this far in advance so they could make the necessary arrangements.

Jason won't like that I invited them, but I want to help him get past his bad relationship with his family, especially before we leave the country.

Based on new information, it is now *if* we leave the country.

Jason's mom was thrilled to hear from me, and for the first few seconds of the conversation, I felt good—until...

"Oh, I haven't heard from Jason in months. I'm so glad you called. I wish he would keep in touch—you gotta tell me your plans. And how are you doing? I'm so sorry again about your grandma—may she rest in peace."

She's a rapid-fire talker for a southern lady, but she didn't run over the first part so fast that I missed it.

I quickly recovered, although my stomach was sick and I wanted to hang up, call Jason and tell him where he can go—and it's *not* Amsterdam. At least not with me and MY MONEY!

However, I controlled myself, remembering what my mother said. I will get more information by being calm, stop blurting shit out, and questioning everyone like I'm interrogating witnesses to a crime.

Although, it appears there may be a crime. Or at least a huge coverup.

Pearly and I had a nice chat, and I updated her on our plans, and told her how we'd love to see them at Thanksgiving. She was thrilled and that was that.

I was not at all thrilled about anything, but I am seeing this train wreck through until the fiery crash. Jason can squirm like the worm he is!

Who the hell was texting him?

Since that week, he's been back every weekend, and he's been sweet but quiet. He's had a bit too much to drink a couple of times, but just slept late for the most part, and I haven't noticed any new suspicious behavior, or asked any more questions. I still want to know why he lied about talking to his mother, but if I ask, he isn't going to tell me, and I'm sick of going around in a circle.

I did not tell him I invited his family for the holiday, and I think that's reasonable given all he is most likely hiding from me.

I am not going to confront him until the time is right. Suddenly I feel like I have all the time in the world, and I will not act until I can say 'AH HA' and not look silly because I made a false accusation.

No, I am going to collect my facts, and lie in wait like a...

Oh, there's Ed's Lincoln Continental. He's at the light getting ready to turn into the shopping center.

I fix my lipstick in the mirror and shake the thoughts of Jason's assumed betrayal, and mentally prep myself for an awkward conversation with Ed.

However, I have a feeling that Ed Franklin knows a LOT more than I ever imagined, and I'm silly if I think I'm delivering some earth-shattering news.

I'm learning that nobody tells me anything that everyone else doesn't already know.

My phone dings again, and I see it's Jason sending me ideas for our Halloween costumes.

Once again, he's trying to make believe everything is fine by acting like the 'fun guy'.

Well, he can wait a minute for a response. Or many minutes.

I may reply tomorrow.

As I get out of the Jeep, I replay another time we had tense words on one of his more recent visits.

I asked him to go to the *Othello* play with me, and he pulled such a face I couldn't help but get annoyed. I told him that he's always complaining that we never do anything alone when he comes to visit, and we're always surrounded by the residents. I told him this would be something for us to do together.

I didn't mention that no one else likes Shakespeare and he's my last resort. But hey, aren't we supposed to do things we don't love sometimes, *for* the people we love?

I explained that Logan's new girlfriend was in the play, and that Logan would definitely be going.

I know I was resorting to provoking him, but I didn't care. I KNOW he's hiding something, and he has some nerve refusing to see a damn play with me.

I've decided that his betrayal doesn't have to involve a woman, and I am (mostly) over my Amy suspicions. If he had another woman, he wouldn't be here all the time, working diligently on our plans, which involve leaving the country, and any other woman who might exist.

Something isn't adding up, but I sure as hell am not going to get to the bottom of this by nagging and/or interrogating.

I'm thinking it's either gambling or drugs. Tax evasion. Voter fraud.

Okay, the last one makes no sense.

I talked to my mom before they returned to Vermont, after the Labor Day party, and she advised me to 'lay low' and 'pay attention'.

I thought I'd been doing that, but I have a hard time keeping my mouth shut and playing along when I think I'm being deceived.

I do want to be sure before ending a five-year relationship, and I'm not completely clear about my own emotions.

And I'm not only talking about Jason.

And most of all (I hate to admit it), I miss Granana's no-nonsense advice coupled with her ghostly knowledge, even if she can't share all of it with me.

However, I was comforted in knowing that when she is let loose to visit the land of the living again, she will see that she can no longer push Logan on me in good conscience. The guy has moved on.

Or at least that's what I had been led to believe by the whole girlfriend thing, until I found out that's also a bunch of crap. More on that later.

Keeping up with the developments in this saga is endless—I should write a book about it.

Ed is finally parked and getting out of his car, jangling his keys, and waving in my direction. I'm hard to miss in this bright vehicle.

I follow him in and after an exchange of pleasantries, Ed starts asking me about the business deals with the factory and applauds Jason's efforts.

"That guy of yours sure is committed to making an impact on the community and your family's legacy. I was sorry to hear that you plan on leaving. But Amsterdam? How exciting!"

We talk about how great 'my guy' is, and I'm not interested in correcting him. I'm not here to talk about my problems, and it's good to hear that Jason has been staying true to *my* vision for *my* inheritance.

The business deals are moving along, and Jason has been meeting with his new guy and Ed, along with Molly, and Maryann, Sassy's organic dog food friend.

Molly's Dollies and Wags and Woofs are both poised to inject a bit more life into this town in a positive way.

Ed crosses and uncrosses his legs, and says, "So, I saw you and a different young man at the *Othello* production the other night? Is that—?"

"Logan from Tonic. Yes, he's my neighbor. His girlfriend is playing Desdemona."

"Oh yes, lovely girl. Top notch performances. But of course, I've been going to plays in this town since my Uncle Arthur took me."

At the mention of Arthur, I jump on my chance to ease into my line of conversation without dropping a bomb.

"That's so sweet. Was your uncle married?"

"Um...no...he was not married. At least not in the *traditional* sense."

He knows.

"Ed, do you know Ian Axton?"

"Why yes, I do. He was a friend of your grandparents."

"More Granana, right?"

"What are you implying?"

"I *know*."

"What do you know?"

"Are you going to make me say it?"

"Axe told you?"

"Yes, it was about time *someone* did."

"I'm sorry, Lia but that wasn't my—"

"—story to tell. I know. I've been hearing a lot of that. But you knew?"

"Not as a child. I thought your grandfather was my uncle's buddy. I had buddies so I thought it was perfectly ordinary. They went fishing together and things like that, and they enjoyed the theater. I had no idea. My parents must have known, but they never discussed it."

"When did you find out?"

"As an adult. I figured it out, and Uncle Arthur and I talked about it before he died. It's unfortunate that they felt they had to hide their true selves, but it was a different time and they couldn't bring themselves to come out."

We agree that it was sad, but Ed assures me that they were happy in their non-traditional relationships.

"It wasn't the norm, but it worked. Oh, and your grandfather wasn't unhappy because he was a closeted gay man. He was just a crotchety guy."

We laugh at that, and he shares more about life in Applebarrow, long before I was born.

I tell him that I told my parents, and my dad took it well, although there is no other outcome I could have imagined. Dad also felt sad that he didn't know his parents as he thought he did, and that they didn't trust him enough to share the truth with him.

I asked Dad how he thinks they hid it from him, and he said he spent a lot of time with only one of his parents at a time when he was young, and as an only child he loved going to friends' houses when he was older. I can relate to that.

Dad may need some therapy, but he'll go to a sweat lodge, get hypnotized, whatever it takes. And he'll accept it. Nothing keeps him down for long.

I leave Ed with a hug and an invitation to come to our Thanksgiving celebration. He says that he usually goes to his elderly aunt's house, but he wouldn't mind escaping the house full of screaming great-grandkids and running dogs.

In the car I smile and send a silent message to my Granana. She had no reason to worry. No one thinks any less of any of them. I only wish they could have known that when they were alive.

In that spirit, I text the only remaining member of their odd foursome and invite him to eat turkey with us, too. I want to hear as many stories as I can before I leave this town, probably for good.

With or without Jason, there's nothing for me here long term.

At least Logan already told me he's going to Chicago for Thanksgiving, so I don't have to worry about any drama there. It will be interesting enough with Jason's family and my new pseudo relations.

Now that I've settled my business for the day, my thoughts return to Logan, and the night at the play.

So obviously based on Ed's not-so-subtle questioning (he clearly thought I was up to no good because he did not come over and say hello at the show), I saw *Othello* with Logan.

Shortly after Jason refused to go with me and made a snarky remark about my mention of Logan, the man himself came by to see if I wanted tickets.

Jason had told me that I should go with Logan, because knowing him, he would be there every night to support his woman.

And this is a bad thing?

I let it go and resigned myself to the fact that I either wasn't going or would go by myself. However, anyone who knows me knows that I don't like to go anywhere by myself.

I've seen *Othello* many times, so I was over it.

But then Logan came by and told me that it was sold out almost every night, but Carla was able to get Jason and me tickets for a Thursday night show.

I was grateful that he was offering weeknight tickets, because it's always easier to make reasonable excuses for Jason during the work week, since it's a two-hour drive from Richmond to Applebarrow.

"Oh, that's too bad," he said. "I know you wanted to go."

I told him it was okay and to thank Carla for being so kind.

I met her briefly on Labor Day, but I felt awkward talking to her, almost like I didn't want to know her.

Also, after all the crap with Jason that day, I wasn't my usual perky self.

Logan said he understood, and maybe next time he'd be able to get weekend tickets.

An awkward moment of silence was followed by, "Hey, you know I'm there most nights. I've been helping with the sets. It's been fun. I could come out and sit with you, if you feel weird going alone. I mean, if you want the company. Either way."

I knew he was trying to be nice, even if he was acting like a middle-schooler asking a girl to his first dance.

However, I knew it had nothing to do with any residual feelings for me, and only his concern over Jason and how he would react if we did another social thing together while Jason was in Richmond.

I was about to launch into my usual martyr routine. 'Oh, that's okay, no one needs to go out of their way for me.'

But then I decided that no, I was going to go. Screw Jason. If he can't make time for me (due to his bookie or dealer—hadn't decided yet), then I am going to do them with other people.

And Logan's girlfriend was going to be on stage, and I was only planning on sitting next to him in a theater for a couple of hours.

The play was wonderful, and I found myself mouthing the words to one of my favorite Shakespearean creations.

Logan was true to his word and came out to sit with me, and even brought me backstage at intermission to meet Carla in her dressing room. He left us alone, citing set movement supervision, and I was wishing he hadn't taken off. It was cool to go backstage, but I was at a rare loss for words with Carla.

What was I supposed to say? "Hey, did you know your new boyfriend has/had a thing for me and now everything is super weird?"

Instead, I complemented her performance and asked about her career.

Luckily, we only had a few minutes to talk before I had to return to my seat for the next act.

I shook her hand and told her to break a leg, even though I always wince when I say that. The performance world needs to come up with better imagery to wish people luck.

She smiled with her one million shining white teeth and said, "Thanks. And Lia, Logan and I aren't dating. You know that, right? It was a quick flirtation."

"Oh no, I didn't know that. But it's none of my—"

She started shaking her head, so I stopped talking. I looked behind me to see if we had company, but there was no one there.

Suddenly, she was towering over me, and I felt compelled to let her take my hands and dispense whatever wisdom she was preparing to impart.

I *wanted* to run out of there with my fingers in my ears, chanting 'lalalalala'.

She looked in my eyes and said, "I'm going back to New York. We had a little fun—*very* little fun." She raised her eyebrows in a way that suggested that the neck kissing at the Labor Day event may have been the extent of their fun.

"I'm sorry it didn't work out."

My eyes dart around the room. Looking into her enormous brown orbs made me feel like I was being hypnotized and might start quacking like a duck.

She's a good actress.

"It was never meant to be anything more than a little fun during this show. I've known Logan for a long time. He was hurting, I knew that. He only wants you, Lia."

"No, that's not true. He may have had a little crush, but I don't believe he's still feeling that way."

No way would a man like Logan wait around for a woman who's taken... and *seemingly* disinterested.

I mean...who's *disinterested*. Period.

She released my hands when she saw the house lights flash, signifying her return to the stage and mercifully, the end of this conversation.

"The show is about to start, but please believe me. I have no reason to lie to you. From one sister to another, that boy has it bad for you. I know you have a boyfriend, and it's complicated. But I couldn't go back to New York in good conscience without telling you."

I took a deep breath and offered her a tight smile. "I appreciate it. I don't know what to do with the information, but no one ever tells me anything.

Thank you, Carla."

Needless to say, the second half of the performance, spent sitting next to Logan, was a bit painful...and confusing.

CHAPTER TWENTY-THREE

Dawson is laughing so hard I'm afraid beer is going to shoot out of his nose.

Emma is smacking him on the back because now he's choking. She's dressed as the Blue Fairy from Pinocchio, and I must say her diet and exercise plans are paying off. She looks fabulous in her long flowing, bright blue gown and sparkly fairy wings.

Dawson holds onto the kitchen counter in the clubhouse and says, "Wooeee...I'm sorry man, but that is some funny shit." He recovers for a moment and looks at Emma and starts howling again. "He looks like a little monkey man!"

Jason has a fake smile plastered to his face.

When he kept messaging me about his costume ideas, all of them were couples' themes where the guy was a hot pirate or fireman. The women were all slutty looking, of course.

Since he was in one of his 'eager to please' phases, I made a suggestion of my own.

Emma shakes her head and her antennae head band almost falls off. Straightening it, she says, "Dawson, he's Mojo Jojo."

He stretches his shoulders, as if the hilarity was quite a workout and says, "Who? Is that like a circus animal?"

I have been trying not to laugh because Jason

is pissed, but I am dying inside.

Because I had been suppressing my frustration with Jason (I know—shame on me!), I had proposed that we come to the Halloween party dressed as characters from my favorite childhood cartoon.

I think Jason was imagining one of the Marvel comics superheroes, or at least someone who looks like an actual man, and not a short primate with a green face, a tail, and a purple striped hat.

I, on the other hand, look adorable dressed as Bubbles.

It's the right amount of sweet and sexy. The platinum blond wig is a fun change, and the best part is the googly, blue-eyed glasses that keep everyone from seeing my eyes rolling…or wandering.

Logan is dressed as a sexy fireman. *Nothing* like a small monkey man.

Hey, I can look. He has a girlfriend.

Well, I'm supposed to *think* he does. No one knows what Carla told me, and he's here alone tonight.

It's too bad Olivia's librarian costume doesn't come with a drool holder. She can't stop staring at Logan. Actually, is she even wearing a costume?

Before Jason decides to drop the 'I'm such a good sport that I'm not going to punch this asshole' façade, I tell Dawson, "You're a little old for *Power Puff Girls*, but you were still a kid when it was on TV. You don't remember?"

Dawson rubs his fake pirate beard and I can almost see the smoke coming out of his ears, as if *he's* in a cartoon. "Oh yeah! Okay, yes. Mojo Jojo. And you're Bumbles!"

"Bubbles. A Bumble is what they called the Abominable Snowman in *Rudolph the Red Nosed*

Reindeer."

"The Bondable what? Like a bail bondsman?"

Emma widens her eyes and leads her man away from this conversation. Hopefully she plans on educating him on classic TV shows and movies that were appropriate for children, in case they get married and have any.

I would love to know what the Swanson brothers grew up watching. Probably *Dukes of Hazard* and *The Beverly Hillbillies*.

Great, now I sound like Jason. Logan is right. I, of all people, need to be more sensitive to other cultures. I plan on building a life in another county and as Logan said, Dawson doesn't know what I know, but I don't know how to bait a hook or shoot a deer.

Oh my God, now I'm quoting country songs.

Dawson and Emma are still laughing as they refill their drinks, so all is well there.

Jason's face is most definitely red beneath his makeup. I want to tell him he's a cute little monkey man, but I don't want another scene tonight. And I feel super guilty after talking to his mother on the way in.

Jason wasn't quite ready to face the crowd in his costume, so I left him to his last-minute ministrations and walked over to the clubhouse to see how the set up was going. I took my phone and received an unexpected call from Jason's mom.

"Hi, Pearly."

"Oh, I'm so glad you answered. You kids never answer your phones. I wanted to check with you and see what we should bring for dinner on Thanksgiving."

"Oh, I don't know. I'm on the way to the Halloween party right now. Can I think about it and let you know tomorrow?"

Based on my experience with Pearly's cooking, we don't want her bringing anything. Napkins. That's about it.

"Oh, sure Sugar. I'm a little nervous because of all the fancy people who'll be there."

"No need to feel that way. No one is fancy, and even if they were, who cares, right?"

"You're such a doll. Is Jason there with you?"

"He's back at my apartment, but yes he's here for the party. Did you need to speak to him?"

"No, but I miss that boy's voice. He hates talking on the phone. It's okay. You kids have fun. You have so many nice parties. I texted Jason on Labor Day morning, hoping I could get him to come to my house, but he was set on accompanying you to your—"

"I'm sorry, what did you say? You texted Jason on Labor Day?"

"Oh my, yes. I blew up his phone, as you kids would say. But he wasn't budging from your side."

"I thought you said you hadn't talked to him in ages when we spoke that week?"

"Right, we haven't *spoken* in ages. I miss that boy's voice, but he'll text all day long. Well, unless he's with you."

Pearly continued while I pondered how much of an ass I was for jumping to the wrong conclusion.

"I'm so glad you and my other boy like to talk on the phone, but I know Jason has a lot on his mind."

"Yes, he does." My voice trailed off as my head ached. Why are Jason and I suddenly so bad at communication?

I think maybe his work troubles are emasculating him. I read about it on Twitter, but it sounded like an old people problem, so I ignored it.

When am I going to catch on that Jason and I are real adults now, and join him in the land of grown up responsibility? It's no wonder he loses his patience.

I look at Jason, and I feel terribly guilty about my costume selection.

However, in my defense every time I question him about anything, he's super touchy and acts suspicious.

Never mind Jason needing therapy. We need couples' counseling.

Since I know that will not improve his feelings of manhood right now (he has the same opinion of therapists as he does New Wave lead singers—creepy), I take his hands and ask him to dance.

His body is stiff, and I ask, "You're not seriously mad at Dawson, are you? Or me?"

He sighs and says, "No, I'm not. But I am taking one for the team here, while all the other guys are walking around like men from some fantasy Playgirl calendar. Even old Fred is dressed as Hugh Hefner. Thank God Hef wore a long robe."

He raises his eyebrow and I laugh as he pulls me onto the dance floor.

We hired a DJ for this event, and so far, everyone has been dancing, and there have been no fights over the music selections. Beth truly set the bar high for this event.

I still can't believe Granana ever thought I would buy that she asked me to come here to help these people with anything. It's like I live in a community of expert RAs and cruise directors.

Well, except for Stan.

As Jason holds me close and waltzes me around the room to the Monster Mash (we're not doing *all* Halloween themed music, but Beth said she likes 'old school'), I feel that twinge of guilt again for making him look silly tonight, when he is just as good-looking as anyone else.

Well, except for one person, but it's a close second. And it's not like I'm a super model in my flannel pjs.

After talking with Ed, I see how much work Jason has taken on, and how ill-prepared he is for this level of project management. He's a junior marketing executive with a failing company. He isn't accustomed to negotiating contracts on a huge scale and managing people who have way more experience than he does.

Since Elevation continues to cause him grief, I am back to suspecting that Amy is the one making his life difficult. Greta is out for herself and wants to work them as much as she can until the end, but he could handle that. This is something more.

Maybe Amy is blackmailing him to sleep with her, and he's caught in a terrible web of deception. He could have made a grave mistake at work, even done something illegal by accident.

I love Jason and he's a go-getter, but he's not always the brightest bulb. He can be careless and sloppy in his work. I edited his essays in college, so I can attest to that.

Hopefully Granana will make an appearance in a few days for actual Halloween. We're having our party on the weekend to make it more festive, and the thirty-first is in a few days.

I talked to Donna recently, and she said I should prepare myself for a visit when the 'veil is lifted'.

Since Granana's veil is lifted all the time (when not in jail), I am confident that if she can figure out a way, she'll be here. She must be 'dying' to give me her two cents on my current troubles.

Or knowing her, it will be more like a hundred bucks.

The dance ends and Jason says, "Don't go anywhere, but I have to wash this shit off my face. It's like greasy slime. You won't be mad, will you? I've been a good sport." He flashes a smile that reminds me of our days at the University of Delaware.

"Of course I won't be mad, silly monkey."

He shakes his head and points at me. "Good one."

I don't tell him I'm not sure the makeup is going to come off with the hand soap in the clubhouse bathroom. Also, it may leave a bit of a green residue.

Shit, I didn't think of that. He may look like he's going to throw up when he goes to work on Monday.

Oh well, nothing I can do now and he's in a good mood.

I'm suddenly starving. I barely eat anymore, and for that reason alone I know Granana must still be serving her sentence. In life, if I lost any weight she'd sit until I ate a plate of meatballs and a few cannolis.

On the way to the buffet table, I almost collide with Mick Jagger, who has his plate piled high with spooky themed foods, such as deviled eyeballs and jalapeno popper mummies.

Beth is a Pinterest genius.

Oh, and the real Rolling Stones front man is not at our party.

"Axe, I love your costume. Are you going to ask the DJ to play some Stones so you can show us your moves?"

"I don't know about that." He laughs and throws back his head and says, "Who am I kidding? Of course, I'm going to do that. You young people need to hear some real music. I'm surprised you haven't requested any Depeche Mode."

"Oh, no I didn't. I didn't think anyone else would like it." I watch Axe's white eyebrows shoot up in horror, as if I said his deviled eyeballs were in fact, actual eyeballs.

"I mean some people probably do, and it's funny...and ironic...Jason always says that British New Wave sounds like 'Halloween music'.

"Huh? How so?" Axe bites into a mummy and waves his hand in front of his mouth to diffuse the hot pepper heat. I think he's still a fish and chips guy.

As he runs to the water to douse his mouth flames, I reply, "Well, he thinks the voices are creepy."

"Creepy? Well, that's bloody stupid. I'm sorry—I know he's your bloke and all, but...creepy?"

Logan walks by and says, "Hey, sorry to interrupt but you look like you could use the fire hose, Axe."

The two men laugh as Logan mimes Axe eating the jalapeno popper and catching on metaphorical fire.

I am sooo grateful for my googly eye glasses because as long as I don't turn my head, I can catch a full glimpse of Logan's assets on display in his sexy firefighter costume without anyone noticing.

I'm surprised he would wear something like this. He isn't preening or showy with his looks. But tonight, he's gone all out.

Poor Jason. I glance towards the bathroom and he's nowhere in sight. I hope he doesn't now have a striped green face.

Logan pops a few mummies into his mouth, and swallows them almost whole, like a dog. That can't be good for his digestion.

"Wow, that's impressive. Did you even taste it?" I ask.

I take in Logan's self-satisfied grin and then I see it. "You're so full of it. No one can handle that much spice. I see *tears* in your eyes."

He sniffles and says, "It's because of you. You're breaking my heart."

My heart pounds instantly and he follows up and says, "I'm kidding, Lia. So where is your monkey man? Did I overhear Axe calling him creepy?"

"No, you heard that out of context. Anyway, he's in the bathroom. Where's Carla?"

"Carla is wrapping up her show tonight. I was gonna go, but she's leaving for New York in a couple of days, and who knows when I'll see her again."

He looks towards the bathroom. Still no Jason.

Logan leads me gently by my elbow to the less populated area, near the soft drinks (the alcohol is seeing more traffic, except for Molly's girls of course, and *they* haven't left the dance floor).

"Listen, um…Carla told me that she talked to you and told you some things."

"Yeah, we talked. Well, she said you guys weren't that serious."

Did she also tell him that she told me he has feelings for me? I guess I should be grateful, since she's a stranger and she's one of the few people, other than Axe, who has told me a damn thing since I moved to Applebarrow.

And *he* had to see a *ghost* to spill his tale.

"Lia, she told me everything she told you. So, back there I *was* making a joke, and I need to make that clear. I'm not crying over you. Carla was telling you the truth, but...I can't wait around for something that's never going to happen. Look, I know this is not the time or the place—"

"No, It's not."

I regret my sharp tone, but if Jason appears now, things are going to go south fast. Logan's expression betrays our intimate conversation, and I'll be forced to tell Jason that Logan was confessing that he has hemorrhoids or used to be a woman.

Yes, I know I shouldn't be thinking of lies, since I was so upset with Jason when I thought he was lying, but I am in quite a pickle here.

"I'm sorry, but I had to clear things up after I found out what Carla told you, especially after the other night, when I brought you the painting."

I haven't told anyone about that (it's becoming a pattern), and it's hiding at the bottom of my closet, under my college yearbooks. Jason would never look at those.

Hiding something isn't exactly *lying*, and I still think Jason is hiding *something* bigger. I don't know if Amy is blackmailing him, and I haven't ruled out a secret vice or habit. I'm hoping it's something more innocent, like a Bingo or cough medicine addiction.

So...the painting.

Logan recently came to my door with a painting of a butterfly that he made for me. It's small and cute, and he said he did it at home, after he saw the butterfly Emma painted on my face—as an early going away present, and a thank you for all I've done for the community.

I had to hold back tears, and I rarely cry.

He also teased me for wearing my ghost pajamas, which did nothing to summon Granana, but I thought were quite stylish for the season.

He left and that was that. Carla's words were spinning in my head.

Still, he hadn't tried anything, not even criticism of Jason, and he knew we had been fighting on Labor Day.

Now, back in the clubhouse, Logan looks at me intently, a little hurt and expectant.

I have been dreading a conversation like this, but I had hoped he would at least do it privately, and not with my boyfriend washing monkey paint off his face a few yards away, and everyone we know making merry all around us, with their real and costume antennae on alert.

"Logan, I don't know what to say. Things have been better with Jason and—"

He raises an eyebrow in skepticism, and I remove my ridiculous glasses. I want him to see my eyes.

"What? I know you saw us on Labor Day, and you assumed we were fighting again. And if you still felt that way about me, why didn't you say something at the play, or any of the other *many* times I've seen you in the last almost two months?"

"I know. I was trying to focus on meeting someone new, but I can't do it, Lia. I mean, I *can* do it. I have to, unless I want to be on my own forever. But I had to tell you how I feel, especially after I talked to Carla."

"You still haven't told me anything other than what Carla said was true."

"Okay, that's fair. I guess I should say it then. I'm in love with you. Okay? That's the truth. And I will do nothing about it because you are so embroiled in your current relationship that you can't see anything clearly."

Logan just declared his love and it's too late. Am I okay with that? I don't even know! However, I am also sick of his presumptuous attitude about me and Jason.

"You know, happy couples argue, Logan. It's not unheard of."

"Not like this. Especially not in their twenties, when they're not even married and they haven't had any kids, or any real-life challenges. Not if it's going to work. But hey, I'm just a bartender, right?"

I fold my arms across my Bubbles costume and realize how silly I must look. "I didn't say that. I'm sorry, but we'll have to finish this conversation another time. Jason is coming out of the bathroom...and oh shit, he's still looking pretty froggy. I need to find Molly—she's my makeup guru."

"No problem. And Lia?"

"Yes?"

"No need to finish the conversation. We're done here. I wish you well. He's not telling you everything, but you'll never believe anything I say now."

He walks off and Olivia grabs his arm, telling him how amazing he looks in his costume, and that she's a naughty librarian because she's wearing glasses and her hair is in a bun.

I don't think she quite understands how that outfit is supposed to work. That's how she looks every day.

What did Logan mean by 'he's not telling me everything'? Does he know about Jason's glue sniffing habit? Or did he tell him something about Amy?

Jason yelled out something about a bitch while he was getting ready to pass out in my living room. I think back to that night and I still don't know what to do. If I ask Jason, he won't remember, and he'll get angry. If I ask Logan, he'll either refuse to tell me, or I won't believe him.

I can't even begin to win.

Jason is searching the room for me, and I duck behind the rest of the guys and pretend I'm trying to dig a bottle out of the bottom of the drinks cooler.

Of course, Dawson runs over to help me.

I love how Emma isn't the least bit jealous. And I thought *she* was the awkward one when we had lunch months ago. I'm a total wreck and she's like a goddess now.

"Thanks, Dawson."

He pops the top off the wine cooler and hands it to me with a little bow.

I'm swigging it as I see Jason talking to Axe, presumably about his poor taste in music.

I think Axe had something to do with the success of New Wave. He's awfully protective of it. Some day when life is back to normal, I'm going to ask him about it.

So, no time in the foreseeable future.

Jason is smiling his creepy fake grin, and I'm

hit with starvation again. That's right—I never ate anything.

No jalapeno mummies for me, and I'm not much of a deviled eyeballs girl, either.

I'm cutting a piece of ghost brownie, which is basically a brownie with marshmallow ghosts on top, when I am startled by a presence behind me.

Nope, it's not Granana. Thankfully, the only ghost I see is on my plate.

It's Molly's girls begging me to dance with them. Beth just requested *It's Raining Men*, and she's pulled all the women onto the dance floor.

Yeah, it's raining men all right. But for me it's either a miserable drizzle and or a hurricane.

I put my brownie down on the table, and join the girls, ignoring the two mopey male faces eyeing me from across opposite sides of the dance floor.

It's not my fault Jason let himself be cornered by someone he doesn't want to talk to, and that Olivia won't dance with other women because she can't stop staring at Logan's chest.

Dancing with the ladies feels freeing, and I'm suddenly caught up in the joy of the moment.

We've formed a sister circle, and each dancer is taking turns doing a solo performance in the middle.

I've never been an exhibitionist, always preferring to set up the fun activities and watch others participate. I'm hoping the song ends before I'm prompted to take my turn. Emma is shaking her stuff, and Dawson is holding his beer and smiling broadly.

Both of my men...wait...did I just say *both of my men*?

What the hell is wrong with me? I have one

man. One!

The song is still playing...this must be some extended remix version, and now everyone is chanting my name.

Crap, I'll have to appease them. I'll do a quick little shake. And I have my googly eyeglasses back on, so no matter what moves I come up with, I'll still look silly.

I start flailing and catch Jason's eye. He smiles and then pulls his phone out of his pocket.

Why do I get a sick feeling every time someone contacts him? He knows lots of people, and it's perfectly normal to answer your phone while your girlfriend is off gyrating.

As I try to move out of the circle (how long is this song? We got it—men are everywhere!), I see that Jason looks super angry on the phone.

So much for him not answering his phone and talking to people. I strongly doubt he'd be that upset with his mother, though. At least I hope not.

I want to break out of the circle and follow him, but everyone is still cheering for me, like I'm the bride at a bachelorette party.

Am I normally so boring that seeing me do one fun thing is fueling this much enthusiasm?

I have no further time for self-reflection.

Logan has broken away from Olivia's claws, and he's watching Jason through the front window, and no...crap, he's following him out there!

I grab Sassy's hand and pull her into the center, slipping through the spot in the circle she just vacated.

I leave her to enjoy the spotlight and let her do her impersonation of disco Wonder Woman.

I take off my stupid glasses as I try to casually

run outside (is there such a thing?) before anyone else notices what's happening.

And hopefully, *before* anything happens.

Why the hell does Logan care who Jason is talking to? He made his big declaration about how he was done with me.

This is getting exhausting and I wish I could put my ghost pjs back on, go home, and talk to...a ghost.

Granana, where are you when I need you?

I open the door and I hear Jason say, "Man, you need to mind your own fucking business!"

Logan sees me and says, "No, I don't think so. How about I tell Lia what I overheard, and she can be the judge?"

"Oh, you'd love that, wouldn't you? You've been trying to get in her pants ever since she moved in."

Now he's in Logan's face...well chest...and even though something I am not going to like seems to be brewing here, I still feel guilty that Jason has to face another man in a confrontational pose wearing a striped purple hat and elf boots.

"No, I actually care about Lia, which is why I've been keeping my eye on you. You don't remember our talk the night you threw up all over my bar, do you?"

Logan points in Jason's face, and I know it's only a matter of moments before there's a brawl, and I can't have that on my watch.

Speaking of watching, all the party-goers are now situated in front of the window. Tucker is even holding back the curtains so more people can get a good view of the show.

I run through a string of filthy curse words in my head in several languages and say, "Enough!

Stop acting like macho idiots. Jason, what is he talking about?"

"You know what Lee, it doesn't even matter anymore. I give up."

He throws his hands in the air and starts walking away, towards my apartment.

"Where are you going?"

I say this only because I don't know what else to say. I can see where he's going. *Where* this is going.

"I am going home. Remember home, Lia? The place you abandoned to come here and play dormitory cruise director for these...morons."

I hope the people inside didn't hear that.

"Jason, you're upset. Why don't I come with you and we'll talk about whatever Logan overheard?"

He laughs and almost sounds a little like the evil cartoon villain he's portraying.

"Yep, Logan *heard* me. Believe what you want, Lia. I'm getting my things and I'm leaving. I'll have Ed get you up to speed on the contracts. After all, it's *your* inheritance."

I watch him walk off. He'll leave my key under the mat and that will be the end of that.

I look at Logan and take a deep breath. I know if I start yelling at him, he'll also stomp off like a Neanderthal baby.

"What did you hear?"

Logan runs his fingers through his thick, dark hair and says, "I'm sure you won't believe me, but despite what...he...says, I respect you, your pants and your relationship. I can't help it if I've fallen for you. I've done my best to stay objective. I've even slept at the bar...alone...many nights...because I can't even stand being near you, even in my own apartment."

What can I say to that? He cares so much that he can't stand to be in the same neighborhood?

None of this is going to end well. Soon I will have no men. See, Weather Girls? Rain can turn to drought pretty damn quickly.

Instead of speaking, I do what my mother advised. I pay attention.

"He was talking to someone, angrily. I followed him out here because it sounded like he was talking to a woman."

"That alone doesn't prove anything. His boss harasses him. She's a scary old bitch. And his mother."

Sorry, Pearly. I know that's not true.

"Sure, I get that. But he said, 'Yes, you can ride me like a pony tomorrow.' Would he say that to his boss or his *mother*?"

"No."

I search my mind for possible misunderstandings or double meanings that could result in Jason's innocence.

I know it sounds bad, but with Pearly I confused *talk* and *text*, and spent weeks plotting Jason's punishment for no reason.

"I know! Maybe someone was riding him...you know...like on his back...up in his grill...giving him a hard time."

"Yes, I'm familiar with the sayings. It wasn't said like that. And if he were innocent, would he break up with you and walk away? I wouldn't do that. And you know what?"

"What?"

"You're not even crying. You didn't run after

him. You're standing here talking to me. What does that tell you?"

I search Logan's eyes while I do an inventory of all he's done for me.

The tickets to the play, helping me buy the Jeep, rescuing me from the side of the road. Twice.

The way he made sure I got home safely, the first night we met at the bar.

The butterfly painting.

He did these things while falling for me, thinking he had no chance.

That's love. It's unselfish. Pure.

My father's tenth Happiness Tenet is—see the love around you.

"Logan, I'm sorry. You're right. Jason and I have been going through the motions for a while now. I didn't want to admit it. I got confused by the changes and the mysterious...it doesn't matter now."

My eyes fill, and as Logan becomes blurry, I reach out to embrace him. "I think I have feelings for you, too."

He pulls back and holds my arms to my side. "No, Lia."

"What?" I wipe my eyes and wish Molly had never taught me to use makeup. It's burning my eyes, and Logan's rebuff is burning my heart.

The irony of his firefighter costume is not lost on me, with all the burning, but he does not appear to have any intentions of dousing any of my flames.

Why do I feel like I'm suddenly starring in a cheesy rom-com? Oh, I know, the audience at the window.

Logan releases his grasp and says quietly, "You go back and forth with him constantly. He may be okay with being a yo-yo, but I'm not. I care more than you even realize, and that's why I am not going to be your rebound man."

He walks away and now I'm bawling.

What did he want me to do? I can't help it if Jason and I didn't have a clean break.

My heart feels like a brick and it's not because Jason is running to his car in the resident parking lot and slamming the door.

Logan slammed the door on what he keeps saying he wants so much, and now I am more confused than ever.

And who in the hell is riding Jason like a pony?

I guess Amy, and I hope she falls off and breaks her bony—

"Get up off that curb, young lady!"

I look up, expecting to see Sassy getting ready to dish out some sass.

Or Beth threatening to fuck them both up, or Emma with an encouraging word.

Maybe Molly with her makeup bag to fix my face.

Olivia gloating?

But no, it's Granana!

"Thank God you're here!"

"Yes, quite literally. I had to cajole and beg to get here before the veil is lifted. I still have a few days left on my sentence, but they let me down for good behavior. Apparently other dead people find a way to poke holes in the endless white void in an attempt to escape."

I jump up to hug my sweet, crazy, loud grandmother, and then realize that people are still watching me.

If I hug the air, I may be in a strait jacket before

the night is over.

"I'm so glad you're here."

I put my glasses back on so no one can tell that I'm looking at Granana. She floats to the side of me facing the apartments and the parking lot, so everyone will think that I'm gazing mournfully at the men who have deserted me.

"That's better. Now they won't think you're bonkers. Now run along inside and talk with the living, wash your face, and all of that. Then meet me in your apartment. We have a lot to talk about."

She shoos me away, and adds, "And I better not find any jar sauce in your pantry!"

CHAPTER TWENTY-FOUR

"Is this Christian music?"

Dawson scratches his stubble, and I notice that he always does that when he asks a question, as if the answer is in his beard, and he can rub it off his face.

The question isn't directed at anyone in particular, so everyone within earshot seems to be ignoring him.

Well, almost everyone.

"My boy, are you alright?" I shake my head at Axe as he chooses to be the one to address the fact that no, "Personal Jesus" by Depeche Mode is *not* Christian music.

Since I am free of Jason's judgments and complaints, I am playing music that I like for once.

Dawson looks puzzled and Axe says, "That's a serious question. Did your mum have slippery fingers?"

Tucker walks over and joins Axe in teasing his little brother, stating that their mother often had her hands in Crisco while making pies.

Emma is coming to his rescue, and I smile at the whole scene.

Olivia, on the other hand, does not prompt many smiles for me.

I let her plan this event because she was so pissy after the Halloween party, claiming I ran off the two best men in the group.

And she said that I play favorites with the event planning assignments, which I don't.

Well, maybe a little bit but I want everyone to have fun!

I decided it's easier keep the peace, and I'm still determined to befriend Olivia and help her pull the stick out of her butt—so I let her take charge of our Thanksgiving celebration.

She's fussing over the turkeys, which she has *named.*

Yes, I'm serious. Well, I don't think *she* named them. When she was assigned this task, she couldn't buy the turkeys from a grocery store. She felt compelled to visit a local farm and pick the live birds that would be our dinner.

I realize this is a fresher option, but when I told her this seemed a bit morbid (I prefer to eat more anonymous meat), she told me that she believes that if you eat meat, you should procure it in the most humane way, which is from a local farm.

I respect that line of thinking, and it's not like *I* was going to pick out the live turkeys who would grace our table.

But then she got weirder.

Apparently, Olivia is a member of a spiritual path I'm not familiar with. I don't know everything, but growing up with my parents in Vermont exposed me to many alternate belief systems.

However, I labeled this one the 'cuckoo' faith.

She said something about merging with Bob's and Melvin's souls as we eat them, and the circle of life continuing.

Honestly, she lost me as soon as I learned my dinner had names.

She had little nameplates made for them, and she's going to put them on the table when she serves Bob and Melvin.

Axe follows me to the kitchen area and is laughing, shaking his head. "That Dawson chap is wackier than—"

"—a woman who names her turkeys?"

I whisper this, of course. If Olivia heard me, the turkeys would probably wind up in the trash, and we'd be going to get takeout Chinese.

We're both laughing so hard that we have to go outside for a second to regain composure, so no one asks to be let in on the joke.

And that's when I see Pearly and Austin Woodcock walking down the path.

Yes, as if Bob and Melvin weren't enough, I allowed Jason's family to come for Thanksgiving.

If Axe thinks Dawson is a nitwit, wait until he meets Jason's brother.

Austin is wearing his usual wardrobe of sweatpants and ill-fitting t-shirt with stains on it, and Pearly is wearing a mini-skirt with fishnet stockings and a body suit without a bra.

I still sympathize with Jason for coping with this while growing up. No wonder he got so screwed up. I wish someone other than the ghost of Granana would have pointed it out to me.

Speaking of Granana, we had a great talk after the Halloween party disaster, after I returned to the clubhouse and did what she instructed me to do—talk to my friends and let them provide comfort and support.

I realized how foolish I had been for not reaching out. At college, I was the one in charge of everyone's problems, and I never shared mine with anyone. But now I know all sorts of people with different life perspectives, and they have so much to offer.

I told them everything. Well, not everything but a lot.

I always complain that no one tells me anything, but I also hide things from people. I'm easing into this new me and it's not easy.

As expected, Sassy gave me some sass.

Beth threatened to beat Jason with Dawson's pirate sword, and Emma did have encouraging words.

Molly grabbed her makeup bag and fixed my face, and Olivia said, "Leave it to Lia to drive off all the good men."

That launched a debate about the quality of the remaining men, and I said good night and headed back to my apartment.

Granana was waiting for me and we talked into the night about her life with Grandpa and Axe. And Arthur.

Such an odd couple of couples.

I was comforted to hear that they *all* got along, and that they lived in eccentric harmony. It wasn't *exactly* as any of them wanted it to be, but it was good.

She assured me that they were all happy on earth, and that the three who have moved on are happy in heaven.

"I do look forward to being with Axe again, but I promise I won't appear to him and cause him to join me prematurely."

I was grateful that Granana doesn't plan on murdering my newfound grandfather figure, and she praised me for getting acquainted with Ed and Axe, and for welcoming them into the family.

I asked if she would give her permission for me to tell everyone the truth about their lives, and she assured me that the departed were now fine with it, and as long as Axe, Ed, and my dad were on board, I should do it.

She expressed regret at trying to stop it from happening and staying stuck in her living mind. "I don't know why I thought I had to continue to protect the secret."

It will be nice for people to truly *know* my grandparents, especially the people who thought they knew them.

I know they'll be accepting and lovely about it.

Even kooky Olivia.

Granana said she wished she could appear and help me tell the story, but she doesn't want to risk killing any of our loved ones, and that might happen if she shows herself.

Plus, she has her Christmas gown picked out and doesn't want to be sent to Haunting Jail for the holidays.

Apparently, she's coming to visit in a dress trimmed with ribbons, tinsel, lights and Christmas balls.

So, she's coming as a spooky Christmas Tree.

To my great shock, she only had two things to say about the events of the night, and how I've managed my love life during her heavenly incarceration.

"Jason is still lying about something, but it doesn't matter now. He's yesterday's news. And Logan. Ahh, that boy is crazy about you. He's your *one*. And you will get to live openly with your *one*, all the days of your life. I was happy, Lia, but I could have been a lot happier."

She kissed my cheek, and I almost felt her touch. It was something a little denser than mist.

I was ready to thank her for her love and advice, and to ask if her studies were allowing her to learn to make physical contact with living people.

However, as she often does, she broke the spell and said, "So don't screw this up."

And she was gone.

Now, standing here outside the clubhouse, on a crisp Thanksgiving Day in Applebarrow, I watch my ex-boyfriend's mother try to extricate her spike heels from the muddy lawn.

Why they got off the path, I can't imagine. Maybe Austin saw a squirrel and chased it.

Yes, he's that bad. And there is nothing actually wrong with him. He's just a nitwit.

Axe walks out to help Pearly, and I can't help but wonder what comments he will have later about this duo.

I should have rescinded their invitation, but Pearly called me last week, crying and telling me that Jason called his mommy immediately after the Halloween party to tell her what happened.

It's funny that it took a breakup for him to finally contact his mother.

She said Jason was devastated, and that he desperately wants a chance to ask everyone for forgiveness.

I told her that it wasn't necessary for him to apologize to anyone but me, and I didn't want to hear it anymore. Jason pushed me too far away, and I'm not interested in going backwards.

But the crying was ridiculous! I do feel sorry for

her, and she said that Jason asked if she would call me and beg me to let him stop by on Thanksgiving, so he could make things right with the others, as if they were all such great friends and he let them down.

This sounded like a ploy to get me back, but if he wants to come and make a fool of himself, I'm not going to stop him.

I said as much, and she thanked me profusely. I told her that she and Austin could stay for dinner, but I expected Jason to say what he has to say and leave.

Now I'm regretting this decision. I am already coping with eating either Melvin or Bob, and Dawson thinks I'm playing Christian music, and Logan is gone.

He didn't move out of Pentagon Place, at least not that I know of, but I saw him leaving for his flight to Chicago early this morning.

I was going to run out and say goodbye, but I knew he would either ignore me or say something snarky about my turkey pajamas.

I still expect him to turn in his rental notice and go stay at the bar, until he finds another home. He's been avoiding me completely and everyone says he's not himself.

Sassy dragged me out to Tonic one night recently, and Logan was working. He came out to talk to one of his employees, saw me, and retreated to his office.

I am starting to get angry with him, too. I get it that he doesn't want to be a rebound guy, and maybe I was too quick to throw myself at him, but I was only coming in for a hug. I wasn't dragging him behind the clubhouse and taking off my Bubbles dress.

The funny thing is—it didn't feel sudden or quick for me. Once Jason left, it's like something broke open inside me and I realized how stupid I had been—about everything.

My feelings for Logan had been building inside me for months, and Jason's behavior that night pushed me over the edge.

In Logan's defense, I had never given him any indication that I was interested in more than friendship, and I guess I wasn't, even though the feelings were stirring.

I wanted to end things properly with Jason, and let that relationship run its natural course. That was foolish and I was hiding from the truth, but it felt like five years made it worth seeing it to the end.

Therefore, I don't think I was impulsive with Logan. He acted like I was a silly girl who always needs to have a boyfriend and latches on to the next available guy when one leaves.

Over the next couple of weeks, I started to feel a little better, and I went out a few times with Emma and Molly, and I started Skyping with Gabby and Taylor on a regular basis.

They are also of the opinion that Jason sucks, and I shouldn't give up on Logan.

If only it were that easy.

At least he won't be here when Jason shows up. I don't think there has been enough healing time for that to go well, and Logan would be uninterested in Jason's group apology.

Yes, things were going a little better. I met with Ed several times, and forced myself to understand the business dealings, and start to put plans in place for how I am going to manage this enormous sum of money that is soon coming my way.

A few days ago, when I was feeling particularly good, I received an email from Jason, thanking me for being so kind to his mother, and for giving him the chance to talk to everyone, one last time.

He also shared that Amy had been pursuing him, and that was what he had been hiding.

He apologized yet again and assured me that nothing happened between them.

I can see where working with someone who is actively pursuing you, and trying to sabotage your work, is stressful. The time to tell me all of this was months ago, not now.

Also, if what Logan repeated was true, Jason is probably still lying. The pony riding bit is hard to justify or explain innocently.

I still don't know if Elevation is going out of business, or if that was another lie, but I don't care.

He ended with flowery crap about how much he loves me, and how sad he is that all our plans aren't going to happen.

Whether or not he's telling the truth doesn't matter to me.

What's notable is that I didn't cry. I didn't feel much of anything. A year ago, this would have devastated me, but I shrugged my shoulders and deleted the email.

I was proud of myself for closing that chapter, and I know it seems like I'm opening it up again by letting him come here, but I'm not. I am so emotionally detached now that I have no need to punish him or keep him from talking to people in my life.

My parents are here—he can apologize to them,

too.

And if someone takes pity on him and asks him to stay for dinner, I'll set another place. Soon I'll be gone from here, and another chapter of my life will start.

It's better this way.

Pearly and Austin greet me, and she hands over her baloney and tuna casserole.

I fight the urge to gag from the name alone, never mind the smell. I tighten the foil around the pan and tell her I'm making sure it doesn't get cold.

Austin explains how it's his favorite. "It's like a surf and turf dish."

Axe is fighting the giggles, and now Sassy has shown up to introduce herself.

Sassy says, "Oh look, Lia. You and Austin are wearing similar pants."

I am *not* wearing sweatpants. I am wearing leggings, but I know she disapproves of my choice because as soon as she saw me today, she said, "Do you want me to finish setting the table so you can change out of your pajamas?"

I said, "These are not pajamas. They're leggings."

"Really? What would happen if you fell asleep in them? Would you be comfortable?"

"Well, yes but—"

"Then they are pajamas. I would be wildly uncomfortable, and possibly injured, if I fell asleep in my clothes. But of course, I gave away all my pajamas. Stan and I sleep in the nude."

Yes, the things that make me gag are plentiful today and Jason hasn't even arrived yet.

Sassy reminded me how fortunate it is that she's staying in Applebarrow, and supervising my *big* wardrobe purchases, once I get my 'loot'.

"We can't have you representing our country in Europe in bunny pjs and exercise wear."

Sassy and Stan are buying a house on Granana's street. That means Stan's apartment will be vacant, then probably Logan's. Then mine. Or maybe Logan will stay and wait out *my* departure.

I do still intend to leave the country, at least for a while.

I am not going to do a whole *Eat, Pray, Love* thing, but I do need to clear my head, and for the love of God—I want to speak to people in foreign languages!

Speaking of that, I am not leaving until the after-school language program is running on autopilot, and there is still work to do.

Also, I am not going to leave Ed Franklin holding the bag with my businesses, either. Molly and Mary Ann deserve my involvement, up until the point where they are up and running smoothly.

It's exciting that my grandparents' factory will hum again, bringing much needed work to the next generation of Applebarrow residents.

Axe and Sassy escort Pearly and Austin into the clubhouse and show them where to sit and get their drinks.

Now that they're here, I'm glad I invited them. It's good closure, and excellent karma.

I am getting a little tense anticipating Jason's arrival. If he has any sense, he will wait until after dinner to show up.

Of course he has no sense, so as Olivia and Tucker carry Melvin and Bob to the table, Jason arrives with a sheepish grin on his face.

I was hoping to gather everyone together and

tell them my story about my grandparents, but that can be the dessert topic.

I never told Jason, and the intimacy of the tale is no longer appropriate for him. Maybe it never was, and that's why I didn't care to tell him.

It doesn't matter if he *knows*—Pearly will tell him for sure. I just don't want to see his reaction or accept any comments or comfort from him.

In short, he will fuck up the moment for everyone.

When all the residents arranged their family holiday schedules so they could be here today, they had no idea they were getting dinner *and* a show.

Well, now it's two shows.

I greet the opening act civilly and ask everyone to quiet down.

Ken complains that he was about to start carving the turkeys, but I explain that Jason came here to say a few words to everyone, and he'll be leaving shortly.

I turn the floor over to Jason, and all eyes are glued to the first act of the show.

"Good afternoon, friends."

Is he giving a sermon or apologizing?

He surveys the room and smiles at everyone. Some return his smile, like Emma and Dawson, but others give him a scowl, such as Sassy, Beth and Molly.

Pearly is smiling at her son, while slapping her other boy's hand away from the dinner rolls, which are covered with a cloth napkin for a reason.

"Thank you so much for letting me come here today. The last time any of you saw me I was not at my best. Actually, I haven't been at my best for some time."

Now the audience is squirming—some because they think he's full of crap, and others because the food is getting cold, and Melvin and Bob are begging to be eaten.

Note to self—stop calling the turkeys by name, or I'll only be eating the mashed potatoes and apple pie today.

Jason drones on. "I won't bore you with all my troubles. And I'm sure you've heard about most of them through the grapevine. But that's all behind us now, and I do hope you will all forgive me as I return to your lives."

Some people nod in agreement and mumble their acceptance of his apology, but others are looking at me for clarification.

He's returning to our lives? How does he figure that?

I glare at Pearly as I assume that if anyone misled him about my intentions in letting him come here today, it was her.

She looks away and continues to smile encouragingly at her firstborn liar, I mean son.

Also, I don't think Austin is a liar. Just a nitwit. And a bit of a slob.

I am ready to thank Jason for coming and ask him to leave, when my father stands up and says, "Jason, what are you referring to? My daughter has expressly stated to all of us, and I am sure to you, that she does not want you back in her life."

If the Happiness Professor is questioning him, I hope he knows he'll be shown the door in about two seconds. My mother is already throwing down her napkin.

Molly's girls are snapping photos, which I am sure will appear on Instagram.

Jason puts his hands together as if in prayer (now Axe is pulling a face like something smells, although the baloney and tuna casserole *did* make it to the table).

"Paul, I appreciate your love for Lia. Please know that I am here with every intention of making things right."

My mother is giving him a 'how do you expect to do that, jackass' look.

And Ken has picked up his carving knife again. I'm hoping he intends to multi-task by listening to the argument *and* carving the turkeys. The knife is awfully menacing in his hungry hand.

I must step in, or we'll never get to eat in peace. This was a bad—

"Lia, my love." Now Jason is at my side, and he's reaching into his pocket and getting down on one knee.

I hope he dropped something, because if he's doing what I think he's doing...

"Ever since I first saw you on campus, a wide-eyed freshman, I knew you were the one."

Pearly clutches her many beaded necklaces and says, "This is so romantic!"

I ignore the interruption and sigh. "Jason, please don't do this."

"No, I want everyone to know how I feel. I've been a terrible partner these last few months. I now see how important your Granana's mission is to you, and I am so sorry for any harm I have caused by my weakness and fear. I should have told you about Amy from the start."

Hands go to faces in the crowd, and Ken drops the knife on the table in disgust.

Pearly relents and grabs dinner rolls for Austin

and herself. Emma hands them the butter. I wonder how romantic Pearly thinks this is now.

Jason holds up his hand and says, "No, it's not what you think. Amy was pursuing me and interfering in my life—in our beautiful love."

Olivia stands up and yells, "Would you get on with it. You're ruining my meal."

Yes Olivia, that's the issue here. She's incredibly selfish, but it's to my advantage today. I'm sure she routinely kicks people out of the library for talking, so tossing Jason for delaying her dinner should be no problem.

"Lia, will you be my wife? I promise that Amy means nothing to me, and I will never—"

"What the hell kind of a marriage proposal includes another woman's name?" Fred finally pipes in. He was busy playing solitaire on his phone, but finally notices this embarrassing display of manhood.

A new voice enters the scene, as I am about to ask Jason to stand and walk away.

"I'll tell you what kind!"

I sit back down in my chair and overhear Ken tell Beth about how he's going to go postal now that this other dumb bitch is here to ruin his dinner. *And* there aren't even any collard greens on the table.

Beth pats her husband's arm and points to the new arrival on stage. She wants her money's worth.

Amy's hair is sticking up all over the place, like she jumped out of bed and flew here on her broom.

Jason holds onto the table and pulls himself up to standing (he has weak knees for a young guy), slamming the ring box on the table. "Amy, get out. You've done enough damage."

Ken picks up the knife and starts carving, and that prompts everyone to begin filling their plates, and passing the salt and pepper.

I see no reason to stop them—there's nothing wrong with dinner theater.

Amy takes her coat off and tosses it on the floor while trying to control her fly away hair. She needs to use a good leave-in conditioner.

"Lia, I'm sorry for coming here today, but Jason is still lying."

All eyes were on Amy and now they've shifted to me. Everyone is chewing and watching the tennis match, and I desperately want to go back in time and tell Pearly that the *whole* Woodcock family needs to stay home. Good karma is overrated.

I look between Amy and Jason and begin to tell them they need to leave, but I am interrupted by yet another new character in this dysfunctional Thanksgiving improv session.

"AH HA! There you are, bad boy! And Amy, you're fired!"

Dawson looks up from eating Bob's leg and says, "Who's this old chick?"

Emma shushes him and he complains. "Well, it's hard to follow."

He looks at the guys for agreement and Ken says, "Truth," and nods his head as he crams mashed potatoes and gravy in his mouth.

Now all eyes turn to an older woman standing next to Amy. Oh crap, that's—

"Greta, you can shove your job up your wrinkly ass!" Amy solidifies her status as a former Elevation employee and I put my head in my hands, willing them all to vanish.

Where's Granana when I need her? I know she

doesn't have magical powers, but maybe she's learned how to throw a table or something, since the last time I saw her.

Greta licks her thin lips and pushes Amy aside. Calmly addressing Jason, she says, "Are you going to tell them?"

Jason is holding his stomach, and if he throws up on Olivia's Thanksgiving table, well...let's just say we'll need to keep the sharp objects away from the hostess.

"Greta, please. I'm begging you. I'll do anything." Jason appears close to tears now and it's not a good look on him. Worse than little monkey man.

Greta places her hands on her bony hips and says, "Really? You'll do *anything*? Well, as I told you, what I want is to continue to ride you like a pony until my saddle is worn out."

Tucker spits out his chewed food, and all sorts of moaning and gagging ensues among the disgusted diners.

Dawson looks around the room and says, "Well, slap my ass and call me Sally!"

Emma translates, "That means he's surprised by the turn of events."

Lots of nodding follows at the table, at least from the people who aren't still fighting their gag reflex.

Marcos looks at Jason and makes a repulsed face. "Oh man, she's as old as my grandma. Seriously dude, what the—"

Amy pipes in and yells, "I saw them doing just that, and let me tell you, it's NOT a pretty sight. I've been desperately trying to help Jason get out of this mess, but he's such a moron!"

My mother says, "That's one word for it." And to Greta she says, "You look older than me. What the hell is wrong with you?" Then she glares at Pearly, who is suddenly fascinated by her green beans. "And what kind of a boy did you raise?"

Now my father is on his feet again, standing between my mother and Greta.

"Sarah, you can't blame his mother. He's a grown man. And *this...person...*is...

He sits back down. My father can't think of anything nice to say, so he is required to stop talking, based on his 'Happiness Tenets'.

In his defense, 'speak kindly' is not an easy one to uphold right now.

You would think I would have questions, but I'm either in shock or so disgusted that it's almost funny. Everything makes sense now, in a sick and twisted way.

Greta is undeterred. "You know, if I were a man seducing a much younger woman, no one would say a word. This is typical sexism."

"No, it's actually sexual harassment, if you're blackmailing him." Ed Franklin is the voice of reason. I forgot we had a lawyer at the table, not that being a lying, cheating asshole is an actual crime.

Although, it surely should be.

Jason looks encouraged by Ed's words. "Yeah, I was harassed. Lia, you're going to vilify me for being coerced into this? She used me and threatened me and—"

Amy looks up at the ceiling and says, "Jason, please! You took off your own pants. I watched you. At least lock your office door, you idiot. Obviously, you'd sell your own mother to get ahead."

Austin wipes his mouth on his sleeve and says,

"That's not a fair statement. He doesn't even like Mom. And she's the best."

In a rare show of sense, Austin earns some encouraging words and agreement. He celebrates by getting up and bringing one of the pumpkin pies to the table.

Olivia's face is beet red and Ken calls out, "I really thought it was the blond. This is quite a twist. I don't even mind missing my sister's collard greens for this show."

Tucker high fives him, and they put their hands down when my mother glares at them.

I pick up my fork and start clicking it on my water glass, as if we were at a wedding and I wanted the bride and groom to kiss.

However, there will be no kissing going on today.

"Hey, can I please say something? Since it's my life?"

Everyone quiets down, and most people even stop eating, in respect for my dead relationship.

If it wasn't already dead enough, the proverbial fork is going in now.

"Greta, you're gross. Amy, you should have come to me. That's what women do for each other. And Jason, you have lied so many times, I don't know how you even know your own name."

Austin stops eating pie long enough to say, "Well it's on his driver's license."

Things are back to normal at that end of the table. "Thank you, Austin."

I continue. "Jason, I want a man I can trust—"

Greta interrupts, "Oh trust is overrated, especially when they can do that thing—"

"Why are you still here?" I glower at Greta, but

she stands taller.

Everyone starts talking again, with half of them rising from their seats. I'm hoping to avoid a mob brawl, but I've lost control of the class.

Suddenly, the most unlikely person emerges as the leader. Emma whistles with two fingers, and after the ear-piercing sound shuts most everyone up, she yells at the top of her lungs, "Logan is here!"

Logan places his suitcase softly on the ground and says, "So, Happy Thanksgiving. What did I miss?"

Dawson stands up and offers Logan his hand. "Happy Thanksgiving, Man. You couldn't stay away, huh?" Dawson glances between me and Logan, as if this is some kind of *Jerry Maguire*, 'you complete me' scene.

Logan accepts the handshake and says, "Uh no...my flight was canceled. There's a huge blizzard in Chicago." He looks around the room and says, "But from the looks of things, there's some kind of storm blowing through here, too."

Dawson is the only one who laughs at Logan's unintentional humor, and says, "Oh, you missed *a lot*. Let me catch you up."

Dawson quickly recaps the events while everyone is silent and frozen in place.

In about a minute, Logan's expression shifts from interested to shocked to disgusted to pitying to overwhelmed.

Dawson winds up with, "And that my friend, is what's going on here. What do ya think?"

Everyone is watching Logan intently, including me. I wanted to see him today, but not like this.

He sighs heavily, gives me a mournful look and says, "I'm going back to the airport to see if they'll get me booked on another flight—to anywhere."

CHAPTER TWENTY-FIVE

"Logan, wait!"

I run after him and he stops. Whew, I knew he wouldn't abandon me. I don't blame him for wanting to get away from that pack of loonies.

As I get closer, I see that his expression isn't inviting. "Logan, why are you leaving?"

"Do you really have to ask me that?" He looks towards the clubhouse with wide eyes.

"Yes, I do." I put my hands on my hips and say, "Logan Mackintosh, don't you see how I feel about you?"

"Frankly, no I don't. All I see is that you are surrounded in drama, and even though hopefully we've seen the last of Jason, how do I know you won't take him back?"

I throw my arms up in the air and say, "Because I am more annoyed that he's ruining our delicious family dinner than I am that he lied to me and had sex with an old lady. If that doesn't say I'm over him, I don't know what does? And, I don't even care if you knew and didn't tell me. I wouldn't have listened anyway. I've been a fool."

Logan's mouth turns up in a slight smile. "You're not a fool, you're just loyal and trusting. And I didn't know about Greta. I knew there was some woman giving him trouble from his drunken ramblings, but I only assumed it was Amy. I'm sorry." He meets my eyes and says, "Lia, I do love you."

He closes the distance between us and takes my hands in his, which I have relaxed and taken off my hips. I'm not feeling indignant anymore. Just mushy...and very warm.

"Why do I feel like there's a 'but' still hanging there?"

"Because there is."

My heart sinks. I don't know what else to do to make him see the truth.

He takes my face in his hands and says, "If I kiss you right now, and this is the start of something for us, it has to be real. I need to walk with you back into that building as a couple. No more holding back and no more Jason. Is this real, Lia?"

"Yes! It's *so* real. I promise that's what I want, too. Logan, I love you. I wasn't willing to admit it—"

My words are swallowed by Logan's mouth on mine, and his lips are every bit as soft and sweet, yet insistent, as I ever fantasized.

Yes, I fantasized about Logan. Who wouldn't?

The kissing goes on and on, and now his hands are in my hair, and I am sure that if there was a back window to the clubhouse, I'd see everyone I care about watching.

Maybe even Granana, although she doesn't need windows.

We come up for air, and I wrap my arms around Logan's neck and close my eyes.

I sense her presence before she speaks.

I open my eyes and behind Logan is Granana giving me the two thumbs up sign and smiling—in a bit of a gloating, 'I told you so' way.

Nonetheless, I know she is thrilled for us.

I owe her so much, but I can't thank her in front of Logan.

Mom appears at the back door, her arms folded against the chilly day. "Hey, I was going to ask if everything is okay, but I would say it is."

I laugh when I see that my hot pink lipstick is smeared all over Logan's face.

I'll talk to Molly about finding some 'kiss-proof' brands. There's going to be a lot of lip activity in my future.

Logan says, "Everything is amazing, Mrs. DeLuca."

"Call me Sarah. And I'm so happy!" She claps her hands and it's sweet to see my mother in front of me and my Granana behind me, both celebrating my new love and good fortune.

My dad joins my mom at the door and says, "Well, that was an unpleasant scene, but some of the others managed to coax the Woodcock family and assorted *friends* out the door. Tucker followed them to make sure they get in their cars."

Poor Dad. He hates conflict.

Mom says, "It sounds like it's safe to rejoin the party. Olivia is pretty upset about Bob and Martin—"

"Melvin, Honey. The turkey's name is Melvin." Dad smirks and Mom smacks his arm.

"Whatever, that woman is a nutjob. I would offer to give her a free massage while I'm here to calm her down, but I'm afraid she might accept."

We all laugh, and Logan and I follow my parents back inside, where we are greeted with a welcome befitting royalty or stars on the red carpet.

Everyone takes their seats. Ken picks up his

knife and carves some fresh turkey, while Sassy and Molly take turns microwaving the sides that have grown cold.

Olivia tosses the pie that Austin had been eating from with disgust. He didn't even use a plate, and no one even noticed. Yuck...

Axe puts the music back on, and Logan says, "Hey Axe, I have a request."

"What is that, my good chap?" Axe puts on an even more formal British accent, and everyone laughs. He's *so* in*formal.

"I'd like to hear Just Can't Get Enough, by my girl's favorite band."

Everyone starts echoing, 'Aww' and 'Isn't that sweet?'

Logan takes my hand and starts dancing with me. It's surely not a waltz, but we're doing some proximity of partner dancing to the New Wave hit.

Everyone else gets up and starts dancing with their own brand of waving and gyrating.

Dawson is really getting into the eighties' New Wave groove, as Emma is teaching him how to do the mime dancing, striking a pose as good as Madonna's.

Logan whispers in my ear, "Sorry to delay dinner yet again, but I know it's going to be true. I'll never get enough."

I squeeze him tightly and the short song comes to an end. The next song on my playlist comes on, A Little Respect by Erasure, and Dawson asks Axe if this a remake of the Aretha Franklin song.

Axe tells him that they are going to meet next week and have some lessons in musical genres. Never one to be easily insulted, Dawson tells Emma that they should have Axe over for dinner.

Before long Dawson will be moving into Emma's apartment and his brother will be on his own. I watch Tucker taking in the scene around him. He's such a quiet guy. I often wonder what he's thinking. Finding him a love match could be my next project.

We all sit back down. Logan places his napkin on his lap with a flourish, and squints at the nametags in front of the birds. "Oh wow, I see I can partake of Bob or Melvin. That's different."

Olivia misses the sarcasm and starts serving him. Hopefully she'll back off now, and I won't have yet another insane love triangle to deal with.

However, I know Logan won't let that happen.

As we get back into the full swing of our meal, I see Axe bobbing his head to the music while Granana is floating around the room, shaking her ghost body with all she's got.

I almost forgot that I never shared their story, but now it seems like it's better to let it wait until Christmas. I can tell they're thinking of each other, and I'll let them have their private moment.

I'm not eating much, even though the food is terrific. What a day this has been.

Really, what a year, but I couldn't feel more at peace.

What happened with Jason wasn't all his fault. He has mother issues, and he needs professional help.

Yes, be behaved poorly and lied about it, but I wasn't 'all in' anymore. I made decisions that led us to where we are now, regardless of Jason's actions.

What he did was horrible, but my choices also set the stage for this day, and I'm not going to hold onto bitterness. I couldn't be happier or more thankful for the way things have developed.

Looking around the table at these people—my parents, new family and friends...I am so grateful for their love and support.

And there's Logan.

I squeeze his hand under the table to assure him that I have no intention of letting go. He is not a rebound man.

And I'll prove that to him, once we're alone. For tonight, and hopefully for all the nights to come.

What we have now, in this moment...couldn't be more real.

THE END

If you loved Lia, Granana, Logan and the gang, please consider leaving a review:

Thanks SOOOO much!!

JOIN ME ON THE EDGE

Go here (http://carolmaloneyscott.com/become-a-fan/) to become an Edgy Reader and receive a FREE BOOK as my thank you for joining!

The fun doesn't stop with the FREE DOWNLOAD!

As a member of my "Edgy Readers Group," you will receive:
- More free books!
- News on upcoming releases!
- Exclusive contests and giveaways!
- Cover reveals!
- Updates on projects and new series in the works!
- Polls asking for your opinion!
- Shenanigans!
- Wiener dog pictures!
- Excerpts!
- Members only sneak previews and exclusive content!

I can't wait for YOU to join the party!

Novels by Carol Maloney Scott

Fun Feminine Fiction

Laughing in Love - Romantic Comedy/Chick Lit

Rom-Com on the Edge Series

Dazed & Divorced (Book 1)

There Are No Men (Book 2)

Afraid of Her Shadow (Book 3)

The Juggling Act (Book 4)

Accidental Makeovers (Book 5)

Valentines on the Edge (A Short Story Collection)

(A Short Story Collection)

Flirting with Fantasy - Paranormal Rom Com/Chick Lit

Love Pixies Series

Love Pixies (Book 1)

Spooky Matchmakers Series

Nobody Tells Lia Anything (Book 1)

Something Molly Can't See (Book 2)

COMING SOON!

Laughing in Love
Romantic Comedy/Chick Lit

Rich Girl on the Run (Rom-Com on the Edge Novella)

Mismated (Rom-Com on the Edge Book 6)

Flirting with Fantasy
Paranormal Rom Com/Chick Lit

Something Molly Can't See (Spooky Matchmakers Book 2)

When Will Olivia Listen (Spooky Matchmakers Book 3)

FREE EXCERPT!

CHAPTER ONE

"Girls, you better get your butts down here or I am tossing your phones in the trash compactor!"

Of course, these are empty threats as I will be the one to replace the ground up phones, *and* the trash compactor, when the apartment handyman sees what I did to the poor innocent kitchen appliance.

However, I have known Pete for many years, so maybe he'd cut me a deal. And I know our sweet little apartment complex owner, Lia, would understand with all the stress I'm under lately.

I glance at the clock on my stove and see that I am going to now be late because I have to drive the princesses to school. My mother was right when she said I shouldn't indulge their every whim and make them walk to school like she did in the old days, uphill both ways, in the snow with no shoes.

I check my tote bag to make sure I have everything for my *whole* day. Sketches for my new doll line, check. Lunch, check. Uniform for my waitressing shift, check. Notes on the new product packaging, check. Grocery shopping list, check.

If it sounds like I have too much going on based on the contents of that bag, you don't know the half of it yet.

"Mooooom, Magnolia stole my lip gloss and it's my favorite cherry kind!"

I sigh and drop my bag and keys by the front door.

"Zinnia Petal and Magnolia Blossom, you get down here right now!"

Yes, I like flowers.

My youngest, twelve-year-old Zinnia appears at the top of the stairs.

"It's not fair! She can wear *real* makeup. All I have is my stupid baby makeup, but at least my lips can look shiny."

My darling girl has her arms folded in a defiant pose and her straight light hair is pulled back in a loose ponytail. She still has a round face and the slightest hint of baby fat. It hurts my ovaries when I think of her...well...becoming a woman with active ovaries.

"Zin, we don't have time for this, baby. Magnolia, let your sister have her lip gloss. Take one of my lipsticks if you want somethin' new. And hurry the heck up!"

Zinnia skips back down the hall to enforce my declaration with her big sister, and they both come down, but not before another excruciating sixty seconds.

Zinnia is first with her unicorn backpack decorated with kitten and puppy stickers, followed by her older sister with her much cooler bag, decorated with band logos and snarky sayings and emojis.

"Magnolia, really? That's the color you picked?"

She's sporting green lipstick that I only bought for a Halloween costume last year.

She rolls her eyes and says, "You said I could pick a lipstick. Do you want me to go back up and pick a different one, because I won't cry if I miss the beginning of first period."

I would count to ten in my head to keep from blowing up, but I don't have the luxury of that kind of time.

"Get in the car with your green lips, then."

I point outside and Magnolia purses her emerald pout and saunters out the door.

I notice that since she turned fifteen a couple of weeks ago, her hips wiggle more than they did before Christmas vacation. My New Year's baby has always been a sass puss, but this is something else.

Note to self—time for a serious sex talk with my oldest.

Yep, the fun times never end.

As I shoo Zinnia out the door, I hear her taunting her sister for having frog lips.

Dear Lord, give me strength.

As if I don't have enough problems, my damn phone has rung about five times in a row. I throw everything in the trunk of my car and try to ignore the daily fight over who gets the front seat. If I had more time (I don't), I would make up a preferred seating calendar and tape it to the inside of the car.

I fish my phone out of my coat pocket and see that Lia has called three times and sent two texts.

"Hey, the new accounting guy is here. Thought I'd introduce you two before your meeting. Are you on your way?"

Shoot, the meeting started about ten minutes ago. Well, not really since I'm not there. Her next text is a question mark and a sad emoji.

I drop my phone on the pavement and smack the hood of the car with my open palm. Oww, that hurt!

I look up and my neighbor, Tucker Swanson, is watching me.

He and his brother live in the apartment next to mine. Well, they used to live in the same one, until his brother, Dawson, moved into his girlfriend Emma's apartment, one door over.

I hang my head in shame for my outburst. I'm glad the kids are in the car. However, I have known the Swanson brothers since they were little tykes. I babysat them for a good number of years. You would think that would have prepared me for the challenges of single motherhood.

Tucker walks over with a slight smile, as if he is amused by my temper tantrum, but not brave enough to assume it's over.

"Hey, Moll. You okay?"

The keys to his Swanson Brothers Auto Repair Shop are in one hand, and a huge mug of coffee is in the other. In his plaid work shirt pocket, a pack of cigarettes peeks out. His hair is still wet from the shower and his stubble is barely there.

It's odd that his appearance is noteworthy this morning, but now that I think of it, I haven't talked to Tucker much in a long time. His brother is the friendly one and Tuck tends to keep to himself.

Except at the New Year's Eve party.

"I'm okay. Just running insanely late. Lia hired a new accountant down at the doll plant and I was supposed to meet him fifteen minutes ago."

I bite my lip as Tucker peers into the windows, and waves at the girls.

"And you have to bring the princesses to school, too. Right?"

I sigh and say, "Yes, we really need to get up earlier, but it's so hard...anyway, I have to go."

As I'm rambling, Tucker opens the car door and tells the girls to hop in his truck. Before I get a chance to protest, he grabs my bag and walks me by the elbow to his truck.

Before the girls can start their front seat argument, Tucker quietly escorts me to the front passenger side and opens the door for me. I slip in and take a deep breath.

The girls climb in the back and Tucker says, "Okay ladies, your stops are on the way to the shop. I am dropping your mama off first."

He peers at my daughters in the rearview mirror and I can't believe how they both nod and smile. Maybe a hot chauffeur would be a good idea for them.

No, on second thought, Magnolia is especially getting too old for that to be safe.

I start my internal scolding—what kind of a mother would want her daughters to be quiet because they're lusting after a man, when said man says, "So, how are things with the dolls? When do you think you'll start production?"

"I hope soon because waitressing at the diner and trying to get this business off the ground is killing me."

"You work too hard, Molly. You need to let loose once in a while." He winks at me and I feel my cheeks get hot.

This is so stupid. This is little Tucker Swanson, the bratty boy who teased me mercilessly for years, and then grew into a sullen young man who was always around, but who kept to himself.

At least as far as I was concerned.

I shift in my seat and glance at the back seat.

Magnolia has her headphones in her ears and Zinnia is playing her game with the puppies on her phone.

"I actually do let loose once in a while; I'll have you know." I pull up the dating app on my phone and show it to Tucker while we are stopped at a light.

"Huh, you sure you should be doin' that? Meeting strangers and all? A woman like you shouldn't need a datin' site to find a man."

I'm grateful for the light turning green so he stops staring at me. When did Tucker develop a smolder? I've always thought of him as a grouchy loner. It's like since he's been living alone, he's changed.

Or maybe I am just noticing him more, especially since the New Year's Eve party. It's been a couple of weeks and I was hoping the awkwardness would subside, but for me it hasn't.

"I'm not saying that I *need* to do it. But I'm tryin', is all."

I look over my shoulder again, even though my 'Mom's eyes in the back of the head' tell me that the girls are oblivious to our conversation.

I lower my voice and say, "Since Ray left, I haven't gotten out much, you're right. I've just been enjoying all the resident events we do at the apartments. Bless Lia for making all of that even more fun for all of us."

He rolls his eyes and I smirk at him. "Now you're acting like my sassy girls."

"Well, Miss Molly, as you may recall, I am a sassy boy."

I huff and try to think of a good retort, when I see that the truck is stopped in front of the old

DeLuca Delicious Delights plant, where my new custom dolls business, Molly's Dollies, is about to take off.

If I can ever get here on time and focus.

I sigh and say goodbye to the girls and thank Tucker for the ride.

"Oh shoot, I really appreciate you dropping us all off, but now I don't have my car, and Lia isn't going to spend the whole day here, so I won't have a ride home. She's just—"

Tucker leans forward into the passenger seat and says, "Shh...girl, get in that building and make your dreams come true. I will pick you all up later."

My face feels hotter and I stammer, "Oh...that's too much trouble. I can't ask you—"

He salutes me and says, "Get your butt in there, girl."

As he drives away, I catch him smiling and waving in the rearview mirror.

That was weird, but I guess I should just be grateful for the kindness of neighbors. I'm one of those women who hates asking for help, but sometimes it's awfully nice to have someone pitch in.

I hoist my overloaded bag onto my shoulder, and shuffle/run to the front door of my new business.

It hardly seems real.

Lia DeLuca moved to our town last year, after her grandmother passed away. For some strange reason, Mrs. DeLuca required Lia to move to Applebarrow to manage our apartment complex, which she owned, and plan social activities for the residents.

It was so odd because we all get along fine at Pentagon Place, and we didn't need anyone to help us. I've lived there for fifteen years, and it's home to me.

Over time it became clear that Lia's dear Granana was meddling from the grave, so to speak, and wanted her to break up with her boyfriend and fall in love with one of the residents.

Mission accomplished—Lia got rid of her lying, cheating boyfriend Jason, and is now very much in love with Logan, Mrs. DeLuca's favorite 'nice young man'.

It was a sweet love story and I have to say it brightened even my outlook on relationships.

Well, just a tiny bit. My loser husband ran off about six months before Lia came to town. I'm still adjusting but I have to do all I can for my girls.

I finally make it to my little corner of this enormous plant site and open the heavy door. Lia was so sweet to invest in my business. I can never repay her. She just saw my handmade dolls at my apartment one night and decided that Molly's Dollies should be a real thing.

My little fledgling business and a new organic dog food company occupy the site of the former DeLuca's Delicious Delights snack cake empire.

It's kind of ironic that my husband, Ray, was one of the many laid off employees affected by the late Mr. DeLuca's sudden closing of the failing plant a few years ago.

Ray never really recovered, but he's still a son of a bitch in my book. When he started with the pyramid scheme, I knew it was too good to be true from a financial perspective, but I hated to discourage him. I just never imagined that he would lose our savings in a year *and* take off with the conniving skank at the top of the pyramid.

I do my count to ten thing, now that I have time on the way to my office.

Yes, I have an office. Me. Molly Jenkins. The one who got pregnant at nineteen and got married, instead of going to college or making any career plans.

Waitressing and bartending have gotten me by all these years, but I don't regret it because I have my girls and I'm still young enough to make a better life for us.

I walk into my office, lay down my bag and quickly run my fingers through my short, spiky blond hair. I chopped it all off when the girls were little to save time, and over the years it's just become my look.

"There you are! Are you okay? Were the girls fighting again?"

Lia sashays into my office in her cute little sweater dress with the chunky heeled boots and swishes her long, dark blonde hair off her shoulders. She turned twenty-five right before Christmas and sometimes I envy her with her youth and her new love.

And the massive inheritance she still doesn't have. In just a few more months, she will be the wealthiest girl I know. Waiting a year has been no problem for her, and she isn't even upset with her grandmother for putting that waiting period in her Will. She's so happy all the time, now that Jason is out of her life and Logan is in.

"Of course, they were fighting. We need to get an earlier start. I'm really sorry. Where is the new accountant?"

She waves her hand in the direction of the other

offices and says, "Oh, Brenda took him in the conference room. She didn't want to wait any longer. You know how she is."

I sigh and slump in my ergonomically perfect office chair. I wish I could waitress at the diner rolling around in this thing. It feels like strong hands are holding me up all day when I sit in it. Kind of like Tucker's hands looked on the steering wheel...

"What did you say, Lia? I'm sorry I drifted off."

And to where I don't understand...I made Tucker peanut butter sandwiches when he was seven years old and I was twelve.

Was I that absorbed in my married life, and then with feeling sorry for myself, that I am just now noticing the guy is almost thirty? And quite hot?

Based on the incident at the New Year's Eve party, I would say he has continued to notice me, or at least he's rediscovered me.

Maybe it's because love is in the air at Pentagon Place. We've had so many couples hooking up and finding love in the past year. He's probably lonely working on cars all day with his brother and going home to a frozen supper. I should really make him some...no, that would just be encouraging him.

Lia waves her hand in front of my face. "Hello, are you in there?"

She sits down in the cozy chair on the other side of my desk and leans forward. "Are you okay? You don't look sick, but I'm sure you're tired. I actually feel bad for helping you now. I am such a newbie at this business stuff that I never thought about all the startup time, and how much work that would be for you while you're holding down a full-time job and being a mom."

Lia and I have had this same conversation several times in the past couple of months, but how can I be upset with her? I knew what I was getting into.

Brenda Wagner, the DeLuca family accountant, was assigned the task of helping with the financial management of my startup. She's about sixty years old and tough as nails. I can't wait to see her face when she introduces this new guy. I'm sure she's mad I was late for the meeting.

But she never had any kids and doesn't even have a pet. She calls herself, 'The Lone Ranger'.

"Lia, honey we've had this talk. Once we get over this hump and we get the first line into production, my involvement will be reduced. And hopefully someday I'll be able to quit waitressing or at least cut back."

Lia crosses her legs and sighs. "You know I could lend you some money to quit now."

I put my hand up immediately. "Nope, I love you like a baby sister, but I do not want to owe anyone anything. And I am not afraid of a little hard work. Plus, I had a little help today."

"Oh yeah, who was the good Samaritan?"

Just as I start to tell Lia about Tucker giving us a ride this morning, Brenda waltzes into my office without knocking, with a skinny redheaded kid at her heels.

"Molly Jenkins, our Creative Director." She gestures towards me and I get up to shake the young man's hand.

"And Molly, this is Shawn Corrigan, our new Junior Accountant."

We shake hands and Shawn tells me that he

graduated at the top of his class at Virginia Commonwealth University in Richmond, and he's excited for the opportunity...

I've zoned out because frankly all this business talk is so boring. I just want to make pretty dolls and sell them to people to bring them joy. Does Shawn think he needs to impress me with his resume?

"Shawn, I am sure you're one smart cookie to get past Brenda and the rest of her team. Welcome to Molly's Dollies."

He winces as if the name of the business is emasculating him. He will probably make up a different name for this job on his resume.

Brenda looks at her phone and says, "Well, I'm off to meet with Mary Ann on the Wags and Woofs side of the house. Shawn, I trust you'll get started on those figures we discussed?"

She raises one grey eyebrow and Shawn turns redder than his hair. "Yes, Bren...I mean, Ma'am."

As soon as she's out of earshot, I say, "Don't let her scare you. She's tough but she'll teach you a lot."

Lia nods her head and we take a moment to be grateful for all the educated, real grown-ups leading this team. With the DeLuca's lawyer, Ed Franklin, and the business consultant, Henry Daley, we should all be looking at some serious return on investment.

Someday, anyway.

Lia senses the awkwardness and chimes in, "Oh and Molly, Shawn has just signed a lease at Pentagon Place, too. Isn't that cool? He's moving into Stan's old apartment."

"Wow, that's great. Welcome to the neighborhood, too."

Stan moved out when he fell in love with Lia's friend, Sassy. Now there's a fun couple!

Shawn turns red again and doesn't seem to be leaving my office. I wonder if he's waiting to be excused or if he's already developed a crush on Lia.

He adjusts his glasses and says, "Thank you. It's a nice neighborhood. After spending the past four years in downtown Richmond at school, I'm looking forward to life in the country."

Lia is still smiling and adds, "And I showed Fred's old apartment to a single middle-aged guy. I think he's going to sign the lease. He's kind of cute, Molly. You might like him."

Now Lia looks uncomfortable as she realizes this is a business and not her college dorm. These young people may have more education than I do, but when it comes to life and common sense...

Shawn barks out an awkward laugh and says, "I'm sure Molly isn't interested in middle-aged men. A woman like you could...anyway, I'll be getting to work now. Bye, ladies."

And he runs out the door.

I slump in my chair again. "I was hoping he was crushing on *you*, not me. I certainly hope that silly boy isn't going to drool all over me now. I can't deal with that."

Lia laughs as my phone buzzes in my purse. It's Tucker.

"Hey Moll, I dropped the girls off no problem. They told me they need rides to friends' houses later. Okay if I drop them off?"

Lia is peering at me and says, "What's the matter?"

I put the phone down on my desk and say, "Oh nothing. Tucker just gave me and the girls a ride this morning, and he's asking if I want him to cart the girls around some more after school."

"Wow, that's awfully nice of him. You trust him, don't you?"

"Oh yes, of course I trust him with the girls. It's not that. Did you notice anything on New Year's Eve?"

"Can you be a little more specific?"

"Never mind. I just thought Tucker was acting a little...odd."

That's putting it mildly.

"I didn't notice, but I think he may be a bit lonely. You've known him all his life. It's okay to let him help you out."

"I guess you're right."

Another text comes through and I let it sit for a moment. Lia has gotten up and says, "Also, I forgot to tell you. I hired a photographer to do a photo shoot with the dolls this afternoon, but I know you have to work at the diner. You don't need to be here. And I feel confident that Ashley can handle it. Her work is really well regarded."

"Sounds great, Lia. Thanks so much, sugar. You're a peach."

She leaves the office and closes my door.

Finally, a moment's peace. I just have to work on a few sketches and then I might have time to eat before I get to The Stone's Throw Diner for the lunch crowd.

Oh, I forgot about my phone, which is buzzing again. I need to reply to Tucker. I'm going to just say thank you and accept this help. I'm being ridiculous.

This text isn't from Tucker. It's from an unknown number.

Oh crap, I think it's that creep I went out with last month. I have since deleted my Tinder app, but not before a few encounters with the less proper men in the area.

"Hey sexy, what's shakin'? How about me and you do some shakin' tonight? Get it?"

Dear Lord, I think I'm put off my lunch now. Once I block this jackass, I'll reply to Tucker.

It's times like this that I really get mad at Ray all over again. Married at nineteen, single again in my mid-thirties. What a bunch of horse shit.

I pull up Tucker's text and see that he's followed it up with a second one. Funny, it's not like him to be the impatient type.

"Hey, I was also thinking—since the girls will be eating supper at the friends' houses and all, how about you and I grab something to eat later? Pick you up at the diner at six?"

How does he know when I get off work? Hmm...well, I will be hungry, and I never want to eat where I work. I just hope he isn't asking me on a *date*.

No, that's silly. I'm just thinking that way because of this Internet dating crap, and now the silly new kid here is making googly eyes at me.

Not every single straight man in Applebarrow is putting the moves on Molly Jenkins.

And now I'm referring to myself in the third person. Loony.

I reply to the text.

"Sure, that would be nice, thank you."

Now I'm acting all formal and weird. This is Tucker—I put band aids on his skinned knees. I helped him and Dawson learn how to swim in the creek.

He writes back with a smiley emoji. Well that's just the icing on the cake. Tucker Swanson is using emojis. What the hell?

I put the phone back in my desk and open up my doll sketch portfolio. I need to focus on tiny, fake women instead of big, real men.

I know I'm being ridiculous. On New Year's Eve Tucker probably had too much to drink and was just feeling celebratory and all.

Tucker is just being a friend. Since so many of the neighbors are coupled up, there aren't as many single people around to hang out with.

And maybe the new guy in Fred's apartment *will* be cute. You never know. Fred found love after losing his wife, and he moved into Martha's house in the village. His apartment could be a good luck charm.

Mine feels cursed ever since Ray left, but I have to get over him. He's not coming back, and would I even want him to, after all the pain he's caused?

PRAISE FOR THE SPOOKY MATCHMAKERS SERIES

"These books are a great escape. I laughed. I cried. I cheered for the main character and found them so relatable. I Highly recommend this book and all others by this author."
AMAZON REVIEWER

CAROLMALONEYSCOTT.COM

ACKNOWLEDGEMENTS

It takes a village to write a book, especially if you want to stay sane.

I am grateful for all the people in my life who help, guide, listen to, and love me through this process.

I thank the ladies of the Abundance Club, especially Patty Washington, for their inspiration and support. Rejoining this group has enriched my life and infused me with the jolt of girl power I need to accomplish my many goals.

My fellow author friends continue to provide me with great advice and a shoulder to cry on, especially when freaking out over marketing and blurb writing. A special thanks to Tracie Banister and Whitney Dineen and sharing their experiences and answering my panicky Facebook messages quickly and cheerfully.

A special shout out to Elaine Kiziah at See Change Studio. Attending her Soulful Time Management retreat in January was the catalyst for me getting my butt in the seat and finishing this book. She's the epitome of the perfect spiritual teacher and practical guide.

My husband, Jim, provides endless patience and encouragement, and I am grateful for his loving support as I navigate my own anxiety on the crazy publishing journey. Writing a book is time consuming, and I appreciate his practical help around the house, as well as his willingness to listen to my late-night rantings about proofreading and advertising.

This book is dedicated to Benny, my sweet little black and tan wiener dog. He joined his big sister, Daisy, in November 2017, and quickly captured our hearts. I often say that they inspire me, but also drive me crazy with their barking at nothing, crawling onto my laptop, and begging for treats. But there is no love like the love of little fuzzy creatures, and their soft, gentle presence is a steady hand on my sometimes-weary head.

My son, Nick, outdid himself with the book cover for Nobody Tells Lia Anything! My pride and love for him is abundant and deep, and I can't wait to watch him receive his BFA degree in Graphic Design in May, on Mother's Day! What a gift! I am not only thankful for his love, humor, and collaboration on my books, but I am inspired by his work ethic and commitment to his craft. As he starts his career at a cool design studio in Chicago, and moves onto his adult life, I know he will continue to kill it in all of his endeavors.

I am so proud of my beautiful, smart and driven stepdaughter, Jaime. She continues to achieve great success at college, and she has big plans for her future, all of which I know she will crush. She reads all my books and is one of my biggest cheerleaders and fans. She is one of the many blessings of my life with her father.

And last, but never least, I love all of my loyal readers, and I enjoy all my interactions with the kind people who read my books and want to get to know me. Writing can be a lonely business, and a short note from a reader, or a great review, can give me that little spark I need to keep going.

I hope you have enjoyed Lia's story, and that you'll stick around and become one of my new book friends! Thank you for sharing your love of the written word with me.

ABOUT THE AUTHOR

Carol Maloney Scott, author of romantic comedy and paranormal chick lit, is a frazzled wife, proud mom and stepmom, and wiener dog fanatic.

She is a lover of donuts, and a hater of mornings. After unearthing a childhood passion for telling stories, she can once again be seen carrying around a notebook and staring into space.

Her stories are witty, fresh, and real—just like life.

Join her on "The Edge" for giveaways, cover reveals, excerpts, contests and members—only content at carolmaloneyscott.com/

WALK THE EDGE OF ROM-COM...ONLINE

Please check out my social media sites and say hello!

Website (http://carolmaloneyscott.com/become-a-fan/)
Goodreads (https://www.goodreads.com/user/show/31420814-carol-maloney-scott)
Facebook (https://www.facebook.com/carolmaloneyscottauthor)
Twitter (https://twitter.com/CMScottAuthor)
Pinterest (http://www.pinterest.com/carolmaloneyris/)

Made in the USA
Monee, IL
23 January 2026